The Thrillville Pulp Fiction Collection
Volume Two:

Lavender Blonde
&
Down A Dark Alley

Will Viharo

Seattle, WA

Copyright Will Viharo

Lavender Blonde Copyright 1987/2011/2016 Will Viharo
All Rights Reserved

Down a Dark Alley Copyright 1992/2010/2016 Will
Viharo
All Rights Reserved

All rights reserved. No part of this book may be reproduced, stored in a retrieval system or transmitted in any form or by any means without the prior written permission of the publishers, except by a reviewer who may quote brief passages in a review to be printed in newspaper, magazine or journal.

First Printing
Printed in the United States of America

Cover art by Mike Fyles mikefyles.co.uk
Formatting by Rik Hall – WildSeasPress.com
Special thanks to Craig T. McNeely

ISBN: 978-0692615256

Published by Thrillville Press
www.thrillville.net

INTRODUCTION TO VOLUME TWO

by Will Viharo

My mother was Miss Houston 1960, runner up for Miss Texas (performing Shakespeare to take the Talent category), and an aspiring actress when she left for New York City (with my father, actor Robert Viharo) to pursue her thespian dreams. I was born April 2, 1963 in Manhattan. During the pregnancy, my mother's schizophrenia kicked in, and, at age 22, her life was basically over. Except for a brief period when she "kidnapped" me, I wasn't raised by her and only met her a few times in adulthood, but I can say without a doubt she is the most tragic human being I've ever known. This sad reality has influenced my fiction more than I can ever measure, in ways I'm probably not even fully aware of myself.

I was raised for my first six years by her relatives in Houston, Texas. The solid foundation they provided no doubt instilled within me the basic survival instincts I would later need to overcome many obstacles. My mother suddenly showed up when I was about five and literally kidnapped me back to New York for several months. My grandfather, who was afraid of air transportation, flew up anyway to rescue me (in fact there was a small plane crash on his way to the Houston airport, I'm told). Not long after this, a guy who called himself my father visited me. I had no idea who he was at the time, either. He was with his current wife, also an actress. Their pet dog, a Doberman

Pincher named "Horse," bit half my face off while I was petting him in front of the television one night. That's what I remember most about that initial reunion. Then a year or so later, I was suddenly put on a plane for Los Angeles to live with this unknown man, who claimed custody. But his latest marriage was on the rocks, and next thing I knew, I was taken away by his current wife who, despite the lack of blood relations, raised me as her own within the bizarre confines of a right-wing religious cult in South Jersey. Suffice to say, it was not a happy childhood. When I was 16, in 1979, my presence was inexplicably deemed toxic by the group, and I was kicked back to my father in Los Angeles. We didn't get along, so I was on my own, in my own apartment, making a living as a Beverly Hills busboy. I hooked up with a young actor friend of my father's, named Mickey Rourke, who became a big brother figure to me, buying me my first car, a 1964 Thunderbird, in 1982 (following a few months spent under the kind auspices of my gracious Houston relatives, where I wrote my first novel, *Chumpy Walnut)*.

In 1980, I saw a film called *Fade To Black*, in which my new friend Mickey had a small supporting role. I became enamored with the lead actress, an Australian Marilyn Monroe lookalike, named Linda Kerridge. I saw the film many, many times, developing perhaps an unhealthy obsession with her, and deliberately hanging out more with Mickey, hoping to meet her. But he had no scenes with her, and this didn't happen. My unfounded fantasies persisted. I designated her my creative muse, because I needed one, and had no other volunteers. Meantime, Mickey was fast becoming a bona fide movie star.

While visiting Houston in 1981-82, again working as a busboy, writing *Chumpy Walnut*, my inexplicable obsession lured me back to Los Angeles. Shortly after my return, I was attending a Marilyn Monroe double feature at the Nuart Theater in West LA, *Gentlemen Prefer Blondes* plus *How To Marry a Millionaire*. A woman sat directly in front of me, even though the theater was nearly empty. I recognized her immediately. It was Linda Kerridge. After the films, I approached her in the parking lot and, identifying myself as a friend of Mickey Rourke's, as well as a huge fan, and asked her for her phone number. Despite the audible warnings of her female friend (who turned out to be Daryl Hannah), she gave it to me —and I wound up introducing *her* to Mickey, as well as his wife at the time, my surrogate sister Debra Feuer (*To Live and Die in L.A.*).

There is much, much more to this incredible but true story than I can't reveal here for personal reasons. Suffice to say, it's all been creatively filtered through the wildly fabricated narrative of my novel, *Lavender Blonde.* Basically, everything in my childhood and teen years has been sublimated into this experimental piece, first written when I was living in a small Berkeley room in 1987, revised rather extensively for self-publication in 2011. My oldest friend, Greg Vargas of Los Angeles, feels it is my strongest work. And he would know, since he was there during many of the travails creatively chronicled if deliberately distorted in this compact book.

In 1992 I visited my mother in Miami, Florida (where 20 years later, ironically, I'd finally meet actor Christian Slater, who wanted to scout locations for his screenplay of my 1993 novel, *Love Stories Are Too Violent For Me,* first published by Wild Card Press in 1995, reissued by Gutter Books in 2013). I'd only visited her once before, in 1989, when she lived alone in the Bensonhurst section of Brooklyn, New York—a Mob neighborhood, meaning she was never safer to walk the streets alone. For years I'd been receiving neatly typed if increasingly unhinged letters from her, with the letterhead of her place of employment, The Cuckoo Clock Company, printed at the top. Irony is often amusingly cruel, or at least cruelly amusing. How she managed to survive on her own so long is a mysterious miracle. She was briefly wed to a Middle Eastern immigrant who married her so he could obtain a green card, but even after their pre-arranged divorce, he looked after her, to his credit. He was later shot dead in the head during a botched robbery as a reward for his magnanimity. I met him only once, when he picked me up at the JFK airport. He was a nice guy, and helped saved my mother's life, for whatever that was worth to her by this time. Fear of death must've been her main impetus for continued existence on this ruthlessly hostile plane.

Anyway, my mother was living relatively peacefully with her mother in Miami by 1992. I also had a cousin that was raised in and around Miami, whom I'd never met. Like my mother, she had been sending me a series of amazing letters—but from prison. They were packed with vivid accounts of her many criminal activities, including setting up suckers for Mob hits. I was always afraid she'd show up at my front door in Berkeley one day, but I've still never met her in person. And I'm okay with that.

When I returned from my Miami trip, I wrote a satirical crime novel called *Down a Dark Alley*, inspired by my brief experiences in the fabled land of *Miami Vice*, my favorite show at the time, even though it had been cancelled by then, as well as my cousin's letters from prison, while riffing somewhat off famous Florida *noir* authors like Carl Hiaasen and Charles Willeford. I was working as a delivery driver for an Oakland blood bank during this period, so this unpleasant reality factored into the narrative as well, along with my earlier experiences living in cheap residential hotels in San Francisco in the mid-1980s. As usual, my beloved male cat "Puss" was at my side as I furiously typed away on my tiny vintage kitchen table. I still miss him very, very much.

Down a Dark Alley became the favorite novel of my good friend Brian Hill, who always suggested I publish it myself, after celebrity editor Judith Regan passed on it, as well as all the manuscripts I sent to her over a two year period, which began shortly after I wrote *Alley*. A well-regarded writer I interviewed, Wally Lamb (*She's Come*

Undone), had recommended my work to her. She expressed sincere interest and eventually asked me to write a memoir, since she enjoyed my letters to her even more than my fiction. It was my natural voice that captivated her. I immediately obliged with an epistolary autobiography called *Graffiti in the Rubber Room: Writing For My Sanity*. But soon after this, Regan left Simon & Schuster, started her own imprint at HarperCollins, farmed my stuff out to a junior editor who didn't get me, and I found all my manuscripts inside a bag dumped in the bushes outside my apartment building.

So when I decided to return to writing after a twelve year hiatus in 2009, once my career as programmer/publicist for Speakeasy Theaters suddenly ended with the company's high profile failure, I bypassed this cold, cruel, corporate system and decided to self-publish. Meantime, my friend Brian Hill, one of the groomsman at my May 2001 wedding to Monica Cortes Viharo —AKA "The Tiki Goddess" of my cult movie cabaret, "Thrillville"—had tragically passed away from ALS. I dedicated the book to his memory (and do so again herein) when I finally self-published *Down a Dark Alley* (with a spectacular cover by artist Rich Black, who created many memorable Thrillville event posters) in late 2010, my third that year, following *A Mermaid Drowns in the Midnight Lounge* (included in Volume One) and *Chumpy Walnut* (Volume Three). The following year I published *Lavender Blonde,* with another provocative cover, this time by famed horror movie host and frequent Thrillville guest Mr. Lobo, in collaboration with his wife, Dixie Dellamorto.

But all this personal jazz aside: if you dig the pure pleasures of sex, or even if you've ever had your heart broken by a failed fantasy, you will enjoy these books. It's really that simple. Cheers.

Will Viharo
Seattle, WA

CONTENTS

LAVENDER BLONDE

A Novel in Dialogue by Will Viharo

For Someone I Never Really Knew

Session One

"I don't even know where to begin." "That's okay. Take your time. Just say whatever pops into your head."

"A sax and a blonde."

"Pardon?"

"Nothin', forget it."

"I did say *first thing*, Eddie. It sounded as if you said, 'sex with a blonde.'"

"Sax. *Sax.* Saxophone."

"And a blonde?"

"Yeah, and a blonde. Right."

"A blonde woman?"

"No, a blonde turnip, for Chrissake."

"No need to get touchy, Eddie. I mean, I don't—that is, we hardly know one another at all. In fact, not in the slightest."

"So?"

"So if there's going to be any progress made here today and in our ensuing hours together, I suggest a more cooperative spirit on your end. Otherwise, what's the point?"

"Beats me."

"Well, I'll *tell* you what the point is, Eddie. You'd be wasting my time."

"I got plenty of time to spare, Doc."

"Well, it's *my* time, too, and if you want more of it, constructively spent, of course, make up your mind right now."

"A tough cookie, ain't'cha?"

"To coin a worn-out anachronistic phrase, I supposed

I am. And apparently you're a—what did old New Yorkers and their ilk say—a 'tough customer'?"

"Jersey, Jersey. Not New York."

"Close enough. It's the regional mentality in question here."

"Say what?"

"Anyhow, Eddie, this is Berkeley, California, far from the Mafia's dumping grounds, and while we tolerate many cultures and attitudes in this area, I must lay down some laws, or, let me rephrase that—uh, I must set certain standards of conduct as far as hospitality and mutual respect are concerned. Do you understand?"

"You've made your point, Doc." Fumble, flip, strike, tsss, puff, drag, whooo.

"If you're going to smoke, Eddie, kindly blow the fumes elsewhere."

"Yeah sure sorry."

"Sincerity would be appreciated in our discussions as well, Eddie."

…

"Did you hear me, Eddie?"

"Yup."

"Then please acknowledge me with at least a heartfelt nod."

"Okay?"

"Thank you."

"No problem, Doc."

"Anyway, to move things right along, 'a sax and a blonde.' Trite as it sounds, it may be a clue to unraveling that compelling psyche of yours."

"If you *say* so. They just happen to be a coupla subjects that I'm into, that's all. I mean, y'know, no big deal or anything."

"Blonde women and the saxophone?"

"Yeah. I'm an expert at both, you might say. Or you might say I'm a *failure* at both. Depends on who you ask— me or anyone else."

"And what's your considered opinion, Eddie? Are you a blues-spouting ladies' man or a complete fiasco in both departments?"

"You keep talkin' like that an' I'm gonna need a friggin' handbook."

"I'm sorry. I don't mean to be pedantic. Or patronizing. We all have insecurities we disguise with different. Anyway, back to this mystique you're obsessed with."

"Mistake?"

"This image, of a saxophone and a blonde lady."

"I didn't say 'lady,' *you* did."

"Then how would you refer to *them*?"

"One thing I've learned, Doc. A broad is a broad. No offense, but that's how I see it. You want honesty, you got it."

"Well, honesty and respect normally go hand in hand."

"If I was normal, I wouldn't be here, would I?"

"What is 'normal' to you, Eddie?"

"Aw, jeez, you talk in circles, you know that? How the hell should *I* know? Ain't *you* the one who's supposed to be tellin' *me* how to be normal?"

"Normality is a myth, Eddie. Everyone's different, approaches life from a different perspective, and responds accordingly."

"Oh, I didn't know that."

"This irreverent tone—did you always have it? Is it a built-in authority complex or something?

"I can't, y'know, I really can't *believe* you're askin' me this. *I* don't friggin' know, Doc, or else I wouldn't be friggin' sittin' here like a putz listenin' to you quote the friggin' dictionary. What're you smilin' at?"

"I don't know. I apologize if I made you uneasy, Eddie."

"I don't give a shit. I'm used to bein' laughed at."

"I wasn't laughing *at* you, Eddie."

"Yeah, yeah, you was laughin' *with* me. Funny how everyone else can be laughin' with me only I ain't laughin'."

"Have I hit a nerve, Eddie?"

"What're you, a rookie at this? You're like an inquiry board already. I thought the idea of this scam was so you could explain me to *me*."

"Well, you're not giving me much to go on. You have to let me get to know you first, Eddie."

"Then let's go out for a drink or somethin'. This joint make me nervous."

"What's the matter with it? It's just a room. Is it the ferns, the goldfish, the sunlight, what?"

"Yeah. All those. It's too, I don't know. *Normal*, I guess."

"You mean sterile."

"Yeah, whatever. It's *boring*, know what' I'm sayin'? Nothin' personal. Add a tiki statue or somethin'. And I don't dig that psychedelic shit, either. Makes me nervous."

"What, the Grateful Dead poster?"

"Yeah. What the hell is *that* doin' in the office of someone like you, anyways? Ain't that a little too, uh, *weird* for shrinks to be advertisin' stuff like that?"

"I'm not a shrink. I'm a counselor, a glorified social worker. And the poster merely expresses one aspect of my musical tastes."

"You gotta be puttin' me on. I happen to know a *lotta* Deadheads and *none* of 'em talk like you do. Not one. Not even close."

"Well, I don't consider myself a Deadhead per se. I also appreciate Mozart and Charlie Parker."

"*Now* you're gettin' someplace. Bird. Now *he* was somethin'."

"An idol of yours, Charlie Parker?"

"I ain't got no idols. They only let ya down like everyone else."

"How? Give me an example of how idols let people down."

"Well, by *dyin'*, for one thing. Jim Morrison. Marilyn

Monroe."

"Marilyn Monroe was blonde."

"No shit. Yeah? No kiddin'."

"I'm merely pointing out, Eddie, that she falls in line with our topic. And so does Charlie Parker, a sax player."

"Are you some kinda genius? You're scarin' me, you're scarin' me, you really are."

"From what I understand, you play the saxophone."

"Yeah, I do a gig now and then. Ain't been hooked up with nobody for a long time, though."

"And why's that? You mean with a band."

"Yeah. I dunno. Nobody likes me, once they get to know me. Same with chicks. You know, they meet me, and, y'know, everything's cool for a while, y'know, we're at the bar, we're talkin', we're havin' a good time, an' then, I dunno, I guess I get too *serious* or somethin' and I scare 'em off. Friggin' bimbos anyway, shit. Why do I waste my— anyways, it's the same old story. People don't mind meetin' me or anything but once they get to *know* me, y'know, *bam*, they lose interest."

"For what it's worth, *I* still like you, Eddie."

"We just met. Give it time."

"True, but you have to give *yourself* time. Maybe you don't know yourself enough to share yourself with others. That's why it'd be good for you to open up more."

"Aw, c'mon, you expect me to buy that crap? Open up and find *yourself*. Get outta the *Sixties* already, c'mon. At least the *hippie* Sixties."

"This is Berkeley, where the Sixties never ended, remember?"

"Tell me about it. I ask myself all the time what I'm doin' here."

"And?"

"I dunno. I mean I just don't know."

"It would behoove you to figure it out as soon as possible, Eddie. Everyone needs to decide what part of the world is their little niche, is the place that offers them the most potential to grow and develop their natural abilities. That's one way of finding yourself, and I'll keep using that phrase till I think of a better one. That's why you're here today, Eddie. That's why *I'm* here. To help people discover their own life's personal motif."

"'Scuse me?"

"Everyone's life has its own motif, Eddie. Certain creative elements, backdrops, moods that bring out the essence of an individual and allow it to flourish."

"Yeah, right. Got any booze around here?"

"No. For instance, what do you think of Berkeley?"

"I don't know yet, I just got here. I live in Frisco— sorry, SAN FRANcisco, anyway."

"What do you think of the City? How does it hit you on a gut level?"

"I only been here a month, give me a break. 'Course, a month in New York and chance are I'd have been *stabbed* at a gut level already."

"Do you prefer New York to San Francisco, Eddie?"

"I dunno. I keep sayin', I just got here."

"Well, why did you come to the Bay Area then, can you answer me that?"

"Two reasons. One is too much time in friggin' L.A. Another is somethin' this guy I used to jam with said to me once about San Fran. He was into, what's that guy, y'know, y'know, 'On the Road' and shit...'"

"Jack Kerouac."

"Yeah, yeah, him. Anyway, this guy played bass like nobody's business, know what I'm sayin'?, and he used to read a lot, y'know, an' he told me that Frisco was like a beautiful woman with only a few weeks to live. Or somethin' like that. Anyway, him sayin' that always made me wanna come up here and check it out. So here I am."

"You've spent most of your life on the East Coast, though, is that right?"

"Yep, sure is. You been doin' your homework, Doc."

"A habit I picked up in college."

"What—you went to school where, here?"

"Yes. But let's stick to you for now. After spending all that time back there."

"You ever been there?"

"Where, the East?"

"Yeah."

"Only to change planes on my way to Europe. Why?"

"'Cause. The way you say 'back there,' like it was another planet or somethin'."

"It may as well be, from what I understand."

"So what does that make me, an alien?"

"Do you feel like one in California, Eddie?"

"Well, now that you mention it, yeah, sometimes. I guess they *are* like two different worlds, huh?"

"So you left your world and came to ours because of what your friend said about San Francisco being like a pretty girl who's dying?"

"I said, 'like a beautiful woman with only a few months to live.' Or weeks or days or whatever. Hours. Don't matter. Not a pretty chick *croakin'*, for Chrissake. It's *how* you say a thing that counts, like in music. It ain't *what* you play, how old it is, or *whose* it is, but *how* you play that matters, know what I'm sayin'?"

"I know *precisely* what you're saying, Eddie, because that's the point I've been trying valiantly to make here with you today. Music, the saxophone, is part of what makes you *you*, and obviously you realize that. And the way you play expresses what's inside of you, is that correct?"

"Yeah."

"So that's part of your personal motif. Your music. But so is the place you choose to grow roots, and the people you spend time with. They all bring out separate but integral facets of your personality. And, well, apparently you think a blonde broad, as you so eloquently put it, would complement your motif beautifully."

"If you say so, Doc."

"It's not what I say but what you *feel* that's important,

Eddie."

"Well, *I* coulda told ya that, that I dig the sax 'n' blondes. I mean, you ain't exactly ready for your own cable show, know what I'm sayin'?"

"Self-therapy may be cheap but it's also lonely, Eddie. It's healthy to have a sounding board. And that's what I am. And I can be a lot more, if you'll let me."

"You can be whatcha want."

"So can you."

"Cute."

"What do you think it would take to get that chip off your shoulder?"

"A bottle of gin."

"That may get it wet, but wouldn't make it disappear. Drowning your sorrows, as they say, in booze won't help in the long run."

"I ain't got no sorrows to drown, sweetheart. You must have me confused with somebody else."

"You don't sound like you're bursting with joy, either. Some people prefer to hang onto their angst, their anger, because they feel neuroses is the key to creativity."

"Some people. I wonder who they are I wonder." *Phtoo.*

"If you were tying to spit in the ashcan, Eddie, may I point out that you missed."

"I wasn't aimin' for the trashcan, Doc."

"You intentionally soiled my rug?"

"Spit dries, Doc, relax."

"Your attitude gets boring, Eddie. Maybe it's the reason people aren't standing in line to be your buddy."

"I can't help it."

"It can't help you either, with this attitude of yours. So why don't you just drop it?"

"'Cause it's *me*, Doc. It's just plain me. Take it or leave it."

"Mock bravado often conceals sentimental sensitivity."

"How reassuring."

"It *should* be. Maybe there's hope you don't have to be an obnoxious cynic all your life. Even if no one else has to live with you, *you* still do."

"Well, there's always the Golden Gate Bridge, ain't there?"

"Are you considering suicide as an alternative to getting yourself together?"

"Uh, yeah, basically. Since you spell it out like that."

"It's not that simple. Death may not be the escape you're looking for."

"One quick way to find out, huh, Doc?"

"The afterlife could be worse, for all you know."

"I dunno. My gig here'd be one tough act to follow."

"What if there are no blondes on the other side?"

"Then things will be a whole lot easier, Doc."

"And no saxophone, either."

"So I'll learn to play the harp."

"What makes you think you'll wind up in heaven? Have you been that good?"

"I guess not. Santie Claus ain't been down *my* chimney, I'll tell ya that."

"Goodness is relative. Everyone is simply reacting to the circumstances they were placed in seemingly at random."

…

"You really like to shrug, don't you, Eddie?"

"Body language, Doc. Ain't that what it's all about? Let me know if I'm turnin' ya on or anything and I'll knock it off, okay?"

"Well, at least you're amusing, Eddie, I'll say *that* for you. Though probably not intentionally."

"Like my old man, ya mean."

"What about your father, Eddie?"

"Ah, what do you really care, am I right? I don't want to get into some big friggin' deal here, okay?" *Sigh.*

"You seem disturbed. I don't mean to, to..."

"Forget it, forget it. It's just that, my old man an' me, we was never too tight, know what I'm sayin'? I mean I ain't afraid of spoilin' his rep or nothin' like that. Ain't nothin' I could do to make it no worse anyways. He was sort of a comic, y'know? In clubs. That's how I first thoughta bein' a musician, hangin' out in clubs an' watchin' the old man bomb night after night. He spent years an' years tryin' to be the funniest guy in the world, and he couldn't even be the funniest guy on stage, by *himself*. The friggin' corny emcees got more laughs than he did, for Chrissake. He was really a sad case all the way around. 'Course I ain't gettin' booked into Caesar's Palace on a regular basis neither, so who am I to talk, right?"

"Maybe your father just wasn't being realistic about his goals."

"Yeah, maybe, maybe. Who cares, anyway. He's dead now, so what difference does it make. Maybe. What a worthless word that is."

"You don't have to discuss memories that are too painful for you, Eddie."

"Memories. Screw memories, Doc. A memory is a memory. No big thing, know what I'm sayin'? Just a thought in your head that could be a dream for all it matters, am I right?"

"But memories are important, Eddie. What is life anyway but a series of images, vaguely pre-conceived at times, dimly remembered at best, and only briefly experienced."

"Well, that's certainly one to chew over, Doc. Let me get back to ya."

"I think you understand me a lot more than you're letting on, Eddie. I know an intelligent mind when I'm talking to it. That's why I refuse to talk down to you. You have what I would call a 'suave savvy.' If only I could find a way to re-mold you, mend your painful memories, it could be quite beneficial to you in the future, particularly in your line of work, which probably helped develop it to begin with. That along with your checkered past of course, which is beginning to fascinate me, I must admit. No need to roll your eyes, I'm being perfectly candid."

"You mean no bullshit."

"I mean no bullshit, Eddie. Tell me, what about your mother?"

"What about her?"

"Well, is she still alive?"

"Yeah. Sorta. I dunno, I guess. We never talk no more."

"Are your memories of her painful as well?"

"Depends on how much booze they're swimmin' in at any given moment."

"Finding solace in temporary escapes makes any peace of mind you may attain tenuous at best."

"A few moments of phony happiness is a lot better than non-stop true-blue depression *all* the time, Doc. Write *that* one down, why don'tcha, for the next bozo on your looney-tunes assembly line here."

"No one here is hopeless, Eddie. *No* one. Everyone's just trying to make an impossible situation work, whatever it may be, which is usually just simply living day to day."

"So what makes *you* so special, huh? How come you think *you're* in a position to have answers the rest of us ain't privy to?"

"I don't have any answers, Eddie. I just ask more questions than you do. Maybe together, we can come up with a few decent answers."

"Well, Doc, I mean, I ain't no wonder sittin' over here. I mean I ain't no mystery. What you see is what I is, like my old man used to say. He used to say alla time, 'My brain is a blank canvas, and my life is an open book.' Or somethin' like that. Well, that's me. So quit diggin' for buried treasure, Doc, 'cause it just ain't there, I'm tellin' ya. I been in there already. There's nothin' inside me at all. If there was...it ain't there no more. So forget it."

"If there was nothing inside of you, Eddie, you

couldn't play a musical instrument. Not with any passion, anyway."

"Ah, passion. *Fuck* passion. 'Scuse me, but that's how it is. Passion. That's what got me *into* this mess."

"Without passion, there would be no art. Don't knock passion, Eddie."

"I ain't knockin' it, it knocked *me*. Like out cold, flat on my ass, know what I'm sayin'?"

"So why are you still playing if you feel you have nothing else to give?"

"So I can tell the cosmos to go fuck themselves, that's why. *That's* art, Doc. Telling time and death and all the rest of it to shove it up their ass."

"You're entitled to your opinion, Eddie. This is Berkeley, we listen to contrasting views. But we also allow people to explore options that enable them to outgrow negative ideas that are bogging them down."

"Well, that's nice. Me, it's too late, Doc. It's just too late. Sometimes, sometimes I wish I could just put my whole past into a time capsule and blow it up."

…

"Eddie, if you're crying, you don't have to feel ashamed. Not here, not with me."

"I ain't cryin', see?"

"Sorry, my mistake. I didn't mean to be presumptuous."

"I got allergies, I got allergies, is all."

"Oh. What are you allergic to, exactly?"

"I dunno. Life. Hey, what's with this room, anyway?" *Creak, pound, pound, creak.* "Jeez, hardwood floors. There's hardly nothin' in this joint, how can ya stand it?"

"Well, it's very old, for one thing. The building. Pace too hard and you'll find yourself back in the lobby. But I like it. It has an almost Edward Hopper starkness to it. Simple, yet eloquent. Spare, yet colorful. Kind of, kind of like *you*."

"Cute." Clop, clop, clop, clop.

"You're pacing like a caged tiger, Eddie. Just sit down and relax. We still have time left."

"I like cats, especially tigers. I need a drink."

"To calm you down?"

"Who said I wasn't calm? I just, y'know, I'm just thirsty, is all. No big thing. I ain't no friggin' *alcoholic* or anything, all right?"

"Have you ever known any alcoholics, Eddie?"

"Are you kiddin' me or what? That's almost funny. I should have bourbon in my veins insteada blood."

"From the bars you've lived in?"

"From the people who made me, Doc. Get the picture? Booze was a big ingredient in the mix."

"You mean your parents, of course."

"No, Doc, I mean the stork that brung me was a lush."

"I see."

"Do you? I really don't see how ya could. Unless you got binoculars on my soul or somethin', if I got one left."

"Everyone has a soul, Eddie. Or at least a heart."

"Ray Charles did, but that's it."

"Someone else you looked up to, Eddie?"

"I don't look up to nobody, for Chrissakes, I keep tellin' ya. But if I did…one time I was in Philly on South Street an' I went into the restroom in this cheese-steak joint, Jim's, and on the wall was this graffiti an' shit, y'know, an' this one guy had written, shit, what was it—'Love is blind, God is love...Ray Charles is blind, Ray Charles is God.'"

"That *is* clever."

"Yeah, I can see you got a big bang out of it. You ain't too emotional, are ya? Kinda cool and creepy, like, I dunno, *Spock* or somebody. Not Doctor, *Mister*. A computer with legs. Nice gams, if I may say so, too."

"Take it easy, Eddie."

"Sorry, no offense."

"I'm sure. Anyway…"

Plop.

"Please go easy on the furniture, Eddie. But thank you

for sitting down."

"Anything for you, Doc, you know that. I'm serious, I didn't mean to offend you or anything."

"It's quite all right, Eddie."

"No, no, really. I mean it. You wanted me to pop off whatever came into my head, right? So I am. And it ain't always pretty. But, y'know, I don't want you to get *pissed* or anything."

"I'm not upset, Eddie. No need to get paranoid. I understand you and where you're coming from a lot more than you think. Maybe I've never been where you've been, maybe I never will, and I certainly don't have a metaphysical telescope to probe your personal regions, awkward as that sounds, but I am trained to deal with human nature on many different levels. I've devoted my life to it. I comprehend human behavior as a series of patterns, however, uh, endless and complex, that can be changed, even stopped, before they lead to the point of no return and waste a precious life worth saving."

"Oh yeah? And you think I'm a contender for this, uh, whatever the hell it is?"

"I think you definitely qualify for salvation, yes. I really do."

"Why? I mean, you have any idea why I'm here, Doc? What or who made me come here, and 'cause of what? I ain't no peach, Doc."

"I didn't say you were an angel. But if I can exorcise your personal demons, as it were, maybe you could be. An angel with a saxophone instead of a harp."

"You gotta nice smile, you know that?"

"Yes, I do, don't I?"

"Cute."

"And yes, Eddie, I am familiar with what brought you here."

"Hm. Well, not much I can say, uh, in my defense."

"You shouldn't feel the need to, Eddie. I mean to explain yourself. Not directly. But the purpose of this whole thing, of me and you talking about matters perfect strangers shouldn't even be hinting at, is so that maybe you can understand *why* you did what you did, and prevent it from occurring ever again. Understand?"

"Yeah."

"Good." *Bzzzz. Click.* "Yes?...Okay, tell him I'm in, um, conference and that I'll get back to him ASAP. Thanks." *Click.*

"Who was that?"

"An acquaintance. I don't take social calls on duty."

"That was social, huh?"

"Even social workers have social lives, Eddie."

"Hard to believe, after rappin' with screwballs all day. What do you do to unwind, anyways?"

"First we talk about you, then maybe later about me, huh?"

"Yeah sure."

"First, let's build this time capsule you referred to, and then later, after you've put as much into it as you care to, you can decide whether to blow it up. Okay?"

"Look, I already know what I wanna do with my memories, but what *you* do with 'em is, y'know, up to you. I mean, I don't wanna *bore* you or anything, now that we're hittin' it off so tremendously."

"Well, I'm glad you feel the ice is melting a bit, Eddie. And don't worry—when you get boring, I'll let you know. Deal?"

"A pretty raw one for one of us, maybe, probably both, but, yeah. Where, uh, where d'ya want me to start? Not at the *beginnin'* I hope. Or else this'll turn into a regular whine-a-thon."

"Pardon, a what?"

"Nothin', nothin'. I just don't wanna sound like I'm feelin' sorry for myself, 'cause I ain't, y'know. *Really*. It all makes no difference to me. As long as, y'know, after we're done, I can walk outta here with my past behind me, where it belongs, *all* of it, in one piece or blown to smithereens, whatever, makes no difference, so long as it's *behind* me. Know what I'm sayin'?"

"I know what you're saying, Eddie. Now, with what time we have left."

"Aw, jeez, there ya go. You're ruinin' it for me, absolutely *ruinin'* it for me. I mean who needs a friend that punches a clock, y'know? Who friggin' needs it. Just forget it, if *that's* how it's gonna be."

"Eddie, you have to understand. I have a life outside of this little room. What's discussed in here stays in here. But I don't. I *can't*. You can't think of me as a computer, but as a person with needs all her own. Otherwise there'll be no real communication between us, because your expectations will be higher than I can maintain. Does that make sense to you, Eddie?"

"More than you know, Doc."

"I certainly hope so. Well, now then. A sax and a blonde is where we began, perhaps it should be our closing note as well. I mean for today. I instinctively feel it tells a lot about your persona. Tell me something, Eddie, was your mother blonde?"

...

"Don't just glare at me, Eddie. It's an innocent..."

"So what if she is? What's that *mean*, huh? I mean don't pull any of this crap like what's her name on TV does, 'cause I ain't buyin' it. Don't give me one of those head trips about my mother's bein' blonde so that's what I meant, I mean, that's why, y'know."

"You're jumping to your own conclusions now. I never suggested any of that. I merely asked if your mother was blonde."

"Why?"

"Well, why not?"

"Well it must be obvious by now that she *was*, huh? So big deal, you score in exhibition. It still don't count, Doc. So my old lady was blonde. So what?"

"I think that'll do it for today, Eddie. Hopefully you'll

cool off before our next encounter and we can start fresh."

"Man, what a putz I was for fallin' for this in the first place. That's me, Doc. Eddie the Putz."

Session Two

Slam.

"You're late, Eddie."

Belch.

"And you look as if you haven't slept since I saw you last."

"I haven't, Doc. I haven't." *Plop.* "'Cause we left on such rocky terms, I turned to drink, to drown my sorrows."

"So your appearance is being attributed to a hangover."

"Several, Doc. But *you,* you look like *roses.* How d'ya do it, Doc? Pills?"

"The smoke, Eddie."

"Whoops! Sorry."

"I hope you don't make a practice of being late, Eddie."

"Naw, don't sweat it."

"I'm not, but *you* should. I'm only here to help, Eddie. And you need as much as you can get. Right?"

Sniff. "Yeah, right. As usual. Only don't get on that 'sax and blonde' kick again, it's boring already. A'right?"

"Fine. Then how about we pick up where we left off? With your mother."

"Aw, jeez, well, what d'ya wanna know? What brand pantyhose she wore? What type tampons? I mean, *what*?"

"Why would I care to know details like that, Eddie?"

"You tell *me.* Last time it was hair color. Now maybe you want her social security number maybe, though I can tell ya I doubt if she ever had one."

"Did she ever work for a living? What are you laughing at?"

"Doc, if you only knew, that's all I can say."

"That's *not* all you can say. You can tell me what strikes you as being funny. I could use a laugh. My week wasn't as rosy as you may think it was."

"Oh, yeah? Why not? Social hang-ups?"

"You, you, Eddie, stick to *you*, not me. Now, why did you laugh when I asked you if your mother worked?"

"'Cause, I dunno."

"That's no answer. A shrug tells me you have something on your chest you're reluctant to release."

"A shrug tells you that, huh?"

"Body language, remember? It was one of my majors."

"Yeah, I'll bet."

"Pardon?"

"Nothin', forget it. Listen, my mother is a touchy subject, okay? Just back off for now. I'll cut loose when I'm ready."

"All right."

"So…what else ya wanna know?"

"Whatever you feel comfortable sharing with me."

"I ain't comfortable with anything *about* this, Doc, so our talks are gonna be more like chats if I stick to the cushy stuff."

"Well, your father. The stand-up comic. Where was it he performed exactly?"

"Florida, originally. He's from Miami. He did the club circuit down there before hittin' Philly an' the Big Apple. He's part Cuban, part New Orleans Creole, part Irish. Whatever the hell *that* is. He met my old lady—don't get excited, I'm still saving the *good* stuff—in Houston, where she's from. I met 'em sometime in the back of an old Buick at a Texas drive-in, or so the story goes. It's so friggin' classic sounds like it was made up to me. But that's what I'm told, anyways. So my old man took my old lady up north where she was gonna be a dancer and he was gonna be a hotshot comic. He was a little scared of tacklin' New York right away so they settled for South Philly, lived in a nice little brownstone, I saw it later when I was grown an' on my own. Every now an' then they'd hit Atlantic City, or other little dives around South Jersey, but mainly he stuck to Philly 'cause it was like bright lights, big city, know what I'm sayin'?"

"I follow you."

"Boring yet?"

"No—but you could be more specific. Illustrate your memories for me, with as little embellishment as possible."

"Bullshitment?"

"Um, that's not what I said, but that's what I meant, pretty much."

"A'right—so anyways, where was I? Oh, yeah, so the old man..."

"Doesn't he have a name?"

"Yeah. Ricardo Patrick somethin'. But he changed it to Seymour when got into the act. He did it in Philly, changed it to Seymour Snatch. Get it? Was he a genius or what? Even though it made him sound like a stripper. His heroes were Lenny Bruce an' Frank Sinatra, only he wasn't funny and he couldn't sing. Seymour loved that Sinatra movie where he plays a comic, 'The Joker Is Wild.' So anyway, Seymour an' Ginny—short for Virginia, my old lady's title, as far as you're concerned, anyway—got sicka the South in general so they took a train from New Orleans after terrorizin' it for a while, an' wound up in Philly with like no dough to speak of. So of course Ginny winds up with some chickenshit gig in a coffee shop busting her ass for a lotta loudmouth construction workers an' old people, an' Seymour, when he ain't hustlin' his act, is like sellin' ties on the street, washin' cars, whatever he can till somethin' better comes along, which it does. Drugs. The old man turns to dealin' to fill in the gaps between club dates. He makes enough to bribe the old lady into spots here 'n' there, these little dinky dance companies, since she ain't no Ginger Astaire, whatever her name was, know what I mean?, so anyway they still wind up goin' broke, livin' in some little hotel room in South

Philly with no heat or anything, no comforts of home, y'know, so what happens but the old man goes into business with Ginny. He becomes her, y'know, manager. So his name comes in handier than he planned. She has a nice figure and the bread starts rollin' in. Plus she pulled a few shifts as a stripper until I got in the way, literally."

"She was pregnant with you?"

"Yeah, I told ya, back in Texas, out on the range."

"And while she was pregnant with you, she was...hm."

"You got the picture. I mean, I don't remember no members, y'know, I mean I can't *remember* anything, but this is what I hear."

"My God."

"Yeah, at least you got one. So anyways, I come along an' the old man, since he couldn't talk the old lady into havin' me wind up on the sticky end of a hanger, started to freak out 'cause he wasn't knockin' 'em dead locally or anything, so after I popped out we headed for New York so he could try his luck there. But it was the same thing, same thing. Seymour and Ginny weren't hittin' it off too wonderfully by this time, y'know?, an' Ginny starts naggin' him about gettin' into real estate or some shit, settlin' down, gettin' a nice little place out on Long Island or up in Connecticut, y'know, somewhere nice 'n' pleasant for little Eddie the Putz to grow up normal. Well, obviously this never happened or I wouldn't be the fine together individual before you today, right? So what happens but of course the old man splits, y'know, he's gone, he's outta here, historyville, know what I mean?, an' the old lady, Ginny, has decided waitressin' ain't her line, tries to get a gig as a secretary, only she has the education of a woodchuck, know what I'm sayin'?, and can't get arrested business-wise, so of course she goes into business for herself, operatin' out of the penthouse of this sort of condemned hotel in Alphabet City. She hangs out sometimes in Times Square, makes a few friends, they form a sort of club, and decide to open their own place, only the rents in Manhattan, even for a whorehouse, are pretty steep, so they all haul ass to New Fuckin' Jersey. And Ginny, she loves me, right, so I go where she goes. Her an' my old man were never officially married so they're never officially divorced, neither, but my old lady never had to go to war for custody of Eddie the Putz, y'know?, only my old man picked me up on weekends sometimes, after a few hot club dates in a row, usually in the Village, Greenwich Village, where there's all types who'll sit through *anything* after enough drinks, y'know?, so he'd pick me up and we'd take off for Central Park and the Bronx Zoo...and, y'know, sometimes it was kinda fun almost. He'd lift me up on his shoulders, y'know, so I could see all the action on Broadway. He took me to the museum, y'know, with the dinosaur skeletons and stuffed animals and everything, and that really boosted my rockets, y'know? I loved that friggin' museum, and the park with all the crazies, and the zoo—y'know, now that I think of it, maybe it was *where* I was and not *who* I was with that such a blast. Y'know?"

"And what about your mother. Did you ever spend time with her?"

"Sure, but not much. She never liked New York from day one, or Philly for that matter. She liked Jersey for some reason. I guess 'cause she was a country gal at heart and Jersey was kinda deserted like that, like it coulda been the moon, at least compared to the big towns. I mean like if a spaceship ever landed there from Mars they'd think they never got off the ground, know what I'm sayin'? I wrote a song about it once, called 'The Moon at Noon.'"

"So you never saw your mother much, you were with your father?"

"Naw, I didn't see him all that much, either. My old lady was pretty protective of me. She hardly let me outta the house, or whatever you wanna call it. Let's face, it was a *whorehouse*. But she didn't want me to end up like her, *or* him. She hadda little room made up for me, and she listened to jazz a lot, y'know, Billie, Ella, the Duke, the Count,

Monk, Miles, Dizzy, Brubeck, Coltrane, *all* those cats, it was the only thing her an' the old man really had in common, besides me, an' I kinda got used to it, that kinda music, I mean, so when I was young I was pretty educated in the blues. In more ways than one. I was alone so much, though. Ginny was paranoid I'd get as fucked up as *she* was. Only she was makin' pretty good dough by the time I was three or four. Her an' the other girls, who were sorta like my family, my 'aunts,' I called 'em, started a kind of escort service for yokels from out of town, in Manhattan on business, y'know, and they were rakin' it in pretty good there for a while. And me, I guess I coulda done worse. I mean, I gotta lotta attention an' everything, so not a *lot*, but some. I was taken care of, let's put it that way."

"What are some of your strongest memories from that period, Eddie?"

"I dunno, I guess. Like, this joint was in Jersey City, the armpit of the world, so I wasn't missin' a hell of a lot outside the house, which was a nice house, I guess, one of those old-style places that looked out across the river at Manhattan, and in the morning I used to watch the sun come up over the skyline there, y'know, and it was sorta pink an' gold an' orange, except on a cloudy day, when it was real misty an' dark, like it was the enda the world almost, an' the fog was all that was left, the fog 'n' the buildings, but no *people*, which wouldn't be so bad, really, sometimes, I think. 'The Moon at Noon.' But, yeah, sometimes I thinka me as a little kid lookin' out at the Manhattan skyline at dawn, an'…I dunno. Sometimes if I shut my eyes I'm there, I can feel it, and, I dunno. Forget it. I must sound like some flake, huh?"

"No, not at all, Eddie. You just sound like there are a few clinks in that armor-clad heart of yours."

"Yeah, maybe. I doubt it, though. Don't get your hopes up about rehabilitatin' me or nothin' like that."

"What makes you think you need rehabilitation?"

"Well, whatever *this* is for, then."

"God forbid we discover you're more like a normal human being than you want to be."

"Say what? You kiddin' me? I *am* what I wanna be. I mean, *I* don't know what I mean. I don't know what *any*thing means. So anyways, what the hell did *you* do since I saw you last time? Did you see that guy or what?"

"Eddie, I hate to be blunt, but that really isn't any of your or anyone else's business."

"But *my* life is public property, right? I mean, I never tell *any*one stuff I just told you, and all I ask is what have you been doin' lately, and I get the iceberg treatment. So forget it, forget it. You said you were gonna be my friend, but you wanna keep it business-like. Okay, sure, fine, I can dig it." *Bam, creak, moan.*

"So you're going to pace again now, is that it?"

"Is there a law against pacing in Berkeley, Doc?"

"Depends on what you're protesting."

"I ain't protestin' nothin', I'm just nervous, is all."

"Eddie, I didn't mean to be rude or abrupt. But...maybe after we know each other a little more, I'll feel more like sharing my week with you. But for now, yes, I want to keep this as business-like, though also as casual, as possible. This is my *occupation.*"

"Yeah, yeah, yeah, yeah, I hear ya, I hear ya already. Whatever, suits me. Hey, this ain't a bad view you got here, of the Bay I mean. Kind of reminds me of what I was talkin' about. You can look out at the bridges and the skyline and everything."

"And lots of fog."

"Yeah, weird."

"What is?"

"Nothin', I was just thinkin' how life is, how you get from one place to another—it's almost like a movie, same characters, some new ones, different scenes and locations..."

"Maybe fog looms large in your personal motif, Eddie. Which could indicate many things."

"Yeah? Like what?" *Strike, puff, drag.*

"Well...being lost in a fog naturally comes to mind."

"Brilliant deduction, Doc, absolutely brilliant. Abso-friggin'-*lute*ly."

"Well, maybe it means nothing at all, then."

"Why does everything gotta *mean* something, Doc? Maybe things are the way they are and we just read stuff into 'em to make it all not seem so friggin' pointless."

"Maybe you're a natural Taoist."

"Huh? Tourist? Like through the world an' life an' shit? Like I don't even really *live* here? Like *none* of us really do?"

"Sort of. That's not exactly what I said but that was a very interesting philosophical extrapolation on its own. Never mind for now. Stop pacing, Eddie, you're beginning to make me anxious."

"Can't have that now, Doc. *One* of us has to have our head screwed on straight here." *Clop, clop, whump.*

"You were talking about life in your mother's house."

"Really think you pulled a fast one, huh? Knowin' talkin' 'bout the old man would naturally probably lead into the old lady. Smooth, Doc, real classy."

"I wasn't counting on you segueing into that taboo topic, but I wasn't about to stop you, I'll admit. I can certainly understand why you'd feel *awkward* about discussing such an unusual situation. But don't feel *ashamed*, Eddie."

"Fuck shame, Doc."

"Actually that's a healthy outlook under the circumstances."

"Thanks, I always thought so. Anyway, you want me to go on or what?"

"Please do."

"Yeah, so anyways, I was raised in this big old house in Jersey City with a lotta very sweet hookers dotin' on me alla time. I mean I coulda had it worse, y'know? I mean I really coulda. And Ginny, my old lady, she was *there* for me, at least. She kept me pent up like a cat or somethin', though. I never even went to school like normal kids. She just brought me tons of books an' she's read 'em to me and she sorta educated me in what really mattered in life."

"Which was what, in her opinion?"

"Ah, I dunno, this and that, y'know. The Golden Rule and crap. Readin', writin', arithmetic, that whole deal. She never let me outta her sight, man. It was almost like she was tryin' to make up for bein' such a screw-up by makin' me into some sorta saint or somethin'."

"To atone for her sins, as she saw it."

"Yeah, whatever."

"Seems rather ironic. I mean considering the unusual manner and environment in which you were raised."

"I guess that's one way to describe it, yeah."

"She must have let you out *some*times, especially when you matured to the point of making your own decisions. There was no way she could've just stifled a boy's natural desire to get out there and learn things for himself."

"She did a pretty good job of it for a while, Doc. She kinda put the fear of God into me."

"You mean to say she actually became religious?"

"I wouldn't go *that* far. She just sorta had little talks with me about the way things was out there, and that if I wanted to not end up like a pathetic but rich wreck like her, I'd best avoid *everything* I saw on TV. She thought the enda the world was pretty close an' to prove it she had me watch the news every night. Shit, she had a pretty good case as far as I could see it. Y'know? Know what I'm sayin'? I mean I really can't believe things have gone on as long as they have. I mean I really can't, y'know? Can *you*?"

"I must admit I'm mystified at times. But there are people out there who care, who want to pull through at all costs. Like me, for instance."

"Yeah, well my old lady didn't much give a damn. Sometimes it was like we was livin' in a friggin' bomb shelter, stocked with typea booze you could think of.

Meantime the old man was fryin' so many brain cells I thought his brain was gonna show up on the menu at Denny's. Denny's. Sometimes the old lady would take me out to eat, to a coffee shop, like on holidays, y'know, at cheap joints, though, where you could get a turkey an' all the trimmings for like a buck ninety-nine or somethin'. She was pretty tight with her bread, for some reason."

"It was her only source of security, really. Her money. I mean she had no husband, no..."

"Oh, she had her guys, all right. I mean like outside of work, after hours."

"She had regular boyfriends, you mean."

"You got it. One loser after another, man. Assholes on parade, it seemed like. I couldn't be*lieve* the jerks she'd disappear with."

"She used to disappear?"

"Hell, yeah. You kiddin'?"

"Where on Earth did she go?"

"I dunno, here and there mostly. Florida, Mexico, the Bahamas. The mountains. A lotta rich guys, old married slobs, y'know, really went for her, an' wined 'n' dined her on their expense accounts. I figured she deserved to have fun, y'know?"

"What about you? Didn't *you* deserve some fun as well?"

"Yeah, I guess. Well, I told ya, the old man took me into the city now an' then, an' I hadda all right time. You know, it was okay. Can't complain, can't complain. I guess, I dunno. I mean who really cares, am I right?"

"Did you ever feel any true love for your mother, Eddie?"

...

"Eddie?"

"What?"

"Did you hear my..."

"Yeah, yeah. I'm thinkin', is all."

"Take your time."

"Okay, I'm done."

"Well?"

"Well, what?"

"What's your answer?"

"What was the question again?"

"I guess that's as good an answer as any."

"Aw, I'm just playin' with ya, Doc. Lighten up. But, y'know, like who really knows, know what I'm sayin'? 'True love.' I mean what the hell *is* that? Do *you* know?"

"Actually I wish I did."

"See? And you're the expert."

"Not exactly. Not on everything. Just listening."

"Yeah."

"You mentioned the other, ah, women looked after you as well."

"Yeah, yeah, sure, sure. Especially when Ginny took off with Howard Johnson or whoever. They were my babysitters. Like I said, I coulda had it worse. They really spoiled me, too. At least most of 'em did. There were a few cunts—'scuse me, bad apples in the bunch, sure, but, on the whole, it was pretty cushy, bein' around all them dames alla time, even though I was too young to really appreciate it, know what I'm sayin'? At least for a while, anyways. But ever since I've always sorta gone for older women. Well, almost always."

"I see."

"You see what?"

"It just make sense, that's all. In an offbeat kind of way."

"Nice that somethin' does, right?"

"Yes. Eddie, tell me: how did your mother get away with keeping you hidden all those years? Didn't you ever have the urge to just run away?"

"I did, Doc. I *did*."

"How old were you?"

"Twenty-three."

"You mean to say you lived in that house until you

were twenty-three years old?"

"Yep."

"Why?"

"'Cause. The old lady. Every time I talked about splittin' she'd lay a big time guilt trip on me. Plus, y'know, there were other things."

"Like what?"

"Ain't you sick of hearin' about this already?"

"I told you I would when I was."

"Nice sentence. Where was it you went to college again?"

"I meant I would tell you when..."

"I know, I know, I'm just givin' you a hard time, is all."

"Thanks but no thanks. Now what other things?"

"What other things what?"

"What factors contributed to you remaining within that fortress of solitude?"

"I *knew* I shoulda quit while I was ahead. Ah, let's see—I guess that's when my blonde problem really got rollin'. Well, I was pretty young the first time it hit me, but..."

"The first time *what* hit you?"

"The blonde thing. Y'know."

"Fill me in, why don't you."

"Well..."

"Was it someone who lived in the house while you were growing up?"

"You got my number all figured out already, huh, Doc?"

"It was an obvious deduction. Go on, tell me all about it. Or as much as you care to."

"Not like you wanna pry or anything, right? Just kiddin', just kiddin'. Yeah...my first blonde."

"Or your second, counting your mother."

"What the hell's *that* supposed to mean?"

"Don't get testy, Eddie. I was merely pointing out that

the first blonde in your life was your mother, that's all."

"Yeah, but it wasn't the same as the rest, know what I'm sayin'? I mean it just wasn't."

"I understand."

"Yeah, sure ya do. Anyways, anyways, so...yeah. The one I was thinkin' of was this one hooker who was sorta my old lady's right hand, uh, whatever. I mean she looked after the place when Ginny was sick or away or somethin'. Her name was Josephine. She had these really big knockers and I remember 'em 'cause she used to bend me over all the time, changin' my diapers..."

"You remember that far back?"

"Well, yeah. Y'know. So anyways, she used to do that kinda stuff for me, and I sorta developed a sorta crush on her."

"When you were still an infant?"

"Well I mean it was innocent kinda thing, Doc. Nothin' *dirty* or nothin'."

"It's still hard to imagine. Or, easy to imagine, just hard to believe."

"Most things are in life, Doc. At least in *my* life. So Josephine was the big-boobed blonde nursemaid who sometimes snuck me out to the park or somethin' when she could get away with it. I still remember her perfume, or maybe it wasn't her perfume, but just her natural b.o. that appealed to me. Kinda...I dunno. *Sweaty* or somethin'. But *nice* sweaty, like she was sweatin' perfume you got from this certain flower that useta grow around the house. Or maybe it was just the *flowers* I remember smellin', and she happened to be there when I first smelled 'em, or...anyways, what the hell. I can't even remember the color of the flowers. But if I'm walkin' down the sidewalk, and I smell 'em, I remember 'em in a flash, and all these pictures of the past creep into my mind, like a friggin' time warp or somethin', only I can't really hold onto the old feeling that long. Less an' less, as I get older. Y'know? And I think of Josephine's knockers, and how warm she was.

Only I can't really remember much else about her, like her face or anything like that. She died when I was pretty young. Botched abortion or somethin', I dunno. I was too young. I remember I cried, though. None of the other dames could shut me up for like a week. I mean I was very friggin' passionate about the whole thing. And it couldn't have been lust, Doc, not at that age, so don't tell me *that*. I don't know *what* it was, but it wasn't that."

"You were simply responding to her kindness, it sounds like."

"Yeah, but, a *lot*ta the girls were kind, Doc."

"Were they also blonde?"

"I can't remember. Some of 'em hadda be, I guess."

"Did she do anything else special for you?"

"What, like whack me off?"

"Eddie, you're spoiling a very tender recollection."

"Sorry. Sorry. I dunno, let's see—ice cream. She used to buy me tons of ice cream. An' comic books. And she let me watch violent cartoons my old lady didn't want me to. You know, those Jap ones like, uh, I dunno, 'Astro Boy' an' 'Marine Boy' an' 'Ultra Man' an' shit. Remember those? An' the white lion, what was his name?"

"I was never much of a cartoon watcher."

"Yeah. Why doesn't that surprise me? But, yeah, so she used to buy me junk food while I dug on 'Speed Racer' while the old lady was takin' care of business. An' toys. She brought me this whole set of plastic dinosaurs, y'know, 'cause I used to be really into dinosaurs when I was a kid. And she read to me from 'The Jungle Book,' you know that book?"

"Kipling, of course."

"Who, what?"

"Rudyard Kipling, the author's name."

"Oh. Whatever. *God*, I loved that woman. Almost as much as the old lady."

"You sincerely loved your mother, Eddie?"

"Yeah, sure! Whaddya, kiddin' me? She was my

mother, for Chrissake."

"That's not an automatic prerequisite for closeness."

"Yeah, I guess. Say what?"

"Just because she was your mother doesn't mean..."

"Yeah, yeah, well I did. I mean I was. Close to her, I mean. She just did what she thought was best for me an' all that. *You* know. You hadda mother once, right?"

"I'd rather not get into my background at this point."

"Didn't think so."

"But, yes, I had, *have*, a mother. But love, *real* love, can differ from respect or…fear."

"Fear? Fear of *what*?"

"I don't know. You tell *me*."

"She wasn't nothin' to be scared of, Doc. Jeez. She never hit me—or hit *on* me—or nothin' like that. Not even the old man ever laid a hand on me. Well, not much. He didn't have the chance. I hardly saw him when I was a kid, and when I got older he knew I coulda kicked his ass without battin' an eye, so…"

"How did your father die, Eddie? If I may ask."

"'If I may ask.' Love it. You kill me sometimes, Doc. Cancer."

"Oh. I'm sorry."

"Yeah, I'm drownin' in your tears over here."

"Eddie, it's very hard to tactfully express regret at a stranger's loss. I was simply…"

"Yeah, yeah, okay. Forget it. Lung cancer, Doc. Or maybe he o.d.'d first, like on purpose. I knew he was dyin' before he kicked off, and so did he. He wasn't that old, either. But I figured, what the hell, maybe he was better off. I mean bein' dead. I know that sounds lousy but he wasn't exactly the happiest sonofabitch in the world, know what I'm sayin'? Anyways, just forget it."

"I truly am sorry, Eddie. As sorry as I can be, at least."

"Yeah. Thanks." Strike, puff, drag.

"Eddie, ah, don't you think maybe you should cut down a bit on the smoking?"

"Smoke gettin' to ya or what?"

"Yes, but, it could getting to you worse, if you follow my meaning."

"Yeah, I get your drift al'right. Like father, like son. Well, that's how it goes sometimes, Doc."

"But you can save yourself, Eddie. You don't *have* to die a horrible death at a young age if you don't want to."

"I ain't that young no more, Doc. Anyway tell that to all the babies getting snuffed in their cribs. Or to gang members on the Lower East Side, or here in Oakland. Or guys who didn't even belong but got it anyway. Or even James Dean, Doc. Or the poor bastards who are born just to die from a childhood disease. They never begged for an early grave, Doc. And I ain't, either. I got enough to worry about without thinkin' about livin' longer than I have to. Like gettin' through the next night. Know what I'm sayin'?"

"Yes, I do. But I still believe it's better to do everything in your power to survive, Eddie, even against terrible odds. Especially when you still do have your health, your best defense against pain and defeat. Preserve your body and your mind, and maybe your soul will be encouraged to stick around longer."

"I got news for ya, Doc. My soul ain't havin' a party inside of me, I don't care what my friggin' blood pressure is. So just get off it, Doc. I don't need no lectures like you was my mother, which you definitely ain't. So please just lay off, huh?"

"Fine."

"And don't pout."

"I beg your pardon?"

"Nothin', let it go."

"I think maybe that's enough for today, Eddie."

"You know best, Doc."

"If you really thought that, you'd listen to my admonition and take better care of yourself."

"Cuttin' down my pack a day would do wonders for me, I guess."

"And from the looks of you, you could use a little less alcohol in your system. Life for you seems tough enough without giving adversity a hand."

"Yeah, well, I'd give a penny for your *next* thought, Doc, but I'm flat broke. No gigs for a while."

"I don't deserve your hostility, Eddie. But I'll put up with it as long as I see a glimmer of hope through this two-bit façade of yours."

"Yeah, well, it's back to Heartbreak Hotel for me, Doc, while you go home to your cushy suburban oasis."

"That's hardly an accurate description of where I live."

"But close enough, I'll bet."

"Goodbye, Eddie, and thank you for being as civil as you were, and for opening up to me."

"Yeah, sure, anytime. Anytime. And say hello to your boyfriend for me."

Session Three

"How do you get here every day, Eddie?"

"Train."

"BART?"

"Yeah, what else?"

"And where is it in the City you live?"

"I told ya, Heartbreak Hotel."

"On Lonely Street, I take it. In the Suicide District."

"Yeah. Naw, I live in the Mission in some dive. When I first got here I wound up in North Beach, you know North Beach?, above some club, or near it, the Stone or somethin', on Broadway, y'know?, but it was so noisy it was drivin' me nuts, so I moved after like a week."

"You like the Mission District?"

"Yeah. Y'know. It's a'right."

"Is the place you live in pretty depressing?"

"Not by *my* standards it ain't. I've lived in worse. I stayed in this one place that like a friggin' bunker in Alphabet City for a while, when I first bailed outta the nest in Jersey. This place in the Mission is like the Ritz by comparison, know what I'm sayin'? Hot an' cold water an' everything."

"Communal restrooms?"

"Yup."

"How do you pay your tab?"

"I still got money saved up from a few gigs in L.A. an' Texas. It's runnin' out quick, though. In L.A. I saved money by crashin' at some dude's pad in West Hollywood, just below Sunset, y'know?"

"Vaguely. I haven't spent much time down there."

"I don't blame ya. It sucks. Too friggin' hot alla time. And you're like stranded without wheels. I was like livin' on an island where I was."

"What do you do for money in between club dates?"

"Pray."

"Seriously."

"Aw, this 'n' that, y'know. I've done everything. Washin' dishes, construction, sellin' fuckin' flowers on Santa Monica Boulevard. Sometimes I even—hey, you ain't a *narc*, are ya?"

"I can fill in the blanks, Eddie. I honor our confidentiality out of professional conscientiousness, but I hope you realize how dangerous and stupid it is to turn to crime to support yourself, even temporarily. One foul-up and you could pay for it for the rest of your life."

"Yeah, I know, I know. I got buddies who done time. One's an actor now. He got the idea in the slammer. Now he's big time, makin' big bucks, and I'm still a bum. And I mean he like made a livin' outta rippin' off cars 'n' shit. He like *lived* on Hollywood Boulevard. He was a pimp, a pusher, you name it. He was like a hero to all the scumbags in Hollywood. I used to hang out with him in this soul food joint on Highland or someplace. He dug soul food, an' he dressed real loud an' everything, like a spade, and his idol was Elvis Presley. He tried combin' his hair like the guy an' he wore rings an' shit and gave everybody orders. Now he's got his own entourage just like Elvis. He even bought one of his guys a car."

"Is he famous? Anyone I might know?"

"Yeah, maybe. I'll just call him Max, okay?"

"When's the last time you saw Max?"

"This past summer in L.A. I looked him up an' he gave me a job answerin' his phone and stuff an' I even crashed at his place a few nights. He kinda felt sorry for me 'cause he knew he'd be *me* if he wasn't so friggin' lucky. He's makin' a regular mint off what his agent calls his 'quality' and his 'look' an' this crap. Whatever's he got he just picked up off the street like anyone else. But the assholes in the movie biz think since he's had a rough life he's some sorta genius, so he's heads and shoulders above these punks raised in Malibu who graduate from high school an' go directly to bein' a movie star. Know what I'm sayin'? It's all such bullshit and I get sick just thinkin' about it. And Max thinks it's a joke too, 'cause he's gettin' paid to jerk everyone off. Or *get* jerked off. If he wasn't discovered by this agent who hyped this hood-with-a-heart image Max'd still be just another Hollywood Boulevard loser. And that's a fact."

"You sound a little bitter."

"Yeah? I wonder why I wonder. I can't imagine."

"Don't you think Max deserves his success?"

"Not any more than the *rest* of us poor bastards."

"Luck is a random, fickle bitch sometimes."

"Yeah no kiddin'. The Universe fucking hates me, and the feeling is mutual."

"Can I ask you, if you're not playing in any clubs now, and you're not working, how do you spend your time?"

"Well, I gotta practice a lot, Doc. I mean I gotta *practice*. I ain't no natural wonder like Max."

"Where, in your room?"

"Yeah sure, sometimes."

"You play on the streets?"

"Yeah, yeah, sure. Alla time. I pick up some change sometimes even in touristy places like Fisherman's Wharf and Ghirardelli Square."

"I didn't know that."

"Well, it ain't like I'm *famous* for it or nothin'. It's just somethin' I do sometimes. I can't make the rent or nothin' with it, but it buys me a few beers with chaser shots now and then at Spec's, y'know."

"Spec's?"

"Spec's, Spec's Bar, across from City Lights an' Vesuvio. You know, in an alley off Columbus in North…"

"Oh, oh. Near Tosca."

"Yeah, Tosca. Jeez, you hang out there?"

"When I'm in North Beach. There or Caffe Trieste."

"Figures."

"Why?"

"'Cause they're the joints everyone *else* hangs out to make themselves more bohemian or somethin'. Now Spec's, Spec's is cool 'cause it's a little joint, y'know, kinda like someone's living room almost, only it's all wood-like, real woodsy, an' the bartenders look like bartenders in old movies, and they play Billie Holiday alla time, an' I can sit there at the bar listenin' to Billie's blues while I slowly pass out on pints and shots, sittin' next to these other characters spillin' their guts to the bartender. There's two I seen, one big guy with a beard who looks like a young Santa Claus and the other one is bald an' has glasses. They're really cool and nice, but not *fake* nice, like an airline stewardess, but no-bullshit friendly-like, like they'll be cool an' rap with you an' all but if you give 'em any crap they'll throw you out on your ass, know what I'm sayin'? I like that. I dig honesty in people. So I spend a lotta time there or down at the Wharf or sometimes in a massage parlor downtown or somethin'. Or a cheap triple-feature at a grindhouse on Market Street. Or sometimes I go practice off alone in Golden Gate Park, y'know, in the woods by a pond or somethin', where it's nice and I can get away and I feel like nobody's listenin' except me and the animals and what do they care, right? One thing about animals, they mind their own business. I like that."

"Always alone?"

"Well, gimme a break, I ain't met nobody up here yet, 'cept at the massage parlor, some cute Chinese chicks, but no one I'd bring home to Mama, know what I'm sayin'?"

"I'll let the irony of that statement pass. How do you plan to get work up here?"

"I gotta make connections somehow. One thing about Max, he got me *connections*. All the work I got in L.A. was 'causea Max. But he can't help me up here, and I don't *want* him to, 'cause then I'd *owe* him somethin', somethin' *more*, I mean, an' I don't dig that, I don't dig that, 'cause next thing you know I'm just another flunky on the payroll an' not an old pal, y'know? So I'll just stick it out on my own till somethin' comes along. I was talkin' to this one really cool black dude in Chinatown who plays there alla time on the street, on Grant Street, which I don't like 'cause it's so crowded an' the Chinese are walkin' around in their own little worlds, y'know, like nobody else is there, y'know, an' they walk right into you an' shit and, anyway, so this guy says maybe he can get me a few bookings at this place called the Saloon in North Beach. Maybe. He said he's gotta talk to a few people first. I've heard that line before, though, so I ain't countin' on nothin' major."

"Why did you leave Los Angeles if you were making money there and Max could help you out?"

"I don't wanna talk about it right now." *Strike, puff, drag.*

"I won't force you to, Eddie." *Slurp.*

"Hey, what's that?"

"Café latte I forgot I had. I picked it up at Café Roma."

"Where?"

"Just a little place on Bancroft. It's frequented by students mainly who want their batteries recharged for school that day."

"I wouldn't know it, then. Only place I really know over here is Café Med. You know that place?"

"Café Mediterraneum?"

"Yeah. I like it 'cause there's a lotta rejects who hang out there and I can sorta fit in but not *hafta* fit into the scene. Know what I'm sayin'? You can be weird but not in a group. You can be weird by yourself."

"I don't consider you weird or a reject, Eddie."

"That's 'cause you probably don't hang out on Telegraph Avenue with the unemployed over-the-hill hippies moochin' off every schmoe who walks by for a quarter or a plane ticket to Hawaii or somethin'. You don't know what the other side of the fence even *looks* like, so how could you recognize someone from there?"

"You hardly know me well enough to make such a judgment, Eddie. I think you'd be surprised to know the places I've been and the people I've associated with."

"Yeah right."

"I'd need a frame of reference if I was going to be allowed to counsel people like you, wouldn't I?"

"People like me, whaddya mean, 'people like me'?"

"People with your...brand of life experience."

"Yeah, well, I'd rather have *my* brand than, than..."

"The generic brand."

"Yeah. What's that?"

"The so-called common lifestyle. The All-American Dream. Two parents who don't divorce, a nice suburban home, a decent education, a lucrative career, and all the comfortable benefits, emotionally and materially."

"I thought that kinda thing was only on TV, Doc."

"In truth, it is. The Sitcom Syndrome, I call it."

"Cute. What about you, was your background screw-up or what?"

"Later, Eddie. Perhaps."

"I ain't got my hopes up, don't worry."

"So what you're saying is you don't regret the life you've had?"

"Oh, I got regrets, Doc. Plenty. Like the first time I got laid—'scuse me."

"No need to blush, Eddie."

"I ain't blushin'."

"Sex is naturally an area to explore if you wish to discuss this blonde mystique you're obsessed with."

"I ain't obsessed with nothin'. I just dig blondes, is all."

"To the exclusion of all other types of women?"

"Well, yeah, basically."

"Are you Jewish?"

"Nope."

"Then you're obsessed. In my professional opinion."

"Fine, have it *your* way, Doc."

"You were talking about regretting your first sexual encounter."

"Man, you really like to harp on weird shit, you know that? I mean I can't figure you out. Okay, so whaddya wanna know, all the horny details or what?"

"Not a blow-by-blow description, as it were, but more of a psychological perspective."

"Oh, yeah, right. My specialty. You don't do much analyzin' for an analyst, y'know. Pretty cushy racket, if ya asked me."

"Again, Eddie, if it's a topic you'd rather avoid."

"Do you understand the word 'manipulation'?"

"I'm familiar with it, yes."

"That's you."

"How do you figure that?"

"'Cause. You're manipulatin' me to talk about stuff insteada just lettin' it come out natural."

"Do you really believe that, Eddie?"

"Yeah. No. *I* dunno. I just feel funny talkin' to one broad about bangin' another, is all. I got *some* kinda half-assed honor, ya know."

"Well, don't think of me as a broad, Eddie, or a woman, that is. Just don't think of me at all. I'm not here. Talk to yourself.

"Oh, nice. Now you got me talkin' to *myself* while you kick back and' pretend not to listen. Sweet racket, Doc, I gotta hand it to ya."

"I'm only trying to make you feel more comfortable, Eddie."

"Yeah, thanks. You're a peach. Anyhow I mean what the hell, Doc. I'm used to bein' discomfortable, or whatever. Life is pain, am I right?"

"I certainly hope there's more to it than that, Eddie."

"Aw, come off it, Doc. You come into this lousy world with pain an' you go *out* with it. And don't look at me like that. Creation wasn't *my* big fuckin' bright idea. That's just how it is."

"But what happens in between birth and death is largely up to us. Take this encounter you're reluctant to discuss. It wasn't like the girl *raped* you, was it? Your first time didn't *have* to be a bad memory, did it?

"Practically, almost, Doc, I'm tellin' ya. I was set up, kinda. It was down in Venice. By this time I was twenty-three an' still cherry, believe it or not. It was like I grew up in a candy store so I was *sick* of candy, *afraid* of it even, even though I still had a helluva sweet tooth. I blew a few opportunities back East, goin' back to when I was fifteen, but my old lady had fucked up my conscience so bad, tellin' me women and sex was basically evil, that every time I came close, so to speak, my boner would deflate like a hot dog balloon. Well, that wasn't *always* the case, but…Anyways, anyways, this chick in Venice—the one down here in California, by the way, not the one over in Europe or someplace, you got that, yeah—anyways, this chick was an artist, and she was gettin' the hot beef injection from *everyone* in this band I was hooked up with at the time, and she came onto me alla time an' everything, at gigs and stuff, an' I kinda liked her, she had big knockers an' everything, only she was like forty or somethin', and she wasn't, y'know, she wasn't *blonde* or anything, so she wasn't really my type. But late one night—none of the other guys in the band knew I was cherry, see—but late one night the broad offers me a ride home, an' I thought she meant my motel, but what she *really* meant was her place near the beach. I was stayin' at the Tropicana in West Hollywood at the time with the other guys in the band, y'know, an' I told her to turn off Sunset on La Cienega and go down to Santa Monica Boulevard where the Tropicana was, right, and she did, I mean she turned on La Cienega, only she goes *past* Santa Monica to Norm's Coffee Shop, and we pull in there and she says she's hungry. It's like three in the morning but I believe her an' once I'm in there I get hungry too. The place is crawlin' with lowlife all-nighters, punks who just escaped from local clubs, winos, teenage brats who think they're big time 'cause they're out after hours in some all night '50s type diner smokin', y'know, some Beverly Hills brats, that whole scene, right?, so, so, me an' this chick— Merva or Minerva or somethin', I don't remember, some half-baked unreal artsy name like that, wants to show me her artwork, so by this time I'm so buzzed on coffee and sugar I say sure, what the hell, let's make a night of it, so we blow Norm's after breakfast and go down Wilshire to the freeway and wind up in Venice. She gives me some weed and blow on the way so by the time we get to her pad I'm sky high, right, so we go into this artsy place right on the beach with lotsa pillows an' throw rugs an' candles an' chimes, and she puts on some Doors or Stones or somethin' and starts to strip. I mean just like that. I got so nervous I get the shakes, right, an' the chick used to be a nurse before she started painting an' sculptin', y'know, an' I'm tryin' to concentrate on this really weird shit she's been workin' on while she stands there naked, sexy as hell, I can *smell* her, she's so sexed up, and I can't stop shakin', like I was epileptic or somethin', right, so she gives me a Xanax or Valium or somethin' like that, on *top* of the weed an' blow, but *that* don't work, so I swallow another one down with some whisky from a bottle, an' by this time I'm so wasted I nearly keel over, y'know, so, so, she pushes me on the bed an' straddles me, takin' my clothes off, an' begins suckin' me off, an' even though I'm turned on I'm so sleepy I can barely keep it up, but eventually I get, y'know, hard an' stuff, and she puts me inside of her and we're pumpin' away, but I was so drugged, like a circus lion, I barely felt anything, a big come down, so to speak, I'm like *numb*, right, inside *and* out, but I keep at it anyway, but I may as well have been beatin' off or dickin' a wet sponge for all I cared, I just wanted to get it over with an' get some friggin' sleep, and finally she starts squirmin' an' moanin' an' everything, and I could tell it was the grand finale, at least for *her*, only I ain't done yet, but I don't care, but *she* does, she's kinda pissed, in a way, like offended I mean, so she starts suckin' me off again and playin' with my balls and I finally I come a little in her mouth but she sorta gags and lets go, so I squirt all over her face and boobs, pretty good wad for a zombie, and then I just collapse.

"Next thing I remember was wakin' up a few hour later, it's like dawn, an' the phone rings an' she's talkin' to some guy who is sayin' he's madly in love with her, while she's lyin' there in all her glory, with my jism still stuck all over her tits, I could see it on her *lips* while she's talkin', for Chrissake, 'scuse me but that's how it was, the room *reeked* of sex, and she makes a date with him anyway, while I'm still right there, like I was a john or somethin', or worse, *not even there*. I felt pretty low, so I got up while she was still on the phone and went to her shower an' washed off. When I got dressed she sends me out for coffee and cigarettes from this little market around the corner, and I keep wondering if the guy behind the counter could smell me, 'cause I can *still* smell her all over me, an' worse, I worry he can *recognize* the smell, an' in fact the smell of her made me hard again, an' I was hung-over but sober so maybe I could actually enjoy an encore, but when I got back, she was in the shower already. I thoughta that dude on the phone, left the cigarettes on the table, took my coffee an' split. I see her later at the club that night with this poor guy, the one on the phone, I figured, an' she hardly even *looks* at me, much less *talk* to me. So after waitin' all those years for some sorta magic, my first time was with this over-the-hill groupie who didn't give a shit about me an' frankly, I didn't give a shit about her neither, so I guess it evened out."

"One-night stands are never much fun, Eddie. Especially if it's your first experience. There must be mutual respect as well as passion for *any* sensual experience to be rewarding on any level."

"Yeah, whatever. Too late now. And the worst part of it is, I *knew* it, I knew at the time that it just wasn't right. I don't know what I was thinkin'. I was thinkin' with the wrong head, is what I was doin', if ya get my drift. And the real bitch of it is, she wasn't even, wasn't even..."

"Blonde?"

"Yeah, right. In fact she had dark hair with lotsa gray already. What a pisser. Nice boobs, though. I still beat off thinkin' about 'em sometimes, but I can't see her face, or I see...someone else's." *Strike, drag.* "But what the hell, life ain't a friggin' poem, right? More like a comic book. I mean what the hell did I expect—Marilyn Monroe, for Chrissake? I tell ya one thing, though, I'd rather done Marilyn in her grave down in Westwood than nail this broad if I hadda do it all over again. I can't think straight just *thinkin'* about it. In my mind, the memory is like this mix of lust and...depression."

"Well, I trust you've at least physically, if not psychically, recovered from the emotional trauma of that encounter."

"You kiddin'? Now I can pop a wad just *lookin'* at a sexy broad, even if I'm in a *coma*. Oh, sorry. Sometimes I forget myself when I'm here, and who I'm with, like I'm rappin' with the guys in the band or somethin', or some joker in a bar."

"That's quite all right, Eddie. I prefer you think of me as such than be prudish and untruthful. Speak your soul."

"And my dick, is that it?"

"If you're so moved."

"It moves all by it*self*, Doc. It's got a mind of its *own*, that thing. But don't worry, I ain't got much to brag about in that department. I ain't Hugh friggin' Hefner over here. Anyways, I wasted too much time in Bimbo City."

"Pardon, where?"

"L.A. Bimbo City."

"Oh. Well, maybe you'll have a more fortunate future here in the Bay Area."

"I ain't countin' on it. I mean my future."

"I can't believe you're that apathetic."

"Believe whatcha want, everyone else does."

"But you have so much to live for, Eddie."

"Aw, you can do better than a corny line like *that*, Doc. I mean one less poor sucker in this world ain't gonna break nobody's heart. Not even God's. He's got plentya *other* people He or She or It can ignore besides me. Anyway sometimes I get the idea I shoulda been dead a long time ago, like I ain't really livin', I'm some sorta shadow of a real person, y'know? Like I fall in love with chicks who can't bother to give me the time of day, I play my guts out on a musical instrument an' who the hell really listens except doped-up drunks in cheap nowhere dives who don't give a fuck about anything anymore than I do. I mean even the jobs, the regular jobs I get, I could get replaced on five minutes' notice. Face it, Doc, I'm one of those faces in the crowd that makes no difference whether I'm there or not, 'cause there's another one to take my place on the assembly line any second."

"What about your mother, Eddie? You believed she loved you. Maybe she still does, wherever..."

"No one, but *no one*, gives a flying fuck about Eddie the Putz, Doc, and that's a *fact*. That's just how it is. I mean, you're *paid* to spend time with me."

"Stop whining, Eddie. I thought you said you didn't like to complain. I have a job to do, true, but I still care. Play your blues for *me*, Eddie. I'm here to listen. It doesn't matter *why*. I'm still here."

"Sorry, I don't mean to sound like a pussy. Survival is for the tough, you're right. I still love Life, even if...y'know. Fuck it. I don't care anymore."

"Feeling like you have an unrequited love of Life isn't the same as apathy. That gives me more to work with, frankly. This strange 'blonde ambition,' to put it colorfully, has caused you to set lofty standards of womanhood for the loves of your life to live up to. *No* one's an angel, Eddie. Not really. I think your mother, with best intentions, instilled this puritanical ideal in you of the perfect female, in order to shield you from all the imperfection of your childhood environment. Although you did mention something else earlier—I didn't want to interrupt you then but it stuck with me—you said something about your mother telling you women in general were wicked? Or just sex with them?"

"Yeah, right. She told me women were basically evil creatures, includin' *her*, an' they had to fight a losing battle to overcome their own badness. 'Course, her mind was so warped, so fucked-up she couldn't help it. She was raised in a very religious family in Texas and it bugged her how she made a livin', though obviously not enough to make her quit. I could never figure that out. An' she sure seemed that *she* liked sex herself, a *lot*, even if it *was* evil and all. Like she'd already given up and gotten used to the idea *she* was gonna burn in Hell, might as well get her jollies while she could. She was just tryin' to save *me* before it was too late. Also she never really got over my old man, I could tell. Ain't that a kick? He was a *bum*, but she sincerely loved that guy, the *only* one she ever loved, I could totally tell. He did okay with the broads after he dumped Ginny, too. Must've been his Latin blood or somethin'. Somethin' *I* obviously didn't get enough of, whatever it was."

"You're hardly unattractive, Eddie. I really can't believe your self-esteem is that low."

"Yeah? Thanks for the vote, Doc, but I was just a twerp, six or seven, when I was first blown outta the saddle by some blonde bimbo. It ain't a quality I've outgrown, neither, whatever it is. Or whatever it *ain't*. Know what I mean?"

"Who is this junior Mata Hari you refer to, Eddie?"

"Aw, just some little dame, is all, some cute little pony-tailed tight-assed neighborhood beauty I used to see when Josephine or somebody would take me to the park near the house. I saw her just before Josephine kicked off, right, so they kinda overlapped. This little chick was like around eleven or twelve, older but in the same ballpark as yours truly, know what I'm sayin', but still too friggin' old for *me*.

I useta try an' play with her, y'know, in the sandbox an' everything, and her old lady was this well-to-do type broad with a fur coat and onea them funny hats that chicks wear at funerals, a *funeral* hat, and it was always kinda funeral weather in Jersey anyways, at least when *I* was out, and after Josephine bit it, my old lady an' this chick's—Greta was her name—Greta's old lady an' mine would sit next to each other on the bench while we messed around. Well, not *messed* around messed around, just *fooled* around, kid stuff, y'know, playin' Tarzan an' Jane an' crap like that, y'know, and this chick Greta was so delicate it made ya wanna cry. I liked to play 'Jungle Book' with her, 'cause Josephine had just finished readin' it to me, just before she kicked off, an' me an' Greta would pretend we was animals in the book, y'know, wolves or somethin' like that, an' crawl around in the dirt like a coupla dipshits, but we hadda gas, in a little kid kinda way, only my heart was bustin' at the seams just bein' around her. I mean really. Whenever my old lady wanted to leave the playground I'd throw a fit, an' Greta would give me this look like I was *retarded* or somethin', right, but I didn't care, I had no friggin' pride whatso*ever*, man. I was a putz even then. But I really loved that little chick. She sorta replaced Josephine in my heart for a while, y'know? And she was so delicate, so, so like a little *girl*. Soft voice an' all, nice skin, like she was tan, even in winter, it was amazing, an' she had this cute little smile, y'know, that made her cheeks sorta fat, or plump, I guess is the word, an' her old lady always dressed her to the nines, real nice, like she was goin' someplace right after, which made me friggin' jealous like a madman, just thinkin' about it, y'know…My stomach was like, like it was cream o' wheat or some slop like that, just bein' around her…

"One time behind a tree I snuck a sorta kiss on her cheek, y'know, an' she smiled an' kissed me back on the nose, only I think she was aimin' somewhere else, but I ain't sure where, exactly, but it didn't matter, an' then her old lady called an' she took off an' then I didn't see her at the playground for a while, y'know, I couldn't sleep or eat or nothin' an' Ginny freaked out an' called this special doctor they used for abortions who worked on convicts an' shit an' he checked me out an' said I was cool, it was all in my head, an' then one time me an' the old lady, after like three months go by, me an' the old lady are at the corner grocery store, an' she's buyin' me some little plastic toy or somethin', an' I see her, I see Greta, an' she's all decked out, as usual, an' she's with some friends around her age, mostly girls, who all look nice, y'know, an' then some guy, some little asshole of a jock or somethin', around fourteen, I guess, shows up with a buddy an' he walks up to Greta an' pats her on the ass, an' she laughs an' then they all kinda group together an' go outside of the store there, an' the punk starts passin' out cigarettes an' the whole gang is smokin' up a storm, right, an' my old lady leads me outside past 'em an' Greta don't even *look* at me, like I ain't there, right, an' I remember the smell, it was pot, but I didn't know what the hell pot was back then, an' my old lady tells me that this chick I useta play with in the park, her old lady told Ginny that Greta was too *good* for me, that she didn't want us hangin' out no more. And there she is with this little half-pint gangsta gettin' stoned on the corner. I started cryin' before we even got back to the house and Ginny told me I was better off without hangin' with trash like her, right, that really *I* was too good for *Greta*. Only I knew my old lady was fulla shit, and so did she. I didn't go to the friggin' park for a year after that."

"Did you ever see Greta again?"

"Yeah, off and on, always with a guy, too. Always some friggin' sleazy motherfucker…An' she got worse an' worse lookin', till by the time she was a teenager she looked like a slut, and even my old lady didn't look like that, an' y'know…But every time I saw Greta, my heart would flinch. I thought I had friggin' asthma or somethin' before I was ten, for Chrissake. I still wonder sometimes whatever happened to Greta…I still dream about her sometimes, only when she was still young an' innocent, in the sandbox in the park, pretendin' we was in the jungle, alone, and she was so tender it made me cry…ah, what the hell. That's ancient history. Except in my dreams, though, I can even feel the weather, it'll be cold, and she'll have her cute little red jacket on, and red hat and gloves, and the wind makes her face sorta pink, y'know, so her teeth look real white, an' it's real overcast an' everything, an' the trees got no leaves or anything, I mean it don't look like no jungle *anywhere*, let's face it, but we don't care, it was just me and her, with my old lady an' the broad I prayed would be my mother-in-law watchin' us, an' everything would be roses as long as Greta stayed young an' never moved or met some pint-sized junkie who put a lotta makeup an' shit on her face an' who the hell knows *what* else…I woulda *never* done that, I don't care what her old lady thought. *Never*. I woulda just kept her just like she was, forever."

"Greta was blonde, is that right?"

"Yeah, sure."

…

"Eddie?"

"Hm? Oh, sorry, Doc, I musta drifted off. I do that sometimes."

"It's quite all right. You don't think, Eddie, that your mother's disapproval of Greta had anything to do with your separation from her?"

"Naw. Least I don't *think* so. I mean I know she wasn't crazy about Greta or nothin', but it was no big deal, she was just someone to play in the park with, it wasn't like we was *engaged*, know what I'm sayin'? Well, to me, it *was* like we was engaged, though, and maybe Ginny saw that. I mean I took it very, very seriously, the whole thing. I really wanted to *marry* Greta. I thought about it alla time, what it would be like, our folks gettin' together at Christmas an' Thanksgiving an' all that, y'know, an' me an' Greta livin' like normal people in a normal house an' havin' normal kids, an' no one would catch on my old lady was a hooker an' my old man a bum, right, an' everything would be roses, like those stupid old shows I useta watch when I was a kid, 'Beaver Knows Best,' or whatever. *Ha*. That *does* sound like *my* house, actually."

"Amusing, Eddie, but I don't think that's what Greta wanted out of life, anyway. I mean if she kept going the general direction she was headed in her youth. It sounds like she got into a disreputable crowd and rebelled against everything you could only dream about, or watch on TV."

"Yeah, ain't that a kick, though? An' her old lady thought *I* was bad news. But, I dunno, Doc. A *lotta* girls go through that, y'know, when they're young. They get over it, when they realize that the guys on the street ain't got bread on a regular basis an' that life in the fast lane ain't such a cushy proposition, know what I'm sayin'? They always go back, they always go back. Believe me, I know. Greta's probably married to some friggin' lawyer an' livin' on Long Island an' raisin' her *own* little delicate heartbreaker by now. That's how it goes, Doc. Everywhere. You want sex on a steady basis, you pay for it. Same with love. The whole world ain't nothin' but a big whorehouse. Security buys love, but love don't buy security."

"Not *all* women are like that, Eddie, no need to insult our whole sex in general because of your own choices in love."

"Aw, come off it, Doc. In L.A. if you ain't got like fourteen major credit cards an' a fancy car an' a killer pad no dame worth a look will even share the air with you. Up here maybe it's different, I don't know yet. Maybe you only need *ten* credit cards to get the time of day from a chick. We'll see."

"So it sounds like you agree with your mother, that women are basically evil?"

"Aw, I dunno. Gold-diggers, yes. Vampire Bitches from Hell? Not necessarily, though I've met a few of those, too. Everyone's tryin' to just get by, any way they can. I can dig it. Fuck it, who cares." *Strike, drag, puff.*

"Frankly, Eddie, I find your criteria for women as shallow as their alleged pre-requisite for wealth and stability—which is a natural instinct, to a point. Women are nesters, so they want a solid nest. But that's isn't as superficial as the color of one's hair, is it?"

"What the fuck ya mean by *that*, Doc?"

"A girl being pretty—and blonde —is the same as a man being rich, isn't it?"

"Well, Doc, wiser men than me have said that, so who am I to say? I guess so. Whaddya want *me* to do about it? I didn't make up the friggin' rules. We're *all* a bunch of bastards, ain't we?"

"I think you're being way too harsh on yourself and humankind in general, Eddie. Take me, for instance."

"'Scuse me?"

"In case you haven't noticed. *I'm* blonde."

"Yeah, I noticed."

"And my boyfriend *isn't* rich. And I don't consider myself a raving beauty."

"A matter of opinion, Doc. Which ain't no indication of *mine*, so don't get excited…You're a looker an' I think you *know* it, an' I think *you* know I think so, you don't need me to *say* it, so no point fishin' in my wet dreams for a compliment or whatever. So your guy ain't well-off, so what? Well then he's on his way, or somethin'. He ain't nothin' like me, I can guarantee that."

"Eddie…" Ding, ding.

"What the hell is that?"

"The alarm on my cell. I'm afraid I'm late for a dinner date."

"Oh, yeah? Where?"

"Yoshi's Jazz Club, matter of fact. The one in the City. Why?"

"Right. Classy joint. For some reason I didn't think it was at no taqueria. Just checkin' is all. Have fun, Doc. See you in your dreams."

Session Four

"What do you call your mother, Eddie?"

"Collect."

"No, I meant, when you refer to her. Mother, Mom, *Mommy*."

"*Mommy*? Are you kiddin' with that crap? I call her Ginny, what else? That's her name."

"Rather unusual for a child to refer to the parent by a first name."

"Not where *I* come from. I know guys who called their parents a lot worse. I knew this cat once who led this band I played for a few weeks in Chicago, at the Green Mill, called themselves Man-Tool and the Flesh-Pistons, sounds like punk or metal but really they played progressive jazz fusion, some funk, anyways Man-Tool called his old man Arty Inseminator and his old lady Sperma Bank. He was pretty creative with names. I think he got into the porn industry next—playin' the soundtrack music, that is."

"I think they played here in Berkeley once, actually."

"Yeah, they got around. Man-Tool was a helluva guy. He was pretty ugly and he was always fallin' in love with chicks who wouldn't bother to spit on him if he wasn't a musician. He got his share but I remember he was hooked on this hot bartender chick who worked at the Green Mill, he sent her roses an' she flirted like hell, but then he waltzes in on the chick in bed with the band manager, an' he says, next time I send that cunt flowers it'll be to her *funeral* after she's gagged on some guy's cock! Helluva guy, helluva guy."

"What a revolting sentiment."

"Hey, I could dig where he was comin' from. I been there where he was, lotsa times, lotsa times. I know guys who *shot* women for less, and vice versa. Love is very violent, Doc. Like, in Texas I played with this country-rock type band and they useta play really raunchy joints in Houston in the worst areas, off the Gulf Freeway, all the way down to Galveston. Called themselves the Texas De-Rangers, or somethin', they changed their name a lot, but that's what it was when *I* played with 'em. Anyway, this one guy, the drummer, was a big fat sonovabitch everyone called Lardbucket. He played drums like nobody's business, man, but he took up the whole back of the stage at every gig. He useta get so excited just *talkin'* to some sweet young thing he'd cream his pants an' hafta excuse himself. I'm dead serious, that's a fact! Right in the middle of a conversation—*gush*! No kiddin'. It was embarrassin' as hell. Anyway I remember this one chick who Lardbucket was losin' sleep over—he even lost *weight* on accounta this broad, for Chrissake—she laughed at him at some bar for creamin' his pants and he picked her up an' threw her out the fuckin' window, an' was about to toss the *pool table* after her, but some good ol' boys got together an' beat him down with bottles an' chairs an' all. He broke the chick's neck an' got sent up. An' another time I was wastin' oxygen blowin' for some Top Forty band in Saint Louis or someplace, Kansas City maybe, an' this guy, called Shades 'cause that's what he wore alla time, like he was blind, Shades robbed the cash register one night at this hotel an' his girlfriend turned him in for the reward money, then changed her mind later, bailed him out, an' he *stabbed* her. Not to *death*, just enough to get sent back to the can for a long friggin' time. And I know *plenty* of broads who shot or stabbed or otherwise maimed their boyfriends too, all for love. Fuckin' guys and dolls, man. Or guys an' *guys*, dolls an' *dolls*, whatever, it's all the same shit."

"None of which explains why you call your mother by her first name."

"Nope, I guess not. Wasn't supposed to. What's the difference, anyways?"

"Even when you were young, you called her Ginny?"

"Aw, get off it, willya already?"

"As you wish. It's just that I've been thinking about some of what you've been saying, about your relationships, your misogyny, your mother..."

"My Miss *Who*? What the hell ya talkin' about now, Doc?"

"You tell me."

"There we go again. Well, I'm not gonna make your job easy today, Doc. I just don't feel like talkin' much today."

"Bad week?"

"Lousy life."

"But if you found the perfect blonde angel, everything would be all right, isn't that it?"

"I ain't even *lookin'* no more, Doc. I mean I just ain't. Especially *these* days, how the world is an' all that crap. If you don't gotta worry about gettin' your heart torpedoed to smithereens you gotta worry about your dick maybe droppin' off in the toilet while you're takin' a whiz at some funky chick's pad. It's germ warfare out there these days, Doc. It's scary. And I *hate* condoms. Like puttin' a trash bag over a saxophone. Just ain't the same. If my jizz is goin' inside a piece of rubber inteada inside some chick's mouth or snatch or even ear drum I may as well just beat off into an ashtray. But then a lotta people are contaminated with VD in my circles, or they might get knocked up if you ain't careful, or you may find out they're hooked up an' now you're gonna get your ass kicked, whatever, always somethin' to worry about. Just a bunch of Venus Fly-Traps out there. Even the blonde ones. An' most of 'em ain't even *real* blondes an' you find out once you got your face buried in their pubic hair. Though I guess carpet don't *always* hafta match the drapes. Anyways, fuck it. Who needs the friggin' hassle? Easier to stay home an' whack off. And *safer*, too.

Even if it's like rehearsin' for a gig that never comes. So to speak."

"It can be a dangerous catalogue to select from, Eddie, I realize that. But intimacy isn't all about the sharing of bodily fluids. You have to risk your heart as well if you don't want to be alone. It seems to me much of your bitterness stems from too many solitary hours brooding about your sundry mishaps."

"You can't play the blues if you ain't *got* the blues, Doc. Am I right? It's part of what I do, what I *am*. You know? It ain't what I do, it's what I *am*. That kinda jazz, know what I'm sayin'?"

"Creativity can be inspired by joy as well as grief, though. Can't it, Eddie? Just think of what a positive effect your music could have on people if you played out of sheer love of life instead of resentment and pain. Think of the infectious joy."

"What the fuck am I, Kenny G for Chrissake? Gimme a break with that Hallmark crap. Nobody in no dive I've *ever* blown in was there to spread peace and harmony an' Good Will towards men. *Or* women. There were all blue as hell when they came in an' they got even lower as they got drunker. I was just background music, is all. We was just sharin' our misery, so it was kinda, I dunno. Kinda beautiful, in a sorry-ass way. I guess. I don't know what I'm sayin' Forget it."

"Maybe your melancholia *is* your joy, Eddie. Maybe you cling to it because it puts you in touch with fundamentals in your life, keeps you in tune, as it were, with the truth in your soul. The saxophone is an instrument of the heart. It can express love as well as loneliness, if you let it, and think of how your artistic horizons would expand as a consequence of this awareness and acceptance of the brighter side of life."

"*Brighter* side? Hell, Doc, that's what *laughin's* for. Know how much I laugh when I'm loaded? A *lot*, unless I'm cryin'. I gotta be doin' one or the other when I'm really shit-faced, know what I'm sayin'? I laugh a hell of a *lot,* don't worry. But sometimes I worry that like in the future, in a few hundred years, nobody'll need to laugh *or* cry, 'cause they'll have all the answers, there'll be no disease, guys an' broads will finally get along, nobody will be fuckin' with each others' countries and shit, everyone will be happy, so there'll be no need for fuck-ups like my old man to get on a stage and make an ass of himself so he can release whatever is inside of him that makes him scream inside, y'know? Don't you ever scream inside? *I* sure as fuck do. Unless I'm laughin' or cryin'. Or playin'. Or fuckin', if I'm lucky. Other than that, I'm screamin' inside like a motherfucker. Sometimes when I play I feel like I'm gonna bust from blowin' so hard, that the piece is gonna explode in my mouth, or the scream will come outta the sax, y'know, and blow the whole joint to Hell. I mean I just gotta blow that thing for all it's friggin' worth, I mean I just do, I just *do.* I mean like I'm makin' it scream insteada sing. My old man useta scream on *stage* sometimes."

"Was he into EST?"

"Naw. Just coke mainly, a little heroin now and then. How the hell should I know? But anyways he useta just come out an' *scream,* an' everyone in the audience would break up 'cause they was nervous, right, like they didn't know what the hell this clown was all about, only it felt good, hearin' someone *else* scream, like he was doin' it for *everybody.* It was like a big relief. At least for me it was anyways. Man, what a trip he was. But guys like him will be outta business in the future, I think. Unless we blow the fuckin' planet up first, natch. Weird, to think of all your little piss-ant problems goin' up in smoke, just like *that.*" *Snap.* "Jeez, life is fuckin' weird, ain't it? I mean is it weird or is it just me? I mean do you ever just wake up an' lie there thinkin' about your weird friggin' dreams an' wonderin' how you got from bein' a little kid to this lonely stupid cocksucker whose hair comes out in the shower an' whose vision sucks so bad he feels like he's always dreamin' anyways, an' it was just last night that he went to sleep as a little kid in Jersey with his whole life aheada him, an' when he woke up he was this nowhere anonymous dickhead with no future an' no money livin' in a fuckin' rat-trap in the middle of San Fran-fuckin'-cisco far away from anyone he knows, far away from the sandbox with Greta, from hangin' out with Max in Hollywood who I only see in the movies now, an' he knows he'll *never* be where Max is, he'll stay right where he is the rest of his rotten useless pointless life while Greta has a good time in Long Island goin' to barbecues and the PTA and shit, and, and…Jeez, I thought I didn't feel like talkin' today. Sorry."

"Eddie, somewhere in that rant you mentioned your weird dreams. Can you describe them for me? I mean other than the ones with Greta."

"Naw, I can't really. They're kinda like acid trips, in a way. Just my whole life thrown into a blender an' then chucked up against a funhouse mirror like in Coney Island. I mean in my dreams I wander from Jersey to California to Texas an' back in a few seconds it seems like, only the places in my dreams don't really look like anything or anyplace when I'm awake, though they're always the same when I go back to 'em at night…always weird an' fucked-up an' distorted an' dark, *really* dark…And nothin' makes sense, y'know. I can't figure 'em out. I couldn't write 'em down or anything even if I could remember 'em. I can't really describe 'em just talkin' about 'em. The best way to describe 'em is they're like nightmare soup, and I'm just swimmin' in it. Sometimes I worry *that's* where I'll go when I die, or if go into a coma, I'll just *live* there."

"Sounds like random impressions from the twisted labyrinth of your past: intense, dark, claustrophobic, because you're trapped in darkest depths of your own mind."

"It's a blast, I'm tellin' ya. If it was a ride I could sell tickets, like in a carnival."

"Maybe your personal demons run amok inside of you

when you dream. All of the people who've hurt you, or whom you feel victimized by, since you're the victim in all cases, it seems, at least to you, come back to haunt you, because the hostility bred in you is unresolved, possibly even compounded as time goes by, like a nuclear stockpile. All that negative energy, and nowhere to explode it."

"Yeah, what a pisser, man. I remember when I was a kid diggin' on shows like 'Voyage to the Bottom of the Sea' an' 'Batman' an' shit, an' that's how I saw the world, y'know, like a comic book, an' you could be or do anything you wanted, an' by the end of every episode you'd come out smellin' like roses no matter what, an' there was always next week to look forward to, a new adventure…When you're a kid, the littlest stupid fuckin' things give ya such a kick in the ass. Now these stupid things just seem stupid, y'know? You outgrow 'em so you can be a swingin' fuckin' hip adult like you're meant to be."

"You mean cynical."

"Yeah. What a drag. I really miss bein' a kid sometimes. Sometimes I go into a comic book store, like that one here downtown, y'know?, just so I can feel like a little kid again with no hassles like I got now, no bills to pay, no bald-panic, no women hang-ups. But things've changed an' there's nothin' you can do about it. Even TV shows are different now. I used to love that cop show 'Miami Vice' because the good guys always got screwed. I'd catch it in whatever cheap hotel I was stayin' in, unless I had a gig. I mean you dress everything up nice an' play some fancy mood music in the background, but underneath it's the same old bullshit, only prettier so you can stand it."

"Like film noir."

"Exactly. I guess. Huh? Never mind. *That's* what I meant about Art, Doc. You're just sayin', okay, God or whoever, fine, just cut us loose in this friggin' nuthouse with no roadmap or handbook and let us knock each other off, okay sure, fine, no problem, we'll just invent this thing called a saxophone an' some stuff called booze an' say to *hell* with it an' have a good time while we can, an' maybe paint a picture of how we *want* life to look, of how it *could* look if everything went right, if life was more like a friggin' poem than a comic book, know what I'm sayin'? Everything sucks, no matter what you do things'll turn out fucked, but at least we can look and sound good, so fuck you *too*, Jack."

"I notice you wear nice clothes for a poor man. The sharkskin, the skinny tie."

"Fashion 'n' style are two different things, Doc. These are my *work* clothes, anyways. Also the only ones I *got*. No dry cleaning for me. I wear 'em till they drop off me. Maybe you notice I rotate the same clothes every week, like I'm a reject from the Rat Pack or 'Reservoir Dogs'."

"A poor man's Mad Man."

"Yeah. Huh? Anyway, you gotta at least *look* good in my line. Chicks dig it, too. I ain't no hip-hop rock 'n' roll slob. You gotta make an impression like you're on top of things alla time, that you got the world by the balls, know what I'm sayin'? It's just an image, a lie, but fuck it. It's all bullshit but what ain't. What ain't."

"What's your favorite color, Eddie?"

"Huh? Who cares?"

"I do."

"Okay. Lavender. I guess. If I *hadda* pick one."

"I thought so."

"Why?"

"The socks. You *always* wear lavender socks."

"I told ya, my wardrobe is slick but limited."

"I still find it an interesting choice for socks."

"Don Johnson didn't wear *any*, and I bet that guy got *serious* pussy. Max liked purple a lot, an' he swatted bitches off like flies, only after he got famous, though. He useta give me purple clothes, hand-me-downs, but I never wore 'em. I kept these socks, though. They got holes in 'em but I still wear 'em, even though they don't match the rest of me. Maybe I need a lavender tie? I guess I'm sentimental. Ginny loved lavender. She wore it *all* the time. This one negligee, I remember…LV loved lavender, too. Funny."

"So did who? I didn't catch that last name."

"I didn't say a name, I said initials. LV."

"What does LV stand for? Love? Lavender?"

"May as well as far as you're concerned. No offense, Doc, but LV *stays* LV, and that's *that*. A'right?"

"Do you want to elaborate just a bit on who this mysterious 'LV' is?"

"Nope."

"Is it a girl?"

"Maybe."

"A *blonde* girl."

"Next subject, Doc."

"All right…it's just that you were on such a roll, like your subconscious was vomiting, to put it in terms you'd appreciate, and I was enjoying having you open up with such passion for a change."

"What passion? Get serious, willya?"

"Do you ever write and play your own material, Eddie? I think it could be very therapeutic for you."

"Yeah, matter of fact years ago I made a tape I got at home—'home,' what a joke—I mean back in my hotel, fulla stuff I just made up, little improv pieces, y'know, with weird titles. Like one is called 'Gasoline Shoes' 'cause I wrote it after this one time in L.A. I was with this chick I was bangin', or *tryin'* to bang, we'd just fooled around some, anyways we were on our way to her pad to finally close the deal an' stopped at a service station, since we were almost outta gas, at least the *car* was, an' I got out to put gas in the car—*her* car, little snazzy sports coupe, real sexy—so I went to put gas in the car like a *real* man would, only I didn't know what the fuck I was doin' 'cause I ain't ever even owned a car, I'm a cheap public transit slut, always have been, don't need the hassle of a car, anyways I take my best shot an' the stuff shoots back out at me from the hole in the car there, I guess I overloaded it like I was about to do to her pussy, or hopin' I would, anyway this thing, the hose is gushin' like a busted condom an' it rains gas all over my shoes an' shit, they got *soaked*, give me a hot foot and I'da *exploded*, an' the broad gets all pissed an' disgusted an' does it her*self* an' she drove home by herself an' I caught the bus an' went home an' whacked off. I felt so humiliated I went home an' wrote this blues piece called 'Gasoline Shoes.' You mighta heard of it, it was top of the charts for like ten years."

"Really?"

"No."

"Any other recent pieces I may or may not have heard of?"

"I get bits of inspiration, normally from times God is pissin' on me like that gas hose on my shoes. Like just the other day, I went to see a movie, which is all I ever do lately, a cheap matinee, some bullshit, an' I gotta pee like a bastard, so I buy my ticket, right, the guy there tears it in half, I run to the bathroom, an' I'm so anxious to go I don't even take the ticket outta my hand, I got my dick in one hand an' the ticket in the other, an' I wind up *peein'* on the damn ticket, so the bitch of it is, when I get to the movie, they won't let me in 'cause I say I lost my ticket, then I say fuck it, I give 'em my wet, smelly ticket an' they look at me like I was a bum, but I wasn't about to waste my bread an' not get a movie out of it, so there ya go."

"Did you go home and write some music about this special experience?"

"Naw. If I did, though, I guess I'd just call it. 'Pee Ticket,' or 'Piss Pass,' or 'Urination Blues,' or some shit. Who cares."

"Doesn't writing music about your mishaps make you feel better, though?"

"Yeah, a little. It used to, anyways. I'd rather just whack off or fuck, though. A lot easier with a quicker payoff. I don't get laid as much as I could, though. I'm a musician so I can pretty much pick some bitch up in a bar anywhere if I'm playin' there, an' I *have*, believe me, but it's kinda like I'm on this mission, to go around fuckin' up an' then writin' music about it, insteada just *fuckin'* an' then writin' about it. It's like any time I score, I can't *score*. Get it?"

"Your mission is to avoid *e*mission?"

"Cute. It's a *failed* mission, but yeah, maybe."

"I'd like to hear some of your own music some day, Eddie. Could you bring the tape to me sometime and let me borrow it, after we've finished sorting through your dirty mental laundry?"

"Yeah, maybe. Thanks. I write mainly for myself, though. Like musical masturbation. And *I* don't even listen to it. What a sick joke I play on myself. Or *with* myself. *I* dunno."

"I think it's a productive way to spend your time and energy anyway, Eddie. You'd be surprised how many people out there are frustrated because they have *no* outlet, artistic or otherwise, for their emotions. Your talent is a gift. Use it to your advantage any way you can, and maybe you'll help others by sharing it. In that sense, at least, you're very lucky." *Slurp*.

"You really dig that cafe latte stuff, huh, that high-falutin' type coffee?"

"I *am* a caffeine addict, I'm afraid."

"Ain't it mostly *milk*, though?"

"Primarily."

"I like it straight up, no bullshit."

"That makes sense for you. That's how you live life, isn't it? Black and acidic, without any cream to soften the taste."

"Cute."

"We all make our own choices, Eddie, whether it's coffee or otherwise. Now I'd *really* wish you'd tell me about this LV person and stop beating around the bush."

"So to speak."

"As it were."

"No dice."

"Your reluctance to discuss her only intrigues me more. I won't give up."

"Who said she was a 'her'?"

"You don't have to. Especially after *that* slip of the tongue."

"Shit, you *got* me. *Again.* A'right. LV was just another broad on the heartbreak assembly line, Doc, no big deal or nothin'. I just call her LV 'cause she's an actress and you may know her, but I doubt it, she's only been in a few B movies an' shit, no big time Oscar-winnin' crap, but that's okay, I like B movies better, since I'm *livin'* one. Y'know, low budget an' loaded with sex an' violence, or at least *sax* an' violence. That's my *life*. People dig what they can relate to. Anyways, LV briefly starred in the B movie of my life. And that's it."

"That's *it*?"

"Yup. Pretty much."

"Were you in love with LV, Eddie?"

"When I say she 'starred' in my life it was more like a walk-on, y'know, a cameo, like."

"But were you in *love* with her?"

"Whaddya think? Why else would I even bring the bitch up?"

"It sounds like it ended on a sour note."

"Why, 'cause I called her 'bitch'?"

"Sounds like you had it pretty bad. So she was an actress?"

"What're you, the Hollywood Reporter all of a sudden? Yeah, she was a blonde bimbo actress, one of thousands down in L.A. With a *guru*. That whole L.A. scene, a package deal. But I loved her like nobody else, for some reason. Or I *thought* I did. She was from the Midwest, raised on some fuckin' farm in the middle of Indiana or Idaho or Ohio or some fuckin' place, I dunno, somewhere with lotsa vowels in it, but she talked with a British accent, but I guess that's just an actor-y kinda thing. Pretentious cocksuckers, they bug the *shit* outta me sometimes. Anyways, to me, at the time, she was like the whole world wrapped up in one dame's luscious body, 'cause she traveled so much, y'know, I mean 'cause she useta be a model an' all that crap, that's how she got into the biz, and after that it was either acting in B movies or porn, so she made her best decision. She hung out with some pretty famous dudes, though, from what she told me, an' some were pretty nuts over her, but not like *I* was. She was so god damn sexy an' gorgeous, but in a natural kinda way, like Marilyn Monroe. No fake boobs or none of that shit, she was all *real*. Inside and out. A natural corndog beauty."

"You mean corn-*fed*?"

"Uh, yeah, I guess. Nobody but nobody was as friggin' bananas over a broad as I was with LV. Nobody but *nobody*, not Tony in 'West Side Story,' not the Hunchback of Notre Dame, not that friggin' artist who cut his friggin' ear off, *nobody*. She was a real, whatchacallit—*muse* to me. She made me see things in my mind, weird sorta visions of other times, other places, maybe New York in the future, or somethin' outta 'Blade Runner—or the moon at noon or the desert at night—the ocean when it's foggy. I can't explain it, but I tried to put it in my music. I think she inspired me to write my best stuff. But it didn't work out, so tough bananas for me. End of story."

"Sounds like just the *beginning* of a story to me, Eddie. Anyone who could inspire such complex, ethereal visions is worthy of some consideration, don't you think?"

"It wasn't really just inside my *head*, Doc. It was the *mood* she put me in. It was kinda like this cat's music she turned me onto, this French guy who did this really weird, moody, electronic music, it felt *just* like that. Jarre or something."

"You mean Maurice Jarre, who did the soundtrack for 'Doctor Zhivago'?"

"Naw, I don't think so. I dig that too but that ain't it. John Michelle or somethin'."

"Oh, *Jean Michel* Jarre. I know his music. *Very* atmospheric and esoteric."

"Yeah, that's it! It sounded all European an' all, right?"

"Well, he *was* European."

"Yeah, but it *sounds* like the way I imagine Europe, is what I'm sayin'. Or the moon or other places I ain't never been. Europe on a rainy day. San Francisco feels like that sometimes."

"I understand the mood you mean. Melancholia. Your motif."

"Yeah, whatever. So anyways, LV made me feel an' see these visions of places I ain't never been but could only imagine, like this cat's music did. Like other *worlds*, man. It put me in this sorta spiritual type mood, like I could see Life for what it really was, it's like I felt my *soul*, like I saw the world through my *soul*. Man, I dunno what the hell I mean. It's all gone now, anyways. Though when it's foggy I think of her and that music and—I get…"

"Mentally transported from your mundane circumstances?"

"You really got my number, don'tcha, Doc? Hey I tell a what—*you* tell *me* about LV, whaddya say? I'm getting friggin' *hoarse* over here."

"I didn't know LV, you did, so only you can tell me about her."

"Tell ya the truth, I didn't really ever know her, neither. She was like…"

"A phantom?"

"Keep finishin' my thoughts for me, why don'tcha? Jeez."

"Sorry. Please continue. I find this fascinating and revealing."

"Whatever floats your boat, Doc."

"Did LV remind you of your mother, maybe?"

"Tricky, Doc, real *sly*. No. Except LV was kinda like how I imagined my mother *mighta* turned out had she been a model insteada just a hooker. Not that there's much difference, they both get pimped out to strangers."

"Astute observation."

"I got my moments."

"Anything else?"

"What're you fishin' for here, Doc?"

"The key to your brain, Eddie."

"It's dark inside this here swamp, Doc. Good luck."

"I'll *drain* that swamp if I have to, Eddie. That's my job. I think LV may just be that key, though, so we don't have to get that drastic. Didn't you also say earlier that both your mother and LV liked the color lavender?"

"Yeah, so? So what? Big fuckin' deal."

"Maybe it is, maybe it isn't. We'll find out. How did you even meet LV, Eddie? Start there."

"Ah, jeez. It's a long ass story, why bother?"

"We have time. Please."

"A'right, you got me cornered. Let's see—it was in a movie theater, of all places."

"Appropriate."

"I guess."

"In L.A.?"

"No, Austin. Texas. This is when I *first* met her—she was on the screen."

"Oh."

"Yeah. See? I told ya this was weird. It'll only get weirder, so hang onto your latte…anyway, I was in Austin an' as usual I go to the movies in between gigs, I went to this place called the Alamo Drafthouse, pizza 'n' beer, loved it, my kinda joint, an' they're showin' this B Movie festival an' LV is in one of 'em, called 'The Apist.' It's about an ape who rapes chicks."

"Haven't heard of that one."

"Didn't think so. Anyway, LV is one of the chicks who gets raped by the ape, or really just a guy in an ape *suit*. See, in the movie, the rapist is this perv who dresses up like an ape, so the cops will be lookin' for an ape, not a dude, an' it gets pretty graphic, he like cuts a hole in the ape suit for his dick, which is really huge though you don't really see it, but you get to see lots of naked women gettin' mauled an' molested by this ape-dude, and..."

"The plot of the movie doesn't concern me, Eddie. Let's move on."

"Anyways, LV was by far the most beautiful of the Apist's victims, and I instantly fell madly in love with her, at first sight. I mean I saw her up there gettin' her boobies pawed by this ape slobberin' all over her an' I just knew she was the *one*. I actually traveled outside of Austin to see the damn movie, it had very limited distribution so it was tough. I drove all the way to Dallas in a rented car just so I could see it in the drive-in there. My band mates thought I was nuts but I didn't give a shit, I was in *love*."

"You mean in *lust*. With an *illusion*, an image on the screen."

"No, Doc, in *love*. Like never before or since."

"Okay. Go on."

"I know I sound like that nutcase that tried to bump off Ronnie Reagan, but this is *different*."

"Okay."

"You don't believe me."

"I'm withholding judgment till I've heard the whole sordid story."

"Anyways, next thing was I'm in a drugstore in Texas and I'm leafin' through the jack-off rags an' I come across, so to speak, a layout on LV advertisin' 'The Apist.' She's all nude an' I'm kinda jealous but kinda proud, too, since in my mind we're like already an item. Don't look at me that way 'cause I ain't *insane*, a'right? This is just how I felt at the *time*. So anyways I buy this magazine an' carry it around with me on the road, only I don't jack off to it, see, 'cause LV is somethin' special. I jack off to *other* broads, but not *her*. She's my angel. I can't even fuck other chicks during this period, Doc. I mean like in my heart, I felt like I was *married*. Weird, huh?"

"Yes, what?"

"Yes, that's weird."

"How so?"

"As in not normal, Eddie. Human beings were not meant to interact in fantasy role-playing as a lifestyle, especially when one of them isn't even in on the game. I'm only agreeing with your assessment, at least in retrospect."

"But it still felt *real*, at least at the time, Doc."

"Delusions often do."

"So you just think I'm fulla shit, huh?"

"No. I think you rather arbitrarily made LV your muse, because your music called for one."

"Yeah, right. What *is* that exactly, anyways?"

"It's from Greek mythology. A muse is a source of artistic inspiration sent by the gods."

"Yeah, that's *it*! Right!"

"But it sounds like you took it very literally."

"I took it any way I could get it, Doc."

"So eventually you actually met your muse in the flesh, I take it?"

"Yeah, I'm gettin' to that. Believe it or not, Doc, I had a *plan*. I *knew* somehow we'd eventually meet, an' by then I'd be famous, so she'd *want* to meet me, an' love me like I loved her. I started writin' songs for her, an' some were pretty good, y'know, an' the band let me play some of my own original sax solos sometimes. In New Orleans I wrote this one piece actually called 'Lavender Blonde'. Which was weird 'cause I had no idea of knowin' how much she loved that color at the time."

"Imagine that."

"I don't *have* to, it *happened*."

"Go on, please. I'm hooked."

"Anyways, this got me through some pretty low times, 'cause I was convinced that me an' LV was eventually meant to be, we were soul mates an' nothin' could keep us apart forever, and this belief kept me goin'. I mean really. It was like magic, Doc. I couldn't fuck other dames, the guys in the band thought I'd gone homo or somethin', but I didn't care, I just kept writin' these solo pieces an' they were a hit with audiences so they put up with me, y'know. One was called 'Blue Destiny,' which I wrote tryin' to imagine a life without ever actually meetin' her. The thought scared me so shitless I couldn't sleep thinkin' about it. I useta lie awake wonderin' if she was gettin' nailed by some slick photographer or slimy movie producer at that very moment, while I was stuck in this fleabag in 'Nawlins jackin' off. I was a maniac, I admit it. I'd wander around the French Quarter pretendin' I was in Paris with LV, and I'd sit in the Café du Monde and sorta talk to her, not out loud like a crazy homeless person, but in my *heart*, y'know? Am I scarin'ya or what?"

"Not, not at all. Maybe it was kismet, or karma."

"Maybe it was *what*?"

"Karma, ever hear of that?"

"Yeah, yeah, LV was into that, that's why it's weird *you* said it. But I'll get to that later."

"Go on." *Slurp*.

"Anyways, 'The Apist' wasn't no runaway hit or nothin', except with me, sometimes I was the only cat in the theater watchin', but eventually it dropped outta circulation an' just sorta disappeared. Later I got the DVD but that was *much* later, even though I ain't got a machine to play it on. It's like sentimental now. At the *time*, though, all I had was this jerk-off rag, an' when I looked at her, if I got hot, which I did, I'd jack off thinkin' about some bitch in a bar, an' eventually it got so bad, my horniness and loneliness, I mean, I had to actually go pick *up* a bitch in a bar, but all the time I was bangin' these faceless broads, I was thinkin' of LV. I kept waitin' for another movie of hers to come out so I could refresh my images of her, but nothin'. I didn't give up the dream, though. I even wrote to Ginny an' told her I'd met this great chick and we was engaged, or *would* be as soon as I actually *met* her. Ginny never wrote back. I didn't even look her up right away when the band wound up in New York, and I would walk around Times Square, hopin' one of LV's movies would turn up at one of the 42nd street theaters, an' sure enough, 'The Apist' made a comeback! I saw it on a triple bill with some Italian zombie movies an' a buncha drunks 'n' dopers. While I was watchin' it, I noticed some raincoat fucker in the corner jackin' off to her an' I went over an' told him to cool it, he made a lotta noise but I threatened his life and he shut the fuck up. I told him that was my *girlfriend* he was beatin' off to, can ya believe it? Well, *he* did, fuckin' idiot."

"Hm."

"So anyways, seein' the movie got me all wound up again, like it was a sign from heaven to keep the dream of meetin' her alive, so I wandered all over Manhattan hopin' I'd run into her. I went down to the Village an' hung out in cafes where I thought actors might hang out. I followed blondes I thought might be her into museums and parks an' restaurants an' bars, even into taxicabs an' busses sometimes. I started flakin' off an' missin' gigs an' got canned by the band manager, so I spent even *more* of my time in 42nd Street movie theaters, most of which are all gone now. No great loss, trust me. Anyways, so I'm sittin' in this one theater, dozin' off, surrounded by winos an' off-duty hookers, an' this flick comes on an' whose name is in the credits but LV! I woke right up an' sat up like someone just stuck a chainsaw up my ass. I sat through this triple feature twice just so I could see it again! This one was called 'Trampires' an' in case you couldn't figure it out, that's a cross between 'tramp' and 'vampire,' since it's all about these vampire hookers, an' Dracula is their pimp an' shit. There was a lotta lesbian scenes in it, including one with LV, which got me worried maybe she *was* a lesbian, which would sorta ruined my plans, of us gettin' married and all, but then I realized, I was confusin' fantasy with reality. She was just *acting* like a lesbian vampire hooker. Very convincingly, too. She also had sex with all the guys in it, before she ripped their throats out. At the end Dracula has sex with her and bites her throat out, and..."

"Eddie, again. The movie plots don't interest me. Back to reality, back to *you*."

"Yeah, okay. I thought maybe the movie plots had some sorta secret meaning that related to my real life, though."

"Then, or now?"

"I dunno. Both? How the hell should I know, *you're* the shrink!"

"Social worker."

"Whatever."

"Did you really think, at the time, that these movies contained some secret messages to you from LV, or about her? Clues to her whereabouts, to your imagined future with her?"

"Yeah, sorta. I guess. But it was tough, I gotta admit it, Doc, watchin' all these strangers slobber all over my angel in these flicks, an' her pretendin' to enjoy it! Kinda hard to find any clues with all that freaky fuckin' goin' on, vampires an' apes an' shit, fuckin' that didn't include *me*, even if it was *fake* fuckin', 'cause I knew deep down she was lonely like me, an' these other people didn't mean any more to her than the bitches I slept with meant to *me*."

"To sidetrack a bit, so you saw Ginny again around this time? What was *that* reunion like?"

"No big deal, except she loaned me the money to go to Hollywood an' find LV."

"Really? She supported your fantasy romance?"

"Literally. At least it gave me *direction*, not just an *e*rection, dig me?"

"And that direction was west, you figured?"

"Yup. Wanna meet a Hollywood starlet, best to start in Hollywood. Hell, it was Ginny's idea!"

"I find that hard to believe, for some reason."

"That's 'cause it ain't exactly true an' I can't fool you, Doc."

"Pardon? Which part isn't true?"

"*None* of it. Well, that's not true either. Fact is, I *did* see Ginny, an' she *did* sorta suggest I go to California to find my true love, even if it wasn't LV, I guess just 'cause it was far from where I grew up, all the bad influences there, but I actually *stole* the money from her. I feel kinda bad about it, even now, so that's why I didn't come right out an' say it right away."

"Hm. Go on, please. No guilt allowed in here."

"Good. That frees me up. So I find myself at LAX, three million miles away, and for all Ginny knows I'm still back in New York, I don't tell her I'm leavin' town right away, 'cause I don't know if she noticed the money was missin' yet or not, it was from her private nest egg up in the attic I always knew about, but *she* didn't know I knew it. I didn't want to burn through it so fast so I could take some time off from giggin' to hook up with LV, even though I wasn't famous yet, not even close, but if jazz teaches ya anything, it's to improvise, so I just skipped that parta the plan since it was takin' too long to come true. Last I heard, my old man was workin' a club in Sacramento, but that was a while before I got back out there, and for all I knew he was dead by then already. My old lady never forgave him for dyin', even though they was long broken up by the time he cashed in. I didn't give a shit, though. I coulda hit him up for some guilt money if he was alive, but I didn't even bother to try to find him. I found out not much later through Ginny he was in fact dead by then, far from California, back in New York, of all places, a mutual friend broke it to Ginny. Cancer, you remember."

"Yes. How sad."

"He was better off and so was Ginny, whether she knew it or not. So anyways, I had LV on the brain, but I had to make it day to day, find some shelter, so after I spent a few nights on benches at bus stops, gettin' to know the local derelicts, my people, I headed directly for Hollywood Boulevard, U.S.A. I remember when I first went out there, to play with a band, the first time I got laid, by the beach, in Venice, you remember, an' I was pretty disappointed. I was thinkin' '77 Sunset Strip' an' Kookie Byrnes 'n' shit, an' it was more like 42nd Street or Market Street here in San Fran, know what I'm sayin'? No glamour at *all*. I nearly got mugged the first night I was there, only the redneck bastards found out I had nothin' to take an' so they just hit me a few times an' took off. I knew to keep my wits around me this time, though. I gotta room in a cheap motel just off the Strip and wandered down to Hollywood Boulevard an' saw a 'help wanted' sign in a doughnut shop. I thought I'd save my stolen stash an' try to eke out a little income doin' mindless work while I was on my quest for LV. They were pretty desperate I guess so they took me in. All the other workers were black an' Mexican so they gotta big kick outta me. I felt outta place so I just took some bread outta the cash register on my first shift and split. I left behind my leather jacket to make us even. It was pretty nice leather an' anyway it was too hot for leather in L.A. Besides, LV wouldn't be interested in anyone who worked in no doughnut shop, know what I'm sayin'? I wanted to save my bread to wine and dine her when we met, which is why I took cash from the cash register, not much, maybe a hundred bucks, less than what the leather jacket was worth, anyways. They couldn't trace me 'cause I lied on my application, anyway. I just wouldn't go back there to buy any doughnuts, is all. I figured it evened out."

"With Ginny, too? You were still a thief, Eddie. A petty thief, but a thief nonetheless."

"Yup, that I was, that I was. And that ain't all, so stay tuned for my *next* exciting episode, same putz time, same putz channel."

"When is that coming up? We're a little over our usual time, but I don't want to stop you now."

"Let's do it. So I'm in L.A., dyin' from the smog 'n' the sun, hatin' every minute of it, so I left Hollywood an' hopped a bus for the beach in Santa Monica, then Venice, to cool off an' get some fresh ocean air an' maybe just run into my first lay an' get that encore, even though I was there to track down LV. It was nice down there. It was in Venice that I first met Max, actually. It was like Fate or somethin'. He was dealin' right there on the beach in Venice, and I walked by an' he asked me if I was a hustler. At first I thought he was comin' on to me but then I found out it was more like he wanted to put me to *work*. I told him I needed bread, but not *that* bad. I didn't know how to take this cat at first, know what I'm sayin'? I mean he dressed really loud an' wore jewelry an' his face looked like a mug shot, but kinda puppy dog innocent, too. We sorta hit it off right away. I told him where I was from an' what I was doin', an' he thought I was crazy so he let me crash at his pad back in Hollywood, of all places! In this scumpit motel, like the one I just left! At least it was *free*. Sorta. He was out alla time an' hookers would call the room at like four in the morning an' wake me up, an' dealers hung out in front of their rooms all hours of the day and night. I didn't really feel safe there, except they knew I knew Max, an' he was like a *god* or somethin' to these lowlifes. *Every*one knew him, man, even the guys flippin' pasta at the little sleazy pizza dives on the Boulevard. He'd tap on the window and he'd wave an' they'd wave back an' sometimes we both got comped a slice. It was *wild*.

"I told Max about where I was raised an' he thought it was hilarious. It gave us a real brotherly connection. He was from New York too, actually, from Brooklyn. He said he came out to be an actor, but all the agents said he was too friggin' weird an' to just go back home. So instead, to get by, he became a pimp an' a dealer, 'cause he'd been pretty much kicked outta Brooklyn anyways, didn't really say why. He'd done time back East for chickenshit misdemeanors, an' it was while in the can he got the idea of bein' an actor, where he could rip off the public but it would be *legal*."

"I think I might know who Max really is now."

"Well, pretend like ya *don't*, 'cause he'd *kill* me if he knew I was spillin' my guts about his past like this. It's mostly all covered up now. But I know the *truth*. I was around when he first got discovered and all. He met this agent in the Howard Johnson's at Hollywood and Vine who encouraged him to take some acting classes, the agent even hooked Max up. He didn't seem to give a shit about acting by then, since he was set either way, he figured. In fact he met some of his hookers in acting classes, actresses who just gave up and needed to make some dough somehow, an' Max was there for 'em. He actually used the acting classes to procure talent, the street-walkin' kind, only Max ran a pretty classy service, caterin' to rich dudes like Ginny did, takin' good care of his women. He was the guy my father only *dreamed* of bein'."

"Ah."

"'Ah', what?"

"Max was a father figure, not just a surrogate big brother."

"Bullshit."

"Okay. Keep going, we have a few more minutes."

"Anyways, one time I'm hangin' with Max in Duke's coffee shop at the Tropicana in West Hollywood, an' some dudes there was hangin' out, musicians, an' that's how I got hooked up with a band an' started giggin' again. I was actually startin' to enjoy myself an' even though LV was still my main purpose for bein' there, I got into this kinda groove without her. I even got a blowjob in a parking lot from this hot little groupie. And meantime, Max is gettin' TV 'n' movie work, small parts, then bigger parts, an' he starts gettin' famous all of a sudden, an' I don't see him as much, but I don't care, I'm meetin' chicks an' havin' a good time anyways."

"That sounds surprisingly healthy, under the circumstances."

"I'm *fulla* surprises, Doc. Anyways, a year goes by like this, then another year, an' no word about LV, no more movies, no *nothin'*, an' I start to sorta forget all about her. Max is a bona fide movie star by now. He also got married, believe it or not, to this pretty hot singer from Reno or maybe Vegas, she was a dancer, too, great body, but she really wanted to be an actress, so Max helped her out by marryin' her an' all, I guess. I kinda had the hots for Mrs. Max but naturally I kept it to myself. She was like a sister to me anyways, the same way Max was like a brother. I'd meet Max and Mrs. Max in our favorite hangout, the Pink Turtle coffee shop in Beverly Hills, in this big fancy hotel, the Beverly Wilshire, I think it's called. We didn't meet often but Max still let me hang around because I was like this connection to the street, to the *real* world, the one he came from and still wasn't too far away from, only in a way, he was like on another *planet* by now. I told Max an' Mrs. Max all about LV an' sometimes I useta bug Max to get me a meetin' with her, get her a small role in one of his movies, but he'd just laugh at me. He was startin' to piss me off, so we sorta stopped hangin' out for a while, plus he was off on location all over the friggin' world, an' I started to get lonely again, an' began missin' LV all over again. I had given up by the time it actually happened."

"By the time *what* happened?"

"I actually *met* her, without Max's help. In a movie theater, of all places. The Nuart, on the west side, near Westwood, y'know?"

"I know of it. It's connected to the U.C. Theater here in Berkeley, or it *was*."

"Yeah. So anyways, I'd just had dinner at one of my favorite joints, Dolores's, right across the street, the eggplant Florentine, my usual, an' then I headed to the Nuart to catch this double feature, 'The Girl Can't Help It' an' 'Will Success Spoil Rock Hunter?', both starring Jayne Mansfield, who was blonde, as you probably know, so, like, perfect, right? So I waltz in there an' have a seat, I'm a bit early so the place isn't that full yet, all the seats in front of me are empty, and who should walk in an' sit *right in front of me* in a nearly empty theater but LV! *Right in front of me*. Like, *directly*. The light caught her face just as she sat down, an' I began like hyperventilatin'. I thought I'd die of a heart attack right in my seat before I got the nerve to speak to her, an' she'd meet me as a *corpse*. She wasn't alone, she was with this other blonde bimbo, an' they were gigglin' like little schoolgirls about somethin', so finally I begin freaking out I'm gonna blow this once in a lifetime chance, so I tap her on the shoulder, she turns around, her face right in mine, in the flesh, no movie screen between us. I can't even friggin' *breathe* but I manage to squeak out some bullshit how I'm a big fan of her movies an' all, all two of 'em, an' she seems genuinely flattered and I start to breath again. Then the lights go down and I settle back and I'm not even watchin' the movie, I'm just in shock. Then the movie ends and they both get up to leave and I follow 'em out to the lobby, stand behind him to buy popcorn, but I can't utter a sound. She smiles at me but sorta ignores me. We go back inside and sit in separate rows now, I don't wanna come off like no *stalker*, but then after the second movie I sorta followed them both out to her car, an old Thunderbird, and I ask for her phone number, just like that! It just popped out. I think we were both so stunned she actually gave it to me, on the spot, even though her friend kept tellin' her to just get in the friggin' car an' drive as fast away from me as possible, but it was too late, I got what I wanted. I'd finally met the girl of my dreams and knew how to find her again."

"Eddie, I'm sorry, this is great but I really have to get going, can you hold that thought?"

"I've been holdin' it ever since, Doc."

Session Five

"So LV is the main reason you left L.A., as well as moved there in the first place, is that how you see it, Eddie?"

"Bingo, Sherlock. Or is that *She*-lock? Anyways, yeah. Her, plus I was just sicka that town in general, alla Max's hangers-on, an' all his sudden newfound friends when he got famous. Just a buncha phonies. I didn't fit in with that crowd, know what I'm sayin'?"

"I still find that story about meeting LV in the theater hard to swallow."

"Well, like I tell *any* chick, swallow or don't, but that's the hard truth."

"But did 'the truth' *stay* firm, Eddie? Or did it soften once it entered the realm of reality?"

"Cute, Doc, *real* cute. Nice to know you can return fire. My life is one big ice cold dirty martini, Doc, though I've had my dry spells."

"So what happened after LV gave you her number? Let's pick it up right there."

"Well, the bitch of it was, I sorta panicked when I called her, 'cause I wasn't famous yet so that was a big part of my plan I hadda do without, so I name-dropped, told her I knew Max, so I was *sorta* famous, right?"

"By proxy, I suppose."

"Uh, yeah. So anyways, it turns out she's a big friggin' *fan* of Max, of course, naturally, *every*body was back then, so I set up a meet with Max and Mrs. Max, the idea bein' to impress LV, not to hook her up with that cocksucker, he hadda enough pussy as it was. I kinda knew he was steppin' out on Mrs. Max by then, but whatever, I think she was steppin' out, too, that's Hollywood, and none of my friggin' business. I just didn't want him addin' no LV notch on his belt, know what I'm sayin'? So I took the chance anyways. LV was a bit older than me, I found out. In fact, without makeup, she looked a *lot* older than she looked in the movies. Still beautiful an' all, don't get me wrong, but in *that* town, she was already pretty much over the hill, which could work in my favor, I figured, since maybe her standards were lower now. The thing is, the night before we were supposed to meet up with Max, I had a gig at Madame Wong's with this band I thought she might dig, sorta jazz-rock fusion whatever, but she gave me some bullshit excuse about a sick rabbit or somethin', so that made me start worryin' she really only wanted to meet Max an' already didn't give a shit about me. But whatever, the point was, I *met* her, against all odds. I mean, she practically sat down right in my *lap*, for Chrissake, outta *nowhere*, once I'd given up on even ever meetin' her at *all*. Fate would take it from there, I figured. Fate is my pimp."

"Interesting philosophy."

"Yeah, I'm a big time philosopher from *way* back, Doc. Anyways, we meet Max an' Mrs. Max at the Pink Turtle for breakfast, an' of course Max gets all the friggin' attention, she don't wanna even *hear* about my so-called musical career or nothin', they all just talk movie shop for *hours*, an' I was just sorta left out in the cold, like a guilty bystander. Every now an' then I offer my insights, which ain't even worth two cents, just to remind 'em I was there, but it's like I was invisible. It was *such* a drag, man, especially after waitin' all those years to meet her, an' in a way, it made me feel worse than ever."

"Be careful what you wish for, as the saying goes."

"Yeah, but that sayin' is fulla shit 'cause how the hell does anybody know what they wish for will *suck*? The only way around that is not to wish for *nothin'*, and if you're not wishin' for somethin' better than what ya already got, what's the point of *livin'*?"

"There's a delicate distinction between the conceivable and the possible, though it is a tricky thing to figure out, I'll grant you that, Eddie. Go on."

"Anyways, I got depressed as hell, I mean I was feelin' a whole lot better about myself *before* I met LV, an' it affected my friendship with Max 'cause it was hard to not *hate* him, I mean, like, *resent* him, y'know? Wasn't *his* fault he was famous an' I was a friggin' loser, though. Anyways, I actually started hangin' out even *more* with Max and Mrs. Max, just so I could invite LV along, like they all came to one of my gigs once, which was cool, but I think LV kinda dug the front man more than me, just the hired gun, the sax player in the back, though I did play a few of the solos I wrote for her, like 'Lavender Blonde,' didn't tell her they was written for her, though, not right away, 'cause I wanted an honest opinion, so I just asked her, 'so how did ya like that?', an' she was always polite an' said, 'yeah, that was great, blah blah,' an' Max was always very encouraging, as usual, an' so was Mrs. Max, especially since she was a singer herself, an' I figured, if Max nails LV, screw it, I'll just do Mrs. Max, who was a knockout an' in some ways, we sorta got along better than me an' LV or even me an' Max, since Mrs. Max was also into music, and in fact, we made out later on, but..."

"Really?"

"Yeah, *much* later, though, after this other stuff happened. Thing is, LV an' Mrs. Max hit it off pretty famously themselves. I even thought maybe they had a thing goin' between 'em, I kept thinkin' of LV in that lesbo vampire flick, but the real reason they get along is 'cause they're both into the same religion sorta, that Indian stuff, not *Indian* Indian, but the *other* kind, over by Iran an' shit, y'know, *that* kinda jazz, with karma an' all, an' they both start goin' to this ashram together, worshippin' the same guru, an' I tag along just 'cause I kinda wanna bang *both* these broads, an' maybe we could have like a spiritual triangle, y'know?"

"A metaphysical *ménage au trois*?"

"Exactly! *I think.* They're rappin' about reincarnation an' shit an' the whole time I'm thinkin', how can I get both these babes in a hot tub? It was *sick*, Doc."

"Where was Max when this was going on?"

"Oh, he *hated* this guru shit, so he *never* went there, which sorta made it safe turf for me. I had these lovelies all to myself. An' not just them. The ashram was like singles' night at a bar, I'm tellin' ya. *So* many lonely broads! If I wasn't so hooked on LV I coulda scored *big* time. I really blew it."

"I gather you didn't benefit spiritually from this environment, either."

"I wasn't there for my soul, Doc. I was there for my heart."

"Are you sure?"

"*And* my dick, okay. I admit it."

"No, I meant, sometimes something happens that we wished for, but it didn't happen for the purpose we thought it would."

"Huh?"

"Maybe you were meant to meet LV, but not for the reasons you hoped."

"Obviously."

"I was thinking maybe spiritual sustenance would be the outcome of this fateful encounter. Whether it's a Far Eastern philosophy or any religion, or just going to AA and acknowledging a Higher Power than yourself, it can be beneficial for your heart *and* your soul, Eddie."

"Are you religious?"

"Agnostic."

"I don't know that one."

"It's not a religion. I just question the existence of God, that's all. But I don't emphatically deny it, either. I'm open to any and all possibilities. The truth is not always the same for everyone. I don't think of it as an absolute. Truth is often fluid."

"Yeah, *speakin'* of which, I'm jackin' off so much thinkin' of LV and Mrs. Max makin' it that I think Max starts suspectin' somethin's goin' on, 'cause guys can sense when other guys are prowlin' around their property. I mean, I talked their ears off about this LV dame for a year before I even met her, an' now *they're* all friends an' I'm just a sidekick they keep around for laughs. So it all got kinda weird, anyways. LV got a good deal outta meetin' *me*—she got the guru thing from Mrs. Max an' a connection with Max for her career an' all, but nothin' ever came out of that, so maybe not. I have no idea why I met her, Doc. I really don't."

"Maybe as time goes on, hindsight will provide the answer."

"Like when I'm dead?"

"Maybe sooner, if we dig deep enough."

"I dig. So anyways, I didn't have much in common with LV, really. I mean I liked her movies more than she did. She really wanted to be a serious dramatic actress and all. And when I suggested places to have lunch, she an' Mrs. Max would wanna go to hob-nobby joints like Joe Allen's, and I'd wanna go to funky dives like Tiki Ti. I liked the Polynesian atmosphere an' all, an' the drinks. It was very exotic but in a cheap kinda way. LV kinda liked it but she'd rather be someplace where she could get discovered."

"Too bad Schwab's Drugstore is gone."

"Where?"

"It's a famous lunch counter in Hollywood where Lana Turner was allegedly discovered. I read about it somewhere. Go on."

"Yeah. We both liked Musso and Frank's an' Café Formosa, though, so we'd often meet there. I'd just basically get drunk while Mrs. Max an' LV talked about their careers and souls. Meantime Max is out and about on the town, hangin' with Hollywood types, bangin' chicks right an' left, but I ain't tryin' to nail Max so I don't care, but the upshot of it is, we ain't that close no more. We sorta grew apart. I'd still hang out with him sometimes, like late at night at Canter's coffee shop, an' he even gave me work when club bookin's got thin, answerin' his phone and fan mail an' shit, but this just made me feel like a loser even more—*me*, answerin' someone *else's* fan mail. I started goofin' off and callin' in sick to his office, which was in his house, and eventually this didn't work out neither, so I hadda start lookin' for odd jobs just to get by, which I kept from LV, I was humiliated *enough* already."

"If she liked you as a person what you did to make a living shouldn't have affected her opinion of you, Eddie."

"It *didn't*, it didn't, 'cause she never thought mucha me *any*ways. I think Max clued her in what a maniac I was about her before we met, an' it kinda scared her. I don't blame her. I mean I could tell she *liked* me, in a little brother kinda way, especially when I went to the ashram with her an' Mrs. Max. I even started chantin' an' meditatin' an' all, just to *make* her like me. I know it was supposed to be good for my karma an' all, so maybe I got somethin' out of it, but I dunno, the whole idea of karma doesn't make sense to me, like it's a point system, tit for tat, I mean, a buncha angels up there keepin' tabs an' score on us? *All* of us, alla time? C'mon. That makes life too, I dunno. Mathematical. Like it's run like a *business*."

"Maybe it is. Who knows?"

"Not me. But LV an' Mrs. Max figured *they* got all the answers they needed from their guru. LV even said to me maybe we knew each other in a past life, *that's* why we met, like we used to be brother an' sister, an' we was pickin' up where we left off, which just wasn't the kinda relationship I was goin' for. I mean, Max was like a brother to me, and Mrs. Max like a sister, at least until we made out that time, so that was plenty enough of a fake family already. "

"Do you care to talk about cheating with your friend's wife? Maybe you're dealing with guilt."

"Well, I don't know if I'd call it *cheatin'*, Doc, since they was separated at the time. I do feel a bit guilty, though.

A *little*, anyways. More afraid than guilty, though."

"How did it happen, and why?"

"I dunno, it was after things with LV just got too intense, she could tell why I was hangin' out at the ashram and it wasn't 'cause I dug the smell of incense, in fact I *hated* it, an' I finally broke down one night an' told her that those sax solos I wrote were *all for her*, an' she seemed flattered an' all, but she started avoidin' me, an' Max an' I wasn't hangin' out as much no more, so late one night, Mrs. Max an' I went to a club, the Roxy, just the two of us, to catch a band I was gonna audition for, an' we went back to her apartment, which Max was payin' for, even though they was split up by now, an' she put on some jazz, mixes some martinis, an' I start cryin' about LV an' Mrs. Max tells me not to worry about it, *plenty* of chicks would love to have me write songs for 'em. I say, oh h?, an' I dunno, we're lookin' at each other and it just happened."

"You made out."

"Well, a little more than that, but yeah, basically."

"A little *more*?"

"How do I know you're not tapin' this? If *any* of this gets back to Max, I'm a *dead* man."

"None of this leaves the room, Eddie. I promise. If you don't want to detail your encounter, that's fine. I just find this to be an interesting turn of events."

"Okay, fine. We didn't actually *fuck*, since we felt too weird 'n' guilty, but bodily fluids got shared. A *lot*. Satisfied?"

"Were *you*?"

"Hell, yeah, she was a fox! She drove me *nuts*! I came everywhere but *in* her, in her pussy, that is, but I really liked comin' down her *throat* more anyways 'cause she was such a good jazz singer, like I was creamin' all over her pretty *voice*, but we weren't in *love* or anything, she could tell I was still kinda hung up on LV, an' she still loved Max, even though she knew he was cheatin' on her, so we knew this was just a one time thing. But that was enough. I mean, well, one reason I left L.A. was outta fear for my life. Sure, the LV thing didn't pan out like I'd hoped, but I still wanna live, y'know? Plus Mrs. Max told me she was sleepin' with LV too, so..."

"What?"

"Yeah, yeah, I wasn't gonna tell ya, but remember how I said I fantasized about them gettin' together? Well, it wasn't no *fantasy*. Since there were no dicks involved she didn't really consider it cheatin'. Whatever. People find ways to justify anything, I've learned that much. But what did I care? I even suggested we do a tag team on LV, a threesome, y'know, wear Mexican masks an' all, no penetration, just, y'know, whatever, fake wrestlin', kinda, but Mrs. Max didn't think LV would go for it. For one thing, no one else was supposed to know about them foolin' around. LV was even more paranoid than I was, since she still kinda hoped Max would give her a part in a movie sometime, and that wouldn't happen if Max found out she was sleepin' with his wife."

"So you and LV had more in common than you thought."

"Like the taste of Max's wife in our mouths? Not enough to move us past the brother-sister phase, Doc."

"Okay."

"Max still wanted me to work for him, too. I didn't want to be his flunky, plus I was nervous around him after comin' all over his wife, so I left. Left it all behind. Now I'm *here*, mainly 'cause it ain't *there*. It was all for *nothin'*. I did leave LV a CD of the music I wrote for her, though: 'Lavender Blonde,' 'Blue Destiny,' coupla others. Dropped it in her mailbox just before I hopped the train outta town. No note. Just *notes*. To remember me by, y'know."

"Did you leave her a way to get in touch with you?"

"How could I when I didn't even know where I was goin'? Not even Mrs. Max knows where I am. It's like I just disappeared. Which is just how I want it."

"Is this really how you want it, Eddie? For the rest of

your life?"

"Well, no. But I hadda leave L.A., Doc. Especially after what Mrs. Max told me about them sleepin' together."

"Do you think perhaps Mrs. Max just made that up to turn you on, or maybe to deflect attention from LV to herself?"

"I don't think so."

"Why?"

"Because I'd rather not."

"Okay."

"But that didn't matter anyway, whether it was true or not. It was the fact that LV didn't love me like I loved her. That's why I left. She just didn't see it, the magic of how we met, of how amazing it was that it even happened at all, much less *how* it happened. She drove around town in her T-bird, wearin' lavender, hob-nobbin' with other actors an' guru people, laughin' it up, an' I was pretty much back to wanderin' around with nothin' in life to look forward to, to *live* for, y'know? I figured if I left and never saw her again, I could pretend none of it ever happened, that we never even met in person, and we could always be together in my dreams."

"Maybe she'll listen to that CD and see you in a new light."

"Too late. I'm already gone, like I was never even there."

"But things have changed, Eddie. *You've* changed."

"How so?"

"I think you know the difference between fantasy and reality now. I'd say that's something to take from this experience. You grew as a person. And you were inspired to make art. I'd hardly call that a waste of time. And maybe you changed her in some way, as well."

"Well, maybe, Doc, just maybe. I introduced LV to people who may hook her up with a better career sometime, and also the spiritual trip an' all, so maybe *she* got somethin' out of it, like I said. Who knows. Who cares."

"Maybe this was mostly about her after all, and not just you. You were meant to introduce her to some important catalysts in her life, and then you both would go your separate ways."

"Yeah, that's great. Just cocksuckin' motherfuckin' sonofabitchin' fantastic for *every*body."

"You did say this brought some magic into your life, right, Eddie? Wasn't that worth it, at least? Magic doesn't have to have meaning to matter, does it?"

"If it doesn't have any meaning, what's the point, Doc? Of *any*thing?"

"Magic for magic's sake. Dreams for the sake of dreaming. I don't see anything wrong with that."

"'Cause it's all one big dream anyways, right, Doc?"

"Maybe. If you *felt* happy, even for a time, that's as close an approximation to real happiness we have in this dream called life, Eddie. *All* feelings, good or bad, are fleeting. And LV put you in touch with a spiritual philosophy that may have enhanced your life, or your view of life, more than you realize at this point."

"Bullshit."

"Open your mind, Eddie."

"I did, and I got a chainsaw stuck in it. Now it's just mush."

"I still think it was a worthwhile experience, no matter how it turned out."

"That's 'cause it was *me* and not *you* who got burned, Doc."

"Freud might say otherwise."

"Fred? Who's that?"

"I think you heard me."

"Yeah, maybe I did, maybe I did. Fuck Floyd or whoever. Who gives a shit what some total stranger has to say about *my* life?" *Whump, clop, clop.*

"Nervous, Eddie?"

"No, why?"

"You're pacing like a caged panther."

"So? I dig cats, I told ya."

"Pacing can be a sign of anxiety."

"Just stretchin' my legs is all, Doc. I also *walked* alla way from the train to here, so what does that make me, a nervous wreck?"

"Sorry if I misread you. You seem to be at an emotional impasse with LV, and the vision of your future together, out of the picture."

"Doesn't really matter, Doc. It's all a dream anyways, we agreed on that, right?"

"I said it's one possible theory. Normally when one realizes they're dreaming, they wake up."

"Is that what Freud would say?"

"Maybe."

"You gotta pocket fulla *maybes* today you're just itchin' to spill, huh, Doc?"

"It's *all* theory, Eddie."

"Yeah, why bother tryin' to figure anything out?"

"Clues."

"Clues. To what?"

"Our purpose in Life. And that's different for everybody. There's no *one* answer to everything for everyone, you see?"

"I *lost* my purpose, Doc."

"Which goes back to what I said. You invested your dreams in a total stranger that you met on a movie screen."

"*And* in a movie theater, in *person*, don't forget."

"Just because you can touch something doesn't necessarily make it real, Eddie."

"It just wasn't meant to be, Doc. No point in over-analyzin' it. Some people was just meant to be alone, I guess."

"You seem to be a loner by nature, anyway."

"Yeah, maybe. What about *you*, Doc? *You're* not alone, are ya?"

"No, but I choose not to be."

"What, like I *choose* to be a lonely bastard?"

"In a way. Your choices dictate your destiny. You chose a fantasy relationship over a real one. That was *your* choice, Eddie."

"What 'real' one, Doc?"

"Well, what about Mrs. Max?"

"How was that *real*?"

"You actually consummated your relationship, for one thing. Maybe you should've written *her* a song."

"She's married to a movie star, Doc. Get real."

"But they're separated, you said. Maybe *they* weren't meant to be."

"Not my problem. I told ya, it was just sex."

"With a sister figure."

"She had a great figure but she wasn't *really* my sister, Doc, ya know, so don't pull *that* shit on me. We was just lickin' each other's wounds. So to speak."

"I see. Maybe you're just in love with the *notion* of love, Eddie, ever think of that?"

"No. I'll tell ya what I'm *not* in love and that's this friggin' conversation."

"Okay, I have to wrap this up early today anyway, I have to get ready for the holidays."

"Nice for you."

"But I have to say, Eddie, I think you're wasting a veritable treasure trove of talent and real passion on the wrong pursuits. I want to help you achieve whatever it is you're after, but in the right way. Do you trust me, Eddie?"

"Yeah. I guess. As much as I trust anybody."

"So not very much."

…

"Is that the size of your trust in me, Eddie? That space between your thumb and forefinger, Doc?"

"Wanna find out the hard way, Doc? Naw, I'm just kiddin'. Sorry I said that."

"All right, I accept your apology."

"I trusted Max to be my friend, an' he left me out in the cold once he got famous. He trusted *me* an' I let his wife suck my cock. He trusted his wife an' she fooled around with both me *and* LV an' who knows *who* else. Mrs. Max trusted Max an' he fucks anything that moves. Lust makes trust rust, Doc."

"Is that a line from a song you wrote?"

"My songs ain't got lyrics, but it could be."

"I think your music *is* your muse, ironically. Your true love."

"Well, even *that* let me down, so in that way, music is like just another broad. I'm nowhere after a lifetime of nowhere gigs with nobody bands. I got nothin' to show for anything. Nobody really cares about jazz no more, Doc. I'm a dinosaur. It may as well be music in an elevator as far as most people are concerned. Everything fades away, Doc. Everything and everybody. What's the point of writin' more music? For *any*body, even myself?"

"Maybe you should just concentrate on the present and let cultural posterity take care of itself, since we have no control over Time. We can just try to live in the moment."

"Who cares, fuck it all."

"Your stubbornly apathetic viewpoint reveals a deeper frustration with the status quo, Eddie."

"Believe whatever ya want, Doc. That's what *every*body does."

"Including you?"

"Sure. But that don't make it true, does it? I learned that."

"Pardon? You *learned*?"

"I mean, I mean…aw, shit, Doc, you *got* me! Yeah, I *learned* that lesson in L.A. I certainly did, certainly did. I learned that life is meaningless. So yeah, you're right, I *did* get somethin' outta all that bullshit. Score one for the Doc."

"Believing in something doesn't make it true, Eddie, but the reverse is also valid. *Not* believing in something doesn't make it *not* true, either."

"Huh?"

"That will be it for this week, Eddie. Do you have plans

for the holiday?"

"Yeah. I might just beat off *twice*. And maybe I'll be thinking of *you*, Doc."

"Don't transfer your fantasies to *me*, Eddie. You'll only be disappointed again. I'm warning you."

"You're warnin' *me*? Against *what*?"

"Just keep your distance, Eddie."

"What, like I'm gonna *rape* you?"

"I didn't say that, but odd you should even suggest that."

"I *didn't*! Though…"

"What."

"Nothin'."

"No, what, Eddie? I have a minute."

"I've had you in my dreams, Doc. A few times. I took you by force. I woke up all wet, from sweat and cum. I took you right here in this room, and you *loved* it."

"Eddie, stay back."

"I'm not sayin' it's gonna happen, Doc. But you *wanted* total honesty, right, Doc? So *there*, you got it. I mean, you're real, right?"

"But your dream wasn't."

"I know. I know."

"Sit down, Eddie. Please stop pacing. You're making me…"

"Nervous?"

"Yes."

"Sorry. So see ya next week, Doc?"

"Yes. Have a nice holiday, Eddie."

"You too."

Session Six

"Is that a gun in your pocket, Eddie?"

"No, Doc, I'm just happy to see ya. *Yes*, it's a gun. It's a dangerous world out there. I can't just defend myself with a saxophone."

"Where did you get a gun, Eddie?"

"Max. Stole it. *Hic*!"

"And you're intoxicated."

"I left a trail of brain cells behind me, Doc, alla way from the bar. Like bread crumbs."

"You show up drunk and armed. That's not a healthy sign of progress, Eddie."

"*I'm* not healthy, Doc. So anyways, how was *your* holiday?"

"Better than yours, I take it. Oedipus."

"Huh?"

"Something struck me over the holiday. You call yourself 'Eddie the Putz', right?"

"Yeah."

"That sounds like Oedipus."

"Okay, whoever that is. Ain't you gonna call a cop 'cause I have a gun, Doc?"

"Not unless you plan to use it anytime soon. Back to Oedipus?"

"Who's he?"

"An ancient myth. A king who killed his father and married his mother."

"I don't get the connection with me."

"Think about it."

"I will, next time I'm on the toilet maybe with nothin'

to read."

"I find it fascinating."

"What, takin' a dump?"

"The fact that your nickname for yourself has this ironic phonetic resonance."

"You're not worried about the gun?"

"Why do you keep bringing it up? I don't want you to ever bring it with you *again*, and I don't want to discuss it now."

"Maybe I'm usin' it to kill my father so I can fuck my mother?"

"So it's a metaphor."

"I got you talkin' about it, anyway. I don't know this cat, Doc. I call myself Eddie the Putz 'cause that's what I *am*. But I aim to change that."

"The story claims that Oedipus killed his father and fell in love with his own mother unwittingly. In psychoanalysis, there's something called an 'Oedipus complex,' wherein the subject—consciously or otherwise—desires to eliminate the parent of his own sex in order to win the favor of the feminine parent."

"So? I didn't knock off my old man and never intended to."

"I'm just pointing out the similarity in the names, Eddie, which just struck me as peculiar, especially given the fact you're attracted to women who remind you of your mother, and you want to save them."

"I may just use this gun on my*self*, Doc."

"Eddie, I know you brought the gun to distract me, it's too obvious a gimmick, so I'm doing my best to ignore it, alarmed as I might actually be."

"LV wasn't nothin' like my mother."

"No?"

"No."

"Beyond the salacious similarities, they were both blonde and liked the color lavender."

"You could say that about a million broads."

"I'm sure you'll get around to those too, eventually, the way you're going."

"Cute."

"I'd go as far as to speculate that had the opportunity arisen, as it were, you would not have been able to perform with LV, since she in fact reminded you too *much* of your mother."

"You mean 'cause they're both prostitutes in their own way—a hooker and a B movie actress, same difference, is that it, She-lock?"

"Or else perhaps you revealed an unnatural longing for your mother which you could morally satisfy through a vicarious liaison with a duplicate. Maybe not LV, but others."

Click.

"Eddie, did you just cock that gun?"

"It wasn't my *cock*, Doc."

"I'm calling the police."

Click. "There, I *un*cocked it.

"Are you threatening me, Eddie?"

"No. I wouldn't do that, you're all I got, Doc. This thing ain't even loaded. Story of my life, right?"

"We're still exploring the story of *your* life, Eddie. Do I need to call the police or not?"

"I'm surprised you haven't already."

"This is a pathetic display of bravado. It's shameful. Don't let me see that gun again, Eddie."

"Ever shoot anyone, Doc? Feels friggin' great!"

"Have *you* ever shot anyone, Eddie?"

"No. But that's what I hear. *Almost* shot my old man once, over a broad."

"Now we're getting somewhere. Tell me about it."

"She was a stripper in a club where he was workin'. Called herself Bluella."

"Bluella?"

"Bluella. A stripper. Just the type of gal my old lady disapproved of, too much like *her*, which is maybe why I liked her so much. This was after I left the nest, though. I was useta seein' grown women walkin' around naked alla time, an' me just jackin' off thinkin' about 'em, but they were off limits. *All* the women that raised me. I called 'em my aunts. Aunt Betsy, Aunt Tina, Aunt Fuckface, whatever. I useta whack off listenin' to 'em comin' in the rooms next to me. We'd all come at the same time. An' Ginny still read to me from the Bible, tryin' to make me stay pure an' all, but some of *that* was pretty sexy too, David 'n' Bathsheba 'n' Samson 'n' Delilah an' all, so if you think I'm attracted to whores, like my mother, can you blame me? I was *surrounded* by 'em."

"I didn't say I *blamed* you, Eddie. What about this time you almost shot your father?"

"I'm gettin' to that. Anyways, sometimes my old man Seymour would come by an' sorta kidnap me, take me out of the nest and out into the real world. So we were kinda close in a way, when I was a kid. He'd take me to his gigs and have me sit in the back while he was on stage, even though I was under-age. He used to even slip me cocktails, no kiddin', when I was like, eleven, twelve. He introduced me to booze, cigarettes, even drugs. Class act, my old man. Anyway, lots of these dives where he worked were strip joints owned by the Mob. So for me, it was like I never left home. More naked broads for my imagination later on when I was alone back in the whorehouse. He even bought me jerk-off rags like 'Playboy' an' 'Penthouse' an' other magazines like 'Vampirella' which were pretty sexy, too. Basically he felt guilty an' got me anything I wanted. Meantime Ginny was back at home worried sick I'd never come back, but we always did, an' she'd be sittin' in a rockin' chair listenin' to that old song 'Those Were the Days' over an' over an' over, it was pretty psycho. Or 'Gypsies, Tramps and Thieves' by Cher, on scratched up old 45s, their grooves worn down to nothin'. Don't ask me why, those were her favorites, even though she mostly played jazz around the house, all her old albums, Sarah

Vaughan an' June Christy an' all. But not as much as just those two songs. I *still* got 'em stuck in my head. When I thinka my childhood, all I hear are those songs an' the sounds of people comin' an' goin' an' comin' again. And jazz. Jazz 'n' jizz. Sex an' music, same thing. Both distractions from death, Doc."

"How so?"

"'Cause they take your mind off the fact that *none* of this shit matters in the long run, Doc. Sax 'n' sex. Jazz 'n' jizz. *That's* the story of my life."

"So if your father was so good to you, why did you try to kill him?"

"I didn't try to kill him, I just shot him almost."

"But why?"

"I told ya already.'

"Bluella."

"Bluella. But that's later, just hang on, Doc. I know you're anxious to get to the dirty parts but there's more to it than that."

"I'm not here for prurient pleasure-seeking by proxy, Eddie. But if you did try to shoot your father, that ties back into the Oedipal Complex I told you about."

"Yeah, we'll just see about that. My old man did a *lotta* nice things for me as a kid, too, y'know. I remember one Christmas Eve, Ginny had to let my old man see me, right, and he brought me a present, like a Batman doll or somethin', an' I played with it under the big Christmas tree out in the lobby of the whorehouse, an' everyone there was exchangin' gifts, like whips an' handcuffs an' perfume an' lingerie an' all, an' everyone was loaded on spiked egg nog, even Ginny, except Seymour, who stayed pretty sober till he snuck me out the front door. Ginny was passed out on her big purple sofa. We stayed out all night an' Ginny never even knew I was gone, Seymour had me back in time for church the next mornin'."

"You went to *church*?"

"On Christmas day, yeah, Christmas services. The

whole gang of us, *all* the broads, all hung-over and fulla cum an' shit. Ginny went to church *all* the time, and dragged me with her, too. All parta the guilt trip, Doc. A round *trip* guilt trip 'cause she always wound up right back where she started, in a whorehouse."

"Where did your father take you that night?"

"Club where he hadda midnight gig, dressed up as Santa Claus, tellin' lame Christmas jokes, gettin' booed, people throwin' bottles an' shit at him. The usual. Then we strolled up Fifth Avenue lookin' at all the displays in the windows of all the closed department stores. Then we threw cherry bombs in the river till the cops showed up an' we ran like hell. It was great. Freezin' cold, though."

"So you do have some fond memories."

"They get fonder all the time for some reason."

"Nostalgic longing for the halcyon complacency of youth."

"Took the words right outta my mouth, Doc."

"I'm still curious how your mother justified her livelihood under the laws of Christianity."

"Beats me."

"Did she ever express any remorse directly to you?"

"Like apologize?"

"In so many words."

"She'd cry the blues in fronta me sometimes, yeah, how she missed Texas, the farm she was raised on."

"Like LV."

"Uh, yeah. But in Texas. LV is from the Midwest."

"And they're both blonde and like the color lavender and engaged in some sort of, shall we say, earthy escapades to make ends meet and then sought solace and absolution through religious or spiritual rituals."

"Um, I think you're reachin' for somethin' that ain't there, Doc, with all due respect."

"Okay. I'm sorry. Please go on."

"Anyways…where was I? Oh, yeah. So Ginny felt guilty about her job, no question, but she didn't wanna lay too much on me, I was her kid, for Chrissake. She just wanted to shelter me from the outside world, an' my old man just wanted to show it all to me at once. So they fought a lot about my upbringin', y'know. My old man thought Ginny was a hypocrite, for not gettin' into some more respectable line of work, even though he got her *into* this line of work to begin with, so they were *both* hypocrites, far as I'm concerned."

"Did your mother even attempt other fields of employment?"

"Yeah, when I was like sixteen she was overloaded with repentance but really just feelin' her age, an over the hill hooker an' all, so she answered some ads in the Times for work in the city. Office work, waitress, whatever. She went into the city a few times an' always came back blue as hell, totally depressed and rejected an' all, even cryin' 'cause all those big city assholes gave her a hard time, laughed in her face. I really wanted to go kick their asses, tell ya the truth. I told my old man but he didn't care, really. And it bugged me, that he didn't care. He didn't even try to help her find other work, I guess 'cause he couldn't hold down a job himself. He actually useta borrow money from her, and she was such a soft touch she always let him. And she was still in love with him, till the day he died, even though he kept tellin' her he was never gonna be no one woman guy. What a coupla bums. No wonder I'm such a bum myself."

"So how does this all lead up to you shooting your father, or trying to?"

"Well, it was on one of these adventures with my old man that I first met Bluella, when she wasn't too much older than me. They called her that 'cause she danced to the blues, had big blue eyes, and blew every bastard who came backstage to see her."

"You met her in a nightclub?"

"Yeah, in the village, called 'the Neon Rose.' Mob joint, for sure. Long gone now. She blew every fat hairy wop who came into that joint. I used to sneak backstage and watch her from behind the curtain. That's how I fell in love with her."

"In lust, you mean."

"Yeah, like there's a huge difference."

"There is, but we'll get to that later. Go on."

"Thing is, see, Bluella had *principles*. She wasn't like all the *other* broads that danced there. She was actually a virgin. Well, *technically*. That's why she got so good at givin' head. She was savin' herself for the right guy, and from the first time I saw her onstage, as a teenager, maybe sixteen, I thought that might just be *me*."

"Why you?"

"Why *not* me?"

"Go on."

"Anyways, I never told Ginny about my love for Bluella 'cause she woulda *flipped*. I think she wanted me to marry a nun or somethin' which makes no sense, but for years I dreamed of marryin' Bluella an' takin' her away from all this, y'know."

"Was she blonde, Bluella?"

"I dunno, she dyed her *hair* blue, too. I think so, yea, underneath, where it counts."

"I see. Go on."

"Nice try. So anyways, my old man's gig at 'the Neon Rose' ends but I still ask him to take me back there, but I'm too young and if he's not workin' the joint he can't let relatives in, see, an' bend the rules, it's a Mob joint right so normal rules don't apply, only *their* rules, so that's the rule, so for a while I don't see Bluella, like years, and it drives me crazy, but I still dream about her alla time, she becomes my, my..."

"Muse?"

"Yeah! I guess. In fact, I ask Seymour to get me saxophone lessons 'cause Bluella liked to dance to blues, like I said, not rock an' disco an' techno an' rap an' all the crap the other dancers liked, only I didn't tell him my secret plan was to learn sax then get a gig playin' at the Neon Rose so I could play behind Bluella an' then kidnap an' rescue her from blowin' all those bastards backstage. So my ol' man hooked me up with this black dude everyone just called Razzmatazz, who played in all the same joints my old man did, an' he taught me how to play. He was a cool cat, man."

"You became a musician for love, then."

"I thought it was just *lust*, Doc."

"Whatever the motivation, you found a way to channel your emotions and sexual energies into something productive. That's very positive, Eddie, and a sign of your own keen survival instincts."

"Bluella inspired me 'cause she was an *artist*. I mean, she didn't just *dance*. She *created*. Like one time I remember her comin' out wearin' nothin' but a string of blue roses, then she took 'em off an' made a *bed* of roses, as she called it, an' she rolled around naked in these blue rose petals with a blue spotlight an' it drove the crowd so nuts an' one time they stormed the stage, so the bouncer hadda save her from bein' eaten *alive*. Another time she came out covered in blue whipped cream or cake frostin' or somethin', an' this oily muscle-bound dude licked it off her till she was naked. It drove me *nuts*. She was a *genius*."

"Did you ever actually *talk* to Bluella?"

"Not for years, not till I came back later an' auditioned as a backup musician."

"And she was still there, at the Neon Rose?"

"Yup, like she was waitin' for me, after all those years. An' by then I was pretty good on the sax after practicin' all during my teen years. It was like my college. And I was majorin' in sax."

"So did you get the gig at the Neon Rose?"

"Yup. I sure did. An' that's when I finally started talkin' to Bluella, who was *still* a virgin. I mean, that's how I finally found out. I heard it from my old man for years but she told me directly, her pussy was *still* locked up, waitin' for Mister Right."

"Did you inform her that might be *you*?"

"Not right away, though I told her I was savin' myself for the same reason, so she could sorta figure it out on her own, that we was meant to be."

"Did she ultimately agree?"

"Not right away, but eventually, yeah. I mean, I *think*. What were the odds two virgins would be workin' in the same strip joint? I useta help her tie her G-string an' shit backstage, in fact I did that for *all* the strippers, I even collected cash off the perverts as they stood in line for lap dances an' blowjobs in the back, includin' Bluella, takin' a fin off some sleazy hippie creep an' then watchin' her get him off, it was...a trip, man. I'd go home and jack off thinkin' about it. But I had faith. I'd already seen everything, anyways, nothin' could shock or surprise me. I was on my own by now, lived in a little room in the Alphabet, basically a crack house, but it's all I could afford, an' so..."

"How did Ginny take it, you leaving the nest finally?"

"Not too good, not too good. But I don't wanna talk about her right now."

"Okay."

"Anyways, so Bluella an' I hit it off but it's like one of those brother-sister type deals at first, like LV an' me, but we still talked a lot, went out for coffee an' whatnot, sometimes uptown to Carnegie Deli, her favorite, or some fast food foreign hole in the wall, 'cause she liked real spicy food, which sorta turned me on, too. It was nice. She didn't wear makeup when we went out, she looked so innocent, an' we talked mostly about kid stuff, movies an' her pets growin' up an' stuff, an' she let me walk her back to her scummy motel sometimes, like we was an old-fashioned couple an' all, an' you'd never think she was the same dame out there wigglin' her perfect ass for a livin'. Only by now she was worried it was startin' to sag a little, by then I was in my twenties an' she was maybe thirty at the most, but in her line, that's pretty old, so she was gettin' worried her best days were behind her, so to speak, which was where *I* came in, I figured, know what I'm sayin'?"

"I can see the pattern, yes."

"Pattern? *What* friggin' pattern?"

"Never mind. Please go on."

"I mean, talkin' to her, she reminded me of Greta, like I could see her as a little girl, playin' with dolls in the sandbox an' shit, all innocent, which made me wonder how she got into a dive like the Neon Rose, takin' off her clothes and blowin' guys for bonuses. She was from a small town upstate and came to Manhattan to be on Broadway, but that didn't pan out so she answered an ad in the paper for a dance gig and here she was, all these years later. Sad, in a way."

"What was her real name?"

"I dunno. She never told me. She didn't want anyone to know. We all just called her 'Blue'. But nobody knew her like I did."

"But she wouldn't even reveal her true identity. That doesn't sound like you had a very intimate, trusting relationship."

"We didn't bother with friggin' *formalities*, Doc, we was too busy talkin' 'bout *important* stuff. Like *Life*."

"So how does this lead to you almost shooting your own father?"

"Hang *on*. Well, for one thing, I got him his ol' gig back at the Neon Rose. *Me*. They hired him 'cause *I* recommended him. They all liked me. He'd been out on the road all this time, I didn't see him as much when I got older, he was gone mosta the time an' he became like a stranger to me. But I helped him out for ol' times' sake. An' I had some clout 'cause everyone thought I was gettin' it on with Bluella, who *all* the guys had the hots for, even my old man."

"Is that why you shot him?"

"I *didn't* shoot him, I told ya, I *tried* to. But I'm still on the *sex* part of the story. The *violence* part is comin' up, promise."

"So you were the envy of the Neon Rose."

"Yeah. I mean, we talked an' all, me an' Bluella, an' everyone thought we were an item but I didn't even hit on her, I swear, not once. She had this great laugh, not a cocktail party phony type laugh, but innocent kinda little girl giggle that just killed me. Even though I watched her dancin' and givin' blowjobs on a nightly basis, I couldn't think of her that way. I could watch her blowin' *other* guys and get turned on, but I couldn't even *imagine* her blowin' *me* like that. I *liked* her too much. We was just friends, really. I useta watch her gettin' dressed, sweatin' bullets, an' she *knew* I was watchin', so she'd take her time slippin' in an' outta her panties an' pasties, y'know, and she'd sorta sing to herself, real soft, an' did her own private strip tease for me in her dressin' room, an' sometimes I'd serenade her with my sax while she was takin' a shower, an' she'd come out all wet 'n' naked, an' then I'd help her get dressed so she could go out there on stage an' get back *un*dressed, an' I was playin' right behind her, lookin' at that heart-shaped creamy ass grind away for all those perverts. And she even stopped blowin' guys backstage now, 'cause she was makin' good bread as the headliner and didn't hafta do that no more, no more deli platters for the perverts to snack on...so...so...eventually, one night in her dressin' room, my dream came true. Sort of. She kissed me, and her lips were so warm an' luscious it made me dizzy, even though I'd seen where those lips had been, but I didn't think about that. She let me kiss her back, and I sucked on her breasts a bit, and she moaned an' I got real hungry and sloppy, but then she stopped me. She was still savin' herself for Mister Right, she says. And I told her I was *still* savin' my*self* for Miss Right, which I hoped would be *her*, but she said she wasn't sure, she hadda be *sure*, she was pretty sure but not quite, she didn't even want to go down on me or nothin' cause I was *special*. I was in *heaven*, I thought. My dream was comin' true. An' then it happened."

"*What* happened?"

"I go to the club one time not long after she kissed me, a week maybe, an' the bouncer tells me Bluella didn't show up for work, an' everyone's worried, 'cause her hotel room ain't got no direct line and the they couldn't get through to her. I tell him I'll to her pad and see what's up. I'm dodgin' muggers the whole way 'cause she lives in this really shitty neighborhood, in this cheap ass hooker hotel, like I *always* do, an' I ran up the stairs past the clerk an' he tells me to stop, visitors gotta pay a fee, so I slapped a ten spot on the desk an' I ask him where Bluella lives, an' he tells me she has company already, an' I run up to her room, an' there's no answer an' some junkie in the hall pulls a knife on me so I kick him in the nuts an' he starts pukin' right in the hallway, but I ignore him, an' then some bald slob sticks his big fat ugly head out his door an' tells everyone to keep it down, but I ignore him too an' find Bluella's room an' start bangin' on the door. No answer. I can hear moanin' an' screamin' inside her her room so I keep bangin' an' finally I just busted in an' Blue's just standin' there naked, an' so is my old man. They're *both* naked. She stands up off him an' stares at me with her big blank blue eyes an' wet thighs an' my old man starts *laughin'*, an' I just busted out *cryin'*. There was blood on the cot, see. There were other stains, too, that looked older, but this was *fresh*. It was her cherry juice. My old man broke her in. After all that time of her talkin' 'bout waitin' for Mister Right. But then she started cryin' an' tellin' me he *raped* her, for Chrissake. He laughs some more an' says he was just givin' her a test drive so she could finally take *my* cherry. He says he was like *interviewin'* her for the job of finally takin' my virginity, since it always bugged him that I was holdin' out. He always tried gettin' one of my aunts to do me, but they were all too scared of Ginny, who'd fire anybody who touched me. So anyways, I went up to him an' decked him once an' then I just split, even though Blue was *screaming* by now. The desk clerk gave me a look an' picked up the phone, I guess to call the cops, but I didn't care, I was gone, out in the night, lost lowlife types circlin' me like hungry wolves. I just ran an' ran an' wound up by the river, pukin' my guts out, an' that's all I remember, really. It was all a blur. I felt like I was in a zombie movie and I was the only person left in the whole world, surrounded by zombies, an' I was friggin' doomed an' alone no matter what I did."

"My God. That's awful."

"Yup. So that's how it ended up, after all that. Bluella an' Seymour. And he *knew* I loved her, too, that sick bastard. He knew it wasn't just lust with me an' Bluella, or else I'da made a move a long time ago. He *knew* I played my sax for her an' her alone, night after night. I still don't know if he really raped her or what, but it didn't matter. She was ruined for me. My old man an' me had touched the same flesh. *Sacred* flesh, to me. It was *creepy*, man. So that's how the story ends. It was all for *nothin'*, my saxophone lessons with Razzmatazz, holdin' out waitin' for Blue to see me as Mister Right, *everything*, all up in smoke, just like that." *Snap*.

"That's tragic, Eddie. So what did you do next? How did you *cope*?"

"For one thing, I quit the club cold, never went back to the Neon Rose after than, even though Bluella kept leavin' messages for me at my hotel, an' then I went out an' borrowed a gun from someone I met at the club an' one night, not long after I caught my old man bangin' Blue, it was rainin' really hard, but I waited in the shadows out front of the Neon Rose, in the rain, all wet, till I caught my old man leavin' the club an' I followed him down the street an' then I just took a shot at him. And missed. On *purpose*. Couldn't go through with it after all. I think. But it scared the hell outta him, that's for sure. He never had any idea what happened, an' *almost* happened that night."

"Did he know it was you?"

"No. It was rainin' and dark and I ran too fast."

"Ran where?"

"Anywhere. *Everywhere*. That's when I started

travelin' the country with different bands as a sax for hire, just to get away from there. That's when I first went to L.A. and got laid myself. That's why I didn't enjoy it that much. It was Bluella I wanted. She was the whole reason I got into music in the first place. What a waste. What a *putz*."

"But once again, Eddie, your pursuit of a fantasy lead you to a more fulfilling reality, just not the one you initially envisioned. You discovered your own musical talents because of your obsession with this woman."

"Big deal."

"I think so. How did Ginny feel about all this?"

"Well, I didn't *tell* her, Doc, jeez. I couldn't tell her I was foolin' aroun' with a stripper an' then I caught her with my old man so I took a *shot* at him. I mean, she'd *freak*."

"But she must've known you were a professional musician by then, right? Didn't that give her some sense of pride?"

"I guess. My aunts seem to dig it more. I'd play for 'em an' all after I got good, and they really dug it. Ginny *tolerated* it, but I don't know if she *loved* it. She always wanted me to go to college, though. Can you imagine? I never even went to friggin' *kindergarten*."

"She wanted you to have the stability she never had. That makes sense."

"Yeah, right. She lived in a total *fantasy* world, Doc. I mean, I was a virgin till I left that whorehouse I was raised in. My old lady is readin' to me from the Bible while my Aunt Matilda is fondlin' some fat slob's balls in the next room. What a joke."

"Did you ever see your father again?"

"Naw. He was already slowly dyin' by then, too. With the cancer. He was coughin' up blood, I seen it by then, an' I felt bad for him till *this* shit happened. I think he knew he was dyin' and just didn't give a fuck about anything or anybody no more. I think he told Bluella he was dyin' and, knowin' her, what a sweet broad she was down deep, she tossed him a sympathy fuck for the road. *Or* he just friggin' raped her. Same difference."

"Hardly."

"Anyway I never saw either of 'em again, I was gone, baby, gone. Razzmatazz got me some connections with some travelin' jazz bands, that's how I got hooked up on the road. One connection leads to another. It's a lifestyle, a brotherhood, a network, like. You just go wherever the money flows, man. If it was up to Ginny, I'd still be locked up in that whorehouse. But instead, I've seen the world, Doc. Or at least the country. I've seen enough, anyway."

"How did you decide to finally move out? You never detailed that decision."

"I pretty much just ran away one day, Doc. When I was twenty-three an' still cherry, well, technically. And kinda for the same reason. My aunts were gettin' to me. I knew if I stuck around I'd give into one of 'em an' that wouldn't be good for *nobody*. It'd be a *blood* bath."

"Did any of your so-called aunts ever try to actively seduce you?"

"Sure! Alla time, of course."

"And you *never* gave in, even *once*?"

"Well, I got a few hand jobs now an' then, sure, startin' pretty much in puberty, but I was sworn to secrecy. My Aunt Tammy useta sneak in my room wearin' nothin' but a green nightie an' slip under my covers an' jack me off while she whispered to me stories about her freaky clients. Man, I'd just *gush* all over my sheets an' she'd just laugh an' sneak back out. I told Ginny I was just whackin' off, an' she let me get away with *that* much at least, I mean, c'mon, considerin' my environment an' all, I needed *some* release. This was when I was like fifteen, sixteen, an' it went on for a few years till one day when I was maybe nineteen Aunt Tammy upped and moved out, just like that. She just vanished without a trace, an' nobody ever talked about it, neither. I always wondered what *really* happened. I mean, Aunt Tammy wasn't the *only* one givin' me hand jobs now an' then. Mainly on my birthday, I'd get a few, late at night, in the dark, after Ginny had gone to bed, alone or not. If Ginny found out she'da had 'em *all* killed. An' Mob guys were a big part of her clientele, so she coulda made *any*body disappear with a snap of her fingers. Cops, too, an' political types. They *all* hung out there, alla time. Ginny had 'em *all* wrapped around her clit."

"Pretty powerful."

"Yeah, I mean, she put the fear of God in me, true, but I was afraida *Guido* a helluva lot more, 'cause he was right *there*. I don't think God was anywhere *close* to that place where I grew up."

"Guido who?"

"*Any* of 'em. They *all* loved Ginny. I think one wiseguy wanted to *marry* her even. But she never gave up on the old man, even when he was sick and dyin'. *Especially* when he was sick and dyin'. She was like that. Fact is, the guy I scored the gun from to take out my old man was a wiseguy client of my old lady's who also hung out at the Neon Rose, which was owned by a New York family, not Jersey, but they all knew each other, those guys."

"So this person just *gave* you a gun?"

"*Loaned*. No questions. I gave it back, don't worry."

"Why did you still a gun from Max."

"Protection."

"From who?"

"Max."

"Ironic."

"Ain't it, though?"

"If I reported you were carrying a gun, you'd be in jail, Eddie. You're on parole. That's why you're here, remember."

"Yeah, I kinda skipped over that part, didn't I?"

"I know all about it. You took a big chance in bringing that here."

"I sure did, Doc. Whaddya gonna do about it?"

"Nothing."

"Nothing? *Really*? Goody-goody like you?"

"You brought that to taunt me, Eddie. I think you *want* to go back to jail, to escape the real world, but I won't let you get off that easy, Eddie. I know the *truth*, Eddie. Do you?"

"You got all the answers, Doc. You tell *me*."

"Next time, perhaps. If I feel you're ready to accept it, though I'd rather you figure it out on your own. And don't have your gun with you."

Spit.

Session Seven

"My life is a bookie's worst nightmare."

"Why do you say that, Eddie? And thank you for not bringing your gun this time."

"I only packed a piece to impress you, Doc."

"I'd have been more impressed if you'd just brought your saxophone, Eddie. It's a healthier form of self expression."

"It's kinda cumbersome on a train. I can *conceal* a gun."

"I would just get *rid* of that gun, Eddie, all things considered. I doubt your friend Max has a hit on you. He has too much to lose now. So why is your life a bookie's worst nightmare?"

"The odds."

"Against what?"

"*Everything.* Me meetin' LV, my old man bangin' Bluella, the way I was raised, *everything.*"

"You see your life as a string of meaningless ironies with no payoff, is that it?"

"You're gettin' good at this, Doc. I may recommend you to the *next* psycho saxophonist who comes down the pike."

"I have quite enough of a work load already, but thank you, Eddie."

"Me, too."

"What?"

"I got work. A gig."

"That's wonderful, Eddie! Where?"

"The Saloon. In North Beach, on Grant, 'cross the

street from your ol' stompin' grounds, Caffe Trieste."

"That's *great* news, Eddie!"

"Well, don't bust open the champagne just *yet*. It ain't steady or nothin'. I'm just gonna fill in for some blues bands now an' then, sorta on call. But if I can get in good with these cats, they might turn me on to some other clubs around town. I already got one possible lead in the Haight-Ashbury, rock joint, but I'll take whatever. So, things are finally lookin' up for Eddie the Putz. Knock on wood." *Knock, knock.*

"One thing always leads to another, Eddie. The domino principal."

"My ol' pal, the domino principal. Maybe they'll fall in the right direction this time."

"How's the romance angle?"

"Whaddya mean?"

"Meet any interesting blondes lately, or even inferior breeds, like brunettes and redheads?"

"Well, actually, now that ya mention it, I hooked up with these two Mod type chicks, y'know, they dress in the tight short skirts an' go-go boots an' all, in Golden Gate Park. They even ride Vespas. Really cute 'n' sexy."

"In the park?"

"Yeah."

"So?"

"So what?"

"So what happened, Eddie?"

"Well, I was practicin' my sax in the park, just playin' with myself in public, y'know how it is."

"Not really, but continue."

"Yeah anyways, so these two chicks, in their early twenties, both Mods with a little Bettie Page thrown in for good measure, typical hipster chicks, in other words, with tattoos 'n' all, they like what they hear so they invite me back to their pad in the Richmond nearby, they're both really into Sixties Brit pop music and old New Wave, Blondie 'n' Devo 'n' Talking Heads an' all, so I play some of that stuff for 'em, and then they ask me if I wanna get high, I say sure, so we light up, have some drinks, then we made out a bit, nothin' major, then they said they hadda go out an' meet their boyfriends, so I split. And that was pretty much *it*. I think they're both Art students or somethin'. I may see 'em again, even though they're hooked up already."

"At least you made some contacts of the opposite sex without any neurotic strings attached. Sounds like progress to me. Were they blonde?"

"Nope, both dyed their hair jet black. I didn't get to check to see if the carpet matched the drapes. Maybe next time, I'll get back to ya."

"Not necessary, thank you."

"I wouldn't mind bangin' *both* of 'em, though. I just won't tell *you* about it, is all."

"I'm only interested in your well being, Eddie, and your adjustment in normal society."

"'Normal society,' you mean like an old Doris Day flick?"

"I don't think those movies truly represented the norm even in their era, Eddie. They were just more fantasies."

"Yeah. Doris Day had nice gams, but not really my type. I'm more of a Mamie Van Doren guy. I went out with a Doris Day type once, when I was a teenager an' I'd escape the asylum I called home sometimes, take a bus down to the shore, Ashbury Park or even all the way down to Wildwood sometimes, during the summer, and I'd see these Doris Day type chicks in their bikinis, an' I just wanted to sorta corrupt 'em, y'know? They were *so* different than the women *I* knew. Like I could hear elevator music and see Technicolor just *lookin'* at 'em. This one chick was named Judy—yeah, a blonde, Doc, ponytail an' all, real Fifties type, innocent, just ripe for some corruption. Met her on the boardwalk in Wildwood, she was with some other chicks, but she stood out—literally, real pointy boobs, musta had one of them bullet bras, just like Mamie Van Doren, but she was more the Donna Reed type, know what I'm sayin'? Or Doris Day, same difference. With a little toucha Ann-Margret sex kitten. She was as different as night 'n' day from my Aunt Tammy anyways, who was whackin' me off to true tales of nasty sex under my sheets back home."

"Aunt Tammy seems to loom larger in your history than you care to share, Eddie."

"Yeah, how so?"

"Well, it sounds like she was the first person you ejaculated *with*."

"Yeah, I guess you're right about that, Doc. Her room was *always* busy with payin' action. She lived just above me, an' I could hear her bed doin' the rhumba twenty-four friggin' hours a *day* it seemed. It drove me *nuts*. I useta whack off like crazy hearin' her an' her johns moan 'n' scream, from the time I was like twelve. I was so jealous of her I wanted to kill every bastard who limped outta her room. This whorehouse we lived in used to be a hotel, see, an' alla bathrooms were in the hallways, so I useta use the upstairs bath just to maybe get a peek at Aunt Tammy comin' in or outta her door with her happy johns."

"She was blonde, yes?"

"Yup, she fit the bill, all right. Though I think she was a *fake* blonde. But that was *all* that was fake. Aunt Tammy useta be a dancer, I don't mean no stripper, I mean like a chorus girl on Broadway, 'Cats' 'n' shit like that, y'know? She had probably the best body in that place. She looked like a cross between Jean Harlow an' Kim Novak, if that's even humanly *possible*. Y'know, the old movie stars? And she made the most of it, too. I mean as a hooker. She got in an accident an' broke her leg an' had kinduva limp so she had to quit dancin'. I heard her old boyfriend broke her leg when he caught her with some guy, but she never really wanted to talk about it. If I even brought it up, she'd get kinda teary-eyed and start cryin' a little, so I'd drop it. I always hadda crush on her, from when she first moved into the house, when I was like ten or so. I was really shy around her until one time when I was older she asked me if she ever kept me awake, an' I said yes, but I don't mind, an' she offered to give me a sampler but I told her my mother would *kill* me, an' she laughed an' said, yeah, me too, then she gave me a kiss on the cheek, like *all* my aunts did, but this one had a different effect on me. I gotta *huge* boner, leakin' through my pants, and she *noticed*.

"One night, it was stormy out, the kinda storm that *makes* you believe in God 'cause He sounds so *pissed*, right, so I'm lyin' there under the covers, an' it's been quieter than usual up above me, so I gotta use my imagination to entertain myself for a change. Or so I thought. Then I hear this knock on my door an' it creaks open real slow and it's Aunt Tammy, in all her glory, wearin' this see-through green nightie, and she asks me, real sweet an' soft, can I tuck her in, the storm is scarin' all the business away an' she's lonely. I was positive I was dreamin' so I figured there was no harm in followin' her back up to her room 'cause it was all a dream anyways, a *wet* one, I hoped. It was neon-red in there, her room I mean, with lotsa big pillows all over, an' she had a huge brass bed with silk sheets, and all this sexy artwork all over the walls, an' Aunt Tammy sorta sprawls across her bed in this real cockteaser pose, totally naked an' says, 'Tuck me in,' only it sounds more like 'fuck me senseless,' right, so I go pull the sheets over her an' then tells me to lie next to her, so I do, an' she asks me to tell her a bedtime story, an' I tell her I don't know any, an' so she says, okay, I'll tell *you* one. And that's how it started. She had really nice feet, too, an' ladies' feet *always* made me dizzy anyways. Still do. Her feet were stickin' outta the edge of the blanket. I didn't lie under the blanket with her 'cause I was so nervous and *hot*, I mean I was sweatin' like *crazy*. Her toenails were painted red an' I'd lie there starin' at her pretty feet while she tells me all this sick shit that was all *true*. So I got the stories behind alla the sounds. I'm tellin' ya, Doc, there are some *sick* bastards out there. But I wanted to hear all about it for some reason. Aunt Tammy just keeps tellin' me detail after detail about how these slobs violate her on like an hourly basis, an' I'm listenin' an' lookin' at her toes an' I can't hold it in much longer, an' she could tell. Then while she's still talkin' she puts her hand softly on my dick, gives it like one pump, an' I came, just like that, all over feet, I mean it shot all the way down to the end of the bed, and I saw my cum drippin' all over toes an' I just about passed out almost. Then there's a knock on the door and it's Ginny, so Tammy panics and tells me to hide under the bed, an' Ginny comes in and says, 'Have you seen Eddie,' and she lies and says no, even though her feet are covered in my cum an' all, but that could be *any*body's cum, since jackin' guys off with her feet was one of her specialties, she even did it to *me* a few times later on. So anyways, they chat a bit an' I'm under the bed completely terrified of bein' found out, but finally Ginny leaves an' I gotta make up some shit why I wasn't in my room, I don't remember what I said, I went for a walk or somethin', which made no sense since it was rainin' out an' I wasn't even wet, but she bought it anyways. So I never went back to her room after that, but Aunt Tammy kept comin' to *my* room now an' then. That was my total sexual experience until I met Judy. Judy kinda looked like Tammy, but before she became a hooker. Maybe that's why I was attracted to her right away. She was like a *nice* version of Aunt Tammy, and far away from the whorehouse, too, so she gave me a chance to get away on a regular basis, with someplace to go, y'know?"

"Judy may have represented the purity your mother wished for you."

"*May* have? She was innocence on a *stick*, Doc. *My* stick, as it turned out. Regular cotton candy. Or so I *thought* till I really got to know what a *freak* she was. That's when I knew all those Doris Day movies my old lady and I useta watch were fulla shit. Rock Hudson in real life was a nice guy who liked to suck cock and take it up the ass an' died of AIDS, for one thing. Funny, he was supposed to be the macho ladies' man but the *other* guy in those movies, Tony Randall, who seemed like the fruitcake, was knockin' out babies when he was like a *hundred*. Ya never know."

"That's what I'm saying, Eddie. Movies are illusions. Like dreams, or even memories."

"Mostly. Except for zombie movies. Ever been to a mall? Totally 'Dawn of the Dead.' Most of the hotels I live in are fulla zombies, too. Welfare moms an' war vets an' laid off union workers an' hookers an' strippers an' junkies, all dead inside, just walkin' aroun' tryin' to find somebody's flesh to munch on. The whorehouse where I was raised was fulla zombies, too. Dead bodies that came there to get reanimated, just a buncha horny corpses. Sometimes it felt like I was suffocatin' inside a coffin, buried alive with all these corpses havin' an orgy all around me, like I was gonna drown in blood, guts and cum one day. So anyways, Judy physically sorta reminded me of Aunt Tammy, who I thought I was in love with, even though I was in love with Bluella by then, too. In fact, my love for Bluella was the only thing that kept me from actually stickin' my dick inside Aunt Tammy. I was savin' myself for Blue. I even told her that an' she thought it was romantic an' all, an' then I'd say so tell me again about how the police chief likes to fuck you up the ass while he pulls your hair an' calls you a cunt, an' tickle my nuts and stroke my shaft while you're tellin' me so I can shoot another load on your feet. That's what I was doin' in between watchin' Doris Day movies, so excuse me if I seemed a bit confused. Then I met Judy who was like from 'Forbidden Planet' or somethin'. To me, *she* was the alien."

"How did you feel about Judy as a *person*, not just an alien object?"

"I was pretty much in love with her *too*, you kiddin'? Even though I was like eighteen an' still dreamin' of Bluella, gettin' my sax lessons from Razzmatazz, an' my *sex* lessons from Aunt Tammy. Judy was so the opposite of everything I knew. She lived in Collingswood. Her folks were from Boston an' her old man was a Philly lawyer an' her mom belonged to all these South Jersey associations an' *every*thing was just like a friggin' *post*card with her. We'd take the PATCO train into Philly sometimes, always with her friends, though. I never fit in. They were all a buncha spoiled assholes, even Judy, but I could tell she wanted to take a walk on the wild side, so I took her for that ride. We'd go to the movies an' hold hands an' pretend we was *in* a friggin' movie. Then she let me give her a pearl necklace in the back of her car at a drive-in once. Not a *real* pearl necklace, but the kind I can *afford*. I came all over tits an' neck an' she scooped it up an' licked it off her fingers. Her tits looked like two big scoops of vanilla ice cream anyway, with cherries on top, an' I just provided the whipped cream. An' with my dick added to the mix it was like her chest was a friggin' banana *split*. She was a perfect angel, or she *looked* like one. It was too good to be true. I didn't know she was just usin' me."

"For what? Sex?"

"Not *just* that. Laughs. Kicks. Cheap thrills. We kept gettin' more an' more wasted together. I scored some mushrooms from one of my aunts and Judy got hooked on 'em, an' then next thing you know, I'm like her pusher, for her *and* all her high-falutin' asshole friends. I brought 'em 'shrooms an' weed at first, but then they wanted more so I went on the street an' scored smack off these lowlifes. I did it for love, Doc. I got all those suburban pussies stoned just so I could cream all over Judy's tits at the drive-in on a regular basis. Again, no dick in her pussy or nothin', I was savin' myself an' she *wanted* to fuck but I said no, I can't, I gotta save myself for my music, I told her, an' by my music, I meant my *muse*. Bluella. *You* know. Anyways, she thought I was crazy but she loved the junk and booze I brought her so it didn't matter...

"One time we all got loaded at the beach in Atlantic City an' started havin' a kinda orgy by the campfire, everybody makin' out with everybody, it was all a blur, but then they *left* me there. I woke up shiverin' with no clothes on. They took my wallet, everything. I never heard from her again. I think maybe her old man got wise she was becomin' a doper, an' I was her connection, even though he never met me, an' he grounded her, even though she was my age. She was about to go off to college to be a nurse anyway, so I was probably just a last fling before she got real. An' she chose me 'cause she *liked* me. At least, that's what I like to think. Better than she just got tired of me an' left me alone by the ocean to freeze to death. I hadda roll some bum for his clothes then hitch back to Jersey City. I learned my lesson."

"Which lesson is that, Eddie?"

"People suck." *Strike, drag, puff.* "Mind?"

"Haven't seen you light up for a while, Eddie. I thought maybe you'd kicked the habit so you could avoid your father's fate."

"No such luck, Doc, no such luck." *Clump, whomp, whomp.* "Cloudy out today. Somethin' timeless about a dark day. Sorta how I envision death. Dark 'n' cool 'n' peaceful. Y'know? I like the weather up here, suits my style. I can wear my suit 'n' shades mosta the time. Down in L.A. it's too hot 'n' smoggy alla time. Houston an' New Orleans are like *swamps*, for Chrissake. Chicago, Philly, New York— too freezin' cold in the winter, too boilin' hot in the summer. And the *fog*, Doc. I dig the *fog* up here. I'm a fog lover. I can get *lost* in it. Maybe I'll wind up in Portland or better yet, Seattle. Life only makes sense to me when it's raining."

"Why don't you just sit down and relax, Eddie?"

"Pacin' makin' ya nervous again? Like I'm a nut? It's because of what I did to be here, ain't it, Doc? The crime. The *atrocity*, the judge called it."

"Sit down, Eddie. Please."

"I'm a homicidal sex-crazed *maniac*, Doc. I can't help it."

"I'm your friend, Eddie. You can relax around me. I didn't turn you in because of the gun, did I? Doesn't that earn me a little trust, at least?"

"I just like lookin' out this window, is all. I'll stand."

"All right. Now that you're working again, have you thought about getting an apartment and moving out of that hotel? It's about time you found a stable place to live, isn't it, Eddie?"

"What, like I'm gonna settle *down* here? Fuck that."

"Why not? You as much as said you feel at home here. Isn't it about time you established some roots? I don't see how this transient lifestyle can be of any further use to you. You can't live your life on the run, Eddie."

"Runnin' from who? Max?"

"Either from one phantom, or towards another."

"Can't afford the down payment on my own pad, Doc. I never even hadda bank account. Cash only. That's my policy."

"Well, maybe you can rent a room in a nice house somewhere, maybe over here in the East Bay. I'm just concerned that the influence of your environment will continue to drag you down."

"Too late, Doc. I'm in the gutter already. I'm a criminal, a madman. I deserve what's comin' to me. I'm beyond help. I don't even know why I keep comin' here. It's a waste of time. Maybe I won't come back."

"But it's a condition of your parole, Eddie. So is staying in the area."

"I ain't goin' nowhere, Doc. I just don't see the point in comin' here. In talkin' to you no more. I think I should just go, back into the fog, and disappear."

"It's starting to rain, Eddie. Stay with me. Even if we don't talk. We can just sit together. Maybe next time you can bring me your music."

"Really, Doc?"

"Yes. I think I'm ready to hear it now."

"Funny, I was just thinkin' of writin' another tune, called 'The Fog Lover,' an' finishin' another one, called 'Diary of a Dreamer'…"

"They sound beautiful, Eddie. Could you get them recorded?"

"Not yet, but I could maybe play 'em for you."

"You mean bring your saxophone *here*?"

"Yeah, why not? You said it yourself. Better than a gun."

"It's a deal."

"Not yet."

"What else?"

"I want *you* to talk to *me* for a change. I mean, who the hell *are* you, Doc? Smart, sexy dish like you. Why'd you even get into a racket like this, wastin' time on nutcases like me?"

"I don't consider it a racket or a waste of time, Eddie. And it would be unprofessional of me to share my personal life with you. That would violate the sanctity of our relationship as dictated by the court."

"Okay, then how about clock out an' we can talk off the record, go our for a drink, how 'about that?"

"I don't think that would be a very good idea, Eddie."

"You think I'm a freak as well as a criminal, don't ya?"

"I think you're a very talented man who got off on the wrong track, and it's my job to help set you straight again."

"Even after what I did?"

"It was ruled an act of, of…"

"Passion. Insanity."

"Yes."

"I should still be locked up, Doc. I should never have been let out."

"Maybe you escaped?"

"Huh? Whaddya mean?"

"That is, maybe you escaped not your past, but your future."

"I don't get it."

"You will. Trust me."

"Sure, Doc. You're all I got in the world."

"That might be true, Eddie. For now."

"So you really want me to bring my sax with me next time?"

"Please."

"I'll play for you, like I played for my aunts, an' Bluella, an' LV. Right?"

"Yes. I'd like that, Eddie. Very much."

"Then what?"

"What do you mean?"

"Can we go out after that? You said you went to Yoshi's once. A jazz club, a ritzy one. I'm workin' now, I can afford to buy you a cocktail."

"I went with my boyfriend, Eddie. My *fiancé*."

"You're engaged? What is he, computer expert? Doctor? Lawyer?"

"That remains none of your business, Eddie."

"Maybe I'll write *you* a song, Doc. And you'll hear it an' fall in love with me an' leave this clown in the dust."

"I doubt it, Eddie."

"You're just my type, Doc. Smart, sexy...an' blonde."

"It's time to go, Eddie."

"Why?"

"It's stopped raining."

Session Eight

"So I wrote you this song, Doc. It's called 'Shadow Music.'"

"That's a lovely title, Eddie. I'm very flattered."

"A title can tell the whole story, Doc. Like I seen this movie once, called 'The Incredibly Strange Creatures Who Stopped Living and Became Mixed-Up Zombies.' If *that* ain't the story of my life I don't know what *is*. I got plenty of others, too. 'The Sea and the Stars.' 'Deep Dark Secrets.' 'Rain in the Night.' 'The Moon at Noon.' I haven't finished alla tunes that go *with* 'em, but sometimes I just like dreamin' up a title first. Nice dress, by the way."

"Thank you. I just bought it."

"It's lavender."

"You noticed. Are you going to play for me now?"

"*Right* now?"

"Yes. Please. I've been looking forward to this."

"Yeah, no kiddin'?"

"No kidding, Eddie. Please play for me."

"All right…."

…

"That was a haunting melody, Eddie. Beautifully melancholy. The funny thing is…it sounds very familiar to me."

"I didn't rip it off, Doc. I swear."

"No, no, of course not. I mean, I've heard it before—maybe in a foggy dream by the sea—a nightmare…"

"Okay, Doc, now *you're* scarin' *me*."

"Really, Eddie?"

"Well, it's kinda feels like, kinda like I've *always*

known you. From before I was born even. I can't put my finger on it."

"Projecting another fantasy, Eddie?"

"Well, you're *real*, ain'tcha, Doc?"

"Am I?"

"Knock it off, Doc. You messin' with my head on *purpose*?"

"I'm sorry, Eddie. I thought you may have figured it out by now."

"Figured what out?"

"Why you're here. With me."

"Because of my crime against inhumanity. Which started with me bein' *born*. And then the *other* stuff. Right?"

"Yes. But that's not all."

"I already decided this is our last session anyways, Doc. I'm leavin' town. Headin' north. Seattle."

"You mean you're going to break parole? I'll have to report that."

"Knock yourself out, Doc."

"Why the change of tune, Eddie? I thought we were making real progress."

"I *need* to escape, Doc."

"Escape from what?"

"Everything."

"There's no escape from yourself, Eddie. You can't hide from what you did. No matter where you go."

"So you're just gonna *bore* me to death as punishment? What's the *point* of all this chitchat if I'm totally fucked anyway?"

"Eddie, why don't we retrace the events that led up to the incident, and we can emancipate your mind, if not your soul."

"What the hell are you *talkin'* about, Doc?"

"Remember the day you first arrived in San Francisco from Los Angeles, Eddie? *I* do."

"*You* do?"

"You were alone, afraid. Hurt, bitter. The only friend you had left was your saxophone. You started playing for tourists at Pier Thirty-Nine, Fisherman's Wharf, Ghirardelli Square. You sat alone at Fort Point, playing your saxophone engulfed in marine mist. You found solitary sanctuary in Golden Gate Park, embracing the emerald enchantment there, the magical solitude, and began to practice putting music to your melancholia. You found a cheap room in the Mission District, and..."

"Jeez, Doc, how long you been followin' me?"

"I've *always* been with you in one form or another, Eddie. Just listen, now. You wanted to know about me, my own deep dark secrets, *now's* the time."

"Be my guest, Doc." *Strike, puff, drag*.

"You wandered around the city, exploring all the colorful districts, soaking up the cultural diversity, and it's the first town you felt comfortable in since you left New York. It's crazy, it's compact, it's complex, it's *you*. You finally feel at home. It's exactly what your friend said it would be, a beautiful woman with only a few months to live. It instinctively reminds of your mother, your *real* mother, your *natural* mother, a paranoid schizophrenic socialite whose bright, prosperous future was decimated at a young age when she became unwillingly impregnated with a son she never wanted, so she put you up for adoption, and a woman named Virginia adopted you when you were just five months old. Your *real* mother, a native New Yorker, was ultimately shunned by her well-to-do Long Island family, then became destitute and homeless for many years before she was arrested for being a public nuisance and wound up a ward of the state, finally dying alone and abandoned in an institution. That part you didn't know, except maybe intuitively, but I know all about it, Eddie. I know *everything*. It's true Ginny was a whore, and that you were raised in a brothel, more or less, but Ginny didn't run a *hotel* of prostitutes, that's just a composite of all the cheap little hotel rooms you've spent your adult life in, surrounded by prostitutes and strippers, junkies and drifters like yourself. No, she eventually worked by herself, after years of establishing her reputation and clientele, based out of her own little two bedroom apartment in Hoboken, not Jersey City, but it didn't matter how she made a living, since she adopted you on the black market and no questions were asked. She never told you that, did she, Eddie? That Ginny was not your *real* mother? That it wasn't an imaginary 'Aunt Tammy' who came into your room all those nights, but it was in fact *Ginny herself* telling you all those bizarre stories while you pleasured yourself until *she* eventually began to pleasure you, *you*, her adopted son, when you were barely a teenager, before finally becoming lovers when you were barely eighteen and she was in her forties?"

"You're fuckin' *crazy*, Doc. They should lock *you* up. Who the hell *are* you?"

"I think you know, Eddie. Your memory is hazy partly because all the alcohol and drugs and pseudo-sex and especially the aching loneliness have warped your brain. I'm here to clear it all up for you, if you'll let me."

"Go for it but so far I don't believe a worda this shit."

"Suit yourself, Eddie. But these are the *facts*. Seymour was indeed a stand-up comedian, *and* a pimp, but he wasn't your actual father. He wasn't a Creole or a Cuban, or whatever he told you, either —he was just a funny Jew from Florida and New Jersey, amoral and apathetic to your plight, or anyone else's; a charming sociopath. Your *real* father was a hungry, half-crazed homeless man who raped your poor mentally ill mother after a party late one night. Her parents, your biological grandparents, whom you've never met, were *very* religious and wouldn't allow her to get an abortion, despite her pleas and pain. The authorities never caught the culprit, so no one ever discovered his identity, the anonymous man who gave you life, Eddie. Her mental illness accelerated after this tragedy. Schizophrenia is often latently activated, sometimes triggered by traumatic events. Her life was effectively over, but she continued to exist for many years, ignorant of you as you were of her, just wandering the streets like a zombie for years after selling you to Seymour, who then gave you to Ginny.

"After many years, your natural mother wanted to track you down, and she gave Seymour letters to give to you, revealing the truth, letters typed in an office where she got a job as a receptionist before the mental strain became too much for her, and she was fired. Seymour lied to her, never gave the letters to Ginny, so you never read them, never knew she existed. Seymour honestly thought he was protecting you, though. Your mother's letters were increasingly delusional and even dangerous, rambling on about government conspiracies, UFOs and other paranoid rants, neatly typed on stationary from the Cuckoo Clock Company in Brooklyn, where she worked. Seymour loved the irony of this until she began making veiled then obvious death threats against Ginny, whom she never met. Seymour never told your real mother who adopted you, so she could never track you down herself. He protected you *and* Ginny all those years, taking the secret to his grave."

"No, no—*please…*"

"Even though he became her pimp, not her husband, Ginny was in love with Seymour for a long time, until you matured and took his place, but he was the man who really broke her heart, since monogamy was not in his nature. They still slept together, though, even after he began pimping her out to gangsters who frequented the Neon Rose, but Seymour *often* sampled his own merchandise. You never took saxophone lessons from a black man named 'Razzmatazz', either. He's just another phantom father figure, a composite of the many black men who laid down with your mother over the years. You're self-taught by ear, which is very impressive, Eddie. That's how you spent your days and nights for many years, when not masturbating, reading, or watching television, that is. Practicing on your instruments, *both* of them. The *truth* is an aged African American musician client died of a heart attack induced by orgasm and too much booze in Ginny's lavender bed, leaving his saxophone behind which she let you keep, and sometimes she even masturbated with the mouthpiece end of it as you watched. That made it a *very* special instrument for *both* of you. You could actually *taste* her when you played it, for years afterward. When Ginny wasn't using it as a vibrator, you began mimicking the jazz records Ginny played over and over, reminding her of her halcyon burlesque days. Some musicians from the Neon Rose visited her and helped you along with your saxophone lessons over the years as you honed your natural talent, which was once considered quite promising, even prodigious. But your obsession with finding the perfect blonde took your eye off the ball, as it were, prevented you from achieving the success you deserved, and it made you bitter, playing the victim, blaming Ginny for everything instead of taking responsibility for your own adult actions."

"I just never caught a break, Doc, that's all. Listen to my lousy life. I was doomed from the start."

"You could've allowed your music, your true gift, to save you, Eddie, but you were too stubborn and self-destructive and unreliable, fired from band after band, club after club, because of your drinking and drug abuse and inability to connect with any other human being. You *shunned* success. It would've been too real for you to deal with."

"That's a lie, a god damn friggin' *lie*."

"There was no 'Bluella' either, Eddie, except in your mind. There was *only* Ginny. She has *always* been your muse. You played for her because you were in love with her. You remember as a child that she would watch over you as you slept, her cigarette light glowing in the dark as she stood vigil, and you thought it was creepy and hid the kitchen knives for fear she'd kill you in the night. But as you matured, your fear grew into respect, then lust, then love. Ginny became the woman of your dreams, Eddie. She wore the color lavender, slept in the color lavender, her silk lavender nightgown you loved so much, her silk lavender sheets, and she drowned you in her lavender love, both of you blissfully ensconced in lavender and perfume. But since you always believed she was your actual mother, deep down it all began to sicken you with remorse and disgust. Ginny never revealed your adoption for fear you'd leave her, both for the devious lie, and the fact that you were not really bonded by flesh and blood, only semen and vaginal secretions, which she shared with strangers. *You* were meant to be special, and hers alone, *forever*. But you couldn't reconcile the situation with your conscience, and finally, at age twenty-three, you became a fugitive from your own unusual upbringing. You stole Ginny's secret stash of cash and disappeared into the outside world, and it broke her heart. But you continued to write and play music just for her, even though she could no longer hear you. You sent her tapes of your music, though, constantly in need of her approval. And to reaffirm your devotion to her, and her alone."

"Fuckin' *crazy.*"

"It was actually Seymour who got you your first musical gigs, in the clubs where he worked, which led to more lucrative connections that helped you find musical work in other clubs around the country, not just strip joints and biker bars but some classy venues as well. He often had sex with the strippers at the Neon Rose, for whom he also procured sexual clients, and you were jealous of his prowess with these women, as well as Ginny. But there was no one named Bluella. She was merely a mixture of strippers from the Neon Rose, the various clubs you gigged in from coast to coast —and *Ginny*. You walked in on Seymour having sex with *Ginny*, Eddie. Not 'Bluella.' *Ginny*. You *hated* Seymour after that. It was bad enough with strangers but not with the one man you looked up to as a mentor. Plus you knew Ginny had once loved Seymour like she now loved you, so he had become a threat, a danger to your relationship with Ginny. That's one reason you finally left home and went on the road. He was like a father to you, and you felt betrayed. You finally couldn't take it anymore, watching and hearing all those men, not just Seymour, having loud, kinky sex with your true love, Ginny—who had female lovers as well, including many of your so-called 'aunts.' She told you all about her experiences, your 'bedtime stories,' because she wanted no secrets between you, other than the ultimate secret, that you weren't really *hers*, not by birth, and because she wanted to vicariously satisfy your inevitable lust for other women by making herself a goddess, sensual womanhood personified, all you'd ever need or desire. It both titillated and traumatized you. She taught you not to be possessive of her, even as she tried her best to control and contain *you*, by putting the fear of God in you, as you accurately put it, but that was a manifestation of her own guilt over her chosen lifestyle. You were intensely attracted to Ginny, yet increasingly horrified by her hedonistic ways, even as they fueled your own feverish fantasies, and even though she 'repented' in church or chanted in an ashram on a regular basis. You were *both* deeply conflicted, to say the least."

"Bullshit. All bullshit."

"Really? I'll tell you something else, Eddie. There's no LV, either."

"How can you even *say* that, Doc? All those *memories*?"

"*Dreams*, Eddie, not authentic memories, just *pieces* of memories randomly re-arranged like a jigsaw puzzle that never reveals a clear picture, because you keep changing it, so you can see whatever portrait of reality you *want* to see. *This* is the truth: Ginny was a transplanted small town Texas beauty queen who was sexually abused by her alcoholic father, a preacher, for many years until she escaped the ranch at age twenty and ran away to New York City, completely changing her identity so her father would never find her. The horrible hypocrite taught her that New York was a modern Sodom and Gomorrah, so she knew he'd never look for her there. After a few weeks struggling on her own, she met Seymour on the subway, they hit it off, and he got her a job as a professional burlesque performer at the Neon Rose, a downtown nightclub where he also worked as an emcee. Later he became Ginny's pimp. Ginny not only danced at the Neon Rose, but she was a cocktail waitress there as well, before she became a backstage prostitute. After the smitten club owner broke her leg one night in a fit of jealous rage, she quit dancing and got into acting, appearing in a few low budget productions that went nowhere and took her with them, down the drain of utter obscurity. That's when Seymour stepped in, first getting her work in porn films and dirty magazines to augment her income, then finally setting up her own private prostitution business, giving up his percentage, an act of friendship if not love. Of course, his biggest gift was that he found *you* for her. 'I can't give you myself,' he told her, 'but I can give you someone else you can call your own.'"

"You're just makin' all this shit up, Doc."

"*You're* the inventive one, Eddie. You see, Ginny *is* LV. Or *was*."

"*What*? How the hell do you figure *that*?"

"When you were very young, twelve, thirteen or so, Ginny showed you the few B movies she starred in before she descended into nude modeling then outright pornography and then prostitution. You were very young when she made them, but not *too* young, so they were still in circulation for a while. First she took you to see them at grindhouse revivals on 42nd Street, and later on video. Later she showed you her porn tapes and the men's magazines she posed for, too, with an odd mixture of shame and pride, and you *loved* them, *worshipped* them, as you loved and worshipped her, even as these explicit materials repulsed you deep down beneath your lascivious libido. She was considered ideal for the porn industry because she was so naturally gorgeous and sensuous and uninhibited, required no breast augmentation, and best of all, even when the seed of strangers were planted in her damaged womb, she could never get pregnant, a source of misery and inadequacy that haunted her always. She had become irreversibly barren, her curvy, childbearing hips a total anatomical, biological waste, from a clinical, procreative standpoint. It remained a medical mystery though it was probably due to all the botched, backwoods abortions she had as a teenager after her father impregnated her on numerous occasions, but even still, she always wanted a *son*. And a *true*, loyal lover, someone she could call her own after years of heartbreak, dejection, loneliness, and men who only wanted her for her body, like Seymour, or her own damaged, demented father. She found both a son *and* a lover in you. A surrogate husband who could never really leave her, because you were also her son, her own flesh and blood, or so she convinced you. She gave up the porn racket to open her own private prostitution practice, with Seymour's help, and that way she could keep you relatively sheltered from the outside world, since she worked from home, and she was there to guide, nurture, and *imprison* you. She was the only person you've ever been truly close to."

"What about Max an' Mrs. Max? You can't tell me *they* didn't actually *exist*. I remember 'em clear as *day*, Doc."

"Both were merely actors in Ginny's films, Eddie. Never became famous. They were never even married, not to each other, anyway. The Max you describe was just a small-time hustler and pusher you met on Hollywood Boulevard, that you *pretended* was really Max, combined with your image of *Seymour*, the father and the big brother you never had, but always yearned for in your lonesome childhood. You never actually met the Max of the movies, or Mrs. Max, who was a composite of several female singers you've crossed paths with over the years, but you obsessively watched Ginny's exploitation films so many times, masturbating to images of a young Ginny, you came to believe that Max and Mrs. Max were your personal friends, just like you convinced yourself Seymour was your real father, because he took you out to the zoo and the park and the museum, and became a surrogate parent, until you caught him having sex with Ginny, your true love, and then you hated him, despite all he did for you."

"That's friggin' in*sane*, Doc."

"*Isn't* it, though? The fact was you were all alone in Los Angeles, and New Orleans, and Texas, and Chicago, and Philadelphia—*always* alone, by your own design, no matter how many opportunities presented themselves, and there were many. Not that you didn't seek out feminine companionship, but they were always fleeting experiences, and you subconsciously chose women who would ultimately reject you because they came from an elite or at least well educated, upper middle class social stratum— ironically, much like your biological mother did. Only certain kinds of women could meet your demands for debasement though, Eddie. Your fetish was masturbation on women's breasts or with their feet, imagining them to be Ginny, your maternal lover, the only woman you were allowed to actually penetrate and unify with—the only woman you allowed yourself to 'violate.' You told yourself you wanted a 'nice' girl but nice girls won't allow themselves to be used in that fashion, like a cheap whore catering to your peculiar sexual preferences. Not the nice girls of *your* dreams, anyway. Even the nice ones wanted actual intercourse, but you were saving yourself for Ginny. You could not be unfaithful to her sacred vagina, the one that you believed gave you life, in more ways than one."

"Sick."

"Yes."

"So that's the true story of Eddie the Putz. I fucked my mother and tried to kill my father, only she wasn't my real mother and he wasn't my real father."

"Yes."

"Sad. I really *am* a putz."

"Yes."

"But what about Greta? *She* was real, right? *That* wasn't sick or sad, was it?"

"Just a little girl in a sandbox, decades ago. 'Josephine' in your memory is a composite of several prostitute friends of your mother's whom you called 'aunts.' They were also her lovers on occasion. And no one but Ginny ever even changed your diapers, Eddie. It was *always Ginny.* She began breastfeeding you even though her bountiful bosoms that loom so large in your sense memory were completely dry, and she *never stopped.* Your body and soul belonged to her from the very beginning. But you had an innocent boyhood crush on Greta, and Ginny was jealous. She was jealous of anyone else who may have loved you and taken you away from her, Eddie. And eventually, you felt the same way about her. Your 'first time' with the artist woman in Venice, the so-called aging groupie? *Most* of the details you gave me were true, but the persona and place have been confused in your revised recollection. The woman was *Ginny.* The place was her lavender bedroom—not 'neon-red,' you're confusing it with the Neon Rose, which was always bathed in an amber light, its sign, literally a 'neon rose,' still flashing incessantly in your subconscious, reminding you of Ginny's burlesque days, which she told you all about. It was *Ginny.* You just stuck another anonymous woman's head on Ginny's luscious body, as you stuck *your* penis *inside* of it."

"No—please, stop…"

"Too late, Eddie. It's time for the truth—*all* of it. It was a stormy night, and you were afraid of the thunder, even as a young man, since you've always feared divine retribution for your sinful ways. Ginny called for you to 'tuck her in' and watch TV together, some Doris Day movie, the idealized antithesis to your own vulgar lives. You went to her room, her lavender lair, surrounded by her paintings and sculptures and other failed attempts at artistic atonement, or at least spiritual sublimation of her sins, where she finally seduced you into actual copulation. It was your eighteenth birthday, or at least the eighteenth anniversary of when Ginny acquired you from Seymour. You left Ginny when you were twenty-three, finally, after the guilt overwhelmed and suffocated you. *And you never returned*, despite what you claim to recall. But you were eighteen when Ginny took your virginity. She waited all those years to seduce you because she wanted to retain her hold on you once you became a young adult, old enough to live on your own, so she physically changed your relationship forever, completing her plan of having both a son and lover, rolled into one package that she could manipulate and dominate forever. She whispered to you as you came inside of her, again and again, that *all* other women were intrinsically evil, and that *she* was the *only* woman you could *ever* trust enough to share this special experience with, to spill your seed inside of. You *belonged* to her, body *and* soul. You were initially quite wary of taking your relationship with the woman you erroneously believed to be your biological mother to this final level of intimacy, even after all of those 'bedtime stories,' but she over-powered you, exploiting your lust for her, for *all* women, channeling all of that pent-up desire into her monstrous vagina. She doped you up and devoured you. You had supposedly incestuous sex with your alleged mother, *unprotected* sex, *intimate*, wet, *messy* sex, finally penetrating her vagina, the one you believed had spawned you, not just masturbating on her feet and breasts as you once did, and you continued to have sex with her, even as she continued entertaining other men in the room next to yours, for money to survive, doing the only thing she had confidence in, in order to take care of you, her son, her lover, even after you became a young adult, with no skills to survive on your own other than your music. But it drove you mad, seeing and hearing her degrading acts of pleasure with other men, so many disgusting strangers soiling her silk lavender sheets, especially after you finally entered her, came inside of her, became *one* with her. It was exactly as she calculated it to be from the time she first adopted you, all part of her master plan to finally evade her own gnawing loneliness."

"That's seriously fucked up."

"But it's the *truth*. Ginny wanted to find truth too, Eddie. She looked in churches, in ashrams, any place of worship that may help her discover why her life had turned out this way, to assuage her own guilt, and she took you everywhere with you, seeking the answers together, but finding none that satisfied her in the end. Ginny was more than a mother to you, Eddie, and you were much more to her than a son. She was a companion, a lover, a muse. She was your one and only lavender blonde."

"And Judy? What about *her*, Doc?"

"There were *many* Judies, Eddie. You simply condensed them all into one pathetic, self-pitying episode. Just anonymous groupies, like the Mod girls you met in the park, many years ago. You met farm girls and small town girls and hookers and strippers, all kinds of girls in your travels, but none could compare to Ginny, who dominated your dreams. They all fell short of the standard she set for you. You were afraid to be unfaithful to the fantasy she had created, even though you had physically left it behind you. So you had superficial trysts to satisfy your base needs, but never to the point of ultimate consummation. You were still saving yourself for Ginny, when you'd eventually have the courage to go back to her, to *marry* her."

"How can you even *say* that?"

"Because it's *true*. Or it was, many, many years ago, Eddie. You've twisted them all up in your warped psyche. Your fantasies and memories have merged into one dense, hazy fog clouding your brain and obscuring the truth. Time no longer has any meaning to you. *Nothing* does now that Ginny is gone. Long gone."

"Is she *dead*?"

"You should know, Eddie, since you effectively killed her. The police psychiatrist found you legally insane, though. So you're no longer in prison, except the one you've built within your own tormented head."

"*None* of this true, Doc. You're twisting it all around."

"You never even had a gun in this room, Eddie. Just another mental prop to pass the time and soothe your shattered psyche. You once owned a gun, many years ago, as a result of your paranoia. You *did* take a shot at Seymour one dark, rainy night in Lower Manhattan, before you left Ginny, but you missed. Not on purpose. You really wanted to *kill* Seymour, permanently eliminate the only true competition for Ginny's sincere affections you've ever known. You were just too nervous to aim straight. You blew it once again, Eddie. But you *did* scare him, and he *did* suspect it was you. Seymour had some unsavory underworld ties so you were afraid if he ever found out for sure it was *you* he'd have you killed, regardless of Ginny's adoration of you, so you stayed on the run, even after you heard through the grapevine that he finally died of lung cancer, and you were free of him at last. You were *really* running from your unnatural, forbidden love for Ginny. You sought moral perfection in other women, an antidote to the sordidness that surrounded you. Either that, or you demeaned them, deeming them unworthy of true love, the love you shared with Ginny alone. You romanticized your life in order to survive it. You embarked on a mission, to find this image of perfection in your head, and you existed in a world of imagined isolation, just you and your dream girl, your lavender blonde. You sought a virginal version of Ginny in other women but could never find her because Ginny could never be truly replaced in your tortured consciousness."

"That can't be, Doc. It just *can't*." *Sob, sniff.*

"This is where it all comes together, or rather, comes apart, Eddie, depending on your point of view. I'm trying to see things from all angles, including yours, which is difficult for someone in my position, but I must, since you *refuse* to. In any case, all of our sessions here, all of the stories you related to me, true and false, now bring us to *the* cathartic experience of your entire life, both proactive and fateful, driven by demons beyond your control."

"No, *stop.*"

"Your imaginary, idealized dream girl, Ginny's purified doppelganger, unblemished by prostitution and promiscuity, is at last completely, undeniably embodied in a girl you meet while playing at Fort Point. Physically she reminds you of a very young Ginny, the one you saw in her movies, when you were too young to appreciate her beauty, only *this* girl is blonde and virginal, saving herself for the right man. You feel like you have gone off the deep end and you are hallucinating. But it is just you and her alone together in the fog at Fort Point, beneath the crimson majesty of the bridge. She tells you she is training to be a nurse but eventually wants to become a social worker or psychiatrist, some field where she can help people, help them *heal*, because her heart is so pure and good, so she is taking some courses at UC Berkeley. She is so beautiful, so innocent, so *perfect*. And best of all, she loves *jazz*. The fog drifts in and deepens, enveloping both of you in a misty shroud, and she is cold, and you stop playing your saxophone, and you hold her. The waves and the wind beat against the parapet, and you begin to gently kiss the girl. She allows you until you become too harsh and pushy. She tries to stop you but you keep kissing her, and she screams. You feel dejected yet again. She is innocence and beauty personified, but instead of wanting to protect and preserve her, you decide to corrupt her, exploit her, like Ginny was corrupted and exploited by this wicked world, and more over: *control* her, dominate her, as Ginny once controlled and dominated *you*. The girl breaks away from you and runs up the hill, and the fog is so dense she looks like a sprinting shadow, but you catch her, throw her down, tear her lavender coat away, and rip her pink blouse open, and begin to kiss the tender flesh beneath, and her warmth is soothing in the icy cold that blankets your offense against purity. You tear her blue skirt down her legs, rip off her silk lavender panties, and you can't decide whether it is her heart or yours that is pounding in your ears, and after her soft breasts and firm hips are suitably exposed for your perverse purposes, you smother her with your body, kissing her wantonly as she screams and struggles, and then you forcibly enter her, the only female you've ever entered besides Ginny, and you become intoxicated with denied, deferred desire as you feel her virginal blood dripping hot on your testicles while you violently violate her pristine beauty with your penis and your semen, filling her again and again until she is unconscious, a limp, broken doll beneath your sweaty, shaky body. You stand up and look at her, and you panic, realizing what you've done, becoming the monster, the ape, the vampire in Ginny's movies. You pick up your saxophone and beat the girl hard across the temple, and then pick her up and throw her apparently lifeless, abused body into the Bay, and the avaricious depths devour her, and she is lost, erased from existence, and you have become a vilified demon, and your lifelong guilt about your lust for the woman who raised you, whom you believed until this moment was your actual mother, is finally justified. It's vile vindication of your villainous self-image."

"How could you even *know* all that, Doc? I mean I never told *any*body all those details, and…"

"Because I *am* that girl, Eddie. Or at least, yet another composite of girls and women you've met, seen in movies, or simply willed into existence over the years since you left Ginny. But basically, I'm *her*, or at least her *essence*, which you so viciously attempted to vanquish, but in which you now seek solace and ultimate absolution. Can't you see that now? *I'm* the girl you savagely raped and left for dead, embellished by your own paranoid projections. I survived your brutal assault, at least in your mind, climbing my way shivering, naked, bruised, bleeding, delirious and near death out of the cold, dark waters of the Bay. I luckily happened upon a kind jogger who gave me his sweatshirt and rescued me—a wealthy, handsome lawyer. We're engaged to be married now. You stole *my* dreams, too, but I've stolen them *back*.

"Eventually I recovered from the physical and emotional trauma, and became the mature, successful, happy woman I was meant to be before I decided to sit down next to you and listen to you play your 'shadow music' that night in Fort Point. I represented everything you love *and* everything you hate. My seeming perfection literally drove you mad. Instead of cherishing me, you defiled me. *I* was your elusive dream girl, but you couldn't handle me in the flesh, so you reduced me to an intangible, ephemeral state. I was too real for you, Eddie, so you killed me. I loved your music and you thanked me by raping me. You wanted to destroy my innocence, and you did, but you also destroyed your*self* in the process. You sacrificed your own happiness, because by killing me, or believing you had killed me, you finally killed your obsession with Ginny, at least in your little foggy mental world. You destroyed your dream girl so you could be free of the fantasy, or so you thought. Instead I became just another ghost of Ginny. After that horrible night, you simply re-imagined your childhood and relationship with Ginny, blocking out the true nature of it. Ginny is gone because she slowly drank herself to death in your absence, and then when she heard of your crime and subsequent incarceration, she didn't care to live any more, not without you, so she added pills and junk to her diet, expediting the process of self-destruction. You were as much a source of fantasy sustenance for her as she was for you, separated only by conscientious denial. In effect, you killed her, too. You blamed yourself for her slow suicide. It was ruled natural causes, not negligent homicide, but is a broken heart really natural? You never forgave yourself. Ginny's ghost still lived inside of you, haunted you, and by killing me, you thought you could erase the memory. But you couldn't. So you simply re-imagined it. Again, that was many years ago, Eddie. You've been alone in this room all of this time. In fact, you hardly ever leave it, except to wander in the yard with the other patients."

"So you *are* a shrink."

"No, Eddie. I'm a guardian angel, a genie, an illusion, an *a*llusion, an apparition, a ghost, a spirit, a shadow figure—a shadow with a *great* figure—from another dimension of time and space, summoned by your screams for salvation. You conjured me up, just like you created LV and Bluella, convincing yourself they were real. But I'm beginning to fade away, Eddie. Then you'll be all alone again. Just you and your saxophone and your memories of things that never happened exactly as you remember them, except in your dreams. I'm getting sucked into the murky whirlwind of your past. You're right, this *will* be our final session, Eddie. There's nothing else I can do for you. Now that you know the truth, my usefulness has come to an end. But you've enjoyed my company, right? I helped you discover the truth, didn't I, Eddie? I took you to places you could only dream of before. I was everything a perfect woman should be—intelligent, compassionate, cultured, sensual, spiritual—everything you wanted Ginny to be, for *all* women to be. Maybe we couldn't make love, you and I, since I have no corporeal being, but nothing is perfect, not even in your damaged, deluded imagination. I can feel myself fading away now…goodbye, Eddie…say goodbye, and blow me a kiss. I'm leaving you alone with Ginny, your true, everlasting love. Maybe I'll see you again someday, in your dreams."

"Fuck you."

"Dream on. I'm so sorry, Eddie. Don't cry now, baby. Don't cry. Everything's going to be all right."

Squirt, splat, squish.

DOWN A DARK ALLEY

A Criminal Romance Novel
by
Will Viharo

For Brian

ONE

The night Johnny Varga met Helen Black was no different from his usual nocturnal routine. On his way to the corner market, he ducked down the dark alley behind it just to see what lurked in the shadows. His life was so boring he almost wanted danger to grab him by the throat and beat him to a pulp. As usual, he was disappointed. Until, that is, he walked into the market and met Helen.

Johnny nodded at the friendly Indian dude behind the counter as he walked in and immediately headed for the Macaroni and Cheese. He was wondering whether he had enough milk at home for the Macaroni mix as well as his Wheaties in the morning when a sudden, obstreperous noise shattered his contemplation.

"Give me all your fucking money and give it to me now!"

Spouting this demand was a shapely, attractive young girl with bleached blond hair. Johnny guessed correctly that she was about twenty-four, with little formal education but plenty of street savvy. She was acting alone, without benefit of a mask to conceal her identity from the camera, which she decided in a belated afterthought to destroy, pumping two well-aimed bullets from her .357 with a grace and ease that impressed Johnny and the Indian in completely different ways.

Johnny was in love, the Indian was not.

Trying to act cool despite an obviously bad case of the shakes, the Indian popped open the cash register and handed Helen a grand total of two hundred dollars and seventy-two cents. "You gotta be fuckin' kiddin'' me," she said.

"That is all I have here," the Indian assured her nervously.

"Don't you have a safe or something?" Helen barked.

"Yes. It is at home."

Helen's trigger finger fidgeted nervously.

"Well, where do you live?"

"In my apartment." The Indian was hoping he could kill time rather than vice versa.

"Don't be a fuckin' wiseass, man, I'll blow you away in the blink of fuckin' eye. Don't think I won't."

This was Miami. The Indian believed her and cut the comedy. In the meantime Johnny was inching closer to the object of his newfound fascination. In her peripheral vision, Helen sensed his presence and quickly swung her weight around behind the .357 so Johnny's forehead was the bull's-eye, just above his black horn-rimmed glasses. Johnny stopped dead in his tracks, but he was too much in awe of her to fear her.

"You can kill me if you want," he said. "My life's a mess anyway. But before you do, I just wanted you to know. I think you're, you're..."

"What? *What*?" He was starting to scare her, a little. She wondered if he was from the psychological wing of the local SWAT team, trying to talk her down to size. Either that, or he was insane.

"I think you're the most beautiful girl I've met in Miami."

At least he was a charming wacko, Helen thought. He was also quite pale, but tall, thin and darkly handsome, in a shy, accessible, low-key, Clark Kent sort of way. Maybe later she could trap him in a phone booth and make a superman out of him. Then she sensed movement behind the counter and swerved toward the Indian in time to take a bullet from his .44 in the arm. As she fell back into the candy display she squeezed the trigger of the .357 three times. The first bullet exploded behind the Indian, shattering several bottles of Wild Turkey. The second hit the cash register, blowing it into a twisted heap of metal on the floor behind the counter. Quite by accident since she was shooting out of blind agony, the third bullet hit the Indian squarely in the chest, bursting his heart like a coconut dropped from a skyscraper. A trail of blood and money was left in the wake of the shootout as Helen staggered outside. Sirens wailed in the distance immediately, probably for something else, but still.

Johnny was momentarily frozen with shock, but he put it together fast enough to assess the hopelessness of the Indian's fatal situation and the precarious predicament of his dream girl. He rushed out after her. "Come on, my place isn't very far from here," he said, putting his faded aloha shirt over her shoulders, and she bled all over his white tank top T-shirt beneath. She looked quite pale in the light of the full moon, and she was shivering despite the warm, humid Florida air. He led her past the dark alley behind the market, and he shivered as well.

TWO

Johnny Varga was stuck in a perpetual state of Virtual Unreality. While the rest of humanity swarmed around him in a frenzied blur, Johnny felt like he was waiting alone on a platform for a train that may only be a rumor, but he already had his ticket. Since he was afraid if he went to take a leak or something the alleged train would come and go without him, he just stood there, holding his pecker, waiting for a phantom choo-choo that may never come to take him to a place that may not even exist, except in his dreams.

It was around two-thirty A.M., and Helen was passed out cold on his sofa, bleeding all over the carpet. But a 1949 *film noir* called *Gun Crazy* was on TCM, and Johnny had been looking forward to it all week, so he flipped it on and pretended he wasn't fascinated by the chiaroscuro mayhem while he tended to his wounded angel. Johnny had read enough crime novels and seen enough late night crime flicks to know how to dress a gunshot wound. He tied one of his favorite old T-shirts—the one with *Attack of the 50 Foot Woman* on the front—around her shoulder to stop the blood flow while he gingerly cleaned the wound with grain alcohol, which was when she had passed out with a scream. The bullet had passed right through her arm, so at least he didn't have to deal with that aspect of the operation. Still, she was in bad shape, and would need professional medical attention in the morning.

In the meantime, he whipped up his Macaroni and Cheese dinner after changing his undershirt, tossing the blood soaked one in the trash with a mixture of relief and pride. As it turned out, he didn't have enough milk for breakfast. After all that, he'd left without the milk, which he could've taken for free, he realized.

Johnny stayed up for most of the movie and then dozed off on the floor beside the couch until dawn, when a loud moan from Helen snatched him out of dreamland, or nightmareville, since Johnny almost never had pleasant dreams while asleep. Only while he was awake.

He got up and put on some coffee. Her eyes were still closed, and she looked like a vampire in an open casket, which kind of turned Johnny on, since he had always loved those bosomy, ivory skinned vampire babes in those old Hammer horror flicks. He flipped on the radio, which was terminally tuned to the Oldies station, just in time for "the Suicide Soundtrack," featuring, in the words of the snide DJ, "all the hits that made you want to slit your wrists." Today's slit list included "Nights in White Satin," "Do You Know Where You're Going To?" "Sorry Seems To Be the Hardest Word," "The Way We Were," and a special tribute to the "Minstrels of Misery," Simon and Garfunkel. It was all Johnny could do not to bust out sobbing as he gazed upon Helen's fading beauty while listening to these melancholy melodies, which brought back painful memories of all those junior high school girls who turned his love into poison. His young life had felt like one long Roy Orbison song. Now, as an aspiring novelist of thirty-five, his past was behind him. The future beckoned brightly. The present, however, still sucked. But as Helen opened her large lovely eyes for the first time since the dark distant night, Johnny felt a surge of hope.

"What the fuck happened?" she said in her soft, girlish voice.

"You don't remember?" Johnny said, offering her a coffee in his collectible tiki mug from the Mai Kai up in Fort Lauderdale.

With great difficulty she sat up and looked around the small studio apartment, "I remember—ohhh *SHIT*! *Ow*! *Fuck*! My *arm*."

"What?"

"It *hurts*, god damn it. Who're you, anyway?

"Johnny. Johnny Varga."

"Johnny Varga? What're you, a fuckin' porn star or a private eye?"

"Sounds like it, huh? I guess my mother had a flair for the dramatic. She liked movies."

"Where is she now?" Helen sipped the coffee greedily.

"Gone," Johnny murmured.

"Where?" she said with suspicion.

"Heaven, I hope."

Helen rolled her yes. "Yeah, right. Prob'ly. You can only go up from this fuckin' world, that's for sure."

"So what's your name?" Johnny asked her.

"Helen Black."

"Oh yeah? Nice. Where're your folks?"

Helen shrugged. "Beats the shit outta me. I was adopted."

"Really? Nice folks?

"I was State raised, stupid. Found my ass in a trashcan. You got anything to eat around this rat trap or what?"

"Yeah. Want some toast?"

"Sure." Her blood sugar had already perked up due to the coffee, liberally dosed with Hazelnut flavored cream. Suddenly she was chattering away the neurotic guest on a celebrity talk show. "This isn't the first time I've been shot, y'know," she said. "It ain't no big fucking deal or anything. You mind if I make a call?"

"Sure," Johnny handed her the phone. "Who ya gonna call?"

"I'm going to call El Doctor. He makes house calls." She dialed slowly, finding it hard to focus.

Johnny was perplexed, as usual. "El Doctor, you said?"

She stared at him like he was a retarded child. "Yeah, right. El Doctor. He's Cuban, so we call him that."

"We?"

"Can the questions for now, okay? I feel dizzy—

Hello?" Helen proceeded to speak in a staccato streak of Spanish, which really impressed Johnny, who only knew a few bad words from immigrant dishwashers in the restaurants where he worked while living in Los Angeles. Helen could do anything. And this wasn't the first bullet she had stopped! What a woman.

During the conversation, Helen picked up an unopened bill on the coffee table and translated the address into Spanish. Johnny didn't interrupt. She hung up after two intensely verbal minutes. "He'll be right over. Mind if I take a quick one?"

"Sure. A quick what, though?"

"Shower, what else? Blowjob?"

"Oh, oh. Okay. Yeah, help yourself."

Despite her valiant efforts to the contrary, she was still quite weak from the blood loss, and as she stood up, she wavered and fell into his arms.

"You had that planned, didn't you?" she said. "Just help me into the shower, okay? I'll take it from there."

With her unwounded arm draped around his shoulders, Johnny walked Helen slowly to the shower, which he turned on while she sat on the toilet. The steam began fogging up his black, horn-rimmed, JJ Hunsecker glasses, which he took off and cleaned. He kept planning to get contacts and never wished he had them more than now. She was wearing a halter-top that featured a broken strap, which went sexily with her cutoff jeans and open toed snakeskin high heels. Dressed to kill. It didn't take much for her to finish taking off the halter-top. She simply let the other strap slide down her shoulder and then wiggled out of it, along with her cutoffs. She was not wearing any panties. All this was accomplished as Johnny was adjusting the water temperature. When he turned to help her into a standing position, she was already nude and ready.

"I'm barin' to go, Johnny," she said with a wan smile. "Help me in, will you? And stick around in case I fall. I don't want to pass out and brain myself on the fuckin' tile."

Consumed with desire, Johnny couldn't muster any words, so he simply followed orders with restrained resolve. He tried hard not to touch her breasts, much less look at them, as he helped her into the water and stood her up, but his massive erection was distracting him from any noble concentration.

The shower revived her energy somewhat, but Johnny never left her side, and he took off his shirt so he wouldn't get it soaked. This was the most erotic action he'd seen in over a year, and he was relishing every wet, wild minute of it.

"This is the first shower I've had in a week," Helen giggled. She held her wounded arm out of the water. Johnny felt a strange urge to kiss it, the bandaged arm, that is, but he held back, unsure how she'd take it. The woman knew how to shoot, after all.

Five surreal minutes flowed by until Helen asked Johnny to help her out of the shower. She stumbled and sat awkwardly on the toilet seat. "Dry me off," she ordered him, and he obliged her without hesitation. *This is so film noir*, he was thinking to himself. A true-blue gun moll in his bathroom, naked as sin, and with a tattoo! He noticed it as he was delicately drying her left boob. Just beneath the breast was a small broken heart. Before he could ask her about the significance of this tattoo, a loud knock on the front door disrupted his thought.

"*Cops!*" he shouted fearfully.

"Probably just El Doctor," Helen said to him calmly. "He lives in Little Havana, I called him on his cell, and he picked right up, lucky for me. He was right in the middle of fucking a nurse in his car, too. That's where he fucks a lot of chicks, since he's married. I fucked him there once, I should know."

Johnny lost his erection, which was a good thing since he didn't want to answer the front door with a raging boner anyway. He put his faded aloha shirt back on as Helen finished drying herself off and then he went to answer the door with mild trepidation.

THREE

El Doctor wasn't nearly as formidable as Johnny had anticipated. He was only about five foot five with a potbelly, balding cranium and thick, tinted eyeglasses. He had a thin mustache and a macho swagger, however, sporting white slacks and a bright orange Wayavera shirt. "Hello, may I please see Lady Scarface please?" he said to Johnny with a gleaming grin, holding his medical bag out in front of him, for I.D. purposes, apparently. El Doctor didn't wait for Johnny to respond. He brushed past him and looked for Helen, who walked out of the bathroom with the towel draped around her curvaceous body.

El Doctor greeted her with a bear hug and then helped her to the couch, where she removed the towel and spread herself elegantly in a supine position, like a sex-crazed patient trying to seduce her horny shrink. El Doctor immediately went to work on her arm, while Johnny stood impassively watching, trying not to imagine this swarthy little mole burrowing into Helen's basket with slimy gusto.

While Johnny was watching this bizarre operation, the crack El Doctor made in reference to Helen, calling her "Lady Scarface," continued to bug him. "Lady Scarface" was not a name he'd have attributed to his dream girls in the past. Suddenly Johnny found himself pining for the company of Loretta Lynx, the beautiful sociopath/waitress at Wolfie's Deli, who had given Johnny nothing but frostbite and inspiration since their one and only date several months back. At least Loretta was relatively normal—neurotic, vicious, a garden-variety fruitcake, yes, but at least she wasn't criminally insane. Unless he counted the death promise she had given Johnny, should he ever call her house again. But that had been an idle threat, made in the heat of passion. It wasn't like she knocked over five-and-dimes for change then whacked out the hapless owner in an impromptu shootout. Loretta Lynx didn't even know that the film version of *The Untouchables* with Kevin Costner was based on the TV series, not the other way around. That's how out of touch she was with actual crime. Johnny wanted to go see her now at the Deli, since she worked the breakfast shift today, and as far as he knew no restraining orders had been put into effect. Besides, he still had her death threat saved on his voice mail. As long as he saved that message, he had her. If his body ever turned up somewhere, the cops would hear that message, and book her for Murder One, Danno. Even if Helen had been the actual shooter. Life is beautiful, Johnny thought to himself. Everything was falling into place at last. Why worry?

"This is all over the news today," El Doctor said to Helen. "The killing, I mean. It's in the *Herald.*"

Johnny's momentary spell was broken by this revelation.

"So? I've made the paper before," Helen shrugged nonchalantly.

"Not by name, Lady Scarface."

Johnny wished he would stop calling her that. He preferred to think of her more as a Robin Hoodette or something.

"What?" she shrieked. "I shot the *shit* out of that camera, man. They got nothin' on me! How the hell could I be fingered? And I don't mean my *pussy.*"

"There were two cameras," El Doctor said. "Everyone in this town is paranoid, you know that. How could you be so fucking careless? Why did you have to shoot him?"

"'Cause! It was just like that narc I blew away in the Everglades, man. Self-defense. You know me—I'm no glory shooter. I just take care of myself."

"But why did you need money so badly you had to rob a fucking grocery? I would've lent you the money, you know that. Why didn't you just call me?"

"I owed somebody, okay? I was just gonna strong-arm the idiot before he started fucking shooting at me! What an asshole—he'd blow my sweet juicy ass away for a lousy two hundred bucks! Ask Johnny if you don't believe me."

El Doctor turned and looked at Johnny, who felt his future sliding into a black bottomless abyss as he listened to this conversation. "Is this true? He shot first?"

Johnny nodded dumbly.

"Turn yourself in, then, and beat the rap," El Doctor said to Helen as he finished dressing her wound. "I'll get our number one top lawyer on it. No time done. Maybe a blowjob for the judge."

"*Fuck that!*" Helen yelled, her large pointy breasts jiggling with indignation. "I ain't no slut, I keep telling you!" Helen sat up and draped the towel around her shoulders with a sudden burst of modesty. "I'll just leave town till this clears up. I'll stay with Tony or Vinnie, one of my old Mob boyfriends. They'll take care of me."

"Tony and Vinnie are married now! *Conjo*, what a mess."

Helen's almond-shaped, emerald eyes were wide with shock. "Married? Like to each other? Didn't know that was legal in Florida."

"Don't be stupid. They can't just take care of you anymore. It is not like you are still a teenager now. You should act your age, take care of yourself and quit fucking around."

"All those fucking favors I did those assholes, and they can't watch out for me now? Like *hell*!" Helen reached for the phone, dialed a number, but then hung up. "Some bitch answered Tony's place. I used to set up hits for those greasy fuckheads, and they go and get *married*! Fucks me *up*! *Shit*!" She heaved the phone across the room, ripping it from the wall in the process. Johnny flinched, but said nothing. Helen was obviously on a homicidal tirade, and Johnny had noticed the .38 sticking out of El Doctor's rear waistband. He decided to let things cool off before intervening on anyone's behalf.

"Tony and Vinnie live in Lauderdale anyway, which is not far enough," El Doctor said to her as she paced the room like a caged tigress in heat. "If you want to leave town leave the fucking state! We'll go to Mexico together."

"Oh yeah? And what will you tell your wife? I'm a patient?"

"That's what I always say! I do house calls, baby, remember?"

"Fuck Mexico. I'd rather go to Hawaii or someplace tropical. Yeah right, nice fuckin' dreamin'. Just forget it. I'll just lay low here for a while till I decide what to do. That okay with you, Johnny?" Before he could answer, she said, "Hey, you got any smokes around here!"

"Uh, no," Johnny said.

"No? Well, anyplace close you can get some for me?"

"Well, there's the corner market, but I don't think it would be a good Idea for me to go there now."

"FUCK!"

El Doctor tried to calm her down. "Sit, sit, take it easy, I'll drive a few blocks and pick some up for you. Right now you need to rest. Hey, you got a bed?" El Doctor asked Johnny.

"Yeah, you think I sleep on the floor?"

"Tonight you will. Put her in it while I go to the store. I'll be right back. And don't go outside. They may want to talk to you."

Johnny was visibly shaking now, along with his voice. "What? Who Me? Why?"

"Because, you were seen on the camera, helping her escape. They probably think you were an accomplice."

"You gotta be kiddin'."

"Do I look like I'm kidding, amigo?" El Doctor stared

into Johnny's eyes with a look of iron, not irony as Johnny had hoped. Yes, his life was ruined, no doubt about it. But at least he could still fix a few things.

"Pick up some milk while you're at it," Johnny told El Doctor.

FOUR

Johnny's couch was a pullout bed, so he set it up for his new, semi-permanent guest while she paced impatiently, feeling simultaneously faint and furious. Johnny was silent as he made up the bed, wondering how he had gotten into this situation and, more importantly, how he could get the hell out. Nothing in his wettest dreams or wildest nightmares matched this strange scenario. Even that dark alley behind the market had never promised anything so seductively evil in its bleak, black vision. Johnny had been dealt far more than he'd bargained for. He just wanted to live long enough to write his tragic baseball lesbian love story *Two Balls and a Dyke*, so at least he'd leave something behind besides a stack of unpaid bills, a bloody corpse and a death threat from Loretta Lynx on his voicemail.

"So is that all true?" Johnny asked Helen as she plopped down nude into the sheets and got comfy. She was built like one of those old Fifties men's magazine models—shapely, but soft. Her deep tan only seemed to accentuate her boldly sensuous femininity. Johnny also noticed she had very pretty feet, though the red nail polish was badly chipped. He also fleetingly noticed scars on her stomach, thighs and shoulders, but chose to ignore these flaws.

"What?" she said with a yawn and a stretch.

"You know, about those Mob guys, and setting up hits and killing some guy in the Everglades."

"I don't want to get into it now, ya mind?"

Suddenly Johnny rose to the occasion. Sitting beside

her gently but with a hot disposition, he fumed, "Yeah, I mind, for Christ's sake. I do mind, a lot. I saved your god damn life last night when I don't even know you, I'm risking my neck now for now good reason I can make out, and the least you can do is talk to me and not act like the god damn Queen of the Nile who's been wounded in battle and has her fucking slaves to take care of her. All right? And don't think of telling El Doc-tor or whatever his god damn name is to threaten me, either. I'm no pansy suburban white bread idiot you can play with like a slinky. Now, you can stay here and I'll try to help you if you're, y'know, like, fuckin' nice to me and all. But I'm fed up with letting myself get humiliated by you flaky psychotic bimbos, whether or not you're packing heat. Got it?"

Helen had it, all right. She reached over and kissed her benefactor flush on the lips. "'Bout time you stood up for your rights, Johnny-O. I was beginning to wonder about you."

The kiss had put a damper on Johnny's temper. "Why, 'cause I harbor felons?"

"No, 'cause you take too much crap off 'em. Just relax and get in the bed with me. Take off your clothes and settle down. I'll give you a massage. I was known for them in the old days."

"You mean when you were in the Mob?" Johnny asked with a goofy grin.

"Yep," Helen answered matter-of-factly. "Now strip down before El Doctor gets back with the cigs."

"Does El Doctor have a real name?"

"Sure."

"What?"

"How the hell should *I* know? What's the dif? Lie down and shut up already."

"It's just that, I get the idea there's something intimate going on between you two," Johnny said as he fumbled with his fly. "I don't want to jeopardize anything, like my life, if he comes back and sees us, y'know, in bed together."

Helen let out a sigh. "Number One: he can go fuck himself if he thinks he can tell me who I can and can't go to bed with. And *Two*, this is *your* house and you can do whatever you want, right? Be a *man*, remember? Or did you lose your hard-on already?"

Feeling light-headed from lack of sleep, lust and too much excitement, Johnny delved between the sheets after shedding his clothes and glasses, lying in a prone position as Helen began to massage him from the neck down. Even though she had showered, she smelled so *fleshy*, Johnny noticed. Earthy. His boner made a comeback and he lay on his stomach and she continued to talk as her surprisingly soft and therapeutic hands relieved the tension he had accumulated over the past three plus decades.

"After all that, I dropped all the fuckin' money on the way out the door," she sighed. "I got nothin' to show for this. I'm so stupid I can't believe it. Two hundred lousy bucks. Shit, I used to drop more than that at lunch in the good old days. Me an' this guy Tony used to rob this jewelry store on Flagler like once a month, just for kicks. I mean, we could afford to buy the whole fuckin' store, but if we did that, we'd be no better than those rich capitalist creeps in North Miami, living in their penthouses above everything like Hialeah doesn't even exist, or Liberty City. At least I'm honest about who and I what I am. Y'know? I'm no phony asshole who pretends to be something I'm not, like these cops and politicos running around Florida waving the fucking flag in everyone's face while they spit on people like me and you when no one's looking."

"What about me?" Johnny asked.

Helen leaned over and Johnny could feel her nipples grazing his shoulder blades as she whispered in his ear, "I know you, Johnny. I can tell just by looking at how your place is furnished that you have dreams that didn't come true, that you're just a regular guy trying to get by. Like me."

He briefly considered his apartment décor, best

described as Target Tropical—cheap bamboo lawn furniture and party tikis were the primary aesthetic. "Like you?"

"What're you, a fuckin' parrot?" She sat back up and continued to rub his tense muscles. "Yeah, like me. Me, I've been on my own since I was fourteen years old. That's when I met Tony, then Vinnie. They wanted to marry my ass, but fuck that, I don't want to be owned like a piece of jewelry for them to show off."

"So did you *really* set guys up to get hit and all?" Johnny was intrigued and incredibly relaxed, intoxicated by her touch and voice. His eyes were closed as he dreamily imagined what she'd just described. His dick was leaking onto his sheets by now.

"Yeah, but so what? Only assholes, nobody, you know, decent or anything. Other crooks, just like them."

"How'd you do it though? Set them up, I mean?" He wanted fuel for his fantasies.

"Easy. I lured them under false pretenses, as the saying goes. They thought they were getting one thing, and BANG!, they got another."

"Another kind of bang."

"See? You're not so dumb after all. What a relief. Florida has too many stupid white guys, starting with our fuckin' governor." Johnny wondered briefly if she'd fucked him too, but decided not to ask. Helen gently rolled Johnny over onto his back and straddled him as she massaged his pecs. He kept his eyes closed, but she was sitting directly on his boner now. It was truly like a dream. "So you mind if I stay here a while now I'm being so nice?" she cooed.

"Until the cops come breaking in, so yeah sure. I'm a lonely guy, except for my cat, that is."

"You got a cat?"

"Yeah, why, is that a problem?"

"Only if he tries to sleep on my head. I hate that."

"Just don't shoot him, okay? He's all I have."

She leaned down and kissed him on the cheek, her

breasts and hair caressing his smiling face. Then she kissed his ear and meowed and licked the lobe. "Not any more."

FIVE

El Doctor would have returned sooner had he not been stopped for speeding on the way back from the supermarket. He was so afraid Helen would seduce Johnny in the interim he had even forgotten to buy the milk. The traffic cop, sensing El Doctor's rude urgency, took his sweet time writing out the citation. El Doctor had been doing seventy in a thirty-five MPH residential stretch. The traffic cop proceeded to give the sweat-soaked El Doctor a lecture on the downside of mowing down schoolchildren and elderly pedestrians who might not be able to leap out of the way of oncoming juggernauts. El Doctor cussed to himself in Spanish, but the Miami Beach cop was bi-lingual and picked up every malicious syllable. This inspired the cop to detain El Doctor even further. He discovered El Doctor's registration had expired. It was all El Doctor could do not to pull the .38 out and whack the nuisance on the spot.

Back at his tacky tiki pad, Johnny and Helen were not engaging in fornication, despite the pulsating pressure to do so. Johnny had no condoms, for one thing, and Helen seemed like the type to be carrying more than just a gun. Also, he couldn't keep it up long enough, despite the full body massage they were giving each other, taking turns with various body parts—you rub mine, I'll rub yours. Helen wasn't in the mood for a full-scale performance, anyway—she was still weak and dizzy, and the bandage on her arm made her feel decidedly unsexy. But her instantaneous rapport with Johnny stirred something in her besides the urge to procreate. Could it be her long dormant maternal instinct? Helen had been thinking a lot lately about having a kid, if only she could find a suitable father, preferably someone in a legit racket. She didn't want her baby to grow up like she had. Johnny seemed so lost and boyish, so desperate for feminine care that Helen imagined him more as her child than as her mate. Except when he turned over on his back—then Helen wondered whether the two could be successfully combined.

"I feel like I'm dreaming," Johnny said, eyes closed, as Helen massaged his inner thighs, teasingly avoiding his genitals, which had taken on a life of their own. "You really are a dream girl, aren't you? Come to life."

"You hardly know me," she purred. "Don't get carried away."

"I don't even care you're a killer."

"I'm only a killer by accident, y'know. I never meant to hurt anybody. If I hadn't shot that guy, he would've killed me. See how it works?"

"Law of the jungle. The female jungle. That was a movie with Jayne Mansfield—'The Female Jungle,' it was called."

"I don't see many movies. Too busy living."

"That's good. I've often wondered what it would be like to shoot somebody."

"Oh yeah? You have anybody in mind?"

"Yeah, sure. Lots of people."

"What're you, fuckin' Charles Manson or some shit?"

"No, no. Charlie Brown is more like it. I mean, I could never actually kill somebody, but imagining it is fun sometimes. In slow motion, with music, like they used to do on 'Miami Vice.'"

Helen had his pecker in a Miami *vise*. But despite his arousal, he didn't come. He kept his eyes closed and kept thinking—about Loretta Lynx.

"Some people imagine killing me, even," he said. His erection went down. Helen pouted but said nothing.

"Your turn," she said, lying on her back, legs wide open. "Do my thighs."

With a groan, Johnny began massaging her legs, still thinking of Loretta Lynx, of the night they made out on this very bed, and she gave him a huge hickey to remember him by, at least until it faded. Then she had abruptly stopped talking to him, leaving him to wonder which wrong button he had pushed, and to second-guess her subsequent determination to deflect all advances from him, even friendly ones. Women.

Then Johnny again noticed the broken heart tattoo, beneath Helen's left breast. "Hey, can I ask you something personal?" Which felt like an odd question, with her wide-open beaver poised in front of him like the web of the black widow.

"Shoot," she said. One-track mind.

"That tattoo of the broken heart—what's the story behind it?"

Helen frowned, but kept her eyes closed, "What do you care?"

"Just curious. It seems like your soft spot. Tough broad like you, and you got a tattoo of a broken heart under your boob. Why—someone broke your heart once?"

"You should be a detective. No kidding."

"So I'm right, then?"

"What do you want, a fuckin' prize? This ain't a game show."

"All right, forget it, if you're gonna get touchy about it!"

"It just brings back bad memories, okay? Just talk about something else for now."

"Well, like what?"

Helen opened her eyes, smiling wickedly, and raised her eyebrows. "Guess what I'm thinking, and I will give you a prize."

Johnny was getting nervous again. He'd never had it so good. Okay, so there were some strings attached—she was a woman with a record and a warrant out for her arrest, but the good far outweighed the bad, at least for the moment. Then the sound of El Doctor's El Dorado peeling into the parking lot in front of Johnny's studio broke the spell.

"Put your clothes on," Helen said abruptly as she hid her body with covers. "Do it quick. Then go in the other room."

"But what about my manhood?"

"Trust me, I recognize the way he pulled in. He's *plenty* pissed. He's a good shot too. If he sees you in the raw, you won't have any manhood."

"Okay, okay. Jesus Christ, what a day." Johnny rushed into the kitchen pulling his pants on as he went. El Doctor burst into the room through the unlocked door, his .38 drawn and cocked.

"I was ready in case the cops were here," he said feebly. Johnny was shaking half-naked in the kitchen, staring into a bowl of dry Wheaties he had just poured. El Doctor stood staring at Helen, then Johnny, gun still drawn.

"Y-you got the milk?" Johnny said to El Doctor in a squeaky voice.

"No, sorry. I forget. I'll get it later," He tucked the gun back into his waistband. "Sorry. I'm a little edgy, forgive me, okay? I got a ticket and it made me in a bad mood."

"How, uh, how long you plan on stickin' around?" Johnny asked El Doctor boldly, stepping out of the kitchen.

"You got my smokes?" Helen said. El Doctor nodded, and handed her a carton of Camels and a box of matches.

"You hear my question?" Johnny said.

"Yeah I hear you, mang, just relax. I want to watch over my patient here, that okay with you?" El Doctor was becoming a serious pain in Johnny's ass.

"Well, I'm a writer, and I need my privacy."

El Doctor laughed derisively, and loudly, for a long time. "A fucking writer, huh? So how you make a living, heh?"

"I'm also a driver," Johnny answered meekly.

"Stock cars in Daytona?"

"No. Blood tests in Miami. I go to work at three, so I gotta leave in a coupla hours. It's over in the Grove, at Mercy. Swing shift. So I usually write in the mornings."

"So who the hell is stopping you?" El Doctor said, climbing into the bed beside the chain-smoking Helen.

Then the sounds of a hungry cat were at the front door. It was The Leopard Man, named after an old Val Lewton flick. The Leopard Man was really a fat, sweet Russian Blue tabby, and the product of a broken home. One of Johnny's old flames had dumped The Leopard Man on Johnny, only then his name had been Bagheera, after the black panther in *The Jungle Book*. Johnny re-christened him The Leopard Man, since the cat obviously thought he was human, and entitled to the same relative luxuries and respect. Johnny let The Leopard Man in and followed him to the kitchen, where he filled The Leopard Man's bowl with premium dry cat food.

El Doctor scanned the room while this went on. The walls were bare except for two movie posters: *Mad Doctor of Blood Island* and *Revenge of the Creature*, two movies El Doctor had never seen, and had no desire to. The cheapjack bamboo furnishing was sparse, the powder blue-painted walls cracked and chipped, but the room was tidy and clean. Just depressingly lonesome. There was a home video system with a stack of DVDs on top. El Doctor scanned the lurid titles: *Faster Pussycat Kill! Kill!, Point Blank, I Eat Your Skin, Blood Feast, Sting of Death, Death Curse of Tartu, The Thrill Killers, John Carpenter's Assault on Precinct 13, George A. Romero's Day of the Dead, The Devil's Rejects, Sin City*. And there were even more beneath the TV. *Fucking crazy ass Americans*, El Doctor thought to himself. So out of touch with reality. Helen was falling asleep. Johnny's hands had soothed her spirit as well as her body. Secretly, she was planning on staying here a long time. But she didn't want to inform El Doctor or Johnny of her plans just yet. They would find out as they happened, anyway.

SIX

Johnny drove one of the few Edsels left in existence, a gift bequeathed to him by his father in New Jersey, where Johnny was born and raised until he was a teenager, before his mother took him to L.A. Johnny's father had died when a car he was working on in his auto shop slipped off its jack and crushed him. The authorities found the incident suspicious but could not find any hard evidence of foul play. No one associated with Johnny's dad had a motive, at least none that anyone knew of. The Edsel had been the old man's pride and joy, and it was in mint condition when he passed on. Johnny's mother wanted to sell it, despite the old man's promise that Johnny would one day inherit it, so Johnny staged a phony robbery one night and hid the Edsel in the barn of a friend's farm way out in the sticks. The friend was a school mate, a strange loner like Johnny, whose parents were old and senile and never really noticed the Edsel till, years later, Johnny returned from California to reclaim his inheritance, which he then drove to Miami, where a girl was waiting for him, or so he had been led to believe. The girl was already married to someone else by the time Johnny got there. But at least he had the Edsel.

Johnny was very paranoid that someone would vandalize or rip off his baby, so he always took extra special precautions with its care and safety. He parked it in the underground garage of his apartment building, where there were very few spaces available. For this privilege Johnny cleaned the laundry room once a week for the landlord, a retired New Yorker living on a pension from a business he never disclosed, although word was he was a former button man for the Mob. Johnny wondered if Helen would recognize him, and vice versa.

When Johnny drove his Edsel to work, he felt like he was in a dream bubble from a Douglas Sirk fantasy world of his own making. The Edsel was like something that had escaped from Johnny's imagination, a remnant of an idealized era that for Johnny only existed on video. The Edsel was the one tangible element of Johnny's dreamland, besides Loretta Lynx, who looked like Donna Reed, and now Helen, who was built like Mamie Van Doren. The best of both worlds, Johnny thought as he drove to work that afternoon, trying hard not to worry about what havoc El Doctor and Helen would create in his apartment while he was gone. At least he wasn't bored anymore.

Johnny loved cruising the Art Deco district just a mile or so from his studio. The combination of the Edsel and the Deco helped Johnny to escape the numbing realities of his waking world, while at the same time depressing the hell out of him, because as time went on he realized that his fantasies were not the answer to his problems. He needed something he could touch.

And now there was Helen. Johnny just couldn't figure out if this was a mixed blessing or flat-out curse. There was a distinct possibility he could get laid, but as he drove down Collins Ave. past Wolfie's Deli, the old familiar ache returned, even though Loretta was not there now. Her shift was over. He'd be visiting her again tomorrow, though. He was even toying with the idea of bringing Helen with him, just to gage Loretta's reaction when he walked in with this bleached bombshell that backed up her bravado with bullets. Real ones, not cowardly voice messages. A real woman. That would teach Loretta all right. The one snag was that when Helen walked out his door there was a good chance she'd be surrounded by a SWAT team and cameras from *America's Most Wanted*. Johnny could do without the publicity at this point, he decided.

Back at his apartment, El Doctor was watching television game shows while Helen slept, waking up groggily and irritably whenever El Doctor shouted at the screen, usually in Spanish. El Doctor called his wife to tell her he'd be late and she hung up on him, but this was S.O.P. El Doctor planned on getting a quick one from Helen later on in the evening before Johnny got home, as payment for medical services rendered. Again, this was S.O.P. But Helen was dreaming of Johnny as she slept, and also of their baby, and their lovely home in a beautiful trailer park, away from the madness of urban mayhem, where she could at last settle down and be the woman she had always wanted to be. Johnny offered her new hope that her circumstances could change. All she had to do was twist his mind around to her way of thinking. So far, so good.

In the hospital lab, Johnny was distant and detached, more so than usual, and his co-workers noticed.

"Thinking about the book again?" asked the Haitian guy whose name Johnny could never remember.

"What? Oh yeah, right," said Johnny, punching the clock with acute disinterest.

"What is it called again? You told me once."

"'Ask the Dust,'" Johnny said. Every time he made up a new, famous title for the Haitian, because he didn't want to have to explain the ironies behind the very American title *Two Balls and a Dyke*. Last week it had been called *The Day of the Locust*. The Haitian never remembered anyway, or so Johnny thought. The truth was, the Haitian was very well educated and had actually read most of the titles Johnny mentioned.

"When may I read it in the store?" the Haitian said with a smile.

"Next year," Johnny said.

"Can't wait," the Haitian said, still smiling as he walked off.

Johnny wasn't allowed to drive his Edsel on the job,

which was all right by him, since he didn't want to cruise through some of the spookier neighborhoods—especially at night—in his coveted dreamboat. The Edsel had recently been painted bright lavender, making it a neon target anyway. Plus the interior was a sparkling pink. Cops often pulled Johnny over, thinking he was a dealer or a pimp with a white bread face. The car Johnny drove on his route was a dull, simple Pinto. His route covered a good deal of Greater Miami, but concentrated chiefly on doctors and satellite labs in Coconut Grove. Johnny liked the Grove and often took his break in a cafe on Grand Avenue, which had the quiet, tree-lined ambience of a sleepy college town. Johnny also drove throughout Coral Gables, the Beverly Hills of Miami, and he sometimes took strolls through the Miracle Mile shopping district, admiring but not buying. Someday, he promised himself, he'd take Loretta Lynx on a whirlwind-shopping spree through Miracle Mile and beyond, once his novel came out to thunderous critical and commercial success. Unless, of course, she killed him first.

Johnny's job consisted of picking up bio-hazardous specimens in plastic bags from labs and doctor offices and delivering them to the mother lab adjacent to Mercy Hospital. He also delivered lab reports back to the clients, as well as sundry supplies. It was not a particularly inspiring occupation, but Johnny enjoyed the freedom and solitude on the road. At least the Pinto was equipped with an antiquated but operating CD player, so he could listen to his favorite songs en route. The CD he had with him tonight was one of his special compilations, all exotic tunes by the likes of Martin Denny, Arthur Lyman, Les Baxter, the Surfmen, the Out-Islanders, mixed with some surf music by Dick Dale and the Ventures. But as Johnny drove through the night this particular evening with a backseat full of bodily fluids, blaring the theme from *Hawaii Five-O*, all he could concentrate on was Helen alone in his apartment with El Doctor. This was good in that it took his mind off of Loretta Lynx, but it was bad in that he was nearly involved in a serious multi-car pileup on 95 due to his preoccupations. He survived unscathed, save for a mess of maledictions hurled his way from several badly shaken motorists.

As he finished his route that evening, he tried an old mental trick his father had taught him the first time his heart had been broken, back in New Jersey, when Johnny was only in the seventh grade. His father had told him, "Son, whenever you start putting a girl—*any* girl, whether she's your wife or girlfriend or just some snob who won't speak to you—whenever you put a girl on a pedestal, instead picture her on a toilet, taking a nice, big, loud, wet, messy crap. That'll remind you she's only human like the rest of us, and de-glamorize your portrait of her as a goddess." Johnny had never forgotten this homespun advice, and had actually put it to successful use more than once, but lately it just had not been doing the trick. For instance, when he pictured Loretta Lynx in such an awkward, vulnerable position, it made him laugh, but it didn't turn him off. And now when he applied the same technique to Helen, he found to his horror that it actually turned him on.

SEVEN

When Johnny returned home that night, the apartment was dark save for the blue light of the TV screen, where Nick Ray's first film, *They Drive By Night*, was playing to an empty house. Both El Doctor and Helen were gone.

Johnny tried not to worry. Good riddance, he said to himself as he cracked open a Coke and settled down in front of the tube. *They Live By Night*, a *film noir* Johnny had never seen, was the story of a young criminal with an innocent heart who falls in love with a simple backwoods girl, and they try to begin a new life together, despite the fact that his past keeps catching up with his present and mucking up their future. They become lovers, then newlyweds, then fugitives. This was a disturbing pattern for Johnny to witness, though he couldn't bring himself to turn it off until the final fadeout, which ends with the guy being shot to death by cops while the girl, pregnant with his child, reads a note he had written her, still clasped in his dead hand. The note told her something he never had the nerve to tell her in person: "I love you." Johnny was all misty when Helen and El Doctor burst in, laughing, drunk, hanging all over each other. Johnny's tears dried quickly as he confronted them.

"I thought you had taken a powder for good," Johnny said with a weak voice. "What the hell's going on? I thought you were wanted by the cops and had to lay low for a while, I don't get this."

Helen bounced from El Doctor's arms to Johnny's. "Johnny—*hic*!—didn't you get my note?"

"Note? *What* note? I didn't see any note."

"Oh, come here, silly." She led him by the hand to the bathroom, where she had written with lipstick on the mirror: *Went for a moonlite swim, be back soon. XXXOOO Me.* "See?" she giggled. "I wouldn't let you worry about me like that. I'm no flake, y'know. What did you think?"

Johnny was already busy wiping the lipstick from the mirror. In the other room, El Doctor was passed out cold in the middle of the floor, his pants down around his ankles. When Helen saw him, she fell down laughing.

"No nookie for you!" she howled.

"*Ssshhh.* The neighbors!" Johnny hissed from the bathroom.

"Don't be such a tightass, Johnny!" Helen said, stripping and hopping into the sofa bed. "Come here and lie next to me, Johnny! I wanna—*hic!*—massage! Right *now*, motherfucker!"

"I said keep your voice down!" Johnny said, giving up on the smeared mirror and shutting off the bathroom light. "Jesus. What's your problem?"

Helen looked hurt. "Are you mad at me, Johnny-O?"

"Mad at you? You come home drunk at two in the morning when you know you should stay indoors, and you want to know if I'm mad at you? You gotta be puttin' me on."

"Well, *are* you?" she pouted, bare-breasted and bedroom-eyed. Her hair, dark roots increasingly obvious, was a tangled mess, but in a sexy way. Johnny felt his will weakening by the second.

"Am I what?" he said, sitting on the edge of the bed, staring blankly at the unconscious man of medicine on his floor, a man who was basically a complete stranger to Johnny, as was Helen, naked and stoned in his bed, beckoning him to enter her web of sin. As if he wasn't already inextricably caught.

"Are you mad at me?" she giggled like a cinema sex siren, lying playfully on her belly, her cleavage pressed against the sheets, glowing in the light of the TV screen. "No one saw me, Johnny, don't worry. El Doc and me just went to visit Tony in Lauderdale real quick, to make plans."

"Tony? The one you were talking about? The gangster?"

Helen giggled some more. "Oh, sweetheart, you're actually worried about me, aren't you? How sweet. You really do care about me, don't you, Johnny?"

Johnny tried hard not to look into her eyes or at her breasts, but it was a losing battle. He surrendered and lay down on his back while she unbuttoned his shirt. His loneliness had sold him out to the enemy, as usual. "So, what are your plans?" he asked as she straddled him and unhooked his pants.

"None of your business," she whispered as she pulled his pants down around his knees.

"It is my business if you're going to stay here," Johnny whispered as she took his throbbing penis in her warm mouth.

He couldn't make out her muffled reply, but he didn't care what it was, anyway. As her hot tongue expertly explored his leaky shaft, he came with a knee-weakening gush down her throat and promptly passed out beside her with a broad smile on his face. Helen licked her chops like a panther feasting on her catch.

EIGHT

The first thing Johnny saw when he woke up the morning after the blow job was Helen polishing her shiny .357 Magnum with the same dexterity and tenderness she had displayed in giving him head. She was quite a woman, Johnny smiled inwardly.

"*Hi*!" she said, kissing him flush on the mouth. He could still taste the hint of his own semen. "I put some coffee on, want some?"

"Um, sure, okay. Where's the doc?" Johnny had noticed right away that El Doctor was no longer prone on the floor, or anywhere in sight.

"He has to go to his office sometimes," Helen explained on her way to the kitchen. "Besides, it ain't like he fuckin' lives here or anything. Want cream and sugar, sugar?"

"Yeah, *lots,*" Johnny said, sitting up. Helen had even placed the Herald at his feet on the edge of the bed. It was still wrapped in the rubber band. With trepidation, Johnny unraveled it, glancing over the front-page headlines and greatly relieved to find only the usual assortment of religious terrorism, natural disasters, racial unrest, economic collapse, and run of the mill chaos. So far Helen had not made the front page. Johnny gave the rest of the news sections a cursory once-over in search of timely topics, such as the suspected whereabouts of the pretty young shooter-on-the-loose, and found nothing that curbed his appetite for breakfast. He really wanted to dine at

Wolfie's, however, since Loretta Lynx was covering the late morning and lunch shifts, and it had been a week since he had gone to visit her. But he didn't want to leave Helen alone for several reasons, including his safety and hers from the long arms of the law, plus he didn't want to offend her gracious sensibilities. He was rapidly growing accustomed to her strong feminine presence, and he wanted her to stick around for as long as possible. His reason emanated from his loins as well as his lonesome heart, both of which were experiencing a rather disorienting sensation of relief bordering on actual pleasure. These were truly days of wine and roses, not whining and neuroses as usual. The outside world made no sense, so why should his life be any different?

Helen made a point of winning The Leopard Man's trust by feeding him first thing. She knew from experience the quickest way to a man's heart is through his pussycat. The Leopard Man was still somewhat distant with Helen, since she was still an intruder in his domain, and a female human one at that, and The Leopard Man was very possessive of Johnny. But for the moment, it appeared Helen was his source of food supply, so he decided to maintain a cautious diplomacy until further notice. With reflexive resolve, Johnny stretched and reached for the remote control, flipping on the TV and running through the various cable channels with a veteran couch potato's agility. For a few minutes he watched a rerun of *Surfside 6*, mainly because he loved the theme song. Then he kept going, finally freezing on the frenzy of images from *La Femme Nikita*, a French New Wave crime thriller about a young, pretty female junkie who happens to be criminally insane. After the cops bust her and she blows one of them away in the process, the Government fakes her suicide and trains her, pretty much against her will, to work for them as a hired assassin. It was sort of a French version of *My Fair Lady Meets The Terminator*. Johnny had seen it about a week before in its entirety, but watching it again now with Helen humming in his kitchen gave the experience a whole new dimension, a sort of 4-D movie with Ultra-Sensurround. Helen, after all, was the real thing, in the flesh. She came in with his coffee just as Nikita was undergoing her first training mission, blowing away a bunch of French guys in a hotel kitchen while synthesized drums and gunfire blared on the soundtrack.

"My kind of movie," Helen said as she slid under the covers with Johnny. Johnny reached over and kissed her shoulder, then noticed the scar on her forearm, in the tender underside of her bicep, which was not as soft to the touch as it looked.

"How'd you get that?" he asked with sincere concern.

"A bullet, what else?" said Helen, mesmerized by the action on the small screen.

"Oh yeah?" Johnny was strangely titillated. "You mean during a shootout?"

"No, I shot myself to get out of the fuckin' Army," she snapped. Then she quickly changed her tone and kissed his cheek. "Don't ask so many questions, Johnny. I'll get suspicious."

"Suspicious? Of *me*? Of *what*?"

"I dunno. I guess I'm a little on edge these days. Being a fugitive isn't what it's cracked up to be." Helen reached for the remote and clicked off the TV. "Enough of that shit already. I *live* it, buddy." She straddled him and began kissing his neck. Johnny dropped the coffee on the floor and The Leopard Man was instantly upon the spill, lapping up the cream-and-sugar laden liquid with relish. "So should you," she said, putting his perpetually petrified penis deep inside of her warm, moist vagina. Johnny didn't have time to even consider putting on a condom. It was too late. Their bodily fluids were mingling. She was consuming him, making him one of her kind, like Catherine Deneuve in *The Hunger*. Johnny's fantasy of being raped by a vampire/gun moll was coming true, and for the moment he didn't care about the ramifications. He came inside of her several times while she rode him like a bronco-buster, gnawing on her own wrist, leaning back her head, her breasts quivering as she continually screamed with her own repeated release. Helen was sucking him dry, body and soul. He was hers.

NINE

Despite her disdain for him, Loretta Lynx was beginning to wonder what had become of her number one fan, Johnny Varga. While she had no intention of giving into his bizarre advances, and had every desire to see him dead, she couldn't help but succumb to this nagging curiosity. Had he finally given up on her, and lost interest completely? She couldn't believe that. Or rather, she couldn't *accept* it. She called his number just to see whether it had been disconnected, and when his machine picked up she quickly slammed down the receiver, somewhat relieved, somewhat disturbed. She couldn't quite figure out what effect Johnny had on her, just that it wasn't pure apathy, more a mix of hatred and something else she couldn't quite discern. Could it be attraction? Of course not, she told herself. She deserved better than him. She had been raised by her wealthy parents in Fort Lauderdale to meet a wealthy young Med student during Spring Break, marry him, and make more rich, snobby Republicans like her heritage dictated. So far, most of the wealthy Med students she had encountered in her young life were too egotistical and obnoxious to deal with past the first date. In some ways, she hated her own whiteness, and secretly she lusted for the Cuban busboys at Wolfie's to gang-bang her late one night in the kitchen after closing. So far, none of the white boys had turned her on very much, and she feared she was frigid and doomed to unhappy bondage with a drunken intern. Either that, or she would die in the gas chamber for the murder and dismemberment of Johnny Varga.

But why did she want to kill him? Loretta had been an English major at the University of Miami before dropping out to pursue waitressing at Wolfie's, and she knew Freud or Jung or one of those smart-ass intellectuals would say she really wanted to fuck him. Everything was *sex, sex, sex*, especially to repressed people who couldn't get any, like the professors that always hit on her. Loretta had told her father, a Princeton educated layer, highly respected in Lauderdale high society, that she was not really dropping out, merely going on hiatus, taking a breather before embarking on the master plan: Harvard Law School. Loretta wanted to be a lawyer about as much as she wanted to be a waitress, but at least Wolfie's didn't require a BA. Loretta had always found South Beach seductive, and the proximity of Wolfie's to the beach and cafes and clubs promised a luxurious decadence she felt she needed to wallow in before settling down to her staid, pre-planned, pre-ordered, pre-paid future.

Maybe she just wanted to kill Johnny out of frustration. Sexual, familial, whatever. Perhaps her anger at the injustice of the world at large was driving her to the homicidal brink, and Johnny was simply a convenient target. Sublimating her rage over oil spills and the senseless slaughter of seals and dolphins would probably not save her from the gas chamber, however, even with her father defending her. After all, whatever she thought of him, Johnny Varga was supremely innocuous. At least he would appear so to the jury, despite the evidence she was compiling against him.

In the beginning, Loretta believed Johnny Varga was stalking her, since he kept leaving her little notes next to his empty coffee cup despite the fact that Loretta was going out of her way to ignore him. When she had finally relented and gone out for coffee with him on Ocean Drive after work one day, she hoped that this would appease the freak and she could then move on to her life without him. But this only stimulated his obsession with her, or what Loretta, who had a healthy ego, perceived as obsession. She was used to frat boys following her around, and as a sorority girl she was famous for both her sobriety and her chastity. The sisters thought she was a heroine, the brothers thought she was an uptight bitch. She did date off and on in college, and liked making out with football hunks when the mood struck her, but she had only actually slept with one boy, a quiet, sensitive loner who later committed suicide, she assumed because she had dumped him one night over the telephone. He didn't even give her time to explain she was going through a bad period—monthly cycle, not school session— and had made a hasty decision based on her mood of the moment. Next day, bang, he'd shot himself. What she didn't know was that the boy was a closet homosexual who knew his macho father, a police sergeant, would have him arrested for attempted sodomy even though he had had only one experience with a boy, and that had been at camp in the Everglades when he was twelve. Loretta was haunted by this, however, and was always plagued by a sense of guilt for driving a love-crazed suitor to blow his brains out in the center of the Student Union, in the middle of the day. Spectators abounded, and Loretta was often blamed for this catastrophe. She'd even been named in the college paper article covering the event as a "possible catalyst." Loretta had put this article in her scrapbook with a mixture of pride and anxiety. She dropped out soon after.

Loretta's father was not proud of her, but still paid the rent on her North Miami Beach apartment, which boasted security guards, an Olympic swimming pool, in-house laundry service, maid service, and even a dating service for singles which Loretta never took advantage of, despite her mother's gentle urging. Loretta wanted to find Mister Perfect or just be left alone. All she had to do was decide just what qualified a guy for this lofty role, and then she'd sink her teeth in him forever.

On afternoons when Loretta didn't have to work, her mother would drive down from Lauderdale and play tennis with her in the apartment building's private court, then go for a swim in the private pool and then perhaps order a pizza and have a pajama party, watching dirty discs rented from the private video outlet downstairs. Her mother's name was Priscilla, but her dad always called her Prissy, and now Loretta did too. Her dad's name, to both of them, was simply Daddy. It had been so long since she had heard her fathers real name she had practically forgotten it.

They were alone on the tennis court today, so they spoke freely while bouncing the ball back and forth over the net with athletic banality.

"I want a grandchild," Prissy said with a huff.

"Buy one," Loretta shot back.

"You're my only daughter, and my only chance," Prissy said sadly.

"I guess you're screwed," Loretta said for effect.

"Watch your mouth, young lady. No wonder you can't find the right man."

"Who said I was looking?"

"How much longer are you going to work at that dump?"

"Wolfie's is not a dump, Prissy. John Kennedy ate there once."

"Damn Yankee liberal Democrat jackass."

"Yeah, that's the one. A lot of famous people ate there. Look at all the movie stars on the wall. Maybe I'll meet one there."

"Dream on."

"I plan to," Loretta said, stopping to catch her breath after once again beating the pants off her mother. "I want to dream for as long as I can before waking up to Daddy's little world."

They walked off the court and toward the private showers for female residents. "You're already in Daddy's little world, Lor," Prissy said in a maternal tone of condescension, "Look around. Who do you think is paying for this? Not Wolfie, that's for sure."

"It won't be forever," Loretta said. "I plan to move out." They both stripped and turned on the shower water. Prissy was in good shape for a middle-aged woman, largely due to tennis workouts with her daughter, but also partly due to the affair she was carrying on with the young stud messenger boy who worked for her husband's firm. He kept her feeling good about herself. Loretta was naturally a shapely goddess, due to heredity and the aerobics class she attended nearby, mainly to work off steam, which would otherwise be channeled into the violent murder of Johnny Varga.

"You plan to move out?" said her mother, thinking of the messenger as she ran her fingers over her body, "And go where, may I ask? Back to Lauderdale?"

"Never. I was thinking of the West Coast, actually,"

"Of Florida?"

"No, Prissy, of course not. I meant L.A. I'm thinking of becoming an actress."

Prissy stuck her pinkie in her ear and drained out the excess water to clear her auditory channels. "I hope I didn't hear what I thought I heard," she said.

Loretta shut off the shower water and grabbed a towel. "You heard me, Prissy. But don't tell Daddy yet. I'm going to tell him I'm transferring to UCLA, and I am, but I'm going to major in Drama, not Law. Face it, I'm not cut out to be a lawyer. I just don't care about that world, Mother. It's boring. I want excitement in my life." Prissy grew frantic as it dawned on her Loretta was not kidding.

"Honey, sweetheart, *listen* to me. You're not being realistic. There's plenty of excitement right here in Miami, even if it is the wrong kind." Prissy had always hated Miami. She was from Atlanta, and her husband was from Virginia, but he loved South Florida. He loved Miami too, but not with his daughter in it. They both wanted Loretta to move back to Lauderdale or better yet, up to New England and go to Harvard, per the original schedule.

"I want the right kind of excitement, though, and I

won't find it here," Loretta said as they walked up to her apartment. Loretta avoided the elevator because the attendant always ogled her blond beauty and it reminded her too much of college. Prissy liked having her blond beauty admired, however, and always flirted with the beefy pool attendant, disgusting Loretta and embarrassing her as well.

"Let's just relax and watch a DVD and sip some Chablis," Prissy said, taking Loretta's arm with a good-natured warmth. "We have time to think about this later. What DVD did you rent?"

Loretta smiled slyly. "'To Live and Die in L.A.'" Prissy let go of her arm and shuddered.

TEN

El Doctor had arranged a meeting with Tony Volare on neutral turf—Hollywood (Florida)—because both were paranoid and had the muscle to back it up. Of course, Tony Volare's muscle was Mob muscle, and El Doctor's muscle was Cuban *Marielito* muscle, which meant instant Latin bloodbath if anyone got too jumpy, though both believed that their muscle was the stronger of the two. Where macho Latino egos are stake, it is best to tread softly. Besides, El Doctor had mutually sensitive business to discuss with Tony—namely, Helen Black, and what to do about this situation she had put herself in, and, inadvertently, the one she had put both of them in. The problem was, Helen knew too much about both the Mob and the Cuban drug syndicates, and if she got pinched and was coerced into cutting a deal with the D.A., she could spill the beans and the pasta right into the Atlantic Ocean. Both El Doctor and Tony loved, or rather lusted for Helen, but this was business. Something had to be done to ensure her silence, even if it meant whacking her, an option neither found desirable. Hence, this informal meeting at a small Hollywood bistro, to talk things out, before any beans or blood got spilled.

"Tony Volare," El Doctor said with a broad, phony smile while quickly scanning the restaurant for signs of camouflaged torpedoes. "Just like the song by Bobby Darin, eh? *Vo-larr-eee*," he sang, annoying the hell out of Tony, who was in a bad mood anyway.

"Dean Martin, you mean," Tony said with strained patience as they both sat down. Tony knew El Doctor had come alone, because he had put a tail on him. And besides, when he had driven up to visit his house with Helen and set this meet, it was clear he was as nervous as Tony about this situation. El Doctor was annoying, but not altogether stupid, at least not where survival was concerned. "Or Bobby Rydell, who did the pussy-ass watered-down white-bread vanilla teeny-bopper *fuck* version."

"Huh?" said El Doctor. "Bobby who? Darin, no?"

"*Rydell*, not Darin. Bobby Darin was a goddamn genius, he sang 'Beyond the Sea,' 'Mack the Knife,' that kinda classy shit, with style. Get your goddamn dead *goombah* singers straight."

"No offense, *mang*," El Doctor said brightly. "As far as dead guys go, I like Perez Prado myself—you too, no? And Tito Puente I know you like. See? Usually when two guys are banging the same broad, especially in our circles, they cannot sit and talk this way. We have more important things in common that hold us together, like mambo music. It is a sign of progress between our two camps, you think?"

"Helen told me last night that she is no longer sleeping with either of us," Tony said flatly. He snapped his fingers and two *cafe con leches* were brought to the table by a humble, silent waiter.

El Doctor appeared shaken by this statement, but maintained some poise. "Of course, she does not want to cause a rivalry between us. Last night was just to catch up on old times, have some fun, not cause a fucking cockfight."

"The point is neither of us got any last night, am I right?" Tony said, looking El Doctor dead in the eyes with the iciness he was dreaded for. Tony was forty-six and handsome in the Armand Assante mold, and he dressed retro, like a disco king, with wide lapels on three-piece suits, and huge sparkling necklaces tangled in his nest of exposed chest hair. He was a charming killer, however, and Mickey Rourke was his friend and idol. They admired each other's style, and Tony always hung out with Rourke when he came to town, up in his penthouse digs on Ocean Drive. Years ago Tony had bankrolled some of Mickey's local fights. Tony wanted to be a movie star, too, but then who didn't.

"You went home to your wife, didn't you?" El Doctor said with a wicked grin.

"Like I said, neither of us got any," Tony said, and they both laughed hesitantly, just to break the ice.

"Anyway, I think she is in love with a little white punk," El Doctor said, swallowing his cafe con leche in one gulp and then snapping his fingers for the waiter and ordering a *coco frio* and some oysters. Tony was not hungry just yet.

"What are you talking about?" Tony asked coolly.

"This punk she's staying with in Miami," El Doctor said. "Young white dude, says he's a writer."

"A rider? A rider of what? Horses?"

"Heh?"

"He's a fuckin' jockey or what?"

"No, what you talking? A *writer*. You know. Of *books*."

Tony's brow was furrowed. "Smart-ass preppy fuck, huh? What's he look like?"

"Ah, you know. Pasty white skin, dark hair, scrawny. Wears glasses. Real loser."

"Huh? What the fuck would our Helen be doing with someone like that?"

"I'm still trying to figure this out myself, you know? Doesn't make sense. He is not her type. He is nothing like me. Or you."

"What does this shithead write you said? Books?"

"Fuck if I know."

"Well, find out. He could be a pain in the ass for us. What if he's a fuckin' journalist? What's *wrong* with you?"

"He's not a fucking *journalist*, Tony, relax. Fuck. He's just a punk, I told you. I take care of it if anything happens. Right now he's keeping Helen out of sight, so it's okay."

"She's holed up with this fuck?"

"Yeah. You got a wife now, remember? It was Helen's idea last night that you introduce her as your cousin, not mine. I don't think she bought it, you ask me."

"She didn't. Like I said, neither of us got any last night. You never did respond to that. You didn't get any last night, am I right or what? Huh?" Tony again looked El Doctor in the eyes, causing discomfort.

"Tony, I told you, *nada*. I sleep in the same bed, but no action, you follow?"

"You slept in the same bed?" Tony stiffened.

"She is my patient, remember? I told my wife I was at the hospital anyway."

"Stupid fuck, she coulda checked up on that."

"I didn't tell her which one, Tony! *Conjo*, I'm no idiot, okay?"

"So this white fuck is nailing our Helen, huh?"

"I didn't see nothing, but who knows? Maybe now, even as we speak. You know Helen. She's no fucking *nun*."

"Well, she better keep her habit to herself, so to speak. If she gets pinched on this chickenshit knock-over and starts bending over for the Man we'll have to have our inside people shut her up, and I mean for good. She's got great tits, but she ain't altogether there upstairs, know what I mean?"

"She is a great piece of ass, no question, but no fucking genius, *es verdad*. Tell me, Tony, why do we stay married to our fucking wives with all this great snatch running around Florida, heh? We *loco*?"

"No," Tony sighed. "Just Catholic. Listen, Doc, if anyone starts rocking our boat, Helen and this white bread fuckhead are the first ones overboard, *capisce*? There's no room for sentimentality here."

El Doctor nodded grimly and slurped down his final oyster. "You not going to eat something?"

Tony rose and straightened his tie. "I didn't come here to eat," he said evenly, and then he walked out with two waiters packing pieces right behind him. El Doctor groaned and shook his head.

ELEVEN

Helen needed new clothes, since she'd bled all over the robbery wardrobe and was tired of wearing Johnny's old aloha shirts. When Helen told Johnny she was going to go shopping that night while he was at work, he panicked.

"Where are you going to find a store that's open and that doesn't have some cop around who'll slap the cuffs on you?" he yelled at her as she relaxed in the bath he had run for her.

"Stop talking like a fuckin' movie, or I'm outta here," Helen said flatly.

"You're out of here?" Johnny laughed. "And where would you go?"

"You think you're my last hope or something? How do you think I got around before I met you, Johnny? Gimme a fuckin' break."

"You know, you shouldn't say 'fuck' so much. It makes you less attractive. Really."

"You ain't my fuckin' mother, alright, so can it. *Fuck fuck fuck fuck FUCK*!"

"You think you're cute, don't you?" Johnny said, sitting on the toilet and pouting at the prospect of Helen leaving his life. "The truth is, you don't have anywhere to run now that you're on the lam."

"On the 'lamb'? You mean like leg of lamb? You mean like I'm into sheep, that what you mean?"

"And the way you say you'll leave, it's like a threat, like you're doing me a big favor to stay here, a real big favor."

"You're gettin' laid, ain'tcha? Quit complainin'. I'm the best nookie you ever had, or ever *will*, so what's your problem?"

"Ha! You really think I've been waitin' around here for you to show up?"

"Me or somebody like me. Only there ain't nobody like me, so yeah, I'd say that. I mean, *look* at you. Look at your pathetic life, Johnny. I mean when was the last time you got laid anyway? I mean with a *real* woman like me?"

"All the time, babe. All the time. The Sheik of South Beach, that's me."

"Yeah, right, Romeo. The Geek of South Beach is more like it."

Johnny didn't say anything else. Helen stood up and opened the shower curtain, and stood in front of him glistening in all her glory. "Hand me a towel?" she said coyly, and Johnny complied without looking at her right away. Helen stood in the tub with the towel around her hefty hips until he finally looked up. She was smiling. "Help me out?"

With a fake sigh Johnny put his arms under hers, and when he did she embraced and kissed him. "How about I give you money and you go shopping for me, okay Daddy?" Helen whispered in his ear.

Johnny pulled back slightly and looked at her through a haze of desire. "What money? You got money?"

"Well, I know where we can get some. All I need is a little disguise so we can go out together to my bank in Coral Gables."

"You got an account in a bank? In Coral Gables?"

She kissed his nose. "You catch on fast, Johnny-O. Now help me get dressed in a disguise."

"I thought you wanted me to go out for you? Doesn't that make more sense?"

"But I can't make you up to look like me, Johnny, and you have to be me to cash a check at my bank. That's the law."

"Funny, you talkin' about the law."

Helen glared at him.

"Sorry," Johnny stammered. "But don't call me a geek again. Okay?"

In response she smiled radiantly and once again enveloped him in her voluptuousness. "I sorry," she said in baby talk. "I wove you, Johnny-O."

Johnny didn't know what to say, and he didn't feel ready to engage in baby talk with her, so he kept silent while he dried her off with the towel.

"I can make myself up to look like a boy or somethin'. Well, maybe not. How about a dyke?"

"Don't say dyke. It's offensive."

"But isn't that the name of your book? Something about a dyke?"

"Yeah, but that's different. That's, uh, y'know. Art."

Helen laughed as she walked into the living room, dropping the towel behind her, and lay on the bed, still unmade, with feline grace. "I have nothing against lesbos. I don't have anything against anybody, as long as they don't get in my face. Hell, I've slept with my share of women."

Johnny was awestruck and turned on. "Oh yeah?"

"You can't eat beef *all* the time, Johnny. A little fish now and then is good for you. Anyway, let's talk about my disguise so I can get money so you can buy me some new clothes?"

"Well, how about I just lend you the money, till you get on your feet?"

Helen laughed again. "Johnny, when I get on my feet, I'm running for the nearest border. And that means you're back to *this*." She pantomimed masturbation.

"Yeah, yeah, yeah, Miss God's Gift to Mankind, but it isn't safe for you to go out yet, in any disguise, unless you got plastic surgery."

"Johnny, just trust me, okay? I like you as much as you like me, and I don't want to get busted again, especially not for a fuckin' murder rap, so take it easy. I've got both our best interests in mind. I didn't get where I am today by being stupid, y'know."

"Neither did I." *And where were they?*, Johnny asked himself. Stuck in his little room with a noisy cat. Truly, they had both arrived.

"So anyway, just listen to me from now on, and we'll be fine. I may even take you to Mexico with me. I was thinking, with all those drug cartels running wild now, they won't even notice you and me, no matter what we do. It's not my first choice, but it's close enough. You take what you can get, that's my motto."

"Mexico? What makes you think I want to go to *Mexico?*"

"Because that's where *I'll* be, and where *I'll* be, my *pussy* will be. Get it?"

"The world does not revolve around your...your..."

"The *world* doesn't, but *you* do."

"The only pussy I care about is the Leopard Man."

"You mean your fucking cat? Your *gato?* Why, you train him to give you head?"

"Stop it, okay? Just *stop* it. I feel sick." Johnny sat on the edge of the bed, but for once he didn't want her to touch him.

She was relentless, though, giving him a delicate massage while she whispered in his ear. "Johnny...you know I'm only kidding. How long have we known each other now?"

"I don't know. Two and a half days, about."

"Well, that's longer than I knew my parents. We're close, Johnny. We're a team. We'll go far together."

"You mean like Mexico or the gas chamber?"

Helen kissed his neck and massaged his crotch until he felt the tension and doubt drain away. "I mean like heaven," she cooed.

TWELVE

Time was running out. Johnny had to be at work in less than two hours and Helen was still trying to come up with a disguise. She had tried various combinations with Johnny's limited retro-hipster wardrobe of bowling and aloha shirts. Finally she pulled out an old jogging suit Johnny had bought once when he had briefly considered exercising to relieve stress. He jogged exactly twice around the block, then decided to stock more liquor in the house instead. She added his Elvis-style shades to the ensemble, and put up the hood.

"All I need is some gold chains 'n' shit," she smiled.

"Jesus Christ, Helen, it's not a costume party. Make up your mind, I have to go to work soon. You look like a rapper, or a white trash terrorist."

"So?"

"You're too pretty to walk around like that. Too bad. Too bad you gotta live like this."

Helen took off the huge gold shades and looked at Johnny with sincere tenderness. "You're sweet." She kissed him once gently on the lips. "You really are a sweet guy. Now let's get outta here so I can get some cash and buy some new fuckin' clothes."

Johnny didn't see the .357 Magnum she had tucked under his sweatshirt.

When he opened the front door, daylight burst into the dark room like laser beams, but the sun didn't destroy Helen. She was no vampire, Johnny thought. Just a crazy, mixed-up kid. That didn't explain his association with her, though. He'd self-diagnose later.

"Let me drive," Helen said when they reached the garage.

"No way, nobody drives my Edsel but me. I don't like this, anyway. I can always go out and buy you more clothes."

"I want to use my own money and pick out my own shit, thank you. You'll dress me like I'm going to a fuckin' sock hop."

Johnny revved up the big engine but still felt powerless. "Let me ask you something. If you have a bank account with money in it, why'd you hold up that store?"

"The bank was closed and I lost my ATM card," she explained coolly.

"Don't you have a checkbook?"

"Lost that too. I got mugged."

"Ah, c'mon. Did you ever have a real job? I mean besides seducing wise guys for hits."

"What, you shittin' me? I'd rather hold up liquor stores than work in one. What do you think I'm qualified to do, anyway? Be a secretary? I had no education except what I picked up in the streets, Johnny. And hey, what is it you do for a living? Drive shit and piss around all day? Yeah, that's *real* fuckin' glamorous."

"At least I contribute to society."

"You contribute shit, you mean. You ain't my fuckin' shrink or social worker, you're just some sweet bored lonesome ass geek with a crappy job who just got real lucky 'cause you met me. Turn here."

"Okay."

THIRTEEN

The Edsel cruised down Miracle Mile like a wayward rocket ship from the past, when the future had seemed so sleek and comfortable. It was a breezy afternoon, a cause for complacency, a reason to stay in South Florida despite the crime, the racism, the tourists, the bugs, and the occasional hurricanes. Johnny felt trapped in a dream of his own design, with a fallen angel by his side. He almost didn't care what happened next.

The Edsel stopped at the corner of Ponce De Leon Blvd. and Helen got out in front of the First Union Bank. "Keep the engine running, I'll only be a minute," she said as she dashed inside. Johnny didn't even have time to tell her how impressed he was that she had an account in such a prestigious looking building. He was parked in a white zone, and couldn't remember what this meant. Maybe it was for white people, in which case he was okay, as long as no one caught on he was white *chocolate*, not vanilla, like the majority of Coral Gables. Even the Cubans here seemed white to Johnny. Too much money bleaches the soul, but doesn't clean it, he thought to himself.

Johnny tapped his fingers nervously on the steering wheel while listening to the oldies station play "I Fought the Law (And the Law Won)." He began to daydream, almost unconsciously, about Loretta Lynx as he sat in the Edsel. The next song on the oldies station was "Since I Fell For You," by Lenny Welch, a song that always put Johnny in tears. For some reason, he did not think of Helen while this song tortured him—he thought of Loretta. Despite the wild sex and promise of sudden violence that Helen offered him copiously, Loretta Lynx was still haunting him. This neighborhood reminded him of her. He loved a girl in California once who was from Palo Alto, who later married a Stanford graduate, and *she* always reminded him of Loretta. Johnny had gone to Palo Alto with this girl once to meet her folks, which turned out to be the kiss of death, since she dumped him soon afterward. She was the one he had been calling from the Surfcomber Hotel just before he got fired. The girl had left Palo Alto to pursue a career as a fashion designer in L.A., or something shallow like that. At least Loretta worked in the real world, in a real diner, and had real aspirations, Johnny told himself. She was down-to-Earth, a woman of the world. Coral Gables reminded Johnny a bit of Palo Alto, even, but this made him uneasy, since he knew these were parties to which he was cordially uninvited. Loretta belonged in a world like this, diner or no diner, and Johnny knew it, even though he hoped she wouldn't mind slumming long enough for him to get his novel published. Johnny recalled another girlfriend who lived in Miami, married to a Real Estate broker or something, who didn't want to wait for Johnny's ship to come in, fearing she'd be too old to bear children by then. Last he'd heard, her husband was sterile and they had not adopted, as far as he knew. He'd lost touch with her, but that was just as well. *Come to think of it, she lives right here in the Gables*, he remembered suddenly. Wouldn't it be funny if she happened to walk by and see the shapely, beautiful Helen getting in his Edsel? Wouldn't that be a gas? Johnny actually began looking around for her, shopping in the area, maybe with an adopted Haitian kid in tow, casually strolling along and then recognizing the Edsel. Then Helen would come running out and...

BANG! BANG! POW!

The sharp reports of gunfire shattered Johnny's daydream. Suddenly, his waking life was a blur. Helen jumped into the Edsel next to him, money bags in hand, and shouted, "*DRIVE*, YOU STUPID MOTHERFUCKER! DRIVE! NOW! *MOVE IT*!"

Johnny was in a daze until Helen stuck the smoking barrel of the .357 to his temple. "*I said drive*," she hissed through gritted teeth. Sirens wailed from somewhere, everywhere. A security guard obviously wounded and cradling his leaking guts, was stumbling towards them, his gun wobbling in the air. Without thinking clearly, Johnny stepped on the gas and the Edsel lurched forward, barely avoiding collision with several oncoming vehicles. He was on the wrong side on the street, as well as the Law. Then he was on the sidewalk. The world around him was complete mayhem, and Helen would not stop shouting at him. He wanted to cry, but couldn't. He was still in shock. The sight of at least three police cars, lights flashing with migraine intensity in his rearview window woke him up. Battling an urge to vomit, he slammed on the brakes and skidded into a parking meter.

"*What the fuck are you doing?*" Helen screamed, but the police were already surrounding them. They were outnumbered and outgunned. Johnny tore the Magnum from Helen's grasp after a brief struggle. Helen was crying now. So was Johnny. Shotguns pointed at them, they were ordered out of the car with their hands in the air. Johnny was commanded to drop the Magnum and he did. Then he passed out cold. Helen kicked and spit on him as he lay unconscious on the ground.

Then out of the blue the sound of more gunfire erupted, as if an Army had descended. Uzis and grenades exploded from several directions, and then came the tear gas. Chaos ensued as the cops began shooting wildly at their attackers, who actually only numbered a half dozen, and they were all packed into one sedan that belonged to Tony Volare. When the smoke cleared, Helen was gone, and Johnny was still on the ground, unconscious of the world crashing down around him.

FOURTEEN

Johnny missed Helen.

It had been a week since the cops had let him walk, convinced that the notorious Helen Black had forced him to offer her sanctuary, then threatened him into being her getaway driver for that daringly dumb daylight bank job. He was still supposed to report in periodically, and his house was under surveillance in case Helen or any of her cohorts tried to return. But he was off the hook. At least with the Law, and at least for now.

Johnny had become something of a hero at work, and he'd even made Carl Hiaasen's column. But this didn't cheer him up. The only thing that might do the trick was if Loretta Lynx had read about his exploits and got so turned on by his heroic confrontation with the forces of evil she'd marry him on the spot before someone else snatched him up. It was worth a shot. Besides, he hadn't been to Wolfie's since the whole Helen business had began. Perhaps it was Fate.

Still, now that Helen was gone, he felt a tremendous gap in his daily life, one that had always been there, probably, but now the emptiness felt more excruciatingly painful than ever, since he realized what he'd been missing for so long. At least there was still Loretta. Maybe. But then Loretta had always been a *Maybe*, whereas Helen was a big, juicy *Affirmative*. He knew it couldn't have lasted, though. And anyway, Helen was probably mad as hell at him for chickening out, when all he wanted to do was stop this trail of tragic missteps and rehabilitate her, once and for all. But now she'd probably put a hit out on him, or maybe she'd even do it herself, blow his dick off and hand it to him. So what. Without her, it was of no use to him anyway.

A big problem with getting to Wolfie's these days was transportation. The Edsel was parked in the garage, but since the bank job and subsequent hysteria, it had become a bullet-ridden hunk of twisted metal. The cops had it towed back to the garage at their expense, since they felt badly for poor Johnny, innocent victim of Florida's endless crime wave, washed up bruised and bloody on the beach of bereavement, though all the bullet holes were from the Uzis of the mysterious attackers, who had not wounded a single cop in the stealth assault. Obviously the attackers' intention had been only to frighten and distract the cops while Helen was being rescued. The fact that they had left Johnny behind had been a major point in his defense, though the authorities also wanted to let Johnny go free so he could serve as potential bait. He had been released without bail for this purpose, but he was still on the local law's shit list, and was being watched carefully. His spotless record and innocent kisser had certainly helped his credibility, but even that couldn't save him from Helen Black. The cops also feared retribution against Johnny, who had eschewed their protection (though they kept tabs on him anyway, in case Helen showed up). Johnny wanted to take his chances on his own, because secretly he prayed Helen would return and steal him away to Mexico or some other mythical paradise. Preferably at gunpoint.

In the meantime, he had his novel to write, which he had re-titled *Up the Fireplace,* ostensibly a metaphor for something, but he hadn't figured that part out yet. He just gave his lesbian protagonist a fireplace. But in case Helen didn't re-enter his life at some point, all he had for a muse was Loretta Lynx. It was time to pay her a visit.

As Johnny boarded the bus for Collins Ave., he was wondering how Loretta would respond to him now that he was an accessory to armed bank robbery, and a free one at that. Hopefully she'd find this an attractive new attribute, though Johnny also wondered whether Loretta was worth the bother. Loretta was beautiful, but cold. Johnny had reached the point where he'd rather have a female firecracker like Helen pistol-whip him into submission. But Helen was out of the picture, at least temporarily, and his novel needed some of that sex-spiced inspiration to get it back into high gear. Johnny got off the bus and walked into Wolfie's with an air of confidence tinged with anxiety. Immediately his defense shields were up, but the devil-may-care veneer was a flimsy vanguard in the face of Loretta's angelic radiance. As soon as he sat down at the counter, he began repeating his mental mantra: Just order, eat, and get the hell out of here. Already he was assuming she'd have a negative response to his presence. Unfortunately, his ESP was A-OK.

In his wallet, Johnny carried several handy clippings of the *Herald's* piece on his derring-do, and he decided that this would be a more appropriate tip than a personally inscribed, easily discarded napkin. After all, he was a veritable hometown hero, albeit susceptible to untimely fainting spells. Fortunately this minor fact had been left out of the newspaper article. The cops had painted quite a rosy portrait of Johnny Varga, Local Hero for the media, though this too was part of their plan to use Johnny as bait to catch the mobsters and the stolen loot, which had also vanished in the mysterious attack. Johnny had no idea who Helen's accomplices could have been, though he suspected El Doctor, but did not inform the cops of this missing piece to the puzzle.

A sudden chill breeze alerted Johnny to Loretta whizzing past him to pick up an order. Usually she split the counter with another waitress, plus serviced a nearby station, so the odds were Johnny would get her as a waitress every other time, and in any case he'd always be visible to her, and vice versa. Whether she waited on him or not, he would always leave her a poem next to his empty coffee cup, and if she had not been his waitress, he would write her name on the backside of the napkin and fold it over. The napkin-poem was always read by eyes other than Loretta's, however, and often read by everyone *except* her.

Loretta often read the *Herald* while on break, which partially explained why her eyes were glazed over with end-of-the-world ennui. She did notice Johnny, however, and went directly into her "ignore" mode, which shone like neon. Johnny had even worn an extra aloha shirt—a *new* one—to catch her eye. He didn't even attempt direct contact with her after he saw her whisper in the other waitress's ear to take his order. She had done this so obviously it nearly made Johnny laugh. He was used to the game by now, and didn't take offense. It proved she had noticed him after all.

Loretta's mind was bouncing with so many conflicting thoughts her head felt like a pinball machine. She had indeed heard about Johnny's travails on the nightly news, though she had missed the newspaper piece, perhaps because her horoscope had been negative that day and she had thrown out the paper in disgust. She was glad that her psycho suitor was at least a mini-celebrity; it made her feel good to ignore someone with notoriety. She made a point of flirting with the Cuban busboy working her station, a short but stocky, sunny but shy teenager supporting his mother on his tip money. His name was Ernesto, or Ernie, as he was known, and he was quite startled when Loretta came up behind him and pinched either side of his waist. He had a crush on Loretta, like most of the busboys at Wolfie's. At the same time, Johnny picked up the *Sports* page left behind on the stool beside him and pretended to be absorbed by the latest *Jai-alai* scores. He acted so mesmerized by these statistics, which had absolutely no bearing on his personal life, that he didn't even look up when his waitress brought over his coffee. He just nodded with an obligatory politeness, and then read on, obsessed by every insignificant statistic. After two years in Miami, he still wasn't even sure what the hell *Jai alai* was.

Unbeknownst to either Johnny or Loretta was Detective Sonny Johnson of the Armed Robbery Division, hunkered down in a nearby booth. Johnson has once been an undercover operative for Vice, but transferred out three years ago for several reasons, one being the ribbing he got on account of his name, which seemed like a cross between actor Don Johnson and his TV alter ego's, Sonny Crockett. The fact that Johnson was black did not deter anyone from calling him "pal" and asking him if they could borrow his Ferrari now and then for a high profile bust. Sometimes they just called him "Tubbs" instead.

Sonny Johnson was in his early '40s and was light-skinned, which accounted for the ribbing he received from fellow human beings both white and black, as well as other officers concerning his insistence that he was Afro-American. He was very soft-spoken and well-educated, did not like Hip-Hop, speak fluent jive or live up to any of the normal stereotypes, plus he dressed and acted very conservatively while keeping his politics to himself. He lived with his wife and six-year-old son on Key Biscayne, where he had recently bought a condo after being promoted to detective. Beat cops were requested to live within city limits for on-call emergencies, but Johnson had won himself the luxury of living any damn place he pleased. His new position garnered new respect, at least to his face, and he took no crap from anyone, particularly the assholes over at Vice, over whom he had no authority directly, but he still outranked his old cronies on the payroll. He harbored very little bitterness toward anyone, but he was terminally sad regarding the state of human life on this planet in general. He was originally a New Orleans boy and had grown up amid a level of oppression accepted as one of the laws of Nature, at least in his neighborhood. He had lived in Liberty City and in Hialeah while a patrolman for the Miami Police Department, pounding beats on both turfs, and when he graduated to a Vice position the depression that had been accumulating reached a breaking point. He couldn't believe his people, or any people, lived this way. Not that he believed Florida was any more tolerant than Louisiana—quite the contrary—but seeing it first-hand had only deepened his awareness of the widespread crisis. Originally he had joined the force as a potential crusader against this evil, working from the inside out, and his Tulane degree in Sociology came in handy on many occasions. He had passed on social work to become a cop because he wanted to fight the battle at ground zero. After seventeen years, his mission seemed hopeless. All he could do was take down enough criminals to make his quota and justify his lofty position. Like most urban centers, but especially here in Miami, the drug trade was wiping out his inner city brothers and sisters. He never talked much about his fears and ideals with anyone except his loving wife Sara, and sometimes his boy Lionel, because if he did he would only incur the same stupid racial jokes from good-natured morons.

Take this Johnny Varga character. Johnson wasn't buying his jive-ass honky routine, with those silly tourist shirts. He believed Johnny was an accomplice, but wasn't sure to what degree. He had arranged to have Johnny freed so he could keep an eye on him and hopefully dig up a lead. The kid's life was so small-scaled that keeping a tail on him during spare time was simple. But Sonny Johnson wanted a break in this case soon, and if Johnny didn't warm up the trail within the foreseeable future, Johnson was going to see to it that his white chocolate ass was tossed back in the cooler, with plenty of butter on the side.

Detective Johnson picked up on the game of charades going on between Varga and that stuck-up waitress. He laughed to himself, remembering his own awkward days of bachelorhood, trying to pick up girls in clubs, though that period of his life had been cut short rather quickly and ahead of its time when his wife nailed him. Johnson had never cheated on his wife, though he often considered it. When she and his boy went down to Key West sometimes to get away from the torrid debauchery of Miami, Johnson would watch the collection of X-rated tapes he had confiscated on a bust while doing Vice years ago. His partner and he distributed some to fellow officers with a penchant for this stuff and kept the rest for themselves. It seemed ironic and somehow wrong to harbor evidence from an undercover pornographic racket stakeout, but Johnson's hormones, pumped up by the sultry atmosphere like everyone else's, made the final call. And these videos weren't store-brought—they were homemade with some of Miami's finest. None were underage, as far as Johnson could tell, so his conscience didn't bother him too much. Like most people, he lived according to his own code of moral relativism. He had the power to take down arrogant white assholes and misguided brothers alike, and he relished in it, but the fact remained: the roots of the social problems he fought against would probably never die.

He didn't drink away his anxiety, nor did he ever do any of the drugs floating around the police property warehouse, nor did he whack out a punk who had beat the system too many times just to let off steam, as too many people he knew and respected did as part of a secret but widespread vigilante underground. No, Detective Johnson just jerked off and made love to his wife. He was a good Christian boy, after all.

Loretta wondered what to do. She was so tired of emotionally retarded academics that a colorful loner like Johnny almost appealed to her in a twisted way. Their single date had been a milestone for Johnny, she knew, but an embarrassment for her, particularly since she had left him with a hickey, physical evidence for him to brag about, if he had any friends, that is. She didn't want to encourage Johnny enough to make him pursue her, but she didn't want to completely turn him off either. She liked having him around, but at a distance. To her surprise, however, Johnny left earlier than usual, in apparent disgust, without even giving her a parting, longing glance as usual. His Shadow followed him out, though only the Shadow knew it was there.

FIFTEEN

Helen walked down Ocean Boulevard on Pompano Beach in Fort Lauderdale enjoying the late winter breeze off the sea and soaking in the soft rays of the sun. It was so much cleaner up here than in Miami, Helen thought to herself. She could only take it for so long. Tony had told her that there was an APB posted for her up here too, but his pals down at the station had "taken care of it," meaning Helen could stroll about unrecognized, or at least un-arrested, if she cared to. Tony had put her up in a beachfront motel until he could figure out what to do with her. They had made love, mechanically, in the motel the night of her rescue, which had completely pissed her off, at least initially.

   Tony's wife still had no idea what was going on, and didn't want to know. She knew Tony was some sort of thug, but she figured he was one of the legit ones who worked for the Government, as he had told her before they were married. Tony had only married his wife because he had knocked her up, and her father was a friend of his father's back in Brooklyn, and this had been the thing to do. He loved her, she had a nice body and all, but she was boring and staid compared to Lady Scarface. Tony was in love *and* lust with Helen, and he hated El Doctor and anyone else who stuck their fingers in her pie when he wasn't looking. This included the punk Helen had been holed up with in Miami Beach. Johnny hadn't known it, of course, but his place had been staked out soon after El Doctor had shown up to tend to Helen. Tony's Miami boys kept tabs on El

Doctor and Helen, so they knew the score before anyone else, but their orders were to lay low and stay out of the picture. Until, that is, Helen pulled this major boner of a bank job. She still hadn't explained why she had knocked over a bank while still hot from the killing, but this was largely because she wasn't so sure herself of her motivations. "If I knew that I'd be a fucking *shrink*, or *fucking* a shrink," she had snapped at Tony when the boys had delivered her to the motel in Lauderdale, direct from Coral Gables. Tony had been angry enough to take her out himself, but instead he had sublimated his rage into humping her brains out as soon as the boys had left, continuing to do so until well after sundown. Helen knew he was mad and let him have his way with her, all the while thinking of Johnny, and wondering why he had turned on her at such a crucial moment.

Had it been because, as Tony put it once, she talked like a truck driver on the rag? Helen's lack of ladylike attributes often made her feel insecure and somewhat depressed. Her ideal man to settle down with was not a mobster, but a nice, straight guy with a steady job, someone who could help her reform when the time came. Helen didn't feel ready to reform or settle down just yet, but Johnny Varga had seemed like a likely candidate for this upcoming role. Until, of course, he had betrayed her so inexplicably.

A couple of Tony's boys, disguised as beach bums, trailed along behind Helen as she ducked in and out of shops, flirted with young and old men alike, played with dogs running around, and generally behaved like Rebecca of Sunnybrook Funny Farm. She still carried her Magnum tucked behind her, despite Tony's admonition not to, so whenever she bent over the handle would gleam in the sunshine, much to the chagrin of the boys behind her, who had orders to make sure she didn't make a spectacle of herself by holding up a camera shop or something. Helen knew who they were and where they were, and was just waiting for the opportunity to make them sweat. She hated men who made a living by kissing someone else's ass. All she was doing as she strolled along the beach in Fort Lauderdale was looking for a quiet way to get into trouble.

Helen was also in a pensive what's-it-all-about mood. While she was all too accustomed to ephemeral affairs with bizarre strangers, her twisted tryst with Johnny had managed to reach her heart. She had thought it bulletproof, like the rest of her. Helen was burdened with a stockpile of bad memories she wasn't sure what to do with; it was like toxic waste. Being molested by caretakers throughout her childhood, succumbing to men like Tony who fulfilled some sick paternal need —being around Johnny for just a few days had helped her to forget all of this. She wasn't sure why. Maybe it was Johnny's innate innocence, and the feeling she got that he really cared for her, at least as much as he could for a virtual stranger.

Yes, she would be seeing him again, Helen decided just before she pulled her Magnum out and pointed it at a street vendor, robbing him of a hot dog, which she ate with wry relish.

Tony's boys were instantly upon her, dragging her into a nearby Ferrari and speeding off towards Tony's office downtown, in a Cadillac dealership, a legit operation and a front for the Mob. Tony was talking to the driver on his cell phone as the boys in the backseat slapped a screaming Helen into submission. "Put her on," Tony said calmly, leaning back in his swivel chair in the dark, deco office. Holding her arms behind her, one of the boys shoved her face into the phone.

"*FUCK YOU TONY!*" Helen shouted.

"You're going on a trip, princess," Tony said simply. "Eddie, meet me at the airport. You're going to New York for a while, as an escort for our naughty girl."

"Sure, chief." Eddie, a muscular, hairy transplanted Brooklynite who hated Florida and missed the old neighborhood, hung up the phone.

"*FUCK YOU*!" Helen screamed again, squirming like a tigress in a trap.

"Tony says either Manhattan or the Everglades," Eddie said to her. "Take your pick. Only with the Everglades, there ain't no return trip."

They had her piece, and Helen had said her piece already, so she calmed down and pouted as the urban landscape gradually turned wild. Instead of screaming, she was scheming. These guys were schmucks; she could handle them. For openers, she wriggled out of her top enough so that her cleavage was more than conspicuous. It was a tired old distraction technique that so far had never failed her. The two guys in back and the driver, Eddie, who watched in the rear view window, knew her tricks and did their best to ignore her as the Ferrari raced for the airport, a private landing strip on the outskirts of Broward County where Tony kept his private plane in the Mob's secret hanger. Helen decided to bide her time, arrive quietly at tie rendezvous, wait for Tony to arrive, then raise Hell.

SIXTEEN

Loretta wasn't sure how to take the newspaper clipping left beside Johnny's cold coffee cup, which had remained untouched during his brief visit, but she knew it was a sign of continued interest, which she would strategically ignore, as was par the course. She saved the clipping, which detailed Johnny's quasi-criminal activities, placing it in a file she was building up for her inevitable court case against him, which would occur after he finally flipped his lid. In the file, a manila envelope hidden behind her bureau where her mother wouldn't find it, were a few dozen poems on napkins, some typed letters in neat envelopes, pleading with her to come to her senses and go out with him again, and even a few dead roses, petals crushed between the tear-and-ink drenched paper.

Sometimes Loretta wondered why she kept souvenirs of this non-existent romance. She was lonely as hell, and at times she even felt something resembling horniness, but she was definitely not hard up. Whenever she went down to South Beach, either to play volleyball on the beach with some airhead acquaintances or take in the dangerous nightlife with a bonehead bogus boyfriend, she was always the center of attention. She was used to it now, however, and no longer felt flattered, only *bored, bored, bored*.

That was it, she decided as she lay in the marble bathtub that afternoon, immersed in bubbles, watching herself closely in the mirrors that lined the walls and ceiling (a security precaution, not a reflection of vanity, the brochure on the deluxe digs had pointed out, as if this had once been the site of the Bates Motel). She was bored, and

Johnny Varga was not boring.

The golden telephone with arm's reach of the tub rang and Loretta answered it on the fourth summons with practiced nonchalance. "Lair of the Lynx," she purred, as she was fond of saying.

"Hi, pumpkin," said the voice of her father. She felt disappointed. She had been half-expecting Johnny to give her a buzz after making such a hasty retreat from the diner.

"Hullo, Daddy," she yawned. "Miss me?"

"Yes, but that's not why I'm calling," her father said in his slow, careful manner that often grated on her nerves because it came off so passive-aggressive. "Your mother told me that you have plans on becoming some kind of movie star."

"*Damn her!*" Loretta said silently, mouthing the words but not voicing them. "I *knew* it!" She just breathed heavily into the phone for a few moments.

"Pumpkin, you still there?"

"Yes, Daddy," she said at last.

"Well?"

"Well *what*?"

"Well, is that true?"

"Depends."

"Depends? On what?"

"On your definition of movie star, I guess."

"Well," he said, laughing softly, "My definition is someone who stars in movies."

"Oh," said Loretta. "Well, I guess that will be me, then. But I won't just be a movie star, Daddy. I'll be a serious actress too. I want to study hard and make something of myself."

"That was my idea too."

"I don't want to be a lawyer, Daddy, unless I'm playing one on a hit how or something," Loretta said firmly. "I've made up my mind. I told Prissy not to say anything to you about it because I knew you'd be upset."

"Upset? I'm not upset. I'm not upset with you,

pumpkin."

"Then stop repeating it so much."

"I can get upset if you insist on talking to me that way."

"Sorry Daddy. Didn't mean to cop a 'tude on you."

"What?"

"Inner city lingo, Daddy. I'm learning a lot about linguistics in the real world lately."

"Pumpkin, listen to me, and listen carefully."

"Yeah, sure, I'm listening." Loretta concentrated on cleaning beneath her fingernails.

"Now, you know I have a college fund set aside for you, and that is something your mother and I have invested in diligently since you were born, and that paid your tuition to the University of Miami, where you dropped out, as you may recall, and that fund is still waiting for you to put to proper use by attending any one of the Ivy League schools to further pursue a higher education and take out some insurance on your future in an increasingly uncertain world."

"Daddy, please speed it up, alright? I mean, really, I don't want to be rude or anything, you know me, but sometimes you talk like Ronald Reagan giving a speech while he's on Quaaludes."

There was a long, uncomfortable pause from the other end. "He's gone, our dear president is gone, but I'm *not*. Not *ye*t."

"Daddy."

"I'm still here," he said with uncharacteristic coldness.

Loretta grew nervous. "Daddy, *look*. I'm not going to disappoint or embarrass you in any way. I want to make you proud of me, believe me, nothing would make me happier, but I want to be happy with myself. Can't you understand that? I need to find a way to make both of us happy. That's all I'm trying to do. Really. Okay? Daddy?"

"What I want to know, young lady," her father said in measured tones, "is how you know what a Quaalude is and what affect it has on anyone?"

Loretta became exasperated. "Daddy, I'm not having wild parties and entertaining dopers, okay? That's just not my style. Tell the truth, I haven't been entertaining anybody in quite some time, especially me. So please don't start with this Little Miss Perfect Lost in Babylon routine. I'm not that girl, and this isn't that place."

"I don't believe you," her father said. "I'm coming up there tonight."

"*Good*!" Loretta shouted, standing up in the tub suddenly like an uncoiling sponge "That will give Prissy a chance to get it on with that hunk that works in your office. You know the one, Daddy? Or haven't you figured it out yet? See, I'm not the only one with a deep dark secret to hide from you. Okay? So yeah, I'll see you soon." She kissed the receiver with a loud smack and hung up, her teardrops making tiny trails in the foamy lather covering her perfect skin.

SEVENTEEN

Here I am again, Johnny thought to himself as he tried
yanking his limp dick into something resembling a hard-on,
so he could come and go to sleep finally, even though it was
only four in the afternoon. On the tube was Wim Wender's
Until the End of the World, an arty, new wave travelogue of
sorts with lots of Euro-pop music on the soundtrack. Johnny
liked this atmospheric stuff usually, but now he just found
it depressing. Once his dream had been to make love to a
girl he cared about in a foreign city he had always wanted
to visit. The movie he was watching while he fondled his
sleeping genitals concerned an adventurous girl chasing a
guy wanted for industrial espionage across the planet; she
wasn't a cop, just a crazy girl in love with life and the
pursuit of the unknown, which reminded Johnny of Helen.
The girl was the sometimes girlfriend of some love-struck
writer working on a new novel and not getting very far
because his muse kept calling him up from weird places and
asking him to wire him some of the stolen money she kept
in a refrigerator in their Paris flat. The guy that the girl was
chasing around the globe wasn't really a spy, just someone
wanted by the U.S. Government because he had this cool
invention, a camera that could take photographs that blind
people could see when hooked up to some computer. The
guy's mother was blind, so he wanted to record the world
for her to see before she died. Anyway, some black
detective was on the trail of the guy with the camera, too.
For some reason this movie seemed eerily familiar to

Johnny, though his own life had never achieved such grand scope. Even though he had a novel in the oven, and even though Carl Hiaasen had mentioned these writing ambitions in his column, Johnny still felt like a hapless, hopeless nobody, in painful contrast to the sexually charged heroics of his brief former life, now dead forever. Unless Helen called him up from some weird place and asked him to join her, providing those guys who had rescued her hadn't bumped her off already, and she was unable to call him because cell phones won't get a signal outside of Hell.

Johnny had been so consumed by these worries he had called in sick to work, for the first time ever. He couldn't really afford this luxury, since he used all his PTO for his vacation last year, which had been spent bar hopping in Bal Harbor without scoring once. All the pretty girls were taken, or snotty, or crazy, or all three. Johnny was tired of this Loretta business. He wanted Helen. That was the girl for him, if only by default.

After the movie and two more hours of failed masturbation, Johnny crawled out of bed and sat at his desk, where a blank page on his laptop screen was waiting to be smothered with breathtaking, Pulitzer-caliber prose. He was roughly a third into his saga, now titled *Up A Warm, Wet Place* rather than *Up A Fireplace* because he hadn't been able to figure out what the fireplace was supposed to signify. And Hell was downward, not up. That was all too deep, too esoteric anyway. Johnny needed a quick sale. He had decided to step up the fictional proceedings and have the lesbian bartender kidnap, tie up, and rape the baseball player because she had decided she wanted to have a baby. The fact that he was a willing victim threw a wrench in this scenario, but Johnny patched it up with a few passages about how the baseball player had found religion and did not believe in premarital sex, not even with the object of his romantic dreams.

Johnny belched and farted and scratched himself, but didn't write a single word. He just went back to bed to resume his jerk-off attempts and watch another movie on cable and wait for the phone to ring. He flipped around and settled on *Lifeforce*, about a sexy naked space vampire from outer space, sucking the life out of her hapless male victims. He got hard again and finished in a messy spurt.

Before Johnny could wipe himself off, The Leopard Man jumped up on his chest and licked himself too, pulling out fleas with his fangs and then coughing up fur balls all over Johnny's bed. It was a disgusting process, but Johnny felt too numb to interfere. He wasn't even watching the screen, just staring into space, praying for the phone to ring.

Finally, it rang. Johnny looked at the clock. It was nearly midnight. Johnny wiped the sticky jism onto the sheet so he could pick up the phone, but the delay was dangerous. It had to either be work or his beloved, phoning from her hideout or a jail cell. Either way, he'd be by her side. "Hello?" he said eagerly.

"Johnny?" The voice was familiar, and female.

"Yeah?"

"It's me."

"Who?"

"Me."

"Me who? Helen?"

"Who? Ellen? No. It's me. Loretta."

Johnny was speechless. She sounded vaguely upset, possibly in tears.

"Johnny, are you there?"

"Yeah, I think so. You want to give me another death threat?"

"No, I wanted to know if you wanted to come over."

"Come over? Come over where?"

"To my apartment. You remember where it is? You picked me up once in that divine car of yours."

"Yeah, well, that car is now deceased. I have no wheels."

"Then can I come over there?"

"You mean *now*?"

"Yes! I know it's late, but..."

"*No, no*! Please. I mean, sure, if ya want." Johnny faked a yawn. "I mean, is this the night you kill me?"

"Don't be silly. I just, I don't know. We need to *talk.*"

"But what's the urgency? I mean, you didn't even say hello to me today when I saw you at work..."

"So? I never do."

"Yeah, so—what's going on? Why now?"

"I have something to say now. Only it has to be in person, and it has to be tonight,"

"Okay, if you say so. I'll, uh, I'll put on some coffee for when you get here."

"Don't bother. I'm bringing champagne." Click.

Johnny hung up the phone in a daze, wondering whether he had just dreamed that whole conversation. He would soon find out.

EIGHTEEN

It was dark and sticky, and mosquitoes sucked any blood from Helen's body that wasn't boiling in her brain. Tony had met the Ferrari at the private airport in one of his Caddys with a group of his goons, all armed with everything from .45s to 9mms. They weren't taking any chances with this wildcat, even though she was armed with nothing but her giant invisible balls. Dusk was just settling on the horizon, pastel slash marks on a black canvas. The sounds of Florida's wildlife croaked, roared, chirped and sang around them, but the only sound Helen could hear was the dissonant hum of the airplane engine, ready for takeoff.

Helen quickly scanned the situation. She was outnumbered, outgunned, and outbound, but she was also out of her mind, which gave her a slight edge. She'd have to think of something quick, lethal, and decisive, and within seconds.

Tony, wearing a black overcoat despite the humidity since he thought it made him look like the Angel of Death, confronted Helen with a smirk. When he bent to kiss her she predictably spit on him. Without even blinking Tony took out his handkerchief and wiped the gob from his brow. Some of his boys suppressed laughter, knowing Tony's good humor could quickly turn sour and deadly in the blink of an eye. Everyone was tense, but restrained. Except for Helen.

"You want to kiss me, how about my *ass*, motherfucker!" Helen shouted at Tony, who only watched her being taken forcibly into the bi-plane with a bemused expression on his face. Helen swung impetuously into action. With a vicious back kick she nailed one guy in the nuts, then with both fists held together she belted another in the jaw, cracking it loudly.

"*Don't shoot!*" Tony yelled as everyone raised their weapons and pointed them at Helen, still busy playing judo with the boys trying to stuff her into the damn plane. Helen was like a cat that refused to be put into its transport box—claws and fangs kept sticking out and puncturing her would-be captors. This airstrip was way the hell out in the middle of nowhere, closer to Pensacola than Miami, and in fact it had once been an adjunct to the local military base before the Mob purchased it via a high-ranking official friend. It often came in handy for getaway occasions, both emergency and casual, though recently it had seen very little use due to the Mob's waning presence in the region. El Doctor's people didn't want even a low profile piece of property such as this, so there was the possibility the airstrip would be abandoned soon. But not before Helen was packed off safely, perhaps permanently, to New York.

"Okay, okay, what about the Bahamas?" Tony said to Helen as three gorillas pinned her down on the ground. "You always liked it there. I'll put you up in my private suite, the one you *like*."

"*Why can't I just do whatever the fuck I want?*" Helen screamed. "What're you, my *dad*? You don't fuckin' *own* me, asshole!"

"Helen. Helen, Helen." Tony tapped his brow and shook his head pensively. "You're giving me a headache. I've always been good to you, and that's what I'm trying to do now. Be good to you and for you. You're in a lot of hot fuckin' water right now, and you just keep sinking deeper. All I'm doin' is taking the anchor off your foot, because there's a chance you could take us all down with you."

"What do you mean, Tony? My snatch don't snitch, you know that. They couldn't show me a deal good enough."

"Even one that saved you from the gas chamber? Or maybe they'll fry your juicy ass. Either way, you're on tape whacking out some unlucky stiff who thought he could outshoot you, and my lawyer tells me he'd have a tough time greasing palms to bail you out of this one after you pulled that incredibly stupid fuckin' bank job. Before he probably could've taken care of it, but now you're Public Fuckin' Enemy Number One and a Fuckin' Half, you dumb *twit!*"

Helen launched a gob of spit, which Tony dodged easily.

"I like when you get me wet, sweet cheeks, but now is not the time."

"*FUCKER!*" Helen screamed, "I'll tell your wife you've been fuckin' me every which way since *way* back! Now let me *go!*"

"No," Tony smiled. He nodded and Helen was again dragged toward the yawning plane hatch.

"Okay, okay then, the Bahamas, but only if it's just me and you!" Helen yelled just as her kicking legs were forced into the door. "I don't want to go with *any* of your fuckin' goons! I want you Tony, or I swear I'll call your wife before you ice me! I *swear*! I want you *NOW!*"

Tony was smirking. He was wary, but weak. Shaking his head, he threw up his arms and approached her. "Let her go," he told the guys holding her. Helen jumped into Tony's arms and bear-hugged him, then began kissing his neck, causing him to blush in front of the men, which made him uncomfortable. She even began to fake heavy sobbing, which Tony bought. He began patting her on the back like he was burping a baby. "Now, now. Tony's here. I'll take care of you. How about I join you there soon, say day after next? I have some business to tend to in Miami, a convention with some old friends. Like Vinnie. You remember Vinnie. Sure you do. Maybe he'll come too." Tony wasn't aware that his lieutenant Vinnie "the Vine"

Vinelli, aka Vino Vinnie, a bigwig in a European wine export business which was one of the Mob's legit operations, had banged Helen on many occasions, several times on Tony's private cruise ship bound for the Caribbean. "It'll be like old times," Tony continued. "Then when this thing blows over, say in a year or two, you can do what you want. Maybe we'll even take that Italy holiday like we talked about. Paris, too. London. Wherever the hell you want. This summer maybe. We could even..."

Tony had become aware of a sharp blade pressed precariously against his jugular. During her struggle with one of the boys she had lifted his switchblade. Tony knew Helen could carve a Michelangelo from a bar of soap, so he motioned for everyone to back off as Helen walked him to his Caddy, made him crawl into the passenger seat. Then, after being handed her Magnum back on Tony's order, she dropped the knife and pointed the business end of the .357 at Tony's temple.

"Scoot over to the driver's seat, and let's get out of here," Helen ordered Tony, who was cussing under his breath. If he weren't so sure Helen was crazy enough to bump him off, he would've signaled for his torpedoes to shoot the shit out of her for humiliating him like this. No piece of ass was worth this aggravation, he had belatedly decided.

"You're just marking time till this mistake catches up with you, you know," Tony said as Helen slammed the door and he started the engine.

"You could say that about anyone," Helen said. "*Everyone* fucks up just by being *born*, 'cause then all that you have to look forward to in the end is biting the dust, one way or another. It's like starting a game you can't ever win."

"You can wax poetical all you fuckin' want," Tony hissed as he began to drive through the darkness, "'cause I'll make you write your own epitaph before I bury you."

"Just keep going another mile," Helen said coolly. "I know we'll be followed even if I can't see anyone. I know this fuckin' outfit too well."

"That's the problem."

"*Shut up!*" Helen commanded. Tony did a slow burn and said nothing, fantasizing about how he'd sexually debase her before cutting her into bite size pieces. "Just keep driving. Get out when I tell you to. And don't try nothin' funny 'cause sometimes I get in this mood, y'know, this crazy fuckin' *mood* where I don't care if I live or die, as long as it's on my terms, and right now *I'm* callin' the fuckin' shots here, Tony baby, so just do as I say and don't make me nervous. Keep driving, then stop when I say, get the fuck out, and I know your fuckin' kiss-ass dorks will pick you up, but that'll give me time to disappear. I don't want anything to do with you assholes anymore. You've fucked me up too much already. You used me, Tony. You never gave a fuck about me. If I had a skinny ass and no tits you wouldn't have given me the time of day. I set up those scumbags to get hit for you, I let you do things to my body, I let you have fun with me, and what do you do? *WHAT DO YOU DO?* You fuckin' treat me like *shit*, that's what. Like I'm a toy you can just put somewhere when you're not playing with it. You don't wanna trust me, fine, *fuck* you. I just wanted to prove with that bank job I don't need *nobody*, I can take care of myself from now on just fine, thank you very fuckin' much, so if you don't mind now..."

"Helen, listen to yourself," Tony said softly. "You're hysterical. Just calm down and stop crying and we'll work this thing out like adults..."

"FUCK YOU! STOP NOW AND GET OUT!"

"Helen..."

"*NOW!*"

"Helen, please. I love you..."

With a scream both primeval and prepubescent in pitch, Helen squeezed the trigger and blew Tony's head right through the window. Blood, brains, bone and glass exploded all over Helen in a shower of fleshy fragments, and the Caddy swerved out of control and sailed through some tall dark grass and into a swamp. Mossy water began seeping into the car as Helen, crying hard, sad but stoic, managed to climb out of the gory wreck as it slowly sunk into oblivion.

She waited by the side of the highway for one of the goonmobiles to show up, and sure enough, within minutes Eddie's Ferrari pulled over and three shadowy figures emerged, obviously puzzled and worried as they followed the broken trail through the grass. Helen aimed carefully as they passed her and shot two in the kneecaps, making them drop to the ground in agony, while Eddie whirled around and let off three shots from his 9mm before Helen turned his yellow shirt to crimson. She ran out of the weeds and quickly found the car keys on Eddie's corpse as the other two groaned on the ground, reaching for their guns and managing to get off a few aimless shots at the curvaceous killing machine revving up the Ferrari engine and leaving them behind in the dusty darkness.

Laughing giddily, streaked with her own tears and Tony's blood, Helen lit up a cigarette from the glove compartment and drove like a bat out of hell toward Miami, toward Johnny Varga. She had an account to settle, and whether she'd have to transfer it or close it altogether depended on how good a story he could come up with in his defense. She was in no mood for fairy tales tonight.

NINETEEN

Drunk and disoriented, Johnny and Loretta sat in the middle of his living room floor, talking and laughing like a divorced couple who had decided to give it another go. They were reminiscing about a love affair that had never actually happened outside of Johnny's imagination. Their one date was only a limited source of material, but they milked it for all it was worth while both Johnny and Loretta tried to figure out, in a roundabout way, just what the hell she was doing in his apartment at three o'clock in the morning.

Johnny was showing Loretta his old video of one of his favorite flicks, 1957's *I Was A Teenage Werewolf,* and trying to explain to her who Michael Landon was.

"You know, the guy on 'Bonanza'," he said to her impatiently as she lay sprawled with him on his floor, empty champagne bottle and two half-filled glasses by their side.

"Never saw it," she said simply.

"How about 'Little House on the Prairie'?"

"Nope."

"'Highway to Heaven'?"

She perked up. "Oh, *that* guy? Yeah, yeah, I know him now. He looks so young here, I didn't recognize him. Especially with that werewolf makeup."

Johnny sighed. He had gone through three generations of Michael Landon before Loretta lit up. She was younger than he thought.

"Anyway, this was my favorite movie as a kid, used to watch it on the local spook show," Johnny explained.

"I like it. You ever see 'Titanic'? That's my *favorite* movie!" she declared proudly.

Johnny suddenly felt ill. "No, I had to work that year," he said snidely.

"You work too much, that's your trouble," Loretta said tipsily. She had been drunk when she showed up at his front door, probably even when she'd called him, Johnny thought. There was a good chance she wouldn't even remember this night. Maybe he should get it on tape somehow, but he lacked the equipment. Even if she slept with him, she'd probably deny everything, even to herself—especially if she slept with him. But that was okay—Johnny would know, and he'd hold it over her head forever, and have a happy memory to beat off to as well. "If you didn't work for wages," Loretta continued, "I mean if you had, like, a career, you could watch anything anytime. Hey, you got TiVo, right?"

"Nope."

"Why not?"

"Can't afford it."

"Exactly. Do you like 'Sex and the City'?"

"It's okay. Only saw it once, maybe. I like 'The Sopranos,' because I was raised in Jersey, but mostly I watch Me-TV reruns."

"Oh, you like old shows only. How about 'Moonlighting,' did you watch that?"

"I don't think so. Wasn't that on the same night as 'Miami Vice'?"

"Not, that was 'Dallas.' I think, I was pretty young back then. I'm afraid we have anything in common," Loretta sighed as she lay back on the floor as the spins set in. She closed her eyes and swallowed back the vomit in her throat. Johnny lay casually beside her, on his stomach.

Johnny cozied up drunkenly beside her, also tipsy though he'd switched to homemade Mai Tais out of a Disney World cup. "Loretta, look. I'm more of a simple, 'Honeymooners' kinda guy. That's just me. But opposites attract. Right? I mean, why else would you be here now?"

Loretta opened her eyes slowly, like a mummy awakened by a forbidden incantation. "What's *that* supposed to mean?"

"Well, well, I just mean, what are you *doing* here, anyway? I mean, not that it matters, I've always enjoyed your company."

"*I'll* say you have!" Loretta said, sitting upright too quickly and suffering a brief dizzy spell. "Can I lie down on your bed? I mean without you in it too?"

"Uh, okay. Sure." Like most males of the species, Johnny agreed to any and all prerequisites and denied any immoral purposes when courting the opposite sex. It was very similar to a politician's promises while campaigning— after the election, or erection, all former promises were null and void.

Johnny helped Loretta into the bed, laying her down gently. Almost unconsciously Loretta kicked off her pumps. She was wearing Capri pants and a thin cotton top, knowing the simplicity of this attire always drove the guys wild, because it was form fitting and so easy to remove. Loretta's eyes were closed but her mouth remained open. "You know why I'm here?"

"No," Johnny said, taking a chance and delicately stroking her hair.

"It's because..." The truth serum known as booze was taking effect, but Loretta had to confess quickly before she passed out and slept and then woke up with a hangover and no explanations.

Johnny touched her shoulder, "Loretta, please. Just..."

"Don't touch me! HELP! RAPE!"

"*Sssshhh*! What are you doing? Are you *nuts*?"

"*You assholes are all alike!*" Loretta shouted. "All you want is one thing! Well you're not going to get it from *me*, buster!"

"Loretta..."

"You really think I came over here to have sex with

you, don't you?"

"Actually, no, no I don't at all. I thought you came over to kill me, like you said."

"Oh, will you get *off* that already? What's your problem anyway? You're obsessed with me, that's your problem." Loretta abandoned her fruitless search for the chameleon-like pumps and lay back on the bed as the room whirled around her.

"Oh yeah?" Johnny said, faking exasperation. "Why don't you get off yourself, huh? You really think every guy you meet is dying of love for you, don't you?"

"No, just you. Well, not just you. But you're the only one who leaves me weird, funky notes in the restaurant."

"Weird? Funky? *Funky?*"

"Yeah, *you* know what I mean. Bizarre, warped, twisted, psychotic. You're probably a serial killer."

"Then why are you in my room in the middle of the night, if I'm so dangerous?"

"I told you why already. Don't make me repeat myself."

"You what? You didn't tell me a damn thing! I have no idea why you're here. All I said was it didn't matter."

"Then why are you harping on it? I'm tired. I should go."

"No!" Johnny caught himself. "I mean, you shouldn't. You're too drunk."

"Then call me a cab, because I'm not sleeping over here. I know that was your plan all along, like most male scum."

"Hey, whose idea was it to come over anyway?"

"Yours!"

"Mine? Where do you get that? You called me, remember?"

"Ha! That's a laugh! Why would I call you? What am I, crazy or desperate?"

"Um, well, I can only guess about the desperate part, but the crazy part seems pretty clear."

Suddenly Loretta was on a crying jag. She was sobbing into her hands as if mourning the cancellation of Friends all over again.

"What's wrong? What's the matter *now*?" Johnny fought an impulse to hold and comfort her, fearing further cries of rape piercing the tranquility of the neighborhood night.

"My father..." she began.

"Huh? Your father? What about him?"

"He, he, he, he...." She was heaving heavily now. "He, he doesn't give a damn about me. He never did. Tonight...tonight..."

"Yeah...?" This new vulnerability made Johnny feel somehow powerful, at least for the moment. He had to make it last long enough to get some reason out of her.

"Tonight, he came over, and...he....told me... if I didn't do what he wanted me to...he'd...he'd..."

"Yeah? Go on."

"He'd cut me off without a cent and disown me! But that's okay, I don't care about the money, it's just that, that he'd do something like that, like I'm just a trained seal or something, and he won't toss me any more fish if I don't perform right for the audience, balance a ball on my nose or something great like that he never cared about me or my mother. That's why she sleeps around I think...and...and..."

"Yeah? Go ahead. I'm listening. It's okay." Very cautiously, Johnny moved Loretta slowly into his arms so that as she spoke, stood her up, and moved her to the bed, where they became cozily entwined. There was nothing sexual about the embrace—Johnny wasn't low enough to take advantage of Loretta's high. Besides, he was perfectly comfortable just holding her. It was an entirely new and rewarding experience, however platonic.

"That's why you called me tonight, I think," Loretta continued, and Johnny didn't bother to correct her rewrite of history. "Because you knew I was lonely, that I needed a friend, someone who didn't want me to be their fantasy of someone I'm not, because I'm not that person to anyone, to my professors, to my father, to all those lame guys...or to you." She looked deeply into his eyes. Mascara streaked her cheeks, but she appeared more radiantly beautiful than ever to Johnny. The intensity of the moment made him dizzy, particularly after the roller coaster ride of emotions they had just endured, but he went with the flow. "You're not like the others, are you, Johnny? *Please* say you're not."

"I'm not," Johnny said dutifully.

"That's what I thought." She just stared into his eyes for several minutes. Johnny wanted to seize the moment and kiss her but the barrier of fear still existed.

"Loretta...why are you so...so..."

"Ambiguous and ambivalent toward you?"

"*Yeah*! Yeah, that's it. Exactly." Johnny sighed, grateful that Loretta was an English major after all.

"I think it's because..." Their faces grew closer. "Because...." Closer. "Because," she whispered just before their lips met.

Then lightning struck and thunder boomed, but not in the romantic sense. The front door to the studio burst open and Helen, panting, painted with blood, sweat, and tears, was standing with her Magnum pointed at them in the middle of the room.

"Who's the bitch?" Helen demanded after a very tense, mood-shattering moment.

"Helen?" Johnny said, rising slowly. "What—what are you *doing* here? Are you all right?" He got off the bed and walked toward her.

"I said," Helen hissed, keeping the gun trained on Loretta's chalk white forehead, "who, is, the, *bitch*?"

"I might ask the same question," Loretta said boldly, though it was really the liquor acting as an untimely ventriloquist.

"You really wanna know, *cunt*?" Helen said as she stepped toward Loretta, who rose as well, unafraid. When Johnny tried to hold Helen back she swung the gun backward and caught him on the jaw, sending him reeling to the floor. At the same time Loretta lunged for her but was quickly stopped by a savage 180 degree turn of Helen's gun, which instantly shattered Loretta's perfect nose. Blood sputtered from her nostrils as she fell backward, and Helen, in a blind rage, pounced on her and pistol-whipped her head and body into a bloody, bruised, broken mess.

"See how many contests you win *now*, Miss Fuckin' America," Helen said as she stood back to admire her work. Loretta was still barely conscious, but that was good—Helen wanted her to feel the pain.

Johnny got off the floor very slowly and whispered, "Helen, what are you doing?"

Helen was crying now, "I don't have time to talk, Johnny-O. I'm sorry if I crashed your little party, but something came up. We gotta go now."

The Leopard Man, sizing up the situation as another typical human catastrophe, dashed out the door and made for safer ground. Johnny noticed him and almost went after him, but Helen's outstretched .357 held him pat.

"Where d'ya wanna talk?" Johnny asked.

"I thought maybe this cafe I know in New Orleans," Helen said evenly, her tears drying abruptly. "Cafe du Monde, it's called. But we'll need cash. Tony hid my money from the bank job, and now I'll never find it."

"Why not?"

"Never mind that now. Just get goin'. Come on."

"Where? Which way?"

"Out the front fuckin' door, bright boy, where else?"

Johnny looked at the motionless heap that was Loretta, and a tear escaped his bloodshot eye "Helen, we can't just *leave* her here!"

"If you don't start moving, I'll fuckin' kill her. I mean it. I told you, I'm in a hurry."

"But, but, what about my life. My *movies*..."

With a whirl of disgust, Helen turned and shot out the screen of the TV, then lodged another bullet in his prized

VCR/DVD player. "Movie's over, Johnny-O," Helen said, swerving back to face him with the gun still pointed out. "Time to wake up and smell my pussy."

"Well, can I at least bring my laptop, and my novel?"

Helen considered this very thoroughly in less than five seconds. "Yes, but hurry," she snapped. "Those gunshots will have the cops here any minute."

Johnny quickly gathered up his equipment, then with Helen walking right behind him, gun pressed against the back of his neck, they marched out the door and into the Ferrari, keys still in the ignition, engine still running.

TWENTY

Detective Sonny Johnson drove across the Rickenbacker Causeway toward Key Biscayne, contemplating what he had seen in Miami Beach that morning. The sight of that pretty young girl—cracked jaw, shattered nose, black eyes, purple polka-dot flesh —had turned his stomach, even if she was a rich white man's daughter. He just couldn't believe that no one under his command or the boys with Homicide had been in the vicinity when Helen Black had finally paid their patsy a visit. True, it had been in the wee small hours of the morning, Frank Sinatra Time, but that should've been when they watched the closest, since Helen was habitually a nocturnal creature. And the State Trooper's report on the astonishing crime scene out by Pensacola had shaken up every local law enforcement agency in Florida, as well as DEA, FBI, and even CIA, since Tony Volare was quite a celebrity in the upper echelon of Government. New York was also quite disturbed by the brutal assassination of their top South Florida general. Even Vino Vinnie, next in line, was somewhat upset by the violent decapitation of his former superior. But now Vinnie was immediately in charge of everything—the operations as well as the investigation. The two boys who were found with the late Eddie were laid up in a private Mob facility, but as fucked up as they were, they could still identify the assassin. Detective Johnson knew where these boys were, since the Mob and the Miami PD had insiders on either side of the fence. Johnson also knew what the Mob knew—that Helen was a marked woman. It was just a question of stopping her from committing further acts of mayhem before she went down for the count.

Johnson had a file on Helen dating back years to her first arrests for Grand Theft Auto, possession, menacing, and assorted misdemeanors. Altogether she'd been in the slammer five times, but had always beaten her felony raps, which had been Johnson's first clue that she was a distant Mob relative. Helen was a well-known bad-ass on the South Beach circuit, and via liaisons with the Miami Beach PD, the Miami Dade PD had linked Helen with a string of robberies, assaults, and even fingered her as a possible accessory in several well-known Mob hits of high profile officials and crime figures alike, usually those visiting the city ostensibly as tourists. Generally these hits had occurred in Miami Beach hotels that Helen was known to frequent, and her tab had always been picked up by mysterious uncles and cousins. Beach Vice had even picked her up a few times for soliciting, though she was no street hooker, and they knew that. Even Helen drew the line somewhere, and prostitution was not her true racket. This was a well-known underworld fact, since several of Helen's alleged assault victims had been pimps trying to procure her services. Deep down, Johnson felt somewhat sorry for Helen, since her history of child abuse and neglect was the classic set-up for the lifestyle she had adopted—or rather, that had adopted her. But if she had really been the one who had knocked off Tony Volare, not even the cops could save her from a Death Row rap. Johnson couldn't help but wonder what had driven Helen to such an extreme act, though it probably wasn't vigilante justice for the public welfare. Tony was viewed more as a politician than a gangster in Florida high society, and while many wanted to see him go down eventually, no one was in a hurry to jeopardize their jobs in the process. It wasn't exactly clear who Tony's real friends were, for instance, and for all Johnson knew, the police commissioner was one of them. So everyone in his unit and the other units focused on the small fry, like Helen, who had been recently promoted to the ranks of Big Fish in this scum-ridden cesspool.

And now Helen had disappeared, probably across state lines, with their primary bait, Johnny Varga. But as far as Johnson was concerned, the line hadn't snapped yet, and if he couldn't reel his catch back in, he'd just swim out after it and capture it by hand. Helen's Cuban connections were far-reaching as well, and Detective Johnson was about to make an appointment with a certain El Doctor to discuss this very topic. Everyone knew El Doctor (real name: Miguel Garcia Lopez Coronado) was crooked. It was generally known that he operated a massive sideline of recreational stimulants, and that his so-called practice was a thin veil for this lucrative operation, but so far no one had been able to nail down enough evidence to secure a warrant. Johnson was hoping that if Helen was nabbed by the law before the Mob got to her, she could help bring down entire networks, though it would take some serious wheeling and dealing to turn her into a prize canary. But that was getting ahead of the game. Right now, the first order of business was to find her, by any means possible, which included those he couldn't file in his official report on the case.

TWENTY-ONE

Loretta Lynx had woken up to a nightmare, so she screamed and screamed until her private nurse ran into her bedroom to comfort her, to no avail. Loretta was hysterical, and had been ever since the ambulance had picked her up and she had refused to be admitted to the hospital, so her father had arranged for a special medical team to set up shop in the familiar comforts of her room, at great personal expense, but worth it to Loretta's terribly shaken father. Loretta's lacerations were only the external extent of the damage, so a special counselor was put on call in case Loretta came around and wanted to talk. Her father had excluded the media from any contact with her whatsoever, and Prissy was drinking like a fish in the living room of the apartment, listening to Wayne Newton records to help soothe her shattered nerves.

Despite numerous, impassioned requests, Loretta had been refused the right to look into any mirrors and view the condition of her bandaged countenance. Though delirious from the painkillers and Valium, Loretta managed to remain alert enough to realize that a shattered face meant shattered dreams in Hollywood, unless she wanted to give it a go as a character actress, in which case she'd have to draw upon an unknown reservoir of hidden acting talent to compensate for her shortcomings in the beauty department. Loretta knew, however humbly, that her looks were her chief meal ticket in the movie world, or would have been. Her father promised re-constructive surgery, but for that she'd have to confine herself to a hospital. Loretta *hated* hospitals. They represented trauma and pain and death, realities she didn't want to deal with. She was still in a state of denial, for her life had offered her a sense of complacency, if nothing else, before that marauding she-creature had ascended from the depths of Hell and inexplicably pulled Loretta, a complete stranger, down into the depths of depravity. It would be a while before the full effect of this detour from dreamland would even touch her. This is what worried her parents: the ramifications concerning her mental state. They had already consulted a top psychologist, and enlisted his future services in the event Loretta went into emotional withdrawal or exhibited symptoms of assorted depression syndromes. The scars would heal in time, but only the ones they could see.

Detective Johnson had given Loretta's father his home number in Key Biscayne to call day or night. Johnson, though limited to Armed Robbery investigations, was working with Homicide not only via his department, but had also dispatched inter-agency memos throughout the state, asking for help. The FBI would probably be brought in soon as an all-out woman hunt went into effect. The *Herald* was scrambling for further details for its morning edition, since it had missed the initial bulletin which went out past press time that day. Discovery of the dead mobsters was already national news, surpassing the daytime bank job, and once America's Most Wanted got wind of this, Helen would be a famous fugitive. *USA Today* was already trying to infiltrate the Lynx family, and Johnny Varga was gaining in notoriety with each passing hour. It was like a steadily unfolding National Reality Show. Carl Hiaasen again featured him in his column, though details regarding his private life were sketchy at best, since his co-workers at the lab refused to talk.

Loretta's father called Johnson at home while Prissy wailed in the background. "It's me," he barked. "Anything yet?"

Johnson had been trying to make love to his wife for the first time in two weeks when the phone had rang. He was trying to forget the outside world, if only for fifteen minutes, to appease his wife's pulsating needs, not to mention his own. "No sir, it's only been a day. But we're coordinating with several agencies and have issued a statewide APB."

"And you haven't found her yet?" Loretta's father fumed. "I want justice *now*!"

It's not like your little princess was kidnapped, asshole, Johnson thought to himself. "I understand your concern, sir, but your daughter is safe now, and we assure you that the person responsible for this unfortunate incident will be brought before a court of law and punished." Johnson hated talking in these phony, stilted sentences, but this was protocol when dealing with the esteemed citizenry of our fine, fucked up land. "Please be patient."

"Don't patronize me, damn it, just get *on* it! Why are you at home, anyway?"

Slow burn. "I have a wife and child to take care of, sir, as if that is any of your business." Johnson was breathing heavily now, pissed off and bored with this obnoxious, over-educated peckerwood. The guy would probably start calling him "nigger" if he hung on the phone any longer. "Whoa! There goes my cell phone!" Johnson lied. "Could be a lead, gotta go, bye now! I'll be in touch." He hung up. His wife had gone to the kitchen to fix herself a drink.

Back in Loretta's apartment, Loretta was screaming and the nurse was trying in vain to calm her down. Loretta's father came rushing in to help.

"I don't want you!" Loretta screamed. "I want Johnny! This is all *his* fault!"

"Who?" asked Loretta's father, intrigued by the name of a new player. "*Johnny*, you said, pumpkin? Who's Johnny?"

"Johnny!" Loretta repeated, then she passed out again.

"She must mean Johnny Varga," the nurse said as she pulled the covers over Loretta.

"Who the hell is that?"

"I heard it on the radio. That's the guy who lives in that

apartment she was in. Isn't that her boyfriend though?"

"Oh, him. No! No, of course not. I've never heard of him before this. For all I know he kidnapped her and was holding her there for ransom before it went haywire. Why else would she be spending time with such a *loser*?"

TWENTY-TWO

Just outside Tallahassee, Helen dumped the Ferrari by the side of the road, flagged down a passing Mustang which contained two young hippies smoking weed and listening to old Grateful Dead songs, forced them out at gunpoint, and then ordered Johnny to get in and drive while she caught up on her sleep. Johnny was tired too, but he was also wired and fearful for his life, so the adrenaline rush would get them at least out of the Florida panhandle and into Georgia, maybe even Louisiana. Johnny had always wanted to go there anyway, though in more relaxed circumstances. Toting his laptop around was a cumbersome drag, but he was anxious to plug it in some dingy hotel room in the French Quarter and chronicle his experiences on the road with a homicidal nymphomaniac. He just prayed that his record of the journey would not be published posthumously. He felt like a cast member of *The Walking Dead.*

Johnny was still too deeply in shock to assimilate all that had happened that night, and as dawn broke over the Gulf of Mexico, he was too intoxicated by the sheer adventure of it all to let himself piss on his own parade down Danger Street. Images of Loretta, both before and after her work over from Helen, haunted his mind, but he blocked them out in favor of thoughts regarding his own immediate welfare and future prospects. He was now without a job, without an apartment, and without his movie collection. This was an indefinite state of affairs, but highly uncomfortable while at the same time strangely exhilarating.

As he drove forward into the jaws of Destiny, he

glanced over at the sleeping demon-angel by his side, awed by her innocent beauty while unconscious. What was the secret behind her schizoid tendencies? It was a mystery which Johnny, willing or not, was already trapped in. While Helen slept—the Magnum lying innocuously on her lap, pointed at Johnny—she dreamed. She dreamed of a perfect world wherein people got away with murder and lived happily ever after. She dreamed of marital bliss with a stable man who would help her overcome her erratic, destructive impulses, who would rehabilitate her spirit. She dreamed that her entire life up till this moment had only been a vicious nightmare, and that when she woke up she would be starting fresh with a young man she loved.

But instead, she woke up with the first rays of dawn in her eyes, illuminating the dirty bandage on her arm, the bloodstains on her blouse, the tearstains on her face. In the driver's seat was the man who had nearly turned her in. *Fucker*.

"All right, stop the fuckin' car," Helen demanded, startling Johnny from his own daydreaming.

"What? Where? Right *here*?"

"Yeah, right here. Right fuckin' *here*, right fuckin' *now*, motherfucker."

"I thought you wanted to talk..."

"STOP!"

Johnny pulled over to the side of the road and they sat amid the peaceful stillness of the morning.

"Climb in back," she commanded. Reluctantly Johnny complied. Helen climbed back with him, forcibly positioned him on his back, mounted him, pulled his Bermuda shorts down, slipped out of her own cut-off jeans, stuck the Magnum in his mouth, cocked the piece, and rode him with animalistic urgency. Johnny's meek protests were muffled by the cold, hard steel bumping against his tonsils, and as Helen, drenched in her own sweat which mingled with the dried blood and tears, began to find her rhythm, she threatened, "*Come before I do and I'll blow your head off!*"

Johnny believed her, so despite the intensity of the moment, or perhaps because of it, he managed to hold back his own orgasm until he was damn sure she'd achieved consummate release, which she did, finally, shaking and shouting with unbridled passion. Johnny came in delirious tandem. When it was over, and Helen lay panting on his chest, Johnny gently removed the barrel from his mouth and pointed it out the window over his head. Abruptly Helen, who seemed to be in a trance, jerked back on the trigger, and shards of glass exploded all over them and the road outside.

"*Shit*!" Johnny yelled, sitting upright, pulling his pants up in a hurry. "You sure know how to spoil a moment, don't you?"

Unfazed by the shards of glass, Helen pinned him back down and sat on him, sticking the gun point blank between his eyes, and then pulling the trigger. *Click*.

She had spent her last bullet. Johnny had still pissed in his pants, though, and a change of wardrobe would be as necessary as a change of scenery. Helen sat on top of him, laughing, drowning in this sea of blood, sweat, tears, semen, and now urine. Johnny felt like all the fluids he had once transported had been poured on him at once, and he was trapped in the backseat with them, being transported to a lab for experiments and tests, to determine what had infected him. But he already knew what was wrong with him.

Johnny resumed driving while Helen scouted for a filling station, since they were running low on gas as well as cash. When they finally found one, she knocked it over while Johnny was taking another piss in the restroom, but there was no money to be found in this little hick pit-stop, so all they got was fuel, enough to continue their journey into a warm, wet place Johnny had only visited in his own dreams.

TWENTY-THREE

El Doctor had lost his patience. Helen was so out of control now she was in orbit around a planet that hadn't even been discovered yet. The extensive coverage of her rampage across South Florida paled beside his throbbing jealousy of her kidnap victim, now widely assumed to be an accomplice, however involuntary. Why Johnny? He was a scrawny, white, poor, white, stupid, white, boring, white, weird, white, know-nothing jerk-off. El Doctor hated the blacks in and out of his trade as well, but not as much as the whites. Blacks were predictable, lowlife jungle bunnies, in his estimation, whereas whites were sneaky, high-class cutthroat deviates that could get away with anything because of the fucking politics of this fucking society. Cubans had made vast inroads during the Reagan and two Bush Administrations, but there still existed a subliminal hostility that prevented them from extending their prowess and message of peaceful co-existence outside of Miami. After leaving Cuba, either exiled or escaped, the Florida Cubans still lived on an island, far away from mainland America, the land of opportunistic white money-talking bullshit-walking assholes.

El Doctor never thought of the bleached blond (but growing out fast) Helen as being white, since she was not only a natural brunette with a deep tan, but she talked like most Cubans who could speak English talked. Plus she was as much an outsider, because of her tragic background and career choices, as most *Marielitos*. This was a Class struggle, not just an ongoing race riot, after all. El Doctor himself had come over on that infamous boat many years ago, and had quickly re-established himself as the local criminals' go-to physician, though in a more civil, law-abiding community, where criminals did not always have to hide as long as they obeyed basic laws of symbiosis. El Doctor's business as a medical practitioner thrived largely due to his under-the-counter prescriptions. Helen had been a frequent client of his services, like the time she was nearly nailed by an undercover narc in the Everglades, one who nearly took her arm off with a concealed .25 at close range before she took it from him and blew his face off. Then there was the time she was nearly raped near the lighthouse on Cape Florida in Key Biscayne, late one summer night while stoned out her wits. She knifed her attacker, a hapless transient who picked the wrong target, and let him drown in the thick, merciless waters of Biscayne Bay. Helen, a knife wound in her ribcage, had managed to call El Doctor's cell, and he alerted Tony, who always knew where Helen was in those days. Tony drove El Doctor out to the lighthouse in his private speedboat, and then took her to one of the supposedly abandoned stilt houses in the middle of the bay, which served as one of El Doctor's medical outposts. Helen stayed there and recuperated with El Doctor by her side. That had been the first time and place they had made love, a move El Doctor had made even in the face of his fear of Tony Volare. Helen seemed worth it, and she was. Until now.

The phone rang in his legit home office on Flagler in Little Havana. It was the day after the news had broken all over the place about Helen's alleged whack-out of Tony Volare, a speculation in the newspapers but a given fact in certain private sectors of the population, up and down the Eastern seaboard. El Doctor was in the midst of the charity clinic work he did to promote his rep in his community, something that had prevented the authorities from cracking down too hard on his suspicious operations. "Hello, who the hell is this? I told my nurse I was in the middle of..."

"Fuck you, it's me. Vinnie," said a strong,

uncomfortably familiar voice. "I'm in Atlantic City now to deal with stuff, but I'm comin' down later tonight to settle this fuckin' mess down there. What I need from you is the dope of where the hell our little friend is right now."

"Vinnie. Vinnie, please, por favor, I am busy right now," El Doctor said, turning his back on the skinny five year old boy's baleful eyes, wide with wonder and empty from malnutrition. A crack baby wailed in the waiting room. El Doctor had no time for these pasta-peckered meatballs. "Let me get back to you, heh? We talk tonight when you get into town."

"I need advance info, Doc, so don't fuck around with me," Vinnie said. Vino Vinnie was barely forty but had already gained a prominent position within Mob ranks, working his way up from torpedo in Brooklyn to Lieutenant and now to General of South Florida operations, if all went well. New York had told him his promotion was not automatic—this wasn't a fucking Wall Street firm—but that if he could ice the bitch that took out Tony, he would be seriously considered for the job. Vinnie had the hots for Helen as much as the next guy, but he needed that promotion, with all its perks and benefits. His wife was pregnant with their third kid, an accident since the Church forbid birth control and Vinnie hated rubbers except with Helen, who insisted on it due to her promiscuity ("I ain't playin' Italian roulette with my twat," she had told him). Vinnie had made some investments that had fallen through, especially in Atlantic City, where he had a piece of a failing casino. He also owned a few horses on a farm in Pennsylvania that ran in Philly on a regular basis, and lost money on an equally regular basis. Vinnie was desperate.

"I don't want to do Helen," Vinnie told El Doctor, "but she fucked up in a major league way. I mean, c'mon, you know the score, you must've heard what she did. She's fuckin' big time wackoville, mang. I mean, have you talked to her? What the fuck is this shit, PBS or what? What's her fuckin' disease?"

"I have lost touch with her," El Doctor lied. "She took up with this strange guy, you know, this fucking white cocksucker, uh, excuse me," El Doctor caught himself, not wishing the five year old to repeat to his mother the nice words he had learned from the nice doctor. "I have not seen her since before she knocked over that grocery and shot that Indian."

"Bullshit. Tony told me otherwise before he bought the fuckin' farm," Vinnie said, sitting in his hotel suite facing the grimy Atlantic, watching his favorite movie, *Angels With Dirty Faces*, on TV with the sound low, since he had seen it so many times since that he had the whole movie memorized. Jimmy Cagney was his idol—he never understood Tony's fascination with Mickey Rourke, who was also pals with Vinnie, though Vinnie secretly thought Rourke was a cheap Brando-Cagney imitator. But then who wasn't in his circles. "Listen, Doc, I got some people coming up in a minute to talk some shop, then I'm flyin' down and payin' you a visit. You got it, *mang*? So if you don't know where Lady Scarface is, you better fuckin' find her quick, cause New York knows you, knows you were doin' her, knows Tony was doin' her, knows I was doin' her, and now she's doin' herself real good, but for the last time. *Capisce? Ciao*." Vinnie hung up just as El Doctor was winding up his heated reply.

Flustered, El Doctor sent his young patient prematurely out to his worried mother, and then hung the NO MAS HOY sign on his door, turning away the poor crack family. But there was one more person in the waiting room, a tall, handsome, light-skinned black guy dressed in an Armani suit and flashing a badge. El Doctor groaned as the cop, Detective Sonny Johnson from Armed Robbery, escorted him back into the clinic and closed the door behind them.

"I know *nada*, okay?" El Doctor said, pacing around the room and fussing with instruments and bottles as if very busy. "Why you hassle me, huh?"

"Cut the crap, Doc," Johnson said wearily, sipping the shitty coffee he had taken from the lobby. "This part of your racket? Poison your patients in the damn lobby with this shit?"

"You don't like it? Pour it out. It's free, right? So nobody bitches. Except you."

"Don't give me attitude, Doc. We got a file on you that could have you practicing medicine from a Rayford cell."

"Then why don't you, heh? Heh? Because you got nothing you can use, *mang*. I know, you know, we all know. So you got nothing on me, don't bother me, I am a, how you people say, a pillar of the community?"

"Caterpillar is more like it. Look, I wouldn't have come down here and embarrassed you if you had've simply returned my call yesterday and just come down to the station. Why are you so paranoid if we got nothing on you, Doc?"

"Who calls back a cop, huh? Nobody *I* know."

"Precisely. Nobody you know would. Like this Helen babe."

"I don't know who you're talking about, so..."

"Can it, alright? Because we know voucher, we have surveillance photos of you together in and out of motels from Bayshore Drive to Key Largo, Doc, so just forget the act and tell me where I can find her."

"Why does everybody keep asking me that today?" El Doctor said in a huff, instantly regretting it.

"Everybody? Like who? Tony Volare's boys? Vinnie the Vine, for instance? We know from the grapevine Vinnie's next in line. It's a small town in a small world, Doc. Everybody knows somebody who knows everybody. Ain't no such thing as a nobody around here. So make it easy on yourself. You help us out, we'll take the heat off from New York."

El Doctor laughed. "Yeah, right, *mang*. In the cooler you'll take the fucking heat off. But even there I am not safe if I play this game, you know? Vinnie—and I am not saying he is my friend, but I have heard things, like the Mob wants *blood*, not your kind of justice."

"So what else is new? We'll give you a fair shake, which is more than New York will give you if you help them out. You think they want to deal with Cubans? Not if they don't have to. You know how they are."

"I know, I know," El Doctor said, laughing more, shaking his head. "One big happy fucking family, this world, heh? Everybody loves everybody, heh? Fuck. But the thing is, you know, I really cannot help anybody. I take no sides with this thing. Helen, I love her, you know? No, you don't understand. Just don't let my wife see no fucking photographs, okay? And if I hear from Helen, I let you know."

"And Vinnie?"

"I will let him know too. I got no choice. Like I said, I take no sides here, except my own. But Helen..." El Doctor let out a sigh. "She fucked up. She's on her own."

"Not entirely."

"Oh, you mean that strange white guy?"

"Johnny Varga. Sounds like he has some Spanish blood, too. You know him?"

"No. I meet him once. He is...I don't know. I don't understand Helen's attraction for him, you know? But I think they are together now, I mean as a team, like. They are their own thing now. No me, no Vinnie, no Mob. She is on her own now. That is why she is fucked, no?"

Johnson laid his card on the table and opened the door to leave. "We'll see," he said, and then he finally left.

TWENTY-FOUR

As New Orleans came into view, it finally began to dawn on Johnny that not only was his movie collection a casualty of Helen's collision course with his destiny, but so were his two other most prized possessions: his Edsel and The Leopard Man. As shock gave way to clarity, Johnny was beginning to realize that his life had been severely, irrevocably altered, with a force and suddenness that made hurricanes seem like sweet, soft breezes from Neverland. At the same time, Helen was coming to terms with the reality of the predicament she had put not only herself in, but also this kind stranger. Fucking his brains out as sublimation of her anxiety was only a temporary solution; eventually, and the sooner the better, she'd have to devise a master plan to extricate them both from this disaster.

They stopped by the Mississippi River briefly to bathe and catch their breath. Afterward, it was time for *café au lait* and *beignets* at her favorite cafe on Earth, Cafe Du Monde, on Decatur near Jackson Square, right on the Mississippi. Helen directed Johnny through the narrow streets, past the old buildings with the ornate balconies, the throngs of tourists and street musicians, and ordered him to park the Mustang on the bank of the River and leave it. They wouldn't be using the same car when they left town, whenever that would be. Later, Helen might go back and drive it out to the bayou and ditch it there, but right now she was too tired and excited about being back in the French Quarter, her favorite refuge from the outside world. Tony had brought her here on several of his business trips, Mob conventions and so forth, and Helen had fallen in love with the foreign-feeling ambience and steamy sensuality of the food and music. Johnny was likewise enthralled by this new world, and for a while he forgot about the Edsel and the poor, lost Leopard Man.

Helen didn't want to sit outdoors, so they went inside to the air-conditioned interior, which offered respite from the sticky, midday heat. Helen was trying to decide which hotel to check them into once they got some money, and she was also trying to think of how to latch onto some quick cash without causing too much of a stir. The *cafe au lait* was sweeter but not as strong as the *cafe con leche* back home in Miami, but together with the powdery beignets a sufficient sugar rush was created which would kick her brain into high gear. Johnny was quiet, in a daze, absorbing the atmosphere as he ate and sipped mechanically, pretending he was on an episode of Bourbon Street Beat. Then Helen broke the spell, as usual.

"So why'd you turn the car around and fuck me up?" Helen asked suddenly, staring him right in the face with fire in her eyes, fire which flickered softly, as if emanating from a fireplace within a romantic setting, but a flame which threatened to rage out of control any second and burn the harmony to ashes.

"I *didn't* turn it around," Johnny said weakly, avoiding her glare. "I just kept going and sort of crashed into the meter. I mean, you have to admit, you kind of took me by surprise with that stunt."

"Yeah, right, Johnny-O, like you didn't know that was what I was gonna do. Don't act fuckin' stupid, I know you better."

"Are you saying I knew you were going to rob the bank?"

"Of course you did. Why else would you have driven me there then actually sit and wait? Why didn't you go in with me to make sure I was good?"

"We were parked in a yellow zone, or a white zone, or..."

"Hell, you're parked in the fuckin' Twilight Zone, motherfucker, that's *your* problem," Helen laughed, polishing off her *beignets* and signaling the busboy to bring her another, if he would. He would, of course, because Helen was Helen. "You're fooling yourself if you think you're just along for the ride now. You're like me, and if you had any balls you'd admit it."

"I don't believe this," Johnny said, sitting back in his chair and trying his best to come off flabbergasted by her character appraisal. "How do you, I mean, where do you get this stuff? You *kidnapped* me!"

Helen howled with laughter. The busboy, a Mexican, laughed as well as he brought her more beignets. Johnny passed when he was asked if he also wanted more. "I put the snatch on you, is that what you think? Well, I put you in my snatch a few times, but next you'll say I *raped* you."

The Magnum was packed under Helen's blouse, in her crotch, and Johnny almost hoped it would go off and really give her a thrill. "You did sort of rape me in the car. Did you really have to stick that gun in my mouth?" Johnny kept his voice low, but nobody was paying attention to him anyway. Only to Helen.

"You *loved* it," Helen declared dryly, flirting with the busboy across the room. "When we get a room you can stick the gun in *my* mouth, if ya want. Or anywhere else, for that matter. Tony used to get me off with his gun all the time." She stopped, and her eyes began to water. "Tony," she whispered to herself. "Oh, well, what's done is done," she said after a moment to mourn, "We need to find a way to get some money fast. Any ideas?"

"Helen, we really have to get something straight here," Johnny said, trying to muster some authority in his voice.

"Oh yeah? Like what?"

"Well, I mean, I miss my cat. I'd like to go back to Miami soon. I mean this is a nice vacation and all, but..."

"We can't go back to Miami. Ever. End of story."

"Why? What happened?"

"Buy a newspaper. It should be in there someplace, even here."

Johnny noticed an abandoned Times-Picayune on a nearby empty table, but felt too sick and weak to walk over and pick it up. "Maybe later," he groaned. "I can't imagine what this could be. Or rather, I could imagine. I just don't want to. Anyway, let's get a hotel room. I'm bushed. I don't want to leave my laptop in the trunk of the Mustang for too long, you know. Might get ripped off."

"So? We can always buy another laptop. Or *steal* one."

"But what about my manuscript? Can't replace that. You don't care anything about me, do you? Not as a person, I mean. I'm just a piece of meat to you."

Helen laughed. "Johnny, believe me, if I didn't like you as a person, you'd be *dead*. Not like you're a sugar daddy. You really fucked me up back in the Gables. My plan was to drive straight here, but instead I had to go through all this other crap that's just gotten me in bigger trouble than usual. So be grateful. Anyway, now you're, whatchacallit, implicated and all."

"Huh? Bullshit."

"You know what I mean. I *hate* when you act stupid. Makes me like you not as much. If I get bored with you, Johnny, you're *fucked*. So stay cool or else you're out on your ass."

Johnny just moaned and put his head down on the table. Helen gently stroked his hair for a few minutes, and he began to fall asleep. Then suddenly she grabbed a hunk of his hair and jerked it hard enough to make him sit up and yell, garnering unwanted attention from the patrons.

"*Ow*! What's the big idea?"

"So how do you know this slut whose face I had to bash in?"

Johnny moaned and put his head on the table again. "None of your goddamn business," he said lowly.

"*What* did you say to me?" Helen said in mock-shock.

"You heard me."

"Good boy, Johnny. I like talk like that. Don't take too much crap off me or I'll lose respect for you, and you don't want that. Now then. Let's put our heads together and try to figure out a way to make some money for a hotel room tonight. I know a few places we can go where they won't remember me or recognize me from when I came here with Tony. Johnny. Johnny. *Johnny?*"

But Johnny was fast asleep on the table by now. Helen let him rest while she signaled the busboy for more beignets, paying for them with the money she took from Johnny's wallet. Then, after about half an hour, she got up and left. With the wallet.

TWENTY-FIVE

Sonny Johnson had toyed with the idea that Helen Black had not been the shooter in the Volare case, and the laid-up torpedoes were only spitting out sour grapes because they had let someone get the better of them. Of course, if Helen had been the shooter—and the Magnum bullet shells scattered at the crime scene indicated this, since they matched the slugs pulled out of the dead Indian—then the Mob boys would have felt even more humiliated, figuratively emasculated by this Annie Oakley from Hell.

Johnson hadn't informed Homicide of his sideline investigations, such as his chat with El Doctor, a figure Homicide had only heard idle rumors about, whereas Johnson had El Doc's number since back in his Vice days. Johnson carried a Browning 9mm in addition to the standard issue .38, and hardly anyone knew about this either, but that was okay, since side arms were regularly confiscated and listed as "missing" from crime scenes. It was a war out there, and artillery was pretty much up for grabs. Such conscientious policies were based on street survival, not rigid Departmental protocol, which was archaic in many respects. At least Johnson wasn't on the take, despite several opportunities, though he knew which of his fellow officers were, and it bothered him, but still, he was no snitch. He had no respect for these guys, especially when there was an underground police family fund derived from drug bust money that went unrecorded. Plenty to go around for everybody who wanted those unofficial "bonuses." Johnson realized many of the cops he worked with in the so-called war on crime were even more crooked than their adversaries, and many others were redneck ex-Marine types who only wanted the power and authority to carry and flaunt legal firearms in dirt bag neighborhoods. These badge-flashing bigots made Johnson physically ill, and there were times when he wished people like Helen were on his side.

Sometimes he admired the Mob's code of ethics, how they stuck to their illegal principals, only killed their own, often laundered money through charitable venues, and would call him a "nigger" to his face rather than kiss his ass like the crackers on the Force often did. But at the same time, he was ambivalent toward the Mob's business techniques—he couldn't condone the exploitation of junkie hookers and gambling gonzos, though whores and bookies were way down on the list of the public offenders.

Secretly, he admired their lifestyle, but hated their methods. In some ways, they fought the same enemy: corporate white bread America, the hypocrites in public office, the yuppie real estate tycoons turning Florida into an amusement park divided into Condoland, Beachland, and Swampland. All of these new tall, gleaming, terrorist target high-rises sprouting up like money trees were an eyesore, too. Johnson and the Mob hated each other, but they also had mutual enemies. And stuck in the middle of this confluence of chaos was Helen. Johnson couldn't help but feel sorry for her, in a way, though dusting that Indian was pretty cold-blooded, even in self-defense, as the videotape plainly showed. A jury would still fry her hot little ass because she was there to rip the guy off and he was only attempting to defend his property. Whether the law or the Mob caught up with her, she was dead meat. What a waste, Johnson thought to himself. If only there was a way to save her, and making her turn on her old cronies was a long shot. The best the D.A. could do for her in exchange for a rollover would be a long-ass prison term with remote possibility of parole. Inside, the bull dyke inmates and pervert guards would ruin her as irrevocably as the gas chamber. The Mob could reach her in the slammer, too, and if by some miracle she was granted a full walk and put in the Witness Protection Program, it would only be a matter of time before she blew her cover. She wasn't the type to settle down and work as a hostess in Omaha or some shit. These was only one way to save her—find her on his own, try to cut her a deal wherein he could nail a few dopers to ease his conscience and do his job, then let her go as a floating informant, not necessarily on the Mob hierarchy, but on smalltime stuff—local pushers poisoning the projects, shit like that. If the Mob, the Government, and the Police Department could invent and reinvent a flexible code of ethics as circumstances warranted, so could he. He'd just have to be crafty enough to get away with it, like they were.

"What in the world are you thinking about?" his wife asked that night over dinner, after he had been silently preoccupying himself with these thoughts for some time.

"I don't know...it's that chick, Helen. Somehow...I don't know. I identify with her."

"What? She's crazy and white. Where's the connection? Escapes the hell out of me."

"Her background file. I'll let you check it out sometime, you feel like it. She was born in the gutter, like we were, sort of, and she's gonna die there, too—unlike *us*."

"There's still the chance some crackhead could gun you down in some dark alley one night, don't forget," his wife reminded him. "Not a night goes by I don't lie awake and think about that. Every time the phone rings and you ain't home..."

"I knew, I know, baby. But I told you, I'm on a quest-like, not to clean up the whole city or change the world, just save a few lost souls if I can. And that little white babe is one lost soul."

TWENTY-SIX

Helen was once again considering her plan of going to school and becoming an accountant, since she was very good with numbers. She couldn't go on like this forever, that was for certain. As she sat on the Moonwalk looking out at the Mississippi, and dusk was settling over Algiers and the steamboats and the dark, decadent Quarter where she felt so at home and at peace, Helen was sobbing secretly to herself. She had another one of those headaches, the first one in over a month. El Doctor had claimed they were symptoms of withdrawal, since she had kicked several drug habits before in preparation for her master plan—to assimilate into a society that rejected her—but a prison quack had told her she had a small cyst on her brain. Nothing deadly, but a minor operation was recommended. The same quack had then offered to perform the operation in exchange for sex, or at the very least a blowjob, and Helen had beaten the shit out of him with a medical tome and then nearly strangled him to death with his own stethoscope before a gang of guards pulled her off him. He waved his right to press assault charges, fearing his advances would gain credence from the female warden, a bull dyke who had the hots for Helen herself, but never did anything about it, since she was a woman with a conscience as well as a mustache. So the upshot of the whole raw deal was that Helen wasn't even sure if the quack had been making the cyst thing up just to get in her pants. The headaches were real, though—and they weren't the migraines that sometimes plagued her, either. These were different, very disorienting and disturbing, like migraines, but deeper, more penetrating, and they seemed to last longer with each successive attack. At least Tony would never have any more headaches. She had done him that favor, if nothing else.

Sometimes she feared she had something really serious, like a tumor, or something a friend of hers in a State home had suddenly died from one night, an aneurism. Helen remembered the agony, the chalk-white death mask of the boy just before he unleashed his final blood-curdling scream. Something in his head had popped, and that was it. Helen wondered if her own brain was equipped with a similar time bomb, another gift from God, whom she still believed in, even though she couldn't figure out what she had done in the womb to piss Her off so badly that She would let her loose in such a hostile world. Helen wondered whether Johnny had woken up in the nearby cafe yet, and if he had wandered off in search of her. She had spent his last few bills on a Hurricane at Pat O'Brien's and some gumbo—some of which she had saved for him in a little to-go cup—but she planned to pay him back sometime before midnight, her deadline for brainstorming a quickie finance plan, short term if not long term, so they could rent a hotel room and fuck and sleep some more, not to mention eat. Helen loved room service, even if it reminded her of prison, except the food was better. At this moment, she felt like she had while on parole for previous busts—still in prison, only on the outside, like an outpatient. An out-prisoner. No matter where she ran or what she did, she felt trapped. It was wearing her down. That's probably why she got so many headaches, she figured. Just plain stress.

Helen got up to look for Johnny, which wouldn't be tough in such a small town, but she believed he had stayed at the cafe, either still asleep or waiting for her to return. When she walked into the Cafe Du Monde, she saw she had been right. Johnny was still sound asleep on the table. The Mexican busboy was just getting off work, and he asked Helen if she'd care to join him for a drink, and she declined.

Then she quickly reconsidered and took him by the hand as they walked back into Decatur Street. Suddenly a plan had dawned on her, and she needed the Mexican's help.

Johnny raised his head and opened his eyes in time to see Helen wandering off with the busboy, and he quickly scrambled to his feet and ran out after them. It began to rain just as he stepped out the door, and Helen and the Mexican blended with the crowd as they headed up past Jackson Square. Johnny, still feeling hazy and confused, waking up in this rain-and-neon *Blade Runner* type landscape far from familiar surroundings, from his movie collection, his car and his cat, was running as if trying to find his way out of a dark alley, an alley he had always wanted to explore, but now he only wanted to escape, even though it was too late, and he was running in the wrong direction.

TWENTY-SEVEN

"I really think you should give her a break," El Doctor said to Vino Vinnie that night at The Palace Bar & Grill on Ocean Drive in Miami Beach. Vinnie loved watching the palm trees sway in the gentle evening breezes. It brought out the poet in him.

"Y'know, sometimes I worry I might have early Alzheimer's," Vinnie said with a scary grin, "because, I swear, I do not recall asking you what you thought, Doc. And why else would you volunteer such useless fuckin' information as what you're thinkin' unless I asked for your lousy opinion? I *must* have amnesia, whaddya think?"

El Doctor, realizing Vinnie's torpedoes were hidden somewhere in the placid setting, said nothing, because if he said what he was thinking he'd be bobbing up in Biscayne Bay the next morning.

"See? Now I remember asking you what you thought, and you have nothing to say," Vinnie sighed. "I should see a doctor. Oh, yeah—you *are* a fuckin' doctor."

El Doctor still said nothing. He just stared into his empty wine glass and pouted. "Y'know, Doc, I know what's eatin' ya," Vinnie said, "Or rather, what *ain't* eatin' ya no more. This Helen broad, you know I done her, right? This Helen broad, see, we thought she was the answer to all our prayers, like God was this big pimp in the sky, right? But God ain't no pimp. The Devil is. See, that chick is the spawn of Satan, Doc. I finally figured it out on the way down here today. That's why she has to be stopped. She's the fuckin' anti-Christ, is what she is. There's no other way a little chick like her could take out Tony and Eddie and nearly waste two other experienced bodyguards without the hand of Lucifer himself behind the whole job. It's Armageddon, Doc. Apocalypse fuckin' now. Not later—*now*. Tonight. She's out there, Doc. The devil's daughter. And it's our job—with God's help —to stop her. She's evil, Doc, pure and simple. She's like this witch, see, this witch that has us under her spell. Well, wake up Doc. Snap out of it. You're possessed. And if you don't come around and see the light, we'll knock those lights out for good. *Capisce?*"

Finally, El Doctor felt prompted to speak up on his behalf. "Vinnie, you are *crazy*. She is just a fucked up little whore, nothing more."

"You ever hear of Santeria, Doc? That voodoo type shit they got down here?"

"*Si,* but..."

"I think she got into it, one way or another. She liked to fuck niggers, that chick. I think an evil spirit got into her through some big black cock one night, and then from then on Satan just took over. See, I got it figured this way: the niggers, 'specially down here, and over in 'Nawlins, where I'm off to next, see, they use this voodoo shit to infiltrate the population and take us over and then out, little by little. That's why they're evil, Doc. I ain't prejudiced, ya understand—not *all* niggers are into voodoo. Some have found God and are saved. But the ones down here—they're out for blood, Doc, and I don't mean just chicken blood. Your people are into this religious shit, too, so take heed, Doc. I'm just tryin' to help out here. Helen is a spy from the other side, Doc. Lucifer's mistress, Mata Hari from *Hell.*"

"You say you're going to New Orleans?" El Doctor interrupted, getting anxious. He'd never realized just how insane Vinnie really was until now. Perhaps the promise of impending power had driven him over the edge, like so many marauders of the past—Napoleon, Hitler, Jimmy Swaggart.

"Yeah, but you ain't invited, so what do you care?" Vinnie said.

"You really think she is there? Why? She never mentioned it to me."

Vinnie smiled like a snake. "Of course not, Doc. She hasn't told you anything, remember? Hell, maybe *you're* the one with amnesia. But I know a quick cure for that, don't worry." Vinnie patted his breast pocket casually.

"Why you threaten me, *mang*?" El Doctor said. "I never fucked you over, or Tony or anyone in jour organization. Our interests have never conflicted, since we have our territories and you have yours, and I always respect that. So why you talk to me like I am a fucking peasant just off a fucking banana boat? *Heh*?"

Vinnie wasn't smiling now, just staring out at the swaying palm trees, thinking poetic thoughts, epic, even Shakespearean. "Tony is dead," he said after a moment, and then he stood up, adjusted his jacket and tie, and walked off. Immediately two swarthy bodyguards who were sitting at the bar dressed like tourists from Philadelphia walked out after him. One walked by El Doctor at the table, pinched his cheek, and then slapped it softly. The other winked at El Doctor as they followed Vinnie up the block to the limo waiting in front of the Carlyle Hotel. Vinnie climbed inside, followed by his boys, and the limo drove off like a hellbound hearse.

TWENTY-EIGHT

Loretta Lynx stared into her little plastic hand mirror with the pink plastic rose petals lining the rim as if transfixed by a late night horror movie, something with lots of gore and walking corpses and imperiled virgins. She was wondering if she would indeed have a future in horror movies with her new face, though the nurse and the doctor and her parents had tried to assure her that the bruises and scars would fade with time. Anyway, "*who cares what a lawyer looks like*?," her father had said, making a major diplomatic *faux pas* and causing his daughter to retreat into a temporary state of self-imposed autism. Prissy camped out on the couch while Daddy Lynx attended his business meetings and made deals and popped in once in a while to see how his princess was getting along, promising her that justice was just around the corner. Loretta knew from recent experience that whatever waited around the corner was often attacked by something unknown and unexpected hiding in the alley.

Besides, Detective Johnson had instructed his wife to screen all calls for the time being, since he regretted giving Daddy Lynx his private number. The man felt free to dial it like it was a neurotic's hotline for salvation. Johnson had changed his number from 1-800-SAVE ME to 1-900-SCREW YOU. So Lynx felt left out in the cold on this one, even as he was lying to his daughter about the temperature of the trail.

All in all, Loretta had mixed feelings about the whole thing. She wanted the psychopath who did this to her apprehended and flailed to death, but she wasn't sure Johnny wasn't as much an innocent victim as she was. She couldn't believe, as her father did, that Johnny was in on this thing, plotting to kidnap her and hold her for ransom, subjecting her to weird sexual deviation while the ransom money was in transit. The idea of being tied up appealed to her somehow. If only that female werewolf hadn't jumped into the arena, interrupting Loretta's scheme to get laid and revenge at the same time. She was planning to accuse him of rape and sic her father on him. After the trial and Johnny's sentence was handed down, she could've jetted off for Hollywood, and everyone would've been happy. Well, only Loretta would've been truly satisfied with this scenario, but that was good enough for her.

But Helen Black, the Bride of Frankenstein *and* Dracula, had changed all that. For all anyone knew, Johnny was inside some alligator by now. Loretta's ambivalence about Johnny had not waned since this crisis—she still secretly hoped he was dead, and still secretly prayed she would see him again, to ignore him and kiss him and ignore him some more before the eventual rape set-up. Despite the temporary disfigurement at the hands of that monster, Loretta's plans for her future as a movie queen had only been postponed, not altered or cancelled, but she was keeping this to herself for now.

Prissy walked in about ten in the morning to change the channel from the slasher flick Loretta was watching, and serve her special breakfast—a fruit basket, with a pint of low fat lemon yogurt, some banana bread, and decaf cafe con leche. Loretta stretched and yawned but stuck to her code of silence, even with Prissy. This did not prevent Prissy from rambling on in a perpetual monologue of grief, hope, and restlessness. "Here we are, Beautiful. I mean that sincerely, sweetheart, you are beautiful—and always will be, at least to me, *and* to the sweet, loving, understanding, gentle, rich man you're going to marry someday...you know, that one doctor is kind of cute. I checked, he's only thirty-eight and single, well, divorced, but—maybe that's because he was meant for better things? Anyhoo, we'll see.

I've arranged to have him return to remove those stitches next week, so you'll get a chance to talk, that is, if you're talking by then. Now, what movie would you like, dear? I brought 'The Sound of Music,' 'Gone With the Wind,' and 'Guys and Dolls,' all long and romantic, so you can just sort of sit there, and—well, since you won't choose, I'll just put in 'The Sound of Music,' then come back in a few hours and put in 'Gone With the Wind'—remember how we used to love watching that together? Maybe I'll just sit in on that one with you, if it's all right. I'm sorry, I can't sit through 'Terms of Endearment' or 'Steel Magnolias' *one* more time, sweetheart. Have you seen 'Guys and Dolls'? It's got Marlon Brando and Frank Sinatra when they were both really cute, and lots of songs, and it takes place in New York in the Fifties, a wonderful place and time, and the characters are, well, maybe it isn't the right time to watch 'Guys and Dolls' just yet. I'll take it back and get—what should I get? Lor? Loretta, *please* talk to me. I've been *so* worried about you. Are you angry with me for telling Daddy about your acting plans? I'm sure he'll come around, dear, just give him time...Loretta? *Loretta*!" Prissy was sobbing now, while Loretta maintained her phony catatonia, staring in the mirror as if in a trance, like the tragic French girl in *Eyes Without a Face*, trying her hardest not to bust out laughing and ruin it. Finally, Prissy left after putting the movie on and setting up the breakfast spread next to Loretta's bed. Once she was gone, Loretta smiled wickedly and settled down into her precious solitude.

TWENTY-NINE

"Oh, I saved you some gumbo!" Helen said to Johnny as he ran up, panting, toward her and the Mexican, who did not like the re-appearance of this gringo interloper. The Mexican was 25 with a wife and baby back home in Guadalajara, to whom he sent half of his paycheck. The rest was spent on tequila and women, since his mother had passed away a year ago. The Mexican was uncommonly handsome and did quite well for himself in the Quarter, and had no immediate plans of returning to his native land, where the presence of his family made it difficult to get laid with anyone other than his beloved wife. He was already thoroughly entranced with Helen, however, and was entertaining thoughts of how to smuggle her into his room in the Garden District mansion where he also worked as a gardener in exchange for room and board. His employer was an eccentric widower with full tenure at Tulane—in fact, he had been one of Sonny Johnson's instructors.

"I don't want any right now, thanks," Johnny said, chucking the to-go container aimlessly by the wayside. "Can I have my wallet please?"

The Mexican laughed as Helen handed him the wallet and Johnny went through it in search of the few dollars that had been in there. "Oh, great, this is just great," Johnny said. "What did you buy, a present for the busboy?"

The Mexican made a hostile move toward Johnny, but Helen stopped him, "See? You shouldn't have tossed away your dinner, dummy, I went out and bought it for you since I didn't want to wake you."

"Oh yeah? Well, thanks. Thanks a million. Only I think

I had more money in here than that little cup was worth."

"Are you saying I stole from you?"

"Hell yeah!"

The Mexican made another aborted lunge for Johnny, then cussed in Spanish and backed off.

"Is the Cisco Kid part of our gang now?" Johnny asked.

"Shut up, Johnny. Don't be so jealous."

"You're a trip, you know that? Anyway, what now? I mean, I should just go back to Miami on my own. Gimme the keys to the stolen car."

Helen laughed. "Are you kidding? Even if I could, I wouldn't."

"What's that supposed to mean—*even if you could?*"

"I chucked them in the river while you were asleep, just in case you got any bright ideas like that. You're stuck for the duration, Johnny-O, so you might as well live it up!"

"Well, what about my laptop and my book?" Johnny fumed. "How can I get 'em out of the truck now, ever think of that?"

"We'll jimmy it open somehow—*relax*, willya? Me and Pancho are going for a drink. If you want to tag along, behave. After all, it's Pancho's treat."

"His name is Pancho?"

"His name is anything I call him. Right, Pancho?"

The Mexican, who real name was Alfonso Cortez, nodded, barely understanding her words or the situation, but enjoying it all the same. They were just passing Preservation Hall and the sound of the hot jumping jazz seduced them inside. The room was small and dusty and stuffy, packed with tourists and locals, elegant and scruffy, black and white and brown and red and yellow. The band of sixty-ish black musicians was doing a mean Joe Turner number that made Helen hornier than usual. She was definitely in the mood for a steamy *menage a trois* when they walked back out into the street.

The blues echoed from everywhere in the night world around them. Johnny was absorbed by the ambience, remembering watching Elvis Presley in *King Creole* with his mother as a kid—it was her favorite movie—dreaming of walking the same musical byways as his boyhood idol. Helen seemed sultrier than ever in this pulsating environment, and Johnny craved her carnal company, but so did the Mexican, both sandwiching her between them as they strolled down Bourbon Street, straying in and out of open bars, watching all the people who were listening to music, drinking, laughing, sweating, flirting, fighting, fucking. Johnny, Helen and their new friend likewise let their own libidos run amok. But their unchecked inhibitions were on a collision course with disaster, as Johnny and the Mexican began taking friendly then unfriendly potshots at each other, first verbally and then physically. Helen had to keep them apart with great effort, while enjoying her role as both object and instigator of this masculine, adolescent, primeval sexual showdown.

She was also working on her plan, and wondering where she could load up her thirsty Magnum too. She felt naked and vulnerable without it. Blues, booze, boys, and bullets—this was Heaven to Helen. Even her headache has dissipated, at least for the time being.

The afternoon rain had turned to light evening showers, then drizzle, but had not adversely affected the moods of the revelers. Rainstorms grand and puny often blew through the city, and natives accepted, even welcomed them as crucial aspects of the ambiance. Johnny, Helen and the Mexican were soaked with booze, rain, and sweat, and none had ever felt sexier. They all wound up sitting on a Canal Street curb at the edge of the Quarter, playfully cutting it up. By now even Johnny and the Mexican were getting along, which was why when the Mexican suggested they all crash at his place, they all agreed enthusiastically. At this point Johnny's jealousy took a backseat to his hedonism.

Loaded with drinks and desire, they boarded the last St. Charles streetcar and headed into the Garden District.

The conductor, an old Creole guy, was friendly but admonished them to settle down or walk the rest of the way. They both complied, taking in the grandiose elegance of the mansions on either side, and in their heads rang mysterious *paeans* to lost Southern gallantry. Johnny wanted to move here, live with Helen, have babies, and Helen was thinking the same thing, while the Mexican kept his eyes on Helen's cleavage and wondered how to get rid of the annoying *gringo*.

The Mexican indicated where to get off, and they jumped off the streetcar and crossed the spacious lawn and walked through some dense, carefully tended foliage and entered the backyard, where easy, unobtrusive access to the Mexican's room was possible. Giggling amongst themselves, they followed the Mexican into the kitchen, where he kept repeating "*silencio*," until suddenly the lights were thrown on and the resident professor, whose last name was O'Grady, was standing in the kitchen entrance looking them over with an expression of fraternal displeasure.

"What's all this racket? I have an early morning..." Then he stopped, staring down the barrel of Helen's outstretched Magnum. Professor Malcolm O'Grady, a large man of mixed heritage, with flowing white hair and a thick mustache of silver, was more curious than afraid. The Mexican was stunned, and Johnny was simply depressed. She had burst his bubble with one swift move. Suddenly, reality came rushing in where once fantasy had flowed freely.

Helen knew the Mexican had to live somewhere, but she never imagined it would be someplace like this. Things were working out even better than she had hoped. She was merely going to rob his house in the first place, but she assumed he lived in abject poverty and could fork over little more than hotel money for one night, if that. If nothing else, she and Johnny would have stayed in the Mexican's little humble abode until she thought of something else. Now she saw the providence in her plan—she must have sensed that the Mexican could lead them to the mother lode. They had hit the jackpot by accident, and she wasn't even gambling. She smiled as she leveled the Magnum at the prof's head and ordered him to his bedroom, which she locked with the key he supplied. When the Mexican tried to kiss her she brained him with the Magnum until he passed out, which did not take long since he was nearly incoherent already from liquor and pent-up passion. Then, while Johnny moped in the middle of the kitchen floor, wondering how he had gotten here from where he had been not long ago, Helen ransacked the whole mansion, looting it for jewels, cash, checks, anything she could stuff into the hefty bag she found under the kitchen counter. The chimes of the ancient grandfather clock in the rustic den struck midnight, and Helen smiled to herself as she finished packing. She had made her personal deadline.

THIRTY

El Doctor ran into the Downtown Miami precinct like the hounds of hell were nipping at his heels. He felt besieged by sociopaths with itchy trigger fingers. He had indeed seen the light. He wanted a new life. He was willing to give up his drug trade in exchange for immunity and protection from Vinnie the Vine, who had all but made El Doctor sign his own whack-out contract. This was beyond Helen. Vinnie was planning on muscling into El Doctor's turf, and while this took some serious chutzpa to pull off successfully, given the ratio of Cubans to Italians down here, El Doctor did not plan on being a POW, MIA, or DOA in the impending war.

"Nice to see you, Doc," Sonny Johnson said as he rose from his office chair to shake hands with his unexpected visitor. "I didn't realize you made office calls. Feeling conscientious this morning for some reason?"

"I need help," El Doctor said, pacing frantically, "and I need help right away. I got a family, you know? Vinnie, he's a fucking lunatic, *mang*, I am telling you!"

"Oh, you two have had words, I take it?"

"Not many, just enough to scare the shit out of me."

"So the Mob's giving you the pink slip, huh? Sixty-day notice? Sixty minutes, what?"

"This is not funny, *mang*."

"I'm not laughing, Doc."

"Yes, but you're smiling. Do not fucking smile. I am not kidding."

"Okay, but watch the rough talk in here. This is my office."

"Sorry. Sorry. I am just nervous, you know? Vinnie, he goes to New Orleans, right? He goes to New Orleans, which must mean Helen is there, right? I was going to go there myself, to warn her, but I never been there, I don't know my way around. But maybe you can save her, mang. And my family, too. Please, right now. Go to my house, send someone, *por favor*."

"I'm surprised you left your family to come down here. I'm surprised you're here at all," the detective said slyly.

"I know, I know, me too, but my wife, she has a gun, see? It has a permit, don't worry. But I am still nervous, you know? So we can make a deal, right? We make a deal, you take care of my family, and I tell you what I know."

"Which is?"

"Later, *mang*. Right now I need you to go my house. Okay? You go?"

"I'll get in touch with somebody who will radio a squad car to patrol the area. That's all I can do right now, until you start singing some serious tunes so we have a reason to suspect the Mob has probable cause to inflict harm on you."

"Fuck that, *mang*! I'm sorry, I'm sorry, okay, okay, okay, but I don't have time. They could hit me on my way home, I'm telling you! They work fast. Vinnie is crazy, *mang*. I am not kidding you, seriously. He's not like Tony. Tony, you could talk to, have reason with, but Vinnie—it's like he's on a fucking Catholic crusade, see! He's out of his fucking *mind*!"

"Calm down, Doc. All right, let's talk on the way to your home." Johnson put on his jacket and straightened his tie. "But I won't be able to offer full protection unless you sign some papers first."

"I know the fucking game, *mang*. Let's just come on."

"Wait for me outside a second. I need to make a call."

El Doctor impatiently closed the door and paced outside the door. Johnson dialed an outside line and booked a round trip ticket to New Orleans, leaving that night, since it was a Friday, and he had a weekend off at his disposal, so he'd tell his superiors he needed a little R&R mixed with personal business. He was from New Orleans, anyway, so the story could easily fly. He was in the middle of an investigation, but then he always was. Two days wouldn't kill anybody, except maybe Helen, and for unfathomable reasons, Sonny Johnson didn't want that to happen. He also made one last quick call to a buddy on the NOPD, telling him he needed both a place to crash and some inside lines on current, very current, Mob activity in the Crescent City.

THIRTY-ONE

Helen had completely shattered Johnny's favorable mental portrait of her as a proletariat heroine, her one last redeeming quality in his eyes. The fact that she had locked the still unconscious Mexican in the bedroom with the professor, cut the phone line in there, left some food from the cabinets and fridge, and then proceeded to make herself at home in the affluent surroundings, all suggested that she was not simply a survivalist, but an unscrupulous materialist, out for mere self-gratification at the expense of anyone trapped in her merciless path. Johnny still ached for her, however—she had indeed infected him, like a vampire, and even while he knew she was evil, at the very least misguided, he couldn't lift a finger to stop her, or himself.

He couldn't argue with her decision to set up camp in the mansion for a while, anyway. It was indeed a luxurious pit stop on their way to violent oblivion, and Johnny tried to relax as he sat in the bubble bath she had run for him and read about their exploits in the *Times-Picayune* that had been tossed out on the lawn by the unsuspecting paperboy just after dawn. Helen was asleep in the guest room, or what she assumed was the guest room, and she had told Johnny not to answer the other phones or the doorbell until she woke up. She was sleeping on a plan. They obviously couldn't stay here indefinitely with the prof and the Mexican held incommunicado. Their disappearance from their regular routine in the outside world would arouse suspicion fairly quickly, especially where the prof was concerned, since he had a school schedule to keep at nearby Tulane. The faculty would have to function without him for the time being, however. Johnny and Helen needed their rest. They also needed a new wardrobe, since Helen could only wander around in public with bloodstains on her blouse for so long, even in the French Quarter. Fortunately, the prof still kept his late beloved dead wife's room intact, and Helen had raided the clothes closet for some very feminine, if slightly archaic, threads. She had also picked some things out of the protesting prof's closet for Johnny, but nothing appealed to him, so he stuck to his bloody-sweat-cum-piss-and-gumbo stained aloha shirt. He realized that since he had not shown up he was already out of a job, as if that mattered now, but at least his employers knew why he had not called in, since the *Herald* had probably explained it to them.

The mansion was over a hundred years old, but in pristine condition. It was two stories with a massive attic and basement, seventeen rooms, including the private guest quarters in the room which now served as the prof's meditation shed, where he wrote in his journal surrounded by candles and pictures of his late wife. They had never had any children, since she had been barren, and they had been real swingers in their day, even doing some partner swapping with liberal-minded high society peers as well as rough trade picked up in Elysian Fields. This stopped when the prof contracted syphilis and nearly died from it. His wife hadn't been so lucky. She was fifty at the time, he was fifty-nine. That had been six years ago. The official medical report didn't attribute her death to extracurricular randiness due to the sensitive nature of his tenure, though the complications that arose from her infection were more due to her fragile health in general than to the disease itself. With her immune system down, she was afflicted with sundry illnesses, though she was found to be HIV-negative, as was the prof. Still, he had been slowly dying of emotional AIDS ever since his wife's demise.

As he lay on his bed waiting for his unwanted guests to leave, he almost prayed that the strange girl roaming his house would decide to bump him off as a potential witness.

He didn't keep in touch with current events much these days beyond local politics that came up in coffee clutch conversations at the college, so he didn't realize he had been targeted, albeit arbitrarily, by a celebrity criminal. The Mexican was still out of it, and probably would remain so most of the day. The prof figured his houseboy could get them out of this somehow—climb down the trellis and alert the authorities or something—but he wasn't counting on it, or even hoping for it. It was time to pass on, anyway. Fleetingly he fantasized about his pretty young intruder humping him to death. His wife would have liked that. Then he could join her and tell her all about it, in case she hadn't been peering in on them from beyond.

The prof's department was History, and Sonny Johnson had been a star pupil in one of the courses—Southern U.S. African American Studies—on his way to a Sociology degree. The prof had no idea what had become of Johnson, nor did he ever really give it any thought. He had no way of knowing that Sonny Johnson had his NOPD connection leave word with the prof's answering service at the University that Johnson would be stopping by to say hello if he got the chance, since he was coming to town on business. O'Grady wouldn't have really cared one way or the other under ordinary circumstances, but a visit now from a friendly ex-student wearing a badge and a gun would have been timely and welcome, even though Johnson would be out of his jurisdiction here. As if that mattered to anyone immediately concerned.

Helen awoke from her catnap and decided to join Johnny in the tub for a quickie. Johnny had fallen asleep himself and was nearly about to drown when Helen rescued him. She then led him, naked and leaving a wet, lathery trail through the halls, to the guest room she had been occupying. She then stripped out of the Southern Belle powder blue gown she had been wearing with only a garter belt and hose on underneath, and proceeded to seduce and mount Johnny with Bettie Page flair. Johnny liked the garters, but after reading that newspaper article naming him as a possible accomplice to mayhem and murder, Johnny wasn't entirely in the mood for love at the moment. He quickly got in the mood, though.

"My life is ruined," he pondered with resignation as Helen licked his neck.

"The whole fuckin' world is ruined, wake the fuck up," she said as she massaged his penis while kissing his face and chest.

He idly played with her breasts as he continued. "Really, Helen. Let's just talk for once, okay? I mean, can we do that? Like, *talk*?"

"I'd rather just, like, *fuck*," she said, sticking her tongue in his ear, then in his mouth to shut him up, but to no avail.

"But that's all you *ever* want to do, besides rob banks and kill people."

Helen suddenly felt drained of all amorous sensations. "What are you saying, Johnny-O?"

"I know you killed that Mob guy. It's in the article. They don't know you did it, but they're pretty sure. There's evidence everywhere. You probably left a path for them to follow us. Not on purpose, but we're *doomed*. Like, *fucked. Totally. I know* it. It's just a matter of time before they catch us. And I'm *innocent*!"

Helen sat up and sighed, running her hands through her hair as her nipples shrunk. "*Are* you, Johnny? Are you really? You gonna tell the hard-ons I kidnapped and raped you at gunpoint?"

"Well, excuse me, but ain't that so?"

"I love you, Johnny." But it sounded more like a curse than a compliment. She got up and walked around the room, picking up antiques and trinkets, touching the lace curtains, suddenly feeling entombed in a Renaissance death chamber, though she didn't even know what that was. She had read a lot of books, mostly True Crime, but also some educational stuff— "How To Get Ahead in Business" type paperbacks she picked up in airports and bus depots—and was actually self-motivated to get ahead in the legit corporate fast-lane one day. She had a keen mind, she knew, but her body and emotions had been mangled, warped, and possibly destroyed. She hadn't done any acid, coke, or crack in nearly a year, just weed, which she considered harmless. This had started because she was on parole for the third time, though she had always broken her paroles with various violations and gotten away with it thanks to Tony's invincible shield. The cops were so crooked in Florida, she believed, that she could get away with anything. She'd actually been astonished when they had swarmed on her *en masse* after the Coral Gables bank job, an impulsive bid for independence, which she regretted. She even felt bad for killing the Indian, even in justifiable conditions, and Tony's death had practically been an accident. If only he didn't tell her he loved her at such a shaky moment, with her finger on the trigger of a Magnum, a birthday present from him after all, pointed at his head, he'd still be alive today to bail her out of this crisis. As it stood, he was the *raison d'etre* for the whole mess. She knew the Mob would get her one day, that her moments with Johnny were numbered, but when Tony had said he loved her, she knew he was lying, and just couldn't take being lied to one more time in her life. Not with a line like that. No one had ever said it to her and meant it. If someone had—*anyone*—she wouldn't be the person she was now. Sitting there on the bed with Johnny, she had finally reached this conclusion. All she ever wanted was for someone to love her, not just desire her. Up till now, she thought Johnny might truly care for her. But now it seemed all he was really concerned about was his own precious hide.

Johnny was reeling from the poignancy of what she had just said to him: I love you. She hadn't said it in the baby talk voice like that time in his studio, either. She said it with maturity and conviction, and something else that sounded like sadness. He wasn't sure how to respond, except honestly, so finally he said, "I love you too, Helen."

Helen looked at him through hardened tears that felt little pearls rolling down her ruddy cheeks. "Don't lie to me, motherfucker," she whispered.

"I'm not lying. Why else do you think I haven't tried to escape? I wouldn't tell them what happened. I mean I'm with you now. We're both doomed, I said. We're being flushed down the toilet together, two turds in a whirlpool."

Helen laughed despite herself. "I think you'd be a great writer, Johnny-O."

Johnny felt a surge of odd warmth. "Yeah? Maybe I can write in prison, like O. Henry."

"Who? Ah, never mind. Don't worry, Johnny, we'll get out of this, you'll just have to write under another name, an alias, but so what? We can go to Houston next, even though I hate it there, but I know some people who can put us up if they're still around, and from there we can easily make Mexico, maybe even South America. Rio! Yeah! Rio'd be good. You ever been to Rio?"

"Can't say I have."

"Well, neither have I, but we can check it out. From there we can take a boat to Australia or somethin,' I never been there either, but all the Aussies I met are real cool. You ever meet any Aussies?"

"A few, I guess. I was in love with one once. Didn't work out."

Helen affected a pout. "Was she prettier than me?"

Johnny leaned over and kissed her with true affection on the cheek, but as he did Loretta's face flashed in his mind. He ignored it, though. "No one's prettier than you," he said. And he wasn't lying, subjectively speaking. Helen had seen to that when she had pounded Loretta's face into oatmeal with the butt of her trusty Magnum, effectively eliminating the aesthetic competition.

Helen kissed him back, long and lovingly, with a depth of passion heretofore missing from their lusty liaisons. Helen felt free to express her real feelings now, for the first time in her life.

"My manuscript!" Johnny said suddenly.

"Huh?" Helen said through puffy lips.

"My laptop and stuff! It's still in the car!"

Helen kissed him again. "Forget it. I'll steal you a whole computer, and you have a new book to write now anyway."

As Helen seduced him into submission, any thoughts of the outside world that had plagued him began to disappear as they made true mutual love for the very first time, oblivious to the Mexican climbing down the trellis, or, back in the Quarter on the banks of the River, the cops breaking open the trunk of the abandoned Mustang and finding a beat up laptop.

THIRTY-TWO

With the Mob giving El Doctor the bum's rush, forcing him to recruit allies on the police force, he didn't feel so dishonorable sitting in his Little Havana home handing Sonny Johnson the lowdown on everything he knew concerning shakedowns, rackets, and various prostitution and gambling rings throughout Dade County. Of course, at least half of it was either made up or vague speculation, which Johnson took for granted, but El Doctor named several key public figures that were known to veil Mob activity in exchange for political clout and protection. Many of them also knew Helen, intimately. Several were deceased after double-crossing the Mob, courtesy of Helen's black widow set-up techniques. Others were on a hit list El Doctor provided, knowing full well his name had been added to it in the past few hours, without giving him official notice, of course. El Doctor hedged on fingering his own people, so Johnson let it rest, at least for the time being. He had already contacted the local FBI office and they were on their way to El Doctor's house to shield him from Vinnie's vengeance. Tony's death had alerted them that a possible restructuring of territories was in order, since Tony had been fairly impassive when it came to muscling new accounts, so to speak, whereas Vinnie already had a reputation for being a dangerous, though business-like, psychopath—just what New York needed for their Miami branch operations. But Johnson's chief concern was finding Helen before anyone else did. He had a plane to catch.

"I really gotta be on my way, Doc. I got somewhere to be." Johnson looked at his watch and whistled. "*Whoa*! It's later than I thought."

"It's later than *I* fucking thought," El Doctor said, rising to pace the room some more. His wife was in the kitchen with the two little ones, barefoot and cooking, just like El Doctor wanted. She didn't seem very nervous to Johnson. Perhaps he was jumping the gun, overreacting. Maybe he was exaggerating because his conscience had finally caught up with him and he wanted to make amends for the good of his tortured soul. Yeah, sure. No, there had to be something to El Doc's paranoia. There was true fear in his voice and eyes. This was his worst nightmare come true. Tony had always been square with him since El Doctor provided him and his extended family free medical services, including access to as much therapeutic cocaine as was desired. Tony's people tried to steer clear of the drug trade, farming out responsibilities to streetwise, unconscionable button men. But Vinnie was a bona fide maniac, power hungry and insatiable. El Doctor had practically forgotten all about Helen. Suddenly his love for his wife and children blossomed with renewed purity and dedication. He was a new man. "I am a dead *mang*," he said as Johnson headed for the door.

"Take it easy, Doc," Johnson said as he opened the front door and looked out across the lawn and the street with eagle eye precision. "The Feds will be here any minute. When they read this stuff on this tape after it's transcribed, they'll love you to death."

"One way or another," El Doctor moaned.

Johnson walked slowly out to his car, wondering what was keeping the suits. They could've hit Little Havana from downtown in fifteen, easy. It had been half an hour since he'd called them. He couldn't wait any longer, realizing he had forgotten his solid gold pen, a gift from his wife, and he was returning to retrieve it when the blast went off. El Doctor's home seemed to implode the second before it exploded. The proximity to the center of the blast sent Johnson soaring back over the top of his Camaro and into the street. Glass, brick, wood, and human body parts sailed through the air in slow motion, and despite the roar of the explosion, Johnson heard nothing. Only deafening silence. It seemed an eternity before he heard something, and then the sounds were muffled, vague, eerie: voices, sirens, screams. Light stabbed him from all directions—white, red, blinding. As someone lifted him up off the ground and deposited him on a stretcher, a myriad of confused thoughts whirled through his numb brain: what kind of wacko would start blowing up the indigenous population of a city he hardly knew, much less had claim to, even before the powers-that-be had sanctioned wartime tactics?

The Feds had told Johnson that their undercover wiseguys knew the Mob did not want a turf war with the Cubans in Miami, or anywhere else. This was Vinnie's doing, independent of New York. He was out of control, trying so hard to prove he was strong enough to take over the operations vacated by the late Tony Volare that he was willing to go all out with a demonstrative act of offensive bravado. This would send a shock wave of signals throughout the Cuban crime community that the Mob was taking over. Vinnie probably didn't even care whether Helen lived or died—but Johnson knew there was a contract out on her, and the way things were going, there was a good chance Vinnie was already pissing on her tombstone.

THIRTY-THREE

"This isn't going to work!" Helen was screaming as she ran around the rooms of the mansion with Johnny on her trail, trying to stop her while at the same time second-guessing her abrupt decision to rant and rave as she pursued a binge of destruction. The timing of this bizarre behavior was what perplexed Johnny the most. Just moments before they'd been in the throes of a deep, secure, romantic embrace, spilling their darkest secrets in between kisses and caresses, when all of a sudden Helen had jumped up and started breaking everything in sight. China, chairs, windows, and chandeliers, anything that stood as an obstacle between her and whatever her long-range objective happened to be. She was crying as she did so, and the racket she made disturbed Professor O'Grady greatly, since he was powerless to stop her until his houseboy had returned with the authorities to contend with this voluptuous, violent vixen. The prof was looking forward to having her tied up and interrogated. He was very curious about her personality and motivations. Something about her raw sense of survival and avaricious style appealed to him, maybe even turned him on in a way that he hadn't experienced since the glory days of adventure with his wife in the jungles of bohemia.

"*What* isn't going to work?" Johnny shouted after her as the prof pressed his ear to the locked bedroom door and attempted to eavesdrop on the random dismantling of his property and precious memories.

"*Us*! What kind of *idiot* am I, anyway?" Helen was now picking up chairs and small pieces of furniture and hurling them into bookcases and out windows. The lawn was littered with discarded items as well as appalled on-lookers from the neighborhood. Helen wore nothing but the dead woman's garter belt and a pair of high heels, which made progress awkward.

Helen was now suffering another headache, and this was in addition to the hangover, which was something she could handle. The murky origin of these headaches was driving her insane, and also serving as a terrible reminder that her life would never be painless or anything remotely resembling "normal." She was suddenly hit with the realization that not only was she cornered in a blind alley and was bound to die, but she had dragged Johnny in there with her, and now they were both trapped. Moonlight and roses were for people with jobs and homes and real, boring lives—not for people like her, who committed atrocities on a regular basis and then expected complete and utter amnesty not only from the Law but also from God Herself. She knew the headaches plagued her as punishment, but then they had started long before she had done anything bad. Her blood mother had dumped her in a trashcan before she could even think of anything illegal, immoral, or otherwise. Perhaps her crimes were retroactive or something, and she was being punished in advance. God knew everything, didn't She? All she knew for certain was that she was royally fucked from the get-go, and now Johnny was too, thanks to her selfish need to be loved by someone so innocent, as if she would in turn become innocent by association. Instead, Johnny had become guilty and condemned by association. Poor, poor Johnny. If she had any more bullets, she would have shot them both. As it stood, she had to wait for the cops to do it for her.

"We're *fucked*, Johnny, can't you fucking *see*?" she screamed as he launched a bold flying tackle and took her down with him. He held her in a bear hug from behind while she kicked and screamed. Outside, the police were swarming all over the well-kept grounds. The Mexican was in their midst, excited and talkative. A bullhorn voice requested that Johnny and Helen give themselves up peacefully, or else they'd storm the place. The police captain radioed for backup as Helen hurled her Magnum out a window, where it landed innocuously in the grass. The cops weren't positive she wasn't bluffing and was holed up with more weapons and ammo. A helicopter from a local TV station buzzed the site, relaying a running commentary on the chaos. Johnny wanted to drag Helen outside and give up, but at the last minute she changed her mind about the whole damn thing. She was still wearing nothing but a garter.

With her free hand she grabbed a flower vase, smashed it on the corner of the kitchen table, and held the jagged edge against Johnny's jugular.

"Wait a minute," Johnny wheezed as she drew a drop of blood and he let go of her. "Aren't we in love?"

"Unfortunately for you," she said as she led him out the back door, exposing herself where several officers were poised with rifles and radios, awaiting the signal to open fire. The helicopter zoomed in close for a shot of the new hostage twist. Live coverage of such an event would make cable news in no time. This was viral footage in the making, loaded with organic sex and violence. It would be an Internet sensation.

"*Back off or I'll throw his fuckin' head at you!*" she yelled at the aroused officers, who received clearance to shoot only when they had clear aim add would not endanger the prisoner. Johnny knew Helen wouldn't really cut him, at least not fatally. Or would she? He was losing faith in her again. Why had she blown it like this? Everything was going so well. Relatively, that is.

The police captain, a half Creole, half Italian named Freddy Rizzo who was Sonny Johnson's NOPD connection and a former high school classmate, walked carefully towards Helen, who was actually trying to pin down his nationality in her mind. He had a deep tan, a very tight Afro hairstyle, heavy-lidded brown eyes, thick lips, and a big honker. Brazilian, she concluded incorrectly.

"Fuckin' back off, man, I'm serious," she said to him when he had stepped within the five-yard danger zone, the boundaries of which could change without warning on Helen's whim.

"What the hell do you want?" Rizzo asked softly, trying not to stare at her bare breasts.

"A fucking clean slate, which you can't give me, asshole, so back the fuck off and let me outta here, or I swear I'll splatter his fuckin' blood all over your faggy suit."

"I know all about you, you know." *Man, she's hot*, thought Rizzo.

"*Like hell*! Nobody knows shit about nobody, cause nobody really *cares*, am I right?"

"No. You're wrong. Dead wrong. Someone I know back in Miami called me about you earlier today. He thinks you can be helped, if only you admit you need it."

"*FUCK YOU*!" If Helen still had her Magnum, it would have been a bloodbath right then and there, and no one would have walked out alive. But she hated the idea of giving up, even in the face of overwhelming odds. Wasn't her style. They'd have to work for it. "Now give me your car keys and ten minutes to get outta here. I don't want no money, no bullshit like that, I just want to be free. That's all I ever wanted. Now *do* it."

"Helen, we'll still catch up with you, sooner or later, so you might as well..."

"*NOW*!" Helen pressed the jagged edge deeper into Johnny's throat, and a trickle of blood escaped and dripped down to his cheat, causing a fresh red splotch to appear under his aloha shirt. He winced with pain. No one but Rizzo noticed, though. Attention was riveted on Helen's nakedness.

"All right, we'll play it your way for now." Rizzo took out his squad car keys and very carefully reached out and tossed them on the lawn. With her eyes on him and the jagged edge still in Johnny's throat, she bent down and picked them up. Then Rizzo led her to his car and let her climb in with her prisoner, waving off the officers as he did so, though they kept their sights trained on Helen with predatory glee. They lived for this kind of shit. Helen had made their day—no, month, maybe even *year*. They were all part of this ongoing national Reality Show, streaming live on the worldwide web. They loved her. If only she had a gun and tried to use it, so she could go out in a blaze of glory and they could riddle her shapely young body into so much bullet, blood and booby soup. Now that would be an international media sensation.

Instead, they watched her drive off with strict orders not to pursue until she was out of sight. Rizzo was confident she wouldn't even make it out of city limits before a police sniper picked her off and Johnny Varga took his chances in the ensuing car crash. Something about her had touched Rizzo in the same way Johnson had described over the phone that morning. She was pathetic, in a very sexy way. He yearned to take care of her, to hold her and tell her everything would be all right, even though he knew he'd be lying.

THIRTY FOUR

Sitting up in bed watching the late night news coverage of the tense standoff/showdown in New Orleans, Loretta Lynx felt consumed by her own significance in this saga, cast in the role of the innocent, beautiful victim, scarred for life but determined to make her dreams come true against all odds. Her life story would make a great TV Movie of the Week, maybe even a HBO mini-series. She could even play herself. This was Plan B, however. Plan A was still to undergo any surgery necessary to restore her natural appearance and then rely on her talent to succeed. Her looks would only be an asset. If for some reason the bandages came off and she was damaged beyond repair, her looks would be the sole basis on which she'd be judged, alleged talent be damned. Loretta knew her father would fix her face at any cost, so she had stopped losing sleep over it. She may even start talking to Prissy again in the morning, if she felt like it. Things were looking up, but that may have only been because she was lying on her back in the sewer. Several of her perfect teeth had been cracked, chipped, and jarred loose in the attack, so a full dental makeover would have to be thrown into the bargain. But that was okay with Loretta, who was already considering writing a book about the experience. "Loretta Lynx: Story of a Survivor." A true-life tragedy that could be serialized in magazines and featured on Oprah's cable network. Why, this had actually been a gift. The girl covering her shifts at Wolfie's had stopped by to express a mixture of sympathy and envy. Loretta's ordeal was natural material for media exploitation. Johnny had inadvertently proven to be her savior by introducing her to the elements of evil. Now her life would never be boring again, to her or to her legion of fans, waiting in the wings for her recovery and then discovery.

Time was running out on her, however, since many of the roles she coveted had already been cast and filmed: Vivien Leigh was forever Blanche Dubois, Marilyn Monroe was eternally herself, Lynda Carter was the *real* Wonder Woman. Loretta would have to forge a new image for herself to carry her onward well into the 21st Century, a symbol of the Millennium for the masses. Her goal—or one of them—was to star in the Best Picture of The Year, a distinction that would guarantee her an indelible place in the annals of cinematic history. Then after that—a TV series based on the movie, which she would also produce and sometimes direct. A triple threat, that Loretta Lynx.

Loretta didn't realize that she was deliriously dreaming delusions because of the drugs pumped into her battered system. Only later would her profound ambitions be seen in the proper light of reality. In the meantime, her dreams were all that were sustaining her.

There was a knock on the door, and in walked Daddy Lynx, fresh from a dinner party on a yacht in Lauderdale, where the topic of conversation had been his dear daughter and the perpetrators of her pain, Johnny Varga and Helen Black, whose names were widely believed to be a media concoction, in line with Machine Gun Kelly, Pretty Boy Floyd, Son of Sam and Engelbert Humperdinck.

"Hello, princess!" he said, clapping his hands together and walking to her bedside. Loretta feigned sleep, unsuccessfully.

Her eyes fluttered open and she yawned, deciding she might as well start talking if she wanted Daddy to start pitching in that surgery moola. "Hi," she said meekly.

"Pumpkin! You spoke! *Hallelujah*! You're going to be okay after all!"

"I still don't feel so hot, Daddy. And my *face*."

Daddy Lynx leaned over and kissed her forehead,

which only had one bruise. Now now, pumpkin. Let's keep our chins up."

"Oh, I still have a chin? How nice."

He laughed insincerely. "As bright as ever, that's my girl! Now, what can Daddy do to make you feel better tonight?"

How about dropping dead?, she thought, but instead said, "Ice cream?"

"Your favorite?"

"Of course. You remember, right?"

Daddy's brow looked bent. "Um, sure. I'll run right out."

"Goody, thanks!' Then she sighed with relief after he was gone. She began flipping around the tube looking for more slasher flicks when she came upon a CNN bulletin regarding a shootout in New Orleans. She masturbated as she soaked in every gory detail, climaxing just before the commercial.

THIRTY-FIVE

Sonny Johnson was released from the hospital after treatment for a mild concussion that produced an annoying, but harmless, ringing in his ears, causing him to check his cell phone needlessly every few minutes. He'd also suffered minor cuts and bruises from hitting the pavement in a storm of shards, but what really bothered him was the fact that he hadn't been in New Orleans for the near capture of Helen Black.

After driving off in Rizzo's police car, she had somehow vanished into the thick Louisiana air. Even cloaked by very heavy overcast, a naked woman in a squad car should not have blended in so easily with the colorful indigenous population of New Orleans. The standoff had taken place roughly the same time as the time bomb in El Doctor's basement—planted surreptitiously the night of Vinnie's Miami visit—had blown El Doctor and his family into the anonymous realm of tragic but instantly forgotten statistics. Vinnie must have wired word to the Mob's people in both towns, and possibly other major metropolitan areas in the region like Atlanta, to find Helen but not to move on her until he arrived. Johnson assumed Vinnie had her at this point.

And he assumed right, though he had no way to verify it just yet.

The basement bomb that had decimated El Doctor was in actuality an act of manic jealousy rather than a carefully calculated career move, though it would have to masquerade as such for the benefit of Vinnie's mental reputation. Now that Tony and the Doc were out of the way,

Helen was all his, and he would personally see to it that the evil within was exorcised before he slipped his salami inside her holiest of holies again.

As for Johnny, Helen had told Vinnie that where she goes, Johnny goes—even to the grave. Vinnie said that would be no problem, as long as they didn't mind a brief stopover in Reno. What the hell, Johnny thought; first he was up and coming in Miami, then down and out in New Orleans. He was a man of the world, and pretty soon it appeared he'd be a man in the earth.

The Mob had staked out the prof's mansion soon after Helen had entered it with the Mexican and Johnny. She had been spotted on Bourbon Street by one of the local boys then followed around the Quarter, discreetly, pending further instructions. Vinnie arrived that night, and dined at Galatoire's in no particular hurry with the head of the local Mob chapter, a beefy, slick, jewel-encrusted exhibitionist named "Leadbelly" Louie D'Amato because he always plugged his enemies in the gut so they could roll around for awhile thinking about their waning life before it painfully ended. Next Vinnie paid a house call on his old pal Freddy Rizzo, the police captain. Vinnie informed Rizzo of Helen's whereabouts but told him not to make a move on her without further word. In the meantime, local cops ran a trace on the Mustang, found the APB posted on it after the hippie owners had reported who and what had happened, and began their own search. Rizzo didn't want to interfere—he was playing both sides of the fence, ever since Leadbelly Louie had leaned on him years before while he was only a rookie street cop, and if it wasn't for Louie's connections within the department, he would never have reached this rank. By the same token, he had to do his job for the sake of appearances, so Vinnie had told him to take Helen into custody—unscathed—and then hand her over later, perhaps faking a jailbreak for the media. But then Helen had wriggled her way out again, and Vinnie, in a rented Mercedes, had overtaken her downtown as she left the

Garden District, and two of his boys, masquerading as "plain clothes men" toting Uzis, had escorted Helen and Johnny into the Mercedes, to the airport, and aboard Vinnie's private jet. This time, though, there was no chance of her escaping—as soon as she and Johnny were stuffed into the Mercedes, Vinnie hit them both with tranquilizers. Helen managed to bite Vinnie in the neck before passing out.

The Mexican had reached the police station just as Rizzo and his men were preparing to storm the mansion, so he wasn't even rewarded for his efforts, except by the grateful prof, who gave him a paid vacation to anywhere the Mexican wanted to go. He chose Chicago, rather arbitrarily. If the boys watching the mansion had not been told to sit tight, the Mexican would have been snuffed before he ever reached the station. Fortunately for him, his run for help was redundant, since by that time the Mob was just marking time until Rizzo bagged Helen for them. The way things had been going, they were all too happy to let Vinnie designate this duty to a cop.

So this was how it came to pass that Johnny Varga was lying in the cramped luggage compartment of the Reno-bound jet with Helen fuming by his side, biding her time, quietly making plans, even in her sleep.

THIRTY-SIX

Vinnie called Rizzo from his jet phone.

"You fucked it up," he said when Rizzo picked up his private line at home. Not even Rizzo's wife had access to this line. Only the Mob and Sonny Johnson, who was completely ignorant of Rizzo's ties with Leadbelly Louie. Or so Rizzo believed. In fact, Sonny was catching on fast. Rizzo was afraid this would happen eventually. As Vinnie's voice whistled down through the air like an arctic tornado, Rizzo realized all the mistakes he had made over the years were culminating this very evening. Sonny Johnson was on his way into New Orleans that very hour. Rizzo was thinking of spilling everything he knew about Leadbelly Louie to Sonny and the Feds. Vinnie had second-guessed him out of sheer, shrewd paranoia, his specialty. "Just like the Cuban in Miami. He fucked up. You fucked up. You had her and you let her go."

"What could I do?" Rizzo said, trying to sound cool and collected. "The eyes of the whole damn world were on me. There was a *helicopter*, for Chrissake!"

"It turned out okay, I got her, but still—you fucked up." The static on the line made Vinnie sound like he was calling from beyond the grave.

"You do? I figured you had. Some of my people caught sight of her being manhandled into a Benz near the stadium. So everything's cool now, right?"

There was malevolent pause. Vinnie was toying with him. He hated crooked cops even more than straight ones. Within the Mob, people like Rizzo wouldn't last a day. No honor. Finally, Rizzo heard him chuckle,

"What's funny?" Rizzo croaked. "Let me in on it. I could use a chuckle right about now."

"What you said," Vinnie laughed. "Your *people*. You *got* no people, half-breed." Vinnie was deliberately pushing his buttons, looking for an excuse to put a hit out on him via Leadbelly Louie, who didn't like crooked cops either, except when they were necessary for business. Vinnie would've wanted to watch Leadbelly do his thing on Rizzo, ventilating the Italian Creole's stomach and letting his life squirt out like Kool Aid from a punctured pitcher.

Rizzo didn't buy into Vinnie's game, however. "Look, Vincenzo, we've had our differences, but I deal with Louie, understand? He's the one I take orders from, not you. Louie told me to play it loose, hold her if I could, but keep her alive and don't blow my cool. But after she pulled off with my car, she was fair game. Louie understands that, and that's all that concerns me. Now if you'll *excuse* me."

"Don't blow smoke rings up *my* ass, you fuckin' monkey. All I gotta do is say the word and Louie will show you why they call him Leadbelly. *Capisce*?"

"I just spoke with Louie, and he's cool about the whole thing. He understands a police captain has a public profile to consider, and there was no way to snag her without letting her ice that kid."

"Fuck that punk. Who cares? What's he to you or anybody?"

"We were on live TV, Vincenzo, remember? You wouldn't want me getting booted off the Force would you? Well, Louie doesn't. He needs me."

Vinnie laughed again. "You think so? We'll see about that, half-ass. Ciao." Vinnie then hung up on Rizzo and tried Leadbelly Louie's line, but only got a lackey who had orders not to disturb his boss, he was asleep, so Vinnie left a message he'd get in touch from Reno. Helen was to be buried somewhere in the Nevada desert. This is what Vinnie wanted his associates in New York and elsewhere to believe, anyway. He would bury her, eventually—but not before he was finished with her.

In the luggage compartment, Johnny and Helen were just coming to. Johnny was hungry as hell. He'd only done a little munching around the mansion, feeling guilty but famished nonetheless, limiting his intake of stolen food to a few snacks while he lounged in the stolen bubble bath. A life of crime had not been his original master plan—unless one considered making a living as a writer somehow criminal in nature. After all, they lived by lies. But a new story was taking root in Johnny's beleaguered consciousness while his stomach rumbled and his brain roared. It would be a true story disguised as fiction, and would feature a female protagonist who was *not* a lesbian bartender. Johnny instead wanted to write Helen's life story as his breakthrough novel. Even as airsickness was setting in, and they were descending into the Reno airport with a connecting flight to nowhere, Johnny's creative juices were sloshing around, soaking his sensibilities.

But first, he had to settle one minor point. "Helen. Helen, *why*?"

"Why what *now*?" Helen murmured, trying not to vomit all over them.

"You know..." He looked down at the huge bloodstain on his shirt, which had rendered the aloha flower patterns unrecognizable. This wasn't what bothered him, however. "You would've killed me. First you tell me you love me, then you almost kill me to save yourself."

"Maybe I'm finally becoming like everyone else," Helen said lowly, trying to reorient herself to reality. "Sounds normal to me, from what I've picked up. Hey—I think we're going down. I hope we fucking crash. This is really fucked. Vinnie's not like Tony—he's a psycho. He's a better lover, too—maybe they're *connected*. Anyway, anything I do is for us from now on, Johnny, just remember that. Look at it like this: Now everyone will think I did kidnap you, since I used you as a hostage. See? It'll all work out."

"I thought you said we were together."

"We are, *forever*, Johnny-O." She reached over and weakly touched his arm, but couldn't sustain the contact. The tranquilizer had made her nauseous. "Then what difference does it make what they think?"

"You still love me, Johnny-O?"

Johnny let out a sigh of surrender. "Yeah. I can't help it, but, I mean, look at us now. Up in the air someplace over God knows where?"

"Reno. He said Reno, remember? Or maybe you'd already gone to sleep by then."

"Were those darts he hit us with?"

"Yeah, guess so. Probably fell out."

"Why didn't he just kill us?"

"He will, don't worry. What's the rush?"

"You're not afraid to die?"

Helen rolled her eyes. "Johnny, come on, you know me better than that. I seem afraid to die to you?"

"Yeah, remember? I know you did it for me and all, but back down on the ground."

"Yeah, yeah, yeah, right. I did that for you. You think I give a fuck what happens to me?"

"I do. I care. I don't want you to die, and I don't want to die, either. I want to see my cat again, and my movie collection, and I want to write a book that gets published, and I want us to be, y'know, together." Johnny started sobbing a bit, but kept his tears at low ebb. After all, he was supposed to be the man in this relationship.

"Oh, Johnny, what have I done to you?" She reached out again and touched his cheek, and he kissed her palm, the same one that held a jagged edge to his throat and pierced the flesh a few hours before.

But that was Helen.

Unpredictable, untamed, unlike any woman he had ever known, or ever would. His memories of Loretta Lynx were draining away like his life's blood, drop by drop, then a torrential release, then back to a steady drip. It was inevitable he would forget Loretta, but it was also inevitable he would die in a way he had never imagined, long before his time. So he'd be a legend. It was just a question of which would come first—forgetting Loretta completely, or buying the farm at gunpoint, an aggressive sale.

Johnny was wallowing in these bleak thoughts as the plane touched down at the Reno airport and a gleaming black stretch limo taxied out to greet Vinnie, his two henchmen, and the "luggage," which had woken up sooner than Vinnie would've thought. When the side compartment door flipped open and Helen came rolling out, spitting obscenities, with Johnny wobbling behind her, Vinnie's boys slapped the shit out of them and threw them into the trunk of the limo. The driver was an old Mob button man named Elmo, semi-retired, who was loyal to the old order and was taking Vinnie directly to his hotel suite at Harrah's where the Mob's Reno delegate, a short, wiry, nervous weasel named Wild West Willie, was awaiting his arrival. Wild West Willie ran two casinos in Reno and wanted to move to Vegas, but he was really on the way out, unknown to him, of course. Vinnie had orders to take him out along with Helen and the stowaway. No one liked or would miss Wild West Willie, who was called such because he shot his mouth off from the hip way too often. Now those verbal bullets were ricocheting right back at him. Benny the Boomerang was also in town, from Detroit, to assist Vinnie's busy agenda while in Reno. But first Vinnie wanted to relax with Helen—alone.

"Yo, Elmo, call ahead and tell Willie I'm tired. I just want to relax a little, huh? I've been all over the fucking country today. Goddamn, I woke up today in Atlantic City for Chrissakes. Oh no—it was New Orleans. Atlantic City was, lessee, yesterday. Anyway, anyway, I wanna relax, huh? Just call ahead and tell Willie not to wait for me in my fucking room. I want Helen with me, that's it." Vinnie leaned back and put his arms over his weary face, flanked by his boys, as Elmo drove into the glittery plastic heart of

Reno. Everyone could hear Helen banging around in the trunk.

"Hey, Vinnie, I don't mean to pry, but orders was to whack the broad ASAP," Elmo said, "Tonight, under cover of darkness. I'm supposed to drive youse outta town after you whack her, or else we can just do it out there, makes no difference, but..."

"*Hey!*" Vinnie blurted, uncovering his face with his arms outstretched expressively. "Elmo, don't fuck with me. I like you, you're old time, you're good people, but we can't just whack her, unnerstand? I keep telling everybody, this chick is possessed by the fuckin' devil himself. I have to make sure that the wicked spirit inside of her is taken care of, and I gotta do it in private."

One of Vinnie's boys laughed, and then caught himself as Vinnie shot him a deadly glare. "Somethin' fuckin' amusing you, dipshit?" Vinnie said. "*Huh?*" He then began smacking the impolite henchman around the face and head.

"Vinnie, Vinnie, okay already," Elmo said from the driver's seat. "Stop slapping him, okay? I'll call Willie right now, we'll do it tomorrow, after you've, you know, whatever you gotta do. Awright? Vinnie? *Awright?*"

Vinnie settled down and sat back, straightening his attire and fixing his thin hair. "Yeah yeah, just fuckin' drive, Elmo, you fuck. I'm telling you, you guys better shape up. There's a new sheriff in town. Tony's history, and I'm gonna make some myself before the night is over. Capisce?"

Elmo, shaking his head subtly, called the hotel suite. In the trunk, Helen was trying to listen in on the conversation. Suddenly, she knew exactly what she was going to do.

THIRTY-SEVEN

Trapped in the back of the limo while Vinnie "took care" of Helen way up in the hotel suite, Johnny was reminded of the scene in *White Heat* where a hapless hooligan locked in the trunk of a car begs for Arthur Cody Jarrett, superbly played by Jimmy Cagney, to give him a little air. "Stuffy, huh?" Jarrett says. "I'll give it a little air." He then pumps several slugs through the trunk, ventilating the compartment as well as the poor sap inside. Johnny did not ask for air for this very reason. He'd take his chances and try not to suffocate, concentrating on his life, his dreams. He started making deals with God, like most cornered, condemned men will do in such a jam, even sworn atheists. He prayed for his novel to be published after he was gone, but then he realized he hadn't written it yet. No, no, this couldn't be—he had to live long enough to write the damn thing, or else his immortal place in cultural history would be stolen by someone else, perhaps the Haitian he used to work with in the lab, who probably had taken over his old route as well. But that was okay—Johnny was thinking of quitting that job anyway and becoming a cab driver. He'd still be transporting the same specimens, only in their original containers. At this point, just surviving as *anything* seemed alluring, except perhaps as a short order cook.

The arid air of the Nevada night made Helen restless. She paced the room at the top of the hotel with the windows wide open while Vinnie tried to get the air conditioner to work. Without such conveniences, Reno was a desolate, neon netherworld.

"Fuck it," he said finally with a sneer. "Just take your

coat off, you'll be cooler."

"Sure, okay," Helen said passively, letting Vinnie's jacket, which he had wrapped around her as he led her through Harrah's lobby with a gun to her back, fall to the floor. Her heels were still in the trunk with Johnny, so all that left was the garter belt. Vinnie licked his chops hungrily. "What do you want me to do now?" Helen then asked with an ingenuous, Betty Boop tone that made Vinnie's prick tingle. His henchmen were outside the door, listening in, but that was okay as long as they manned their station with alert enthusiasm, and weren't distracted by wild mating sounds from within. Helen's cooperative spirit made Vinnie suspicious, but as usual, desire obscured his reason.

"Get on the bed and spread your legs wide," Vinnie ordered hoarsely, seeing how far he could go before she snapped. But she did as she was told with flirtatious giddiness.

"I was hoping it would turn out like this," Helen giggled as she rolled around the king size bed. The suite was decorated in garish red and purple tones, befitting cheap royalty. Vinnie loved it. He took off his tie and shirt, shoes and socks, then slowly removed his trousers as he sat on the edge of the bed, staring at his prize, "I only did Tony so we could be free," Helen said as she playfully dodged his advances.

"Yeah?" Vinnie said, wanting so badly to believe this. "No shit. But I gotta check somethin' first. Let me see up your poon tang a minute, willya?"

Helen frowned. "Huh? I been checked out. No VD here, bub."

"I ain't checkin' for that. I'm lookin' for the evil spirit inside you. Where'd you pick it up, 'Nawlins or Miami? Someplace else maybe?"

"Huh? What the fuck you talkin' about?"

Vinnie sighed with spiritual indignation. "Helen, I know you can't be a regular fuckin' broad and knock off big shots and get away clean without some backup from the

Devil. Satan fucked you, didn't he? Jesus, won't you say no to no body?"

"Vinnie, have you lost your last fuckin' marbles? Next you'll be pullin' out a fuckin' cross and sprayin' holy water on me."

"Naw—what do you think I am, an *idiot*? I don't buy into that shit."

"I don't think you're an idiot. A lunatic is more like it."

"*Hey*! Be nice. I still gotta kill ya, you know. But I can make it painless. So be polite." He suddenly lurched forward and held her down while he mounted her.

Helen squirmed beneath the hairy, sweaty weight. Vinnie's massive boner probed but couldn't make contact with its objective. "Vinnie, get offa me. I ain't gonna let you fuck me then do me! Like I said—I only did Tony so's we could be together—and *now* you give me this shit? What kinda man are you anyway?"

Vinnie relented slightly, but still kept her pinned beneath him. "Listen, you little slut, don't try to fuck with my head. I don't give a *fuck* about you, you don't give a fuck about me, but you're the best piece of ass I've ever had, and I'm gonna screw that demon right outta you before I bury you so you won't rise from the goddamn grave like a fuckin' zombie slut and haunt my ass. *Capisce*?" Then Vinnie started licking her breasts and neck and face while he again attempted to penetrate her.

Helen reached down and grabbed his hard-on with both hands, then dug her nails in until she drew blood. Vinnie screamed and rolled off of her. Helen shot a foot out and hit him square in the balls, and Vinnie saw white lights as he fought to retain his strength. He stumbled after Helen as she jumped off the bed and took his .45 out of its holster, hanging on a chair by the dresser. "One more move and I'll blow your dick off and hand it to you, you fuckin' *SCUMBAG*!"

"You, you wouldn't *dare*, you fuckin' satanic *whore*! Satan's *slut*!"

Helen jerked back on the trigger. Vinnie tumbled forward and then lay in a heap on the floor, holding his arms between his legs as he lurched into a fetal position, soaking in a billowing pool of blood. Outside the door, Vinnie's henchmen were pounding on the wood, jiggling the lock, and trying to get in, not sure who had shot whom. Vinnie had been too stunned to scream. It was only when Helen walked over to the far side of the room, picked up a bloody sausage-like stump, and then deposited next to Vinnie's bulging eyes that he realized he had been emasculated.

"Here ya go," Helen said as she casually dropped his detached pecker on the floor beside his gasping mouth. "See, Tony used his head, you thought with your dick. I aim for the brain." The henchmen were on the verge of breaking the door down when Helen walked up to the door and fired four point blank bullets right through it and into the henchmen. When she heard a slump and then silence, she opened the door, stepped over the prone bodies, walked back and removed the jacket. Then she put it on, walked to the elevator, pressed L for Lobby, descended serenely to the casino, and walked out into the limo, where Elmo was still waiting. Wild West Willie saw her exit the casino, and followed.

"Hey Elmo, what gives?" Wild West Willie said on the sidewalk. But Elmo just nodded and shrugged, then rolled up his window and drove off with his passenger, who had the .45 trained on the back of his head. Elmo knew better than to argue with her. In fact, he kind of admired her spunk. He knew Vinnie had to be dead or worse if she had been able to just walk away like that, and in a way, he was glad. He never truly liked Vinnie, but he somewhat liked Wild West Willie, who would see the dawn after all. Elmo would do whatever Helen said, to a point.

Helen ordered him to pull over a few miles outside town and let Johnny out of the trunk. They embraced and kissed and Elmo could see it was true love. He was touched. Helen told Johnny she'd explain everything later, then told

Elmo, nicely, without the gun pointed at him, to kindly drive them to the nearest filling station, fill up the tank, then call a cab back to town. Helen would be taking the limo from there. Elmo nodded and shrugged. He had nothing to lose. He planned on telling Willie Helen had inadvertently foiled a hit out on him, and that Elmo and Willie should split for parts unknown, maybe a small Italian villa, raise sheep and live the simple life. Wild West Willie would believe Elmo, and heed his advice. Helen had saved the day.

"Where are we going?" Johnny asked her as the limo pulled out of a 24-hour gas station on Interstate 80. Elmo waved at them from the pay phone, and Helen waved back.

"San Francisco," Helen answered, "Ever been there?"

"No," Johnny said, thinking: every nut, fruit, and flake wound up in Frisco. It was like a huge bowl of nutritious breakfast cereal. Johnny smelled the fumes of Fate. "What are we going to do there?" he asked her.

"Live, I hope," Helen said as the first rays of dawn shot over the horizon behind them.

THIRTY-EIGHT

Sonny Johnson was met at the New Orleans airport by his old friend Freddy Rizzo, who drove them straight to Brennan's restaurant in the Quarter, where Rizzo had made reservations. "This keeps up, the CIA will hire her to take out fuckin' Al Queda," Rizzo laughed as they sat at his customary table in the elegant main dining room, surrounded by old New Orleans money. Rizzo loved it here, because he had once been a busboy here, while going to high school and supporting his family. Boring, basic, bullshit survival. Rizzo had enough of that, which is what had seduced him into Leadbelly Louie's clutches to begin with.

"Let's cut the crap," Johnson said, perusing the menu. "Riz, I know the Mob got to you, that's why you let her go. Just tell me where you think she is, and I'll walk away from this table and never look back. Deal?"

Rizzo was stunned speechless for a beat. Then he said, "Sonny, you don't understand, man, you just don't get it."

"Yeah I do. There was this Cuban in Miami, a doctor who patched up Tony's people on occasion. Vinnie blew him up yesterday, which was why I was detained. I'm not even supposed to be here. I still hear bells from the blast. I was there, you see. I saw Vinnie's handiwork close up. He's completely insane, but smart in a way, which is what scares me. Anyway, the gist of what I'm saying, old buddy, is that the Cuban gave you up while waiting for the Feds to show up and protect him. Of course, they showed up late with some lame ass excuse, but that's not my problem anymore. I know our Government is corrupt, nothin' I can do about it. I know there are dirty cops. Some are friends of mine."

"Sonny, please, man, just *listen* to me for a second."

"Shut up a minute, Riz. We go back a long way, I'm not going to blow the whistle on you. Not yet, anyway. First I gotta know where this little white babe went."

"Sonny, I swear, I don't know. I know Vinnie has her, but that's it. He called me from a goddamn plane a coupla hours ago, so God knows where he went. New York, maybe."

Johnson shook his head. The waiter showed up for the order, but was told to come back. Then Johnson said, "Listen to me first, Riz. Okay? I'm just trying to save a few souls here, that's all. I know Vinnie has here. Everyone does. People are going to put two and two together and the IAD will come down hard on your caramel ass you'll be sorry you ever met Leadass."

"Sonny."

Leadbelly Louie had just walked up to their table. He'd been following Rizzo ever since the Helen fiasco at the mansion. He seemed bemused, as always, by life in general. At this point in time, Vinnie was still alive, up in the air someplace in his jet, speeding toward an appointment with disaster.

"Evening, gentlemen," Louie smiled. "Bottle of vintage on me?"

"Yeah," Johnson said, "I'll break one over your head if you don't beat it. You're spoiling my oxygen."

Louie laughed. "You smug spear-chuckers kill me." Everyone stiffened, nobody moved. Rizzo looked at Johnson and shook his head. "Anyway, you're out of your league, Miami. Yeah, I know who you are. You got the hots for this crazy little dame same as everybody else. I don't get it. Must be some piece of work in the sack. Anyway, Rizzo, call me later after you dump this piece of shit, okay? Vinnie's going to call me from Reno later, when he lands. I think you'll want to hear about our conversation, since I'm sure your name will come up. All right?" Louie patted

Rizzo's tense shoulder. Then he sauntered off and out of the restaurant.

"Nice friends you got," Johnson said. "He just came over here to blow your cover in front of me. He probably ran a check on me already, knows I'm not dirty."

"Sonny, god *damn* it!" Heads turned in the restaurant toward the outburst. "Can't you see how deep I'm in it, man? It's too late. For me, and for this stupid chick"

"She's not stupid. I feel sorry for Vinnie, tell the truth. Ten to one she'll waste him, same as Tony."

"Unless he does her first, which will probably be the way it plays."

"I wouldn't bet on Vinnie, Riz."

"Just don't call me dirty anymore."

Johnson just looked sadly at his old friend. "Well, guess I'll just head back for Miami."

"So soon? Sonny, can't we just talk, man?"

"About what? You let that scum talk to us like that? You're right, Riz. It's later than I thought. Anyway, I came to find Helen. Obviously she isn't even in Louisiana anymore. Say hello to Professor O'Grady for me. Hell— small world, ain't it?" Johnson got up and walked out. Even in a shrinking world, Rizzo felt puny.

THIRTY-NINE

Crossing over the Bay Bridge, the pop-up storybook skyline of San Francisco loomed before Johnny and Helen behind the wheel of the limo like a glistening beacon from beyond the rainbow. Finally, things were falling into place. Helen beamed with pride and satisfaction. As she took the 5th Street exit and entered downtown, she felt at home in this land of the beautiful and the bizarre. She'd always wanted to come here, lured by the City's reputation for liberal, open-minded acceptance of all types of warped individuals and fugitives from their own pasts. Plus she could take a ferry out to Alcatraz, one of her lifelong ambitions. The idea of a prison as a tourist attraction amused her. Normal citizens found people like her so fucking fascinating. They wrote books and made movies about her kind. She could never understand why. She wanted to visit a prison as a tourist and try to see what the attraction was. To her, an abandoned prison was like an empty zoo. Helen couldn't figure out whether she was an outsider or an insider. It depended on perspective, she supposed. Sometimes she felt like she was outside looking in at everyone having a nice, normal life; other times, she felt like she was trapped inside a bubble floating through space, and everyone else on the outside was looking at her, trying to figure out what she was, what made her tick, like she was a UFO—an Unconventional Fucking Oddball.

She followed the signs into North Beach, drove down Columbus Ave. straight to Fisherman's Wharf, and parked the limo. It was a breezy spring day. The Bay was a vivid blue against the mountains of Marin and Alameda Counties.

Alcatraz looked like a palace surrounded by a massive moat full of sailboats. They could see the Golden Gate Bridge being enshrouded by an encroaching fog bank. The weather was cool and invigorating, unlike anywhere Helen had ever been before. The fact that she was walking around in a man's jacket buttoned up over her naked voluptuous body didn't seem to faze many people. Johnny's blood splattered T-shirt was likewise tolerated. Helen felt at home, though she did want to put something on under the jacket, which barely covered her private parts, reaching down to the tiptop of her thighs only. The sea breeze wafted up her goose-pimpled flesh and gave her visible chills. She had on her red high heels that she had retrieved from the trunk along with Johnny. Johnny felt conspicuous in his blood-soaked aloha shirt, but he was also overwhelmed by his brand new environment. He felt at home as well. Still, new clothes, and food, were definitely in order.

Helen was considering their prospects as they walked along the Wharf, being gawked at by several tourists as typically eccentric native Californians. They even had their picture taken, unknown to them. They wound up on Pier 39 looking out at the seals and the Bay. They kissed passionately, absorbed by the romantic ambience, temporarily forgetting the death and destruction left in their wake.

"If only we had lunch money, I'd be a completely happy guy," Johnny said with a sigh. "Well, almost."

"Whaddya mean—*almost*?" Helen said, narrowing her eyes playfully.

"I still miss my cat. And I'll have to start a whole new book with a whole new laptop. If we finally get a chance to breath and take it easy."

She kissed him and bit the end of his nose like a kitten. "Don't count on it."

Suddenly Johnny felt his heart sink. Was this it, then? Was this to be his lifestyle until he was gunned down in some alley by the cops? He needed to contemplate his options, and quickly.

A pair of aging punk rockers stopped by to pay tribute to Johnny's shirt. "The blood's a great touch!" one of them said. He'd inadvertently inspired the Tiki Zombie Look, destined to become a popular new counterculture hipster clothesline. What a town, Johnny thought. But he still vaguely ached with the notion that he was clear across the country from everything sacred to him, including his aborted love affair with Loretta lynx—dull, but stable. He had to block her out as he kissed Helen again.

"Time to go shopping," she said.

"Please be careful," Johnny said, following her back toward the heart of North Beach. Different town, same shit.

They walked up Powell and into Washington Square. The cathedral in its center was complemented by Coit Tower up on Telegraph Hill. Trendy cafes, bustling bars, and fancy restaurants flanked the park, which was populated by serene street people, tourists, and happy residents. The fog was drifting into the City now, and Helen was starting to shiver. Johnny put his arm around her tightly, so her body partially covered his stained shirt, which was beginning to cause him real embarrassment now, despite its heartfelt reception by the punkers.

"We have to live in the limo for a while," Helen said as they walked up Columbus and then turned on Grant, passing The Saloon and then Cafe Trieste, both bohemian landmarks. Mad poets and wild musicians abounded. This was an entirely new universe for both Helen and Johnny. If only they had clothes, they'd feel so much more comfortable. "At least I didn't steal a Volkswagen," Helen noted.

She led Johnny into a Grant Street boutique that specialized in vintage hipster threads. Helen had left her .45 in the limo, which had already garnered a parking ticket sitting out by the Wharf, but that was not an immediate problem. Sooner or later the SFPD would run the plate and trace the ownership to one "Wild West Willie" Romero of

Reno, and by then Helen and Johnny would be safe and secure in their love nest. In the meantime, Helen didn't want to tempt herself, so she had left the gun in the limo.

Johnny and Helen browsed around the store. The clerk, a young girl with pink hair and a phony Marilyn Monroe mole on her sad, bored face, pegged the two shoppers as street people. She didn't care if they looked around as long as they didn't get the merchandise dirty or steal anything. The clerk went back to her movie magazine, playing with her long, golden earrings and snapping her gum. The clerk was dressed in black leotards, matching her perpetually gothic mood.

"Excuse me miss, do you take credit?" Helen asked her sweetly. Johnny cringed, but said nothing.

"Just cash or check," the clerk said without looking up. She could tell Helen had no underwear on beneath the main's jacket, and thought Helen was either very cool or very sick. Maybe both, which would make her someone to know. "You guys doing your laundry or somethin'?" she then added, smiling but still keeping her nose in the magazine.

"No. All of our clothes burned in a fire," Helen said with surprising sincerity. "We lost everything."

The clerk looked up. "Really? I'm sorry to hear that. What a drag. I lost stuff in a fire once. What a nightmare."

"Really? Then you know how we feel." Helen's eyes were wet with synthetic grief. Johnny just shook his head and sighed, trying on an oversized broad-shouldered '50s detective style jacket, like something out of *77 Sunset Strip*—or *Hawaiian Eye*, especially when combined with his bloody aloha shirt. If only he could afford it. He dreamed on while Helen's conversation with the clerk turned into a distant drone. He didn't hear Helen fabricating their life stories, telling the clerk about their abused child-hoods as well as more recent traumas. After fifteen minutes of this crap, Helen walked up behind Johnny and hugged him. "Pick out what you want," she said. "Within reason. Just one set of clothes. We'll pay later, don't worry. This is on the up and up for once."

Astonished, wary, Johnny picked out some cool '50s style trousers to match the jacket. Helen then picked out a sparkly blouse, a leopard-spotted mini-skirt, black leather knee-high boots, and some fishnet stockings. She also found a cute, form-fitting pink sweater to protect her from the chill. In exchange for these duds, Helen had promised to help clean the place up after closing, though that was obviously a euphemism for sexual favors. The clerk was bi-sexual and very attracted to Helen, and definitely planned on taking out some of this generosity in trade at some point in the very near future. Helen's allure was universal. If only she liked herself as much as everyone else did, she'd be a content human being, she thought to herself.

Helen did manage to steal two items: black, super-spy shades for herself and Johnny to look cool as they walked down the street, even though he couldn't see too well without his normal glasses. Helen would just yank him using his pecker as a leash anyway, the blonde leading the blind. The clerk asked Johnny if she could wash his soiled shirt and take it for the store, for a price, of course. Johnny said sure, and after a brief negotiation, pocketed another twenty bucks for a night on the town with his best girl. On the way out, he watched Helen French kiss the clerk, and it made him tingle all over.

The clerk had given Helen her phone number and told her to call if she wanted to crash at the clerk's flat in the Mission District later that night. Helen thanked her, and then she and Johnny went out for a pizza and sodas, like an old-fashioned, All-American couple. Then they splurged on a cab and took in the movie at a theater in Chinatown, a revival of John Woo's Hong Kong hit man classic *The Killer*. After the movie they went to a nearby café, sipped cappuccino and acted like frustrated artists. Johnny wasn't really acting, though at the time he didn't feel frustrated for the first time in many years. He was simply an artist enjoying his muse.

They had spent most of their money already, but decided to blow the rest on two pints of Bud at Spec's bar, which had the ambience of a beatnik living room. Johnny then dragged Helen into City Lights bookstore, which Helen found interesting as a people-watching place, whereas Johnny was struck with grand literary stimulation. He wanted to live in this town forever with Helen. He had finally found paradise.

It was after midnight when they walked back down to the Bay. They sat on a bench in the glade in front of Ghirardelli Square and listened to the waves lap the shoreline. The fog was very thick now and the lights of the Golden Gate twinkled in the distance.

Then they went back to the limo and made love and slept more soundly than ever before in their lovelorn lives. Visions of the future obscured memories of the past. To them, the Bay Bridge had linked them with a promising destiny. Too bad it was a two-way bridge.

FORTY

Ever since she was a child, Loretta Lynx, a notorious sleepwalker, had been afflicted, or as she saw it, blessed, with strange, surreal dreams of death. In many of these dreams a madman was pursuing her with an axe, which chased her to the edge of the storm-swept cliff. Looking below, Loretta saw bloody corpses strewn across the rocks. When she turned to face the murderer, as he raised his axe high in the air, poised to chop her to pieces, then toss those hunks of pretty flesh into the raging turf, she always woke up—*wet*. So far, these had been the only orgasms she had ever experienced.

These dreams had deserted her for almost a year before Johnny entered her life. Then her beloved axe murderer returned, only this time his murky countenance began to resemble Johnny Varga. Her nightmare lover now had a daytime doppelganger identity. Of course, she could never seriously date a psycho killer, but it would be fun to flirt.

While lying in bed waiting for her face to heal from radical cosmetic surgery, her natural beauty almost fully restored, though in a plastic sort of way, which would fit right in around Hollywood, Loretta dreamed constantly of her axe-wielding lover boy. Except in the new dreams, the axe made contact. She could feel it penetrating her chest with a nauseating squishy sound, geysers of blood bathing both her and her attacker as she pulled him over the cliff with her into the jagged rocks below, joining a marine graveyard of withered cadavers. Sometimes the cadavers would be repugnant zombie rapists who then molested and devoured her as she screamed with ecstasy. Then something would happen—her parents would call or visit—and ruin this morbidly erotic fantasy. No one else knew of her darkly secret passions. She knew if she shared them with anyone, they might get the wrong impression of her, as a freak or something.

While awake and not teasingly fending off slasher suitors, Loretta was making phone calls to Los Angeles. A sorority sister was living there now, married to some kind of wealthy-by-inheritance asshole in Pacific Palisades. Another sorority sister was shacked up with an aging movie actor in Malibu, trying to make it as a singer-actress-fashion-designer-environmentalist. Saving seals and making deals, that was her life story. Loretta wanted to join her, and was doing this advance long distance networking to properly plan her prospects in Tinsel Town. Both of her sorority sisters were already tired of domestic life and considering single-hood again, especially in this land of model hunks, so there was a chance Loretta would have two roommates come autumn. By then she would have been operated on and rejuvenated, and she could get on with the business of fame and fortune. Loretta didn't inform anyone of this—not even Prissy, who had betrayed Loretta's trust once already.

So, whenever Daddy Lynx talked about Harvard Law School or some kind of similar nonsense, Loretta always smiled sweetly in complete accord. If she could stand waiting tables in Miami Beach, she could stand it in L.A. Besides, all the upcoming starlets waited tables out there. She'd be in good company. Being a waitress was practically a prerequisite for stardom, it seemed. The way she saw it, she was already ahead of the game.

When Prissy wasn't around, Loretta read her books on the Method and the Madness. She'd take aerobics and acting classes on the West Coast, hobnob with agents at wild parties, run the whole gamut of schmoozing until she forced her dreams to happen. After all, she was no Johnny Varga. Poor sap. Thirty-something years old and still carting human waste around the suburbs. Well, not lately. There was a chance he was dead by now. That Helen Black bitch had put on a convincing show of hostility toward him in New Orleans. Johnny was no longer considered an accomplice, but a kidnap victim. Loretta wondered how those two had ever hooked up in the first place. Didn't matter, really. Her brief, violent encounter with Helen had changed her life forever, and Johnny had been the accidental catalyst. Loretta, too, could smell the fumes of Fate permeating her existence. But she had to be careful she didn't inhale too deeply, or she wouldn't just be sniffing, she'd be choking.

And unknown to Loretta or anyone else, four hundred miles north of Loretta's ultimate destination, her two unwitting career boosters were lost in a fog of their own making. The fumes of Fate just mixed with the mist. But Loretta didn't hate them anymore, wherever they were. Thanks to Helen, Loretta would no longer have to rely on vicarious thrills. She finally had the blues because she'd paid the dues. She now felt ready for her close-up—once the bandages came off, that is.

FORTY-ONE

Sonny Johnson had lost all respect for the Mob now. They were ruthless, greedy, big-mouthed bigots who didn't hesitate to kill anyone who pissed them off. Of course, this was not news, but somehow Johnson had always blocked out the truth because they talked, walked, dressed, and acted so damn cool, at least in the movies. This wasn't *Goodfellas* or *The Sopranos*, though. Their true-life ugly underbelly had been exposed in the light of rampant corruption. Johnson felt sorry for Rizzo, but was powerless to step outside his jurisdiction—personally and professionally— and help him. If Leadbelly Louie were a Miami wise guy, Johnson would've been severely tempted to exact vigilante justice. Maybe he was burning out after all, like his wife Sara always told him lately, every night over dinner, when he made it home in time, that is.

The newsflash of Vinnie's mishap in Reno spread rapidly through the *goombah* grapevines. Even New York, while upset about losing another battle with the notorious Helen Black, was somewhat amused by her methods. Vinnie didn't bleed to death after all. Wild West Willie had found him and taken him to a hospital and they'd saved him, but having to piss through a tube and not being able to screw ever again made life meaningless for a macho religious horn dog like Vinnie. The shame and humiliation that accompanied the loss of his number one appendage was unbearable. Helen had literally robbed him of his manhood. He was a joke now, to his own people and to the Law. He'd have resigned his post even if the Mob had not asked him to retire, moved somewhere out of the country preferably, since his presence was deemed annoying and only served to remind everybody of how this young girl was making a laughing stock of Mob prowess. Not even New York knew where she was at this point. Elmo wasn't talking. He and Wild West Willie had skipped the continent soon after the whole incident had hit the airwaves. The media at large was ignorant of it, naturally.

The Mob could do without such bad press. Vinnie the Vine had blown it when he had blown up El Doctor anyway. But there was to be no subsequent bloody turf war with the Cubans, especially now with Vinnie out of the picture. Mob delegates had been dispatched to assure El Doctor's survivors that the Mob had no intention of crossing any lines without talking shop first, and that Vinnie had acted on his own, out of personal passion, a lie which happened to be true. The Cubans took a cash settlement and war was averted.

Sonny Johnson sat on El Doctor's tape, unsure whom to trust with it now. Miami was brought up to speed within days of Vinnie's infamous comic tragedy, and Sonny Johnson felt strangely relieved, even vindicated. Like Leadbelly Louie, Sara suspected Johnson had more than rehabilitation on his mind while pursuing Helen, and Johnson had denied it, to everyone, even himself. He only knew her through surveillance photos and her file, for God's sake. It wasn't like he was obsessed with her or anything. However, he thought of her quite often in the ensuing months, and wished Helen Black well, wherever she might be.

FORTY-TWO

Pleading *nolo contendere* and throwing himself on the mercy of the courts had occurred to Johnny as a viable option, but as time went on and his love for Helen deepened, he quietly resigned himself to a life of constantly looking over his shoulder while Helen went down on him. He couldn't decide whether it was heaven or hell. Somewhere in between, probably. It was like a line from a song by one of his favorite groups, Blondie: "*I'll give you head and shoulders to lean on.*" And in between sex acts with his beloved, he was actually writing and completing his book about her, called *Down An Alley, Darkly*. Helen had suggested he shorten the title to *Dark Alley*, or just *Alley*, either one a graphic metaphor for the true star of this saga, her pussy, because movie makers seemed to like short, succinct titles, as she pointed out. Already she was looking forward to the movie sale. "Maybe I'll just call it *Al*," Johnny said.

They were living now in a residential hotel in Chinatown called The Blue Bamboo. To pay the tab, Johnny pulled graveyard shifts as a desk clerk and Helen did the weekly laundry for all residents, most of whom were either retired strippers, old Chinese living on a pension or single mothers of various races living on welfare. Helen had been the one to swing this deal, naturally. She met and wooed the Chinese owner of the hotel, Mr. Shun, in a North Beach bar a few nights after she and Johnny had arrived in town. They were getting tired of living in the limo and begging for spare change, and Helen had sworn to herself as well as to Johnny she would not resort to crime unless totally necessary.

Going straight was going to ruin them, however, unless honest resourcefulness came to the rescue. Johnny had needed a shave and a bath badly, so he couldn't even look for a job until he found a place to wash up. Mr. Shun was on a drunken excursion into North Beach, an Italian neighborhood bordering Chinatown but gradually undergoing radical integration and gentrification by sundry ethnic and social groups. He was sitting at the bar of the Bohemian Cigar Store when in walked Helen and Johnny in their new old duds, wrinkled and dirty after days and nights of wear, and Helen made the rounds of the loner types until she struck up a conversation with Mr. Shun, who was married but played the field when possible. Mr. Shun liked white women, especially ones stacked like Helen, since his Chinese wife and mistresses were so small chested.

Helen explained her situation, describing Johnny as her long lost brother, recently reunited, and before an hour was up Helen had found them a new home. Besides laundry, Helen also did some maid work which she despised, and for this she was given cash bonuses. She also tolerated Mr. Shun copping a feel now and then, and eventually occasional hand jobs, which she preferred to odd jobs, but she didn't tell Johnny, who assumed it anyway. But he was so consumed by the laptop Helen mugged off a yuppie in the Financial District that he almost didn't care. He was writing for his life now. Even while on duty in the quiet office of the Blue Bamboo Hotel, Johnny was busy scribbling notes based on Helen's life and near-death experiences. Helen often sat with him, sometimes hiding beneath the desk and giving him head and inspiration while he wrote. Johnny couldn't have been happier.

This pleasant situation lasted throughout the summer and into the fall. No Feds, cops, or hit men showed up to crash their private little party, and Helen felt content for the very first time in her life. However, she was not entirely satisfied with her arrangement with Mr. Shun, who smelled funny, like an old fish. But more than anything, she wanted

Johnny to finish his book, get it typed, and submit it before they left the hotel. Mr. Shun bought their groceries as long as Helen complied with reasonable sexual demands. For the first time in her life, she felt like a real whore. But she was justified it since she was doing it for Johnny's sake, more than her own.

Johnny channeled his anxious imagination into the book with a vengeance, so they could move out and up. Helen was growing increasingly impatient as weeks became months. This was not her dream come true by a long shot. Johnny was almost perfect, at least by her sorry standards, but their lifestyle had to change. She wasn't used to this kind of shit. She'd risked her life and rubbed shoulders with mobsters to avoid it. Her fantasies of earning a GPA degree were dwindling rapidly. She'd lost her motivation. When she'd applied at San Francisco State, they laughed her out of the office because she kept giving different names and places of origin during the course of a fifteen-minute interview. It seemed hopeless. The strain and stress induced more and more of her odd headaches. Also, she'd been monogamous with Johnny, not counting jacking off their landlord once a week, for much longer than she'd ever been, and it felt strange to her, even uncomfortable. She took to going out nights when he was asleep and playing pool with bikers and dopers, getting drunk and making out with a few but always managing to make it home with her panties still on. She still loved Johnny. She just didn't love her life with him anymore.

Their hotel room at The Blue Bamboo overlooked a dark alley littered with stray cats, garbage cans, and leaking bums who sometimes made too much noise. The blue neon hotel sign was visible from an angle on the corner of the building facing the street. An ancient sax player blew tunes for tourists within earshot on a daily and nightly basis. Johnny loved it; Helen thought it was okay but not exactly home sweet home. Johnny asked Helen if she cared to skip down to Palo Alto one day and pay a visit on his married ex-girlfriend who had spurned him. Helen said she'd only wind up killing the bimbo as well as her entire family, which was fine with Johnny, but it never happened. Helen was like a caged tigress, pacing back and forth, back and forth, waiting for the right moment to escape. Sometimes when they made love Johnny felt like he was injecting her with tranquilizers, to soothe the savage beast within her, hungry for freedom.

"Where do you go nights?" he asked her out of the blue one night while he was sitting at his post in the office. It was 2 A.M. and the whole world felt like a Tom Waits song.

"What do you mean, where do I go nights?" she snapped, avoiding eye contact. Julie London sang on the portable CD player, a bonus from Mr. Shun. "Cry Me A River" was the right tune at the right time.

"Look at me Helen," he said. "Just tell me. If you see other guys (he swallowed hard) I'll understand, believe me. You're restless, I can tell."

"Fuck you Johnny," Helen said petulantly.

"What's that for? I was just askin'. I gotta right to wonder, right?" Jesus, late night dialogue could get corny, he thought. He let it rest while he watched the action on the TV mounted in the corner. Some soft-core porn was on, but with the sound low. Mr. Shun didn't want his desk clerks becoming too distracted by the TV, but he also didn't want them falling asleep on the job. The images seemed so sad and depressing all of a sudden.

"I play pool sometimes, ya mind?"

Johnny looked up from his stolen laptop, containing he first draft of his book, which he spent days and nights typing. "You play pool? With other people?"

"Yeah, bright boy. I didn't say I played *pocket* pool." Johnny idly flipped channels and found *The Big Sleep* on TCM. He felt like Bogart. But if he got cute with Helen, she'd slap the shit out him. "Can we change the fuckin' station? I'm sick of this old shit," she said suddenly.

"Helen, c'mon, what's wrong? I'm just wondering."

"Mind your own fuckin' business, Johnny. It would serve you right I went out and fucked a few sailors on a pool table."

Johnny froze. "Helen, just tell me if you did, that's all. I mean, since we don't use rubbers and all, if you were to pick somethin' up, y'know, that could suck for both of us. "

"You mean like a *baby*?" She was glaring at him now with chilling intensity, yet her vulnerability was bubbling beneath the wounded surface.

"No, like a virus. Well, a baby too, but you told me you were on the pill."

"I lied."

"You *lied*?"

"Yup. Sue me, why don'tcha."

Johnny didn't feel like writing any more tonight. "Helen, why can't you just tell me? Just tell me. I love you, you know that. I want you to be happy, and you don't seem very happy lately."

"Are you happy?"

"Well, yeah. Pretty much. But..."

"Then don't fuckin' worry about me, just write your fuckin' masterpiece and let me live my own fuckin' life over here."

"But I can't be happy if you're *not*, don't you see?"

"I thought you just said you were happy."

"I am, I guess, pretty much, but..."

"So then you're full of shit, is that what you're sayin'?"

"No, not at all. I just want to find out what's been bugging you lately. I mean, like, why don't you ever ask me to play pool with you?"

"Aw, fuck it. You're either workin' or asleep or workin' on your fuckin' masterpiece."

"But I'd drop it if you asked me to."'

"You would? What a wimp. You should tell me to fuck off."

"But Helen, I *love* you."

"*DON'T FUCKING SAY THAT ANYMORE*!" Helen

shot upright and paced the office. Johnny hoped the scream didn't arouse Mr. Shun or any of the residents, most of who were insomniacs and visited him when Helen wasn't around. "I need a cigarette," she said, going through the desk drawers. "*GIVE ME A FUCKING CIGARETTE! NOW!*"

"Helen, please, cool it."

"*DON'T FUCKING TELL ME WHAT TO DO, MOTHERFUCKER!*" Helen was crying now, and shaking like she needed a fix. She hadn't smoked in a month, but this was not cold turkey hysteria—it was a symptom of something far more disturbing. Things had been too smooth, too calm for too long. Helen was suddenly unraveling before Johnny's fogged-over glasses. Finally, she collapsed on his lap and sobbed into his shoulder. "I'm sorry, Johnny-O. It's just that I feel so *desperate*."

"For what, sweetheart?" Johnny whispered soothingly in her ear.

"I don't know," she whimpered. "I just don't fucking know anymore."

Suddenly Johnny felt an aching pang for The Leopard Man. He felt lonesome, stranded in a strange town full of even stranger strangers. Many nights he had lay awake missing The Leopard Man, wondering what had become of him, but at this very moment, as Helen so completely revealed her stubborn unhappiness, Johnny missed The Leopard Man more than ever. The abrupt tidal wave of loneliness was devastating, and he felt weak and nauseous. Helen had another one of her headaches, an affliction she had never revealed to him, and as she cried her heart out on his shoulder, it only grew worse.

Mr. Shun came downstairs to find out the origin of the commotion, fearing Johnny was dealing with a drunken hotel guest. But when he saw Helen in Johnny's lap, shaking with sobs, he decided to let it wait. He figured Helen had finally told her so-called brother she'd been blowing the boss, and Shun didn't want any rumors bouncing around the hotel. He planned to kick them out in the morning. He just went back to bed.

"I wove you too," Helen whispered to Johnny in the baby talk she had spoken in months before in Miami. Sometimes while making love she did it too, and it always turned Johnny on for some reason, but now it gave him the heebie-jeebies. "I weely do, Johnny-O. I wove you, Daddy." For the first time, it was creeping Johnny out.

Johnny knew Helen had never known her father and sought a surrogate in other men, formerly gangsters boasting non-conformist attributes and power, and now she'd chosen Johnny for the role, for some random reason. "I'm not your Daddy really," he said softly, taking a chance. "I'm just a little kid like you inside."

"I know, silly," she sniffled. "But you're also the daddy of the baby inside of me."

Stunned into silence, Johnny stared at Bogey and Bacall on the tube, wishing he could leap inside of it and leave this dimension behind forever.

FORTY-THREE

The next morning Mr. Shun gave Helen fifty dollars and her walking papers. She and Johnny had to leave to make room for some family of his coming in from Shanghai, he told her. Since there was no lease and their arrangement had never been put on paper, there was no binding legal agreement, so Johnny, Helen, and the month old fetus were back on the street. Johnny carried his stolen laptop with him everywhere. At this rate, he'd make Jack Kerouac look like a literary paraplegic.

Helen felt very much relieved after her confession. She did ask Johnny if she should get an abortion, but he said no, realizing she had always wanted a kid, someone to raise properly, to spoil and adore, someone who could have the childhood she had always wanted. Also, it would create a lifelong bond with her, which would ensure some sort of lasting relationship between them, no matter what else happened. But already he was wondering whether this was a blessing or a curse.

Helen became convinced she was pregnant after a visit to a North Beach clinic for corroboration. Morning sickness had been the first clue. She was now very glad she had been faithful to Johnny all summer, relatively speaking, because she had no doubt he was the father. Johnny's love for her made everything seem right. Her restlessness turned into contentment again, verging on happiness. Even as they roamed the streets wondering how best to spend the fifty bucks, Helen was practically overcome with something that felt like real joy.

"I think I'm going to be happy now," she said, kissing

Johnny as they sat on a park bench in Washington Square. Helen couldn't stop crying. It was all so beautiful, he could hardly stand it. She felt a power within her that rivaled the feeling she got from shooting people. It was frightening and wonderful at the same time.

"Let's take the boat to Alcatraz!" Helen said, clutching his wrist tightly with excitement. "It won't cost much. We'll still have enough to eat on. At least for today!"

Johnny didn't see the prudence in blowing her severance pay on a tourist trap, but if it made her happy, so be it. As for himself, Johnny experienced mixed emotions about their predicament. A novel and a baby on the way at the same time could be terminally stressful, mainly because there was the chance the first wouldn't make any money, whereas the second would definitely cost a bundle.

"Sure," he shrugged. "Why not?"

Helen kissed him with an urgency he'd never felt from her. For once, a woman's love for him made Johnny even queasier than the absence of it. This was a stark turnabout from the night before, when she had seemed so cold and distant. Now he knew he'd never get rid of her. Not that he wanted to. But the proximity of such passion was even more overwhelming than he could've ever imagined. The responsibility, both for Helen's fragile emotional state and the welfare of their child, made his heart drop into his stomach like an overripe tomato into a churning blender.

Hand in hand, sweaty palms and all, Johnny and Helen walked down to the pier where the tour boats cast off, signed up for their ride, paid for the tickets, and waited in line for the next boat. They were surrounded by people from all over the world, mostly families and couples. "We're like everyone else now," Helen whispered as she kissed Johnny's cheek tenderly. He clutched onto the laptop as a strong sea breeze whipped about them. Fleecy clouds hung like celestial cottontails in the perfect azure firmament. The City was positively scintillating on such a day. Johnny struggled for appreciation of the moment, knowing it would slip away all too quickly and get absorbed by the quicksand of his past, which contained very few memories such as this one.

As the boat whisked them across the choppy Bay waters, and seagulls hung in seemingly frozen suspension above Johnny and Helen as they embraced on the deck, both grew very silent.

While the tour of the prison and the grounds was conducted, Johnny and Helen hardly exchanged a few sentences, except to remark on the frightening, claustrophobic conditions of the cells. "We had it good compared to this," Helen said in awe, recalling her days in Florida jails, which seemed like another lifetime, on another planet. Helen watched the people looking at the landmark more than she noticed anything else on the island. When the tour guide revealed civic hopes to some day turn Alcatraz into a private resort, a kind of theme park, and that there had been several movements to legalize the island as a gambling outpost, turning the prison into a grand casino, Helen burst out laughing.

"Normal people are so funny," she said lowly to Johnny. He didn't reply. She was very moody and pensive as the boat returned them to the mainland.

"What now?" Johnny asked her after a pregnant pause.

Helen looked out toward the Golden Gate and pointed. "I've always wanted to walk across that bridge," she said with a little girl smile.

Johnny let out a sigh, and then kissed her cheek. "Let's do it. Do it while we can."

"That's what I always say," Helen said eerily, slipping her hand into his as they walked all the way past Ghirardelli Square, the Presidio, and the Marina to Fort Point just beneath the bridge. "This is where Kim Novak tried to drown herself in *Vertigo*," Johnny pointed out as they stood watching the waves crash and break against the platform. The grandeur of the orange monument was breathtaking so close up. "It doesn't even look real, with me standing right underneath it," Helen said. "Looks like a painting, huh?" Johnny smiled and held her, as if they were immobile, immortal figures in this painting.

"So this is where that chick, Kim whatsit, jumped in the water, huh?" Helen said, staring into the foamy waters, murky, thick, and windswept, almost inviting in its mysterious majesty.

"Yeah," Johnny said softly.

"She drown?"

"Jimmy Stewart saved her."

"Nice guy."

"Yeah. He loved her, but she didn't know it yet."

Helen turned and looked at him with an expression of such sad tenderness he thought his heart was going to pop right there. She touched his face.

"I know you love me, though," she said.

Johnny held and kissed her, taking a mental Polaroid picture of the moment. Lovers against a romantic backdrop, he called it. Looking back on it, he would never believe he was the guy in the picture.

They walked up the steep hill and onto the pedestrian walkway of the bridge. Johnny experienced his own vertigo as they walked beneath the towering arches, and then stopped to look back at the skyline of the City. It was too perfect. He almost couldn't relax enough to enjoy it. He took more mental pictures for his scrapbook, and held onto Helen like she was going to disappear any second.

"I never thought this would happen to me," Johnny said, his laptop and novel under one arm, Helen under the other. "I have everything. No money, no place to sleep tonight, but everything that counts. Y'know?"

Helen didn't reply. She was weeping as she stared down into the Bay. Despite the idyllic setting, she could feel another headache coming on.

"What's wrong?" Johnny asked her. "Aren't you happy now?"

"Oh, Johnny," she said brokenly. "I'm so sorry"

"What for, sweetheart?" He stroked her hair and face.

"My whole life," she said, "Look what a mess I've made of it. All those guys I slept with—none of them meant anything to me. I was just looking for you in the wrong places."

"I know. I know that. You don't have to explain anything."

"Johnny, it's still inside me, though."

"What? The baby?"

"*No*. The *other* thing. Whatever it is that made me do all those awful things. It's still there. It's trying to eat our baby." She dug her nails into his palm like she was slipping away into an abyss. "We can't let that happen, Johnny."

Johnny wasn't sure what to say, so he just held her, but she was rigid to the touch, unyielding.

"Remember my tattoo?" she said.

"The broken heart one? Yeah, sure. You never did tell me why you have that."

"It's under my boob, y'know? Right where my heart is, or where I thought it was. I found out later the heart is more in the center of your chest. Doesn't matter, though, I guess."

"So *why*?"

"Because that's how I'll always feel, Johnny. No matter what. Some things you can't fix. Someone dropped me in a trashcan when I was a baby, like ours, and broke my stupid little heart. Not cracked it, not dented it, but they broke the fucker. It'll never be fixed."

Johnny swallowed nervously. "Helen, but what about us? Our baby? Doesn't that help at all?"

She clutched his arm for dear life. "Yes, Johnny, at this moment I'm perfectly happy, more than I've ever been. That's why I don't want it to end, to get ruined, and I know it will if I can't kill this thing inside of me that's trying to eat our baby. I don't want my baby to be born without a heart. And this thing in me...it wants our baby's heart. This guy Vinnie? He thought I had a demon inside of me. I think he was right. I don't know how it got there. I only know one way to get rid of it."

"How?" Johnny whispered. "*Kill* it?"

"How are we gonna do that? Get religion?" Helen smiled wanly. "Maybe. We'll see what happens." Johnny felt relief. At least she talked like she'd be around for a while now.

"Don't ever leave me," he said hoarsely. "I love you."

She turned and they held each other for a long time. "I love you too," she said as she kissed his face over and over. "We'll always be together. I promise. Goodbye."

Before he could react, Helen pushed him away and jumped over the railing of the Golden Gate Bridge. As Johnny lunged after her, he let go of his laptop, and the wind carried it away along with Helen. Johnny heard screams behind him as he watched Helen disappear into the dark waters below, falling in slow motion, whipped by the winds, loose and free, her naturally dark hair a diminishing point of reference as she merged with the Bay like an anonymous drop in the big, blue ocean.

FORTY-FOUR

Time passed, like a bus with an unknown schedule, rushing past its passengers waiting at the depot and not giving them a fair chance to catch up. Johnny finally caught his bus, however, hanging onto the rear fender and going the distance. Now he was known as John Varga, author of *Down An Alley, Darkly*, a cult crime novel that everyone knew was based on his experiences with Helen Black, whom he refused to discuss in interviews. He was living out in L.A. now, in Westwood, the community surrounding UCLA, because he had been hired to write the screenplay for his book, which the producers insisted on calling simply *Dark Alley*. Helen's instincts were always sound where it concerned people and money, Johnny recalled fondly. Hanging onto his bus and sucking in the fumes of Fate, Johnny never failed to remember Helen, who was now probably *driving* the damn bus.

Johnny decorated his Westwood studio almost exactly the same as his old place back in Miami Beach, though with more upscale bamboo and tiki products. He found a new haunt at Tiki-Ti, corner of Hollywood and Sunset. Amazingly, The Leopard Man had been waiting for him when he'd finally returned to his Miami digs. So was Sonny Johnson, who was there more as an outside observer than a cop. Johnson just wanted to know one thing: was Helen still alive? Johnny told him everything about his trip, from A to Z. Johnson listened in silence, shaking his head. While Johnny was away, Johnson had given El Doctor's tape to the Herald anonymously, and now many of the Mob's minions were under indictment—except for Captain Rizzo in New Orleans. Johnson had deleted his name from the tape after making Rizzo swear he'd do everything in his power to take down Leadbelly Louie. Johnson felt good about the case, despite the death of Helen.

"It was her only way out," Johnson told Johnny.

"I know," Johnny replied stoically. Then Johnson took him out to his Camaro for a surprise: Johnny's original laptop, retrieved from the NOPD personal effects warehouse. Johnson had asked Rizzo to give it to him so he could return it to Johnny Varga, innocent kidnap victim, given up for dead.

Helen's body was never recovered, however, so the identity of the suicide was never made public. Johnny had immediately hitchhiked out of town and across country. Normally, the idea of hitchhiking struck Johnny as foolish and dangerous, but in the state he was in, being picked up by a psycho killer would have felt like mercy. On the contrary, a cute, wholesome, buxom gal from Colorado driving a pickup truck picked him up. She invited him to spend the night with her when they reached her home in Denver. Johnny suddenly had a new and intriguing sex appeal, and the Colorado girl made his stopover in her apartment a memorable experience to write about. But all Johnny wanted to do was get back to Miami and see The Leopard Man. The Colorado girl even loaned him some money, which Johnny promised to pay back. She gave him her address and phone number, and Johnny caught a bus for Houston, a train for Atlanta, and rode with an itinerant indie rock band all the way back to Miami.

Once there, he was greatly relieved to find a sympathetic landlord and a starving, but living, Leopard Man. The landlord never told Johnny he was an ex-button man, or that he had retired early because he had fallen in love with a nun who asked him to change his habits. The landlord even lent Johnny some money to eat on, and gave him work to do around the apartment complex to pay off the back rent. Johnny spent nights writing since he no longer had a TV and DVD player—he had forgotten that Helen had shot the shit out of them on their way out the door—and before long had virtually recreated his lost manuscript for *Down An Alley, Darkly*. He didn't even apply for his old job at the lab. He finished the book in two months, working for the landlord off and on, and sold the book to the third publisher he sent it to, thanks to the fame his name had garnered during his wild adventure with Helen, which now seemed like a long, sad, wet dream.

The book was not an instant bestseller but gained a steady following and went through several printings, enough to keep Johnny healthily in the chips for some time. The media caught wind of it and Johnny was besieged with phone calls, requesting his appearance on talk shows and exclusive newspaper and magazine rights to his story, but he waved them all off, telling them he had escaped from Helen and had no idea what had become of her. All he knew about her, he said, was that she was not the person they made her out to be. The character in his book was a sympathetic orphan who took a wrong turn and got lost down a dark alley. The book said everything he had to say about the subject.

When the Hollywood offer came, he moved back to L.A., a city he had sworn never to return to. Before he left, Johnny had called Loretta Lynx several times in the dead of night, but always hung up when she answered. Sometimes he received hang-up calls as well, and knew it was Loretta. He really didn't know what to say to her now, and he wasn't even sure how he felt about her in Helen's wake. He was in mourning, anyway.

On his final night in Miami, he called Loretta's number and got a recording saying her number had been disconnected. He resigned himself to the possibility he would never see her again. He should've talked to her when he had the chance, he lamented. It was just as well. Helen had ruined him for any other woman anyway. Not that Loretta Lynx was weeping by the wayside, praying for

Johnny's return. She probably hated him, holding him responsible for what had happened to her. At least she was still alive. That was something, he supposed. Even with the success he had always prayed for coming his way at long last, Johnny was still an unhappy, lonesome puppy.

With his royalties, Johnny was able to soup up the Edsel and not only restore it to its former glory, but modernize and enhance it with a new engine. Johnny was then able to drive all the way to L.A. in his Edsel, Leopard Man in the passenger seat. Helen was with him all the way. The movie deal would finance time to write a new book, though he wasn't sure what that book would be. Perhaps *Up A Warm, Wet Place*, about the minor league baseball player and the lesbian bartender. It was worth a shot, anyway. Without Helen, he was running out of material fast.

His L.A. routine, post-success, was eerily similar to his Miami life, pre-success: watching movies, writing his screenplay, beating off, playing with The Leopard Man. Why had he thought success would change his life, anyway? He needed to get out more, meet people, advertise his growing fame, since writers were not visible, identifiable celebrities. Johnny got along well with the director of the movie, and Mickey Rourke had just been signed to play the chief mobster, a combination of his former, deceased friends, Tony Volare and Vino Vinnie. Rourke liked Johnny and wanted to set him up with a groupie starlet, but Johnny was shy, still haunted by the ghost of Helen, so Rourke let it rest. Johnny later reconsidered this offer, however. He was now in his late thirties. His body ached for satisfaction, a woman's touch. He even called the girl in Colorado, and asked her to come visit him, but by now she was engaged. Same old story.

The part of Helen's character, called Ellen in the book, had not been cast yet. The director wanted an unknown to play the part, and even allowed Johnny some input on ideas. So far, no one who had read for the role from Johnny's first draft had the right combination of sensuality, cynicism, and empathy. Mickey Rourke came up with a few suggestions, but the director, known for low budget thrillers, wasn't satisfied with them. He knew she was out there somewhere, though. "Help me find her, Johnny," the director told him. "Hang out with Mickey, go to clubs. Get out more, for Chrissake. Live it up. Meet women. You can meet lots of struggling actresses in this town who'd love to play opposite Mickey in this part. They like guys who may beat the shit out of them. Learn something."

So Johnny haunted the coffee shops of L.A., reading the *Times* and Raymond Chandler novels, eschewing Rourke's biker parties for his own lone werewolf ways. He took to wearing old '60s suits with white dress shirts and skinny black ties. He found his "look." But inside, he felt as lost and naked as ever.

One day Johnny went to his favorite diner, Dolores' on Santa Monica Blvd in West L.A. It was a typical time machine—booths, a counter, waitresses in cute uniforms dishing out burgers and milkshakes. Considering all of civilization's achievements, the coffee shop was Johnny's favorite. Besides movies, coffee shops were the pinnacle of modern life, and had been since the 1950s, still Johnny's favorite era, the one his head lived in forever. His heart lived with Helen Black so he wasn't sure where the hell it was these days.

He sat at the counter, opened his paper, and then looked over the menu, still wearing his Ray-Bans for camouflage. He made a quick decision—the Eggplant Florentine—and then returned to the paper while he patiently waited for his waitress to show up and take his order.

"May I help you sir?" said a sweet, pretty voice.

Johnny looked up and his jaw dropped while his eyes strained for release from their sockets. A wave of *deja vu* made his skin ripple and his hair tingle. Standing before him with pen and pad in hand was the one and only Loretta Lynx—damaged goods, her visage somewhat altered by the surgery, but it was definitely his Loretta. Despite the few scars on her chin and left cheek she was instantly recognizable.

"*Johnny*?!" she exclaimed, her tan fading into white shock.

"What the hell are *you* doing here?" Johnny said after regaining control of his vocal chords.

"I work here," she said, her pen shivering in her grasp. "What are *you* doing here? Stalking me again?"

Johnny had to smile. "Yeah, right. Moved out here, hired a private dick, tracked you down. You should see the photos of you in the bathtub. Very nice."

Loretta half-smiled. "I could always renew my death threat, you know."

"At least you'd be speaking to me."

"So what are you doing way out here? Are you retired from the medical profession?"

"Well...I don't know if you heard, but I had a book published finally."

"Yeah, I know. I read it."

"You *did*?" Johnny beamed triumphantly. "Really? What did you think?"

"Hmmm, pretty violent. Sexy too, though. And sad. But also funny."

"So you liked it or what?" Johnny wanted to know.

"*Hmmm*, yes and no."

"Still non-committal, I see."

"Only where you're concerned, because I know it bugs you."

"Gee, thanks." Different town, different diner, same old bullshit banter. "Glad to see some things stay constant in life."

"Yeah, I guess. Like what?" she teased.

"You're still dying of love for me, for one."

"Oh, you could tell?"

"It's in your eyes. That crazy look I admire so much."

She narrowed those gleaming peeps. "Traitors. So why

wasn't *I* in your book?"

"Huh? You were expecting to be?"

"Well, since you were obviously writing about your experiences with that really crazy girl..."

"She wasn't crazy."

"Oh, excuse me. I guess that really makes *me* crazy."

"I'll buy that. Anyway, I'm writing my next book exclusively about you. I was saving up."

She lit up. "That's better. Maybe it will make up for what you did to me."

"What *I* did to *you*?" Johnny looked around. "You're blaming *me*, still?"

"I guess now you'll say you're completely innocent."

"I don't know about that, I always think so, but I'm always being told otherwise."

"Poor baby. Would you like some coffee?"

"Yeah, sure. But tell me somethin': what are you doing way the hell out here?"

"Well...it's a long story. What are you, writing a book?"

"Could be."

"I'm an actress now."

"Oh, obviously. *All* waitresses in L.A. are actresses."

"Very funny." Loretta got the coffee pot and filled Johnny's cup. It was steaming hot. "I have to at least look like I'm working."

"So have you gotten many parts yet?"

"A few. I was a semi-regular on this series that got cancelled mid-season. A reality show."

"Yeah? Which one?"

"It was called 'Scarred For Life.' About how people who've had tragic accidents cope with life afterward. Like me."

"Huh. Don't know that one. But I don't watch T.V. that much anymore, except for 'Mad Men.'"

"Even *I* watch that show. I can tell by the way you're dressed. It's better than those stupid Hawaiian shirts. Maybe you're finally developing good taste, thanks to my influence?"

Johnny grinned. "Must be it. You look good, Loretta. As pretty as ever."

Loretta's eyes teared up. "I better get back to work."

Johnny grabbed her arm gently, then let go. "Loretta, I'd like to be friends. Nice to know someone out here, someone I can talk to."

"Oh, is that what we are? Friends?"

"We could be. Hey, how would you like to read the screenplay I did for my book?"

"Are you going to write it on your napkin and leave it for me?"

"No, it's at home. You can stop by later and pick it up, if you want. Or else I'll drop it off at your place. Where are you living now?"

"Why?"

"Okay, forget it then."

"No, wait. I'm sorry, Johnny. Actually, I live in Hollywood, in a dumpy place with two of my sorority sisters. Well, one now. The other just moved out. She's marrying a producer."

"Great."

Loretta narrowed her eyes again. "So you think I'd be right for a part in your script?" Loretta asked seductively.

"Maybe."

"What part would that be?"

"You'll see. I'll have you meet the director tomorrow or something. Mickey Rourke's already been signed for it, too."

Loretta squealed. "Oh! He's so sexy! For an old guy."

Johnny rolled his eyes. "Yeah, whatever. So you wanna come over tonight and pick up the script or what?"

"What time?"

"I dunno. Eight. Here's my number."

"Oh, I have to call you."

"If you want the part."

"I want it, believe me. Whatever it is."

"Oh, you'll like it," Johnny said with a wink. "It's right down your alley."

"You mean *up* my alley," she said. He grinned and nodded. Loretta smiled, poured Johnny another cup of coffee, and he returned to his paper. Then she went back into the kitchen and when the chef wasn't looking, slipped a butcher knife into her purse.

-FINIS-

www.ingramcontent.com/pod-product-compliance
Lightning Source LLC
Chambersburg PA
CBHW061303170626
46817CB00001B/30